PROOF THROUGH
THE NIGHT

PROOF THROUGH THE NIGHT
A Supernatural Thriller

Lt. Colonel Toby Quirk

ELM HILL

A Division of
HarperCollins Christian Publishing

www.elmhillbooks.com

Proof Through The Night
A Supernatural Thriller

Published in Nashville, Tennessee, by Elm Hill, an imprint of Thomas Nelson. Elm Hill and Thomas Nelson are registered trademarks of HarperCollins Christian Publishing, Inc.

Elm Hill titles may be purchased in bulk for educational, business, fund-raising, or sales promotional use. For information, please e-mail SpecialMarkets@ ThomasNelson.com.

Library of Congress Cataloging-in-Publication Data

Library of Congress Control Number: 2018953416

ISBN 978-1-595559128 (Paperback)
ISBN 978-1-595559227 (Hardbound)
ISBN 978-1-595559364 (eBook)

Contents

Spring in America, 2015

CHAPTER ONE

Akebe Cheron prayed into the somber grayness above the Pacific Ocean. "My Lord *Ogoun*, master of the darkness, grant me patience to deal with these inferior underlings. They exist in blind ignorance of you, my god. I give you thanks for overseeing our master plan to shape America into a herd of mindless sheep. I am eternally grateful to you, *Ogoun*, for enlisting me as chairman of the Directorate, endowing me with your black power and secret wisdom. As my board of directors travels to my yacht today, I ask that your mighty hand would hover over our world-shaping deliberations. Amen."

"Samuel," Akebe shouted across the expansive deck of his 100-meter superyacht, *Medusa*, "get over here and clean this up."

The deckhand quickly bagged up the remains of the chairman's pig sacrifice to his Voodoo God.

Old Gabriella watched the sand crab desperately try to escape from the seagull's beak, slashing his pinchers at the gull's eyes.

"Mr. Crab, for nine decades I've watched your ancestors struggle to escape seagulls' clutches. You are not going to win this one."

The Atlantic had calmed down from last night's spring rain. Gabriella felt the gentle rhythm of the ocean lapping against the granite shelf below her ledge where gulls dined on sand crabs all summer. She set her face to the soft breeze. Her thick black hair danced on her shoulders.

"Up you go, Mr. Crab," she said.

The seagull soared into the soft morning twilight with the flailing crab in her beak. At the perfect altitude, she let it fall and smash open on her rock table. The gull swooped gracefully down to her breakfast. She turned one of her black eyes in Gabriella's direction.

"Most coastal folks consider you a troublemaker, dear bird, and I'm sure all the crabs think you're evil. But you and I know you're one of the Master's fine creatures. Enjoy your breakfast. I'm receiving another assignment."

Gabriella stared at the glimmering horizon and listened. *"Protect Anna Stone,"* said the voice.

"Let me see how I can stop these evil murderers one more time."

Akebe watched Donald Snow pilot his seaplane through the white shroud of cloud cover to *Medusa's* starboard boarding platform. He grinned as the pudgy director of Weather and Agriculture waddled up the gangway.

"Greetings in the name of American excellence," said Akebe.

"Hello Akebe; great venue," said Donald.

The two men shook hands and Akebe offered Donald a scotch.

"No ice, Akebe, just neat. Thanks."

Donald Snow: pudgy, white, and bald was the physical opposite of Akebe Cheron, a full-blooded Nigerian from the Yaruba tribe, tall, raven-skinned, and muscular.

"So, Akebe, how goes the vetiver empire? How fascinating that your Haitian grass generates such substantial profits."

Akebe inspected Donald's face for traces of sarcasm. "Western culture cannot satisfy its lust for luxury, my friend. Perfumers and their overindulgent customers can't get enough of my rare fragrant vetiver oils.

The prices of perfumes like Le Labo's Santal 33 and Ermenegildo Zegna's Florentine Iris keep soaring.

"Here comes Olivia," said Akebe over the thundering clack of helicopter blades. "Frances O'Donnelly flew in with her."

Doctor Anna Stone put the breakfast dishes in the dishwasher, dried her hands, and called upstairs to her husband and daughter. "I'm taking off now."

"Okay, bye," said Paul.

Anna's mouth bunched up when she was perturbed. "Hey, you guys forget something? I said I'm leaving the house now."

Paul appeared on the landing with Melissa perched on his hip. "Mommy wants her kisses," he said.

He made his way downstairs. "Oh, I forgot to tell you something your daughter said yesterday."

"What?" said Anna.

"So we're picking up the clothes from church. Four boxes of stuff from the clothing drive, right?"

Melissa twirled her little pink finger in her father's ear.

"Cut it out, kid."

The four-year-old grinned at her mother.

"Anyway, we put the boxes in the van, right? And deliver them to Salvation Army. I strap the kid in her car seat and guess what she says?"

"Can't imagine."

"She says, 'Daddy, are we thieves'?"

Anna looked at her little cherub, shook her head, and laughed. "Where do you get this stuff?"

Paul leaned over. He took the left cheek, Melissa took the right, and they gave Anna her kisses.

"I'll see you tonight."

"My god, that helicopter makes a racket," said Donald.

Olivia Kingston, director of Food Production, piloted the AW119 to the yacht's helipad, cut the engine, and climbed out of the cockpit.

"Yes," said the chairman, "and my crew has to secure the deck furniture or the downwash scatters everything into the ocean."

"Greetings, ladies," said Akebe, "in the name of American excellence."

"Frances, our director of Education Control, how good to see you," said Donald.

"Hi, Donald, Akebe. Quite the boat," said Frances.

Akebe handed each lady a glass of Chablis. "Thanks," said Olivia, her khaki shirt, slacks, and aviator sunglasses somehow incompatible with her New England patrician visage. "Akebe, what a grand vessel."

"100 meters of pure luxury," said Akebe. "I could live out here indefinitely. But we have important work to do on the continent, eh?

"Ah, must be our director of Healthcare and Pharmaceuticals," said Akebe, looking over the port side to the northeast where a high-performance motor yacht approached. "He'd be sailing from Puget Sound—Romano Goldstein."

"And another boat to the southeast. Look at those beautiful sails," said Frances.

"Okay," said Akebe, "all present and accounted for. That's Randal Sanford, our director of Business and Finance."

In a few minutes, the six billionaires who formed the Directorate's executive board assembled on the bridge.

"My crew will show you to your staterooms. Make yourselves comfortable. Chef Gerard will serve us a sumptuous dinner in the saloon at sixteen-hundred before our meeting," said Akebe. "Do not discuss any Directorate business until we get to the saloon. My security team has shrouded that room with security measures that protect our highly classified conversations from prying eyes and ears, all right? See you all at four."

Anna cruised through her hometown of Cabot, Arkansas, and swung up the onramp to Route 167 South toward North Little Rock. Winter was all through with Arkansas. For the first time since November, Anna opened the Camry's moonroof, pressed the buttons to lower the windows, and let the spring air ruffle her long auburn hair. Willie Nelson's version of *Uncloudy Day* blasted out of the new Kenwood sound system Paul installed for her birthday. Traffic was light on Anna's familiar commute to North Little Rock.

About a half mile before her exit onto Kiehl Avenue, Anna saw a ragged mother ahead sitting on the guardrail cradling a baby in her arms. *What the heck?* Anna clicked off the music. She pulled into the breakdown lane, stopped the car, and jogged back to see if she could help the woman when the shock wave knocked her on her face before the explosive roar reached her ears. She flew into the air and smashed hard onto the pavement. Shards of asphalt and concrete dust fell all over her back. Still conscious, Anna inspected her skinned palms, elbows, and knees. The woman and baby had disappeared.

Akebe's crew set up the saloon as a combination boardroom - dining room. At four o'clock, each member of the board sat comfortably in leather seats with wine glasses and an array of appetizers before them on the thick glass table.

"I suppose we must wait for Randal," said Romano Goldstein, "late as usual."

"Please," said Akebe, his Haitian accent barely perceptible. "Tell the waiter your wine preferences and enjoy some hors d'oeuvres. I particularly like the seared steak lettuce cups."

"Akebe," Frances O'Donnelly said, "I have a quick question while we're waiting."

"Yes, Frances."

"As far as I know, we never resolved the question about these radical Muslim groups in the Middle East—ISIS, Al Qaeda, and the others. Are they in any way affiliated with us?"

Akebe nibbled on his d'oeuvres. He looked up at Frances, knowing how strategically her mind worked.

"Frances, we must consider ISIS and the fifteen other radical Islamist groups who are working toward a worldwide Caliphate as long-range competition. However, as you know we've used their publicity as cover for our operations. Over half of our assassinations have appeared to be the work of radicalized Muslims."

Frances nodded and laid a piece of brie on a cracker. "Right. Thanks."

"Glad you could join us," said Romano to Randal Sanford as he took his seat.

Akebe ignored the adversarial body language between Goldstein and Sanford. He filled his wine glass with pinot noir, lifted his glass, and said, "A toast to American excellence."

"To American excellence," the Directorate's executive board repeated.

Chef Gerard announced the menu, "Ladies and gentlemen, may I present: glazed salmon with pineapple salsa, green beans, rice pilaf, assorted breads, and sorbet for dessert, along with several wines."

After the meal, the cigars, and snifters of Remy Martin all around, Chairman Akebe Cheron began the official proceedings with their organization's pledge.

"Let us stand."

All stood and recited, "We are the Directorate. We humbly accept our role as the overseers of the free world's institutions, and where necessary we will carry out our duty to prune out those hindrances that prevent the healthy advancement of the American culture. Duty. Honor. Oversight. Always loyal to the Directorate." They took their seats.

Each executive poured over the spreadsheets from the operations center. The successful entries were highlighted in green, the failures in red. Alarmed at what they were reading, they murmured their surprise and looked at Akebe.

"Tonight we decide if our current operations officer, Andrew Johansen, lives or dies. You have seen the monthlies. In the last month out of seventeen attempts, only two succeeded at removing an obstructionist. So, directors, tonight you will present two items: first your reports on your areas of expertise, then state your position on Johansen's termination. I'll go first, then around the table to my right."

Andrew Johansen, the Directorate's operations officer, leaned back in his black graphite ergonomic office chair, eyes glaring at the six-foot, high-definition screen on the wall above his operations console. He kept playing the North Little Rock explosion over and over searching for Anna Stone's red Camry, but no matter how many times he analyzed the video, he could not see any vehicles crossing the bridge on Highway 167 when his explosion went off.

Then he widened the view and there it was, Anna Stone's car. It was stopped by the guardrail fifty feet away from the smoking crater. He ran the recording again and saw his target lying on the pavement, covered with grey dust.

"Maybe I got her," he said.

Andrew zoomed in on Anna's prone form. He leaned forward and peered into the big flat screen above his console. *Are you dead? Are you dead? Please, be dead.*

"Oh, crap. You're moving. You're alive. You're getting up. Why can't you just die like you're supposed to?"

Andrew banged his fists on the console. He put his hands against his temples and leaned his elbows on the countertop.

Despite his fury at the blown assassination attempt, Andrew still remembered to post the false notifications on the internet giving ISIS credit for the bridge explosion in Arkansas.

"Got to be some explanation."

Something went wrong again. He flicked the space bar on one of his keyboards activating a spreadsheet listing all current operations. In the last five weeks, only two of seventeen hits were successful. All six of his squads had at least two failures. Bravo and Echo Squads had three each and Delta Squad now had three failures, including this one.

So far Andrew was able to lay the blame on his squad leaders, but now he was sensing a need for a more definitive strategy to deflect responsibility away from him. In this risky line of work, the consequence for poor performance was terminal, literally.

One of the phones on his console buzzed. It was Bubba Whiting, the leader of the operational unit in charge of Anna Stone's assassination.

"You messed up, idiot," Andrew shouted into the phone.

"I don't ignite the charge, Andrew, I just identify the target and place the explosives. And as you can see I did an excellent job," Bubba said, his voice not displaying the slightest concern. "Stuff happens."

"I'm going to put this to you in terms your Neanderthal mind can absorb, Bubba. Your squad has failed three attacks in a row. Your earlier successes mean nothing in the face of all these failed attacks. America deserves better."

Akebe Cheron's eyes scanned each director's face for traces of betrayal as he reported on his ever-increasing control over senior governmental officials. He briefed the board on specific departments: Defense Department, National Security Agency, Central Intelligence Agency, and all law enforcement agencies from the US Attorney General, the FBI, right down to police officers on the streets.

"I estimate an increase of our hypnotic control over government agencies from twenty-five percent this time last year to forty-two percent this year. Too slow for my liking. We gained the most control in the area of the White House. Today's president continues to advance a communist agenda, weakening our local police forces and ushering in an unprecedented era of chaos. The US military suffers from indecisive senior leaders who fall impotent to our hypnotic stream. Devoid of any coherent strategy, these DOD bumblers have infected the military culture with social experimentation rendering every US war-fighting unit nondeployable.

"The rest of my report dovetails with all your departments, since government now controls every aspect of American life. I will hold my comments on those specifics until after your briefings.

"Now about Andrew Johansen, our operations officer. Here's how we will proceed: Romano, since you trained and recruited Andrew, I will ask you to recuse yourself from the final vote, but your comments on his viability are most welcomed. I will have a vote on his continuation or termination when it comes time for that.

"I will say this: you can see from the reports there's a fly in the ointment, my comrades. You know where that expression comes from? Anyone?"

Vacant stares from the directors.

"Well, if you illiterates knew your Bible you would recall Ecclesiastes, the tenth chapter, the first verse, and I quote, 'Dead flies make a perfumer's oil ferment and stink; so a little folly outweighs wisdom and honor,'" said the chairman.

"A fly?" said Olivia. "Whoever or whatever prevents our pruning operations from succeeding is more effective than a bug. Our system is broken. We need to examine every link in this chain and find out where the disconnect lies."

Randal Sanford agreed. His voice slurred from the wine, "There's a fly. A real aggressive, dangerous fly, and it has corrupted our systems. Some evil cockroach keeps attacking our operators."

Donald Snow asked, "What does our operations officer have to say about all these failures? Fifteen losses against two wins—pathetic."

"Finally, the right question," said Akebe.

Chapter Two

Bubba Whiting occupied his favorite table at the Generator Coffee House and Bakery on Shackelford Road in West Little Rock. He devoured his second piece, their famous chocolate walnut pie, and a cup of iced coffee. "Yeah, so what are you sayin', Andrew?"

"I'm not sayin' anything, Bubba—I'm doin'."

Bubba dropped his cell phone as the glass wall that separated him from the sidewalk exploded from the gunfire of three AR-15 automatic rifles. One round grazed his right shoulder and Bubba screamed, the pain searing his right side. He went to his knees next to two women who lay bloody beside him. He watched the three men in ski masks fire their weapons with grim smiles fixed on their mouths. Bullets zipped and cracked over Bubba's head. Then everything went black. He never heard them yell, "Allah Akbar," or saw them jump into the van they had stolen that morning and drive away before the North Little Rock S.W.A.T. team responded to yet another "Jihadist" mass shooting in America.

An urgent knocking at the saloon door.

"Not now. We're in session," said Akebe.

The muffled voice from behind the heavily padded, secure door, insisted, "Sir, a report from the operations center. It may bear on your meeting."

"Get in here."

Gene Philmore, the *Medusa's* captain, shuffled into Akebe's presence.

"Read it, Captain."

"Today, zero eight hundred, Central Time. Subject: Failed Assassination Attempt on Doctor Anna Stone...."

Akebe growled and slammed both fists on the glass table. Veins in his neck and forehead bulged through his dark skin. A tiny slip of saliva oozed from the corner of his lips. He forced a phony smile, breathed deep, and became suddenly still as stone. He peered around the table at his subordinate directors. They were all stunned. Frozen.

"All right dear Captain, please proceed with the message from our operations officer."

"Direct from Andrew Johansen, Operations Center: 'Anna Stone eluded our attack. This so-called holistic healer has a set daily routine. She drives from her house in Cabot, Arkansas, to her office in Sherwood Monday through Friday, same route, same time every morning. This time, for some unknown reason, the woman stopped her car a quarter mile short of the bridge where our squad placed the demo. I activated the charge from this remote location with precisely the right lead time for the speed Anna Stone was driving, but Stone stopped her car and got out precisely when I triggered the demo. She avoided the explosion and still lives.'"

"Why would she do that?" asked Randal.

"Shut up, Randal. Continue, Captain."

"'The following is a recording of her cell phone call right after the explosion hit the local news:'

"'Are you okay, honey?' (Paul Stone)

"'Yeah, I stopped my car just before the bridge blew up.' (Anna Stone)

"'Why?' (Paul Stone)

"'There was a woman with a baby on her lap sitting on the guardrail there. I thought I could help her, so I stopped. Then the bomb went off and I was tossed in the air, and I landed on my face.' (Anna Stone)

"'Dear Lord. Are you all right?' (Paul Stone)

"'My hands, elbows, and knees are all scraped up, but nothing serious.' (Anna Stone)

"'What about the woman?' (Paul Stone)

"'Never saw her again. Weird. She either hopped the guardrail with the baby and ran for it, or she disappeared into thin air.'" (Anna Stone)

"She's covering for somebody," slurred Randal. "She knows damn well why she stopped her car. Somebody tipped her off, and we gotta root him out and get rid of him."

Frances O'Donelly weighed in. "Take it easy there, slugger. Anna had no reason to be secretive on the phone with her husband. This naive little country doctor had no idea that her phone was bugged. If someone warned her about an attack on her life, she would have stayed home and called the police. It took nearly five minutes for the cops to respond. No, she never got an actual warning. She sounded convinced that she saw a mother and child in distress, and she stopped to assist them."

"Enough, people," said Akebe. "What else, Captain?"

"Yes, sir, last paragraph here: 'I have eliminated the operations team that failed the mission, Bubba Whiting and Team Kilo. Made it look like an attack by radical Islamist. Although the target of the mission still lives, we succeeded in causing chaos in North Little Rock with two violent incidents. Traffic on Route 167 will be stopped for days, and the population is reeling from the shooting in the cafe.'

"End of message, sir."

"Get out," snarled Akebe.

The chairman's countenance turned stony. The drumbeat in his brain pounded against his skull. He closed his eyes and watched a horrifying parade of cackling demons swirl around the invisible realm, accusing him, taunting him, calling him a miserable failure.

Akebe's trance lifted. He surveyed the stunned faces at the table, then he shot a quick bolt of telekinetic energy at each director that erased the last few minutes from their brains.

"Well, another failure. The fly in the ointment has interfered again. The question before us is whether or not Andrew Johansen continues as the Directorate's operations officer. I say remove him.

"That concludes my report. Next is Romano Goldstein, director of Healthcare and Pharmaceutical Control. Give your report first, then your assessment of Johansen."

"I'll be brief," said Romano.

"That'll be a first," said Randal.

"For over twenty years we have successfully invaded America's medical establishment—from their schools to the legislation governing their practices to the unbreakable ties they have with large pharmaceutical corporations. The new overarching Affordable Care Act, expertly engineered by our chairman, effectively shackles health insurance companies to government bureaucrats and health care providers. Doctors no longer diagnose illnesses or injuries and look for cures. They just read our detailed protocols and prescribe chemicals, thereby discharging an unceasing flow of mind-numbing chemicals into the brains of American citizens.

"People like Anna Stone who refuse to accept the medical establishment's protocols and those few well-educated physicians who have somehow escaped our brainwashing mechanisms in med school pose the biggest threat to our plans."

"Sorry to interrupt," said Frances, "but who, for instance? Can you name anyone?"

Dr. Goldstein stammered, "One of them is running for president; can't recall the name. He clings to radically conservative views, devoutly religious principles, and unconventional medical practices."

Olivia jumped in, "Yes, and how many times has our brilliant operations officer tried to take him out? Four? Five?"

"As our chairman has mentioned, we've failed too often, and this 'fly in the ointment' seems especially protective of this doctor turned politician. Andrew must remain in command of his pruning squads to ensure our ultimate success.

"So, my assessment of Andrew...."

"Briefly, I'm begging you," said Randal.

"In Andrew Johansen," continued Romano Goldstein, "I developed a rare amalgamation of human traits. My staff at the Loving Center, where I preside over the world's most brilliant staff of psychologists, certified Andrew as a sociopath. He possesses genius-level intelligence. An orphan, he suffers from a pathological dissociative disorder that keeps him from caring about any other human being. He works for days without rest. Andrew Johansen is a cocktail of psychotic disorders, the perfect specimen to serve as our operations officer.

"That, Randal, is my brief description of Andrew Johansen. My only advice to the board is that when you consider your vote for his elimination, remember it will be very difficult to find a replacement."

Akebe said, "Thank you, Romano. Randal, you're up next."

"Yeah, okay," said Randal, "business and finance have seen a couple major leaps forward, thanks partly to Akebe's influence over congress with the passing of the Patriot Act despite all the misguided attempts to repeal it. This law gives us unprecedented access to just about every list in America. We have deep roots in all the databases where the NSA and the FBI are rapidly harvesting personal information on every US citizen. The illegals are causing us some problems, though. I don't know what we're doing accepting so many of them. They're hard to track.

"Anyway, as you know I have been elected chairman of the board at Columbine Capitol and I have installed my people in all the key positions. We have enhanced our capability to digitally invade every TV network and alter their broadcasts so the public gets only the information we want them to get."

"Example, please," said Donald.

"Sure. One of the networks, I think it was Fox, did an interview with this freethinking jerk of a Navy Seal veteran. He's telling the audience that his treatment for PTSD at the VA is all messed up. He says all the doctor does is look in his cook book—that's what he had the gall to call it—and dish out meds. Then he talks about how he went to a homeopathic practitioner for treatment and he gets better—healed, he says, from the mental trauma. Well you know we don't want to spread that kind of garbage, so my guys just grab the broadcast out of thin air, reprogram it, and have the soldier tell the world how great his VA doctor is.

"On top of that, we now have identified several new targets that are obstructing our successful campaign of controlling the minds of all Americans."

Frances O'Donelly asked, "Any names, Randal, in the business world?"

"Well, most notable is a New York billionaire and TV personality. He's making noises about running for president."

"Ridiculous," said Frances, "Such a peacock couldn't get nominated, never mind elected. Don't waste our resources going after such an imbecile."

"Fine, then I'll take the name off Andrew's list then," said a sulking Randal.

"But I want to weigh in on what to do with Andrew. I say we keep him. He has created an entire network of ingenious technological advancements without which my operations would be impossible. Just last month he came up with that plan to use structures that look like cellphone towers to broadcast mind-controlling microwaves. Good plan. That's it from me."

Akebe listened intently to his board. He heard nothing new from Olivia Kingston who briefed on her programs to expand the food industry's degradation of the nutritional value of processed food. Her only advance seemed to be in the increased popularity of energy drinks that are successfully poisoning the younger age groups. The chairman was mildly impressed when she mentioned her direct control over Montasso Incorporated and, like Sanders, she has placed Directorate agents in key positions in that agrochemical company.

"My research shows," Olivia said, "that over sixty-five percent of the US population buys into Montasso's propaganda. I'm reading from their website here, 'Monstasso works with farmers from around the world to make agriculture more productive and sustainable. Our technologies enable farmers to get more from every acre of farmland. Specifically, we are working to double yields in our core crops by 2030.'"

"Right," said Randal, "but you have your threats. The Organic Consumers Association has to be taken out. And we need more visibility on the protestors. By my last count we have only terminated a dozen or so of these radicals. You have more problems than you realize, lady."

Olivia cast him a look of superiority from her well-bred, nearly masculine face, molded by centuries of aristocratic DNA.

Akebe said, "And your position on our operations officer, Olivia?"

"Randal's so misguided on this. We need to get rid of the arrogant slob."

Randal said, "Olivia, you can't see beyond your bigotry. Andrew is an essential asset to the Directorate."

"That's enough, people," said Akebe. "Donald, your report on climate control."

"Well our latest pilot program to cause continuous cloud cover is ready to go national. We've blanketed the northeast US with almost continuous clouds for eight months. The only reason we allowed an occasional day of sunlight is so the locals wouldn't realize how bad we are making it for them. The effects are phenomenal. We're seeing a spike in clinical depression and suicides. We're still studying the effects on how the lack of sunlight is having on general mental capacity.

"I want to thank Randal for manipulating the local and national weather broadcasts on TV. His people have been able to alter the weather reporting so when meteorologists report on the unusual stretches of cloudy days, our agents have effectively kept that information from the public. Even internet articles on the lack of sunshine get buried.

"The other program we have initiated since our last board meeting is causing droughts in those areas in California where the large organic farms have cropped up.

"And, Chairman Cheron, your ingenious strategy of brainwashing key leaders in the government regarding global warming has created a marvelous smokescreen that has effectively concealed our meteorological manipulations. We have an iron grip on the scientific community. Not only are they publishing peer-reviewed papers and articles that support the climate hoax, they have also spread their influence globally. And any freethinking scholar who tries to publish or teach the truth gets ostracized, and often loses tenure.

"Now about Andrew Johansen: Olivia, you need to get some long-range perspective on this. The young man has served us well for what—fifteen years? Give the boy a break. Keep him on."

Olivia stood up and banged the table. "He's a failure. He's the fly in the ointment."

Randal said, "Pipe down, woman. You don't know what you're talking about. The fly is external."

"Don't you dare talk to me like that, you miserable drunk. I deserve more respect than that."

Akebe raised his hand, just slightly. He smiled his disturbing grin. "Let's stay on point, folks."

Akebe watched the two powerful executives comply with his rebuke like children to a stern father. *Thank you, Ogoun, for giving me this controlling power.*

CHAPTER THREE

A cross the continent on a granite outcropping just south of Cape Ann, Massachusetts, Gabriella stood with her face to the wind, focusing all her prophetic energy on the Directorate's meeting. Their high-tech security measures obscured the details of their conversations from her, but Gabriella was able to catch the gist. She leaped her way up the rocks to her cottage on the bluff where dinner was almost ready.

"The Directorate will be searching for us," Gabriella stated quietly as she placed the serving bowl of pasta on the dinner table. Before sitting down, the aged woman turned her back to the room, looked out the bay window, and took her time scanning the Atlantic horizon beyond their rocky point. Past the visible realm, Gabriella "saw" the shimmering formation of the angelic platoon she had requested. They halted in the air above Cielavista where they would establish their war room.

Gabriella's granddaughter and grandson-in-law waited respectfully for their perduring Nonina to take her seat at the head of the table. Accustomed as they were to the ancient Sicilian's agility, they still marveled at her inexhaustible energy. Gabriella spun on her toe, dipped onto her chair, and slid it forward to the table, her lips murmuring in prayer.

"Who are these people?" said Sandy as she dished out the pesto pasta with chicken into three bowls while Sandy's husband, Henry, poured the wine.

"The ones who are orchestrating all these murders," Gabriella said.

"Well, maybe we just have to hold off for a while," said Henry after his first sip.

"Oh, no, no, no," said Gabriella, "many good, important people will die. We cannot let that happen. I have to continue protecting their targets. They have attempted to kill an important presidential candidate several times. But we must initiate countermeasures. Henry, you will take charge of that."

"No problem," Henry said.

Gabriella read his eyes. He didn't have the slightest inkling of what she was talking about. Gabriella knew that in twenty-eight years Henry Baker had never become comfortable living here with her and her granddaughter, where every daily event burst onto the calendar with unpredictable spontaneity.

Gabriella could see it coming—another raging episode roiling up in Henry's gut. *Lord, I know that but for your grace, this marriage would never have lasted a year.*

"Frances, your report on education control?"

"We're well entrenched in all levels of public education from preschool to postdoctorate. The leverage we have with government funding keeps them all in line. From the top down, professors and teachers provide very little thought-provoking instruction. The students are not rewarded for understanding the principles behind the facts, just rote memory. Every curricula simply provides the formula for repetition and test-taking. The whole idea of standardized testing gives us a tremendous tool for control.

"We must continue pruning out the freethinkers who pop up all over the place. Although we have over ninety percent of public school teachers and college professors totally brainwashed into our mold, the resistance is coming from stubborn students and their parents. When we hear of these dissenters we attempt to hypnotize them, but if that doesn't work we target them for elimination.

"Requiring the homeschoolers to register with local school boards has been somewhat effective. We have installed solid Directorate servants as gatekeepers who impose bureaucratic barriers that frustrate home-school parents. Andrew has my target list of these obstructionists.

"Now, on the issue of terminating Andrew: I can't honestly judge him without seeing him. I've never met the man. I have to delay my vote."

"All right," said Akebe. "Let's take our vote with Romano recused and Frances holding off for more information. I yield my chair to Romano."

Romano began, "The issue before us tonight is whether to keep Andrew on as our operations officer, with the sole duty to execute our directives to prune out those independent thinkers who are impeding our progress toward the new American excellence.

"All those in favor of keeping Andrew Johansen in his position say 'aye.'"

Randal Sanford, "Aye."

Donald Snow, "Aye."

"All those opposed say 'nay.'"

Akebe Cheron, "Nay."

Olivia Kingston, "Nay"

"Frances?" said Romano.

"I'm sorry to hold up this very important decision, but before I can cast my vote I must meet with the man. I intend to go directly from here to Missouri to interview Andrew and view his operations center. I will notify the board of my vote afterwards."

Romano said, "Well with that delay in place, we will table this discussion and I yield the chair back to you, Akebe. Looks like Andrew will live to work at least a little longer."

Akebe spewed out a sigh of frustration. "We're deadlocked. I was hoping we could dispense with this matter quickly, but I suppose we'll have to live with Frances' deliberations.

"Ladies and gentlemen of the board, we are being opposed by a fly in the ointment. It is a force that has found a way to thwart our noble efforts to change the face of America into a land free of dissent and obstructionist thinking. We will find the source of this force and eliminate it. In the meantime we will continue to control every institution, every organization, indeed every human being in this country. We will right this floundering nation and set it on a new path of greatness under the control of our brilliant minds.

"We are the last remnant of great American patriots. Stand tall, my brothers and sisters, in the battle for the new American excellence.

"This meeting is adjourned. Please enjoy your stay on *Medusa* for as long as you desire, then return to your posts refreshed and renewed."

The board finished their meal and repaired to the ship's auditorium to watch the German film, *Goodbye Lenin!,* then to their plush staterooms.

A few minutes past midnight there was a soft knock at Akebe's door. He opened it and welcomed the stately Olivia Kingston into his bedroom.

Henry's nervous nature compelled him to create lists and calendars, budgets and charts, so when tomorrow broke every eventuality was covered: enough food, gas, money, time, the right clothing, equipment, supplies, everything. But not here. Not at Cielavista.

For the thousandth time Henry constructed a calm veneer over the fire building in the left hemisphere of his brain as he observed his wife pour her affection on his grandmother-in-law.

From the kitchen, Henry called to his wife, "Sandy, honey, would you come in here for a sec?"

"What is it?" said Sandy. She could feel the tension radiating from Mister Neatness.

"Not a big thing, just thought I'd tell you. See this butter container?"

Sandy indeed saw the square plastic tub that contained a butterlike substance—supposed to be healthier than the real stuff made with cow's milk. She recoiled from the heat of Henry's anger, and she braced herself for the ambush she knew awaited in Henry's literal mind. "Yes, what about it?"

"Okay; see, this side of the butter tub is obviously the front. And when the lid is on the container, the printing on the lid should be properly aligned with the printing on the front of the tub, right?"

"I'm not sure what you're getting at, Henry. There's no right way to put the lid on the butter as long as it's seated properly. It's a square, so whichever way you put it on, the lid fits."

"Well, maybe, darling. But the way this product comes in the store, the lettering on the lid is aligned with the front, so if it's worth putting the lid on the container, it's worth doing right. I mean it doesn't take a few seconds to make sure the printing is readable from the front and the top now, does it?" said Henry.

"Here's another thought," said Sandy. "Let's say I remove the lid like this and place it on the counter right next to the tub with the lettering facing front. And I dip two fingers into the butter and gob it on your shirt like this? How 'bout that?"

Henry made no effort to remove the big glob of butter from his immaculate white golf shirt. He just glared at his mischievous wife and let the hot rage build up in his head.

Sandy backed quickly out of the kitchen, smiling.

"Not funny," he said.

Henry changed his shirt, cleaned up the kitchen, and put everything away, including the butter with the lid properly secured on the tub.

"I'm going to walk my rounds," said Henry. "Meanwhile, dear Gabriella, how about coming up with some guidance for me to keep the bad guys from the gates."

Henry heard Gabriella whisper to Sandy, "I'm afraid you've upset your husband again."

He refilled his wineglass, left the cottage, and strode through the yard toward the stone mansion at the center of Villa Cielavista.

In the soft twilight drifting into the dining room, Sandy said, "Nonina, sometimes I don't know whether to admire you or have you committed."

She draped her arm softly over her grandmother's bony shoulders.

"You eat three bites of dinner, take a sip of the vino, and walk out to your rock. You stay out there on the point until after midnight and then you sleep a couple hours. Then you nibble a slice of black toast, sip your espresso, and out you go to your ledge to pray and wage war in the heavens. Yet you are stronger than any of us. How do you do it, my love?"

Gabriella feathered her calloused hand over Sandy's arm. "You are the one to be admired, my daughter. I thank my God for you. You and that obsessive Henry of yours. You take care of everything."

Dusk was approaching the shoreline, dissolving the joyfully brilliant sky into a chalky amber-grey. Gabriella rose from her coffee and biscotti at the dining room table and turned again to the big bay window.

"What?" Sandy asked, recognizing the power radiating from Gabriella's body when she was "seeing."

"Get your laptop, dear."

Sandy went upstairs to her room, returned to the dining room, sat down at the table, and waited for her grandmother to turn around. Sandy closed her eyes. A strange silky warmth brushed over her mind. She felt Gabriella sit down beside her.

"See if there's a news alert about an attempted murder on a chief justice," the old lady said with a wave of her boney fingers toward the computer.

Sandy glanced at Gabriella's face then at her screen, tapped some keys, and the CNN website came up.

The headline read, *U.S. Takes Cuba Off State-Sponsored Terrorism List.* The women waited a few seconds. A red banner coursed across the top of the page: *News Alert: Chief Justice Escapes Attempt On His Life.*

Sandy clicked on the banner and a brief paragraph gave scant details of the incident.

Supreme Court Chief Justice Allen Scales was the target of a sniper attack this afternoon at his home in McLean, Virginia. Justice Scales was getting into his car in the driveway of his home in the secluded neighborhood of Colony Estates when three rounds struck the car's driver-side window, inches away from Scale's head. The elderly judge miraculously escaped being struck down by the sniper. More details of this story to follow.

"Snipers don't miss," said Sandy. "What did you do?"

"I've been doing this for over eighty years, and every incident amazes me.

"The Spirit prompted me to create a wall of energy in the path of the bullets between the sniper's rifle and his target. Evidently this mass of vibrating ions slightly deformed each projectile, causing them to deviate from the victim in the sniper's crosshairs."

"Why wouldn't you just eliminate the murderer?"

Gabriella turned her face to her granddaughter and she looked into her eyes. "My precious Sandy. Did you feel anything in your soul a few minutes ago?"

Sandy took a deep breath, inhaling some of Gabriella's fragrance and aura. "Yes, Nonina."

"Soon you will be inheriting this spiritual gift, and then you will understand those mysteries that you cannot understand.

"Our enemy is getting better at masking their brutal plans. I'll be on my rock, dear. Our heavenly helpers have arrived. Have a peaceful evening."

Gabriella kissed her granddaughter on the forehead and walked softly through the french doors and down her path to the granite ledge on the water.

CHAPTER FOUR

This majestic thirty-acre rock, covered with manicured forests and gardens, comforted Henry's engineer mind. He had studied how the natural footings of granite were permanently embedded in the bowels of the earth. A masterpiece of hydrogeology, the massive outcropping stood impenetrable to the relentless crashing waves that battered its bulwarks. The solid landmass provided Henry a counterbalance to Gabriella's unpredictability and the chaotic lifestyle she spawned.

He approximated Gabriella's age at over one hundred and five. She was Sandy's grandmother and Sandy was fifty two. Add about twenty-five years for each generation and the old lady had to have been born just after nineteen-hundred. And she could be a lot older, given the fact that some of those Sicilian families had a dozen children, and she talked about some of her younger brothers and sisters. Her history and her origin were shrouded in mystery and murky legends.

From where he stood at the edge of the lawn behind the cottage, Henry looked down and watched Gabriella descend the ledges on the cliff like a teenage gymnast. Despite his animosity for her, he was fascinated by the old lady's physical ability to climb down the natural uneven rock stairway. She ended her descent at a shelf of rock, split in two by a deep crevice that she had to jump across to get to her meditation spot. Henry was amazed watching her take two graceful running steps and leap over the wide gap with her tiny right foot outstretched and her left leg trailing, until she landed down softly on the opposite ledge. He knew it was there, on that one rock, that his grandmother-in-law waged her invisible war with the wealthy elitists who systematically targeted and destroyed mindful men and women whose noble character and curious minds posed a threat to their insidious stratagems.

Henry's anger dissipated as he sipped his Burgundy and strolled through the herb garden taking in the fragrances of basil, mint, and thyme. He looked up at the tops of the blue spruce trees inexplicably waving to him against the sky without a breeze to disturb their branches. He dismissed what he saw as just one more curious fluke he had no desire to explain.

The angel assigned to protect Henry stopped shaking the treetop and watched his reaction.

Henry was thinking back to the summer of 1985. He and Sandy were both twenty-three.

Henry had found himself breezing through all his coursework at Northeastern University in Boston and the job they assigned him as part of the university's work-study program. The US Federal Bureau of Investigation, Boston Office, hired him for twenty hours a week during the school year and full-time during semester breaks.

"Give him a brush on the cheek," Michael said to Tobias. Tobias turned to the archangel and smiled. He floated down through the spruce branches and fluttered his invisible fingers across Henry's face.

Henry wasn't startled. He absently flicked his hand at the feeling and chuckled to himself.

Henry was recalling when he joined the understaffed engineering division of the Boston branch of the FBI. He soon realized that this division occupied the lowest priority in the budget.

Tobias, drifting above Henry's head, hummed a few bars of Henry's favorite song, "Up Where We Belong." Henry found himself softly singing the lyrics.

Unfazed by the spiritual interruption, Henry continued his reverie, remembering his impression of the engineering division chief, Shirley Devens. She could serve as the poster child for all that's wrong with federal employees. Rarely moving her ponderous body from her chair, she ruled her nearly-irrelevant division of the Boston FBI office with astonishing incompetence and an iron fist.

Tobias tried something else. He rose aloft above the towering spruce trees that bordered the herb garden and spoke Henry's name. "Henry."

Henry calmly looked around but dismissed what he thought he heard, too deeply involved with his memories.

Within a few weeks at the Federal Bureau of Investigation, Henry realized that as long as he arrived on time and stayed until 5:00 p.m., he could do pretty much whatever he wanted, so he explored the Bureau's databases with the fervor of a zealous monk. Eventually he purchased three high-capacity hard drives and downloaded the information on them so he could study them at home.

"Having fun on the computer?" Mrs. Deven's gravelly voice inquired from her corner cubicle through the cloth and metal partition to Henry's work station next to hers.

"Just learning what I can, ma'am," Henry said, suppressing his familiar bursts of anger.

"How 'bout delivering these reports to the director's office?" she said.

"Right away," he responded and quickly logged out of his internet search and stepped into her cube.

"These?" he picked up an inner-office envelope.

"Yeah, time sheets and a bunch of forms we have to fill out weekly. Hurry up."

Henry navigated the maze of alleys through government-grey cubicle partitions on the fifth floor of the O'Neil Federal Building on his way to the director's office. He walked by the agents' area. Henry had little use for the Neanderthals who investigated federal crimes and chased down criminals. He knew they perceived him as a paper-pushing pansy of a clerk.

He heard snickering and a crusty voice call, "Hey, Wussy."

Henry's trigger went off in the deep recesses of his brain. A torrent of epinephrine gushed through his nervous system. He controlled it and he kept on walking, keenly aware of the drumming in his head and the churning in his gut. He was sweating and red-faced when he delivered the forms to the director's secretary's desk.

"Thank you," the young woman said without looking up.

On Henry's way back through the maze, Billy McCarthy stood leaning against the pillar of his cubicle, his coffee mug handle looped in his trigger finger. "How ya doin', Wuss?"

A blinding white light flashed inside Henry's eyes and he found himself on the floor straddling over Billy, whose nose was surging blood. Billy's service pistol was in Henry's hand, cocked and aimed at Billy's terrified bloody face.

"Keep your weapons holstered," Henry heard himself say to the agents who had rushed to the ruckus, "or this little incident will get a lot more serious." His voice was calm, his words measured.

"We're cool," the senior agent said. "This moment has already been forgotten. Let's just get back to our jobs, okay?"

Henry hopped up, stepped back from the trembling field agent who was trying to grovel to his feet. He set the Beretta pistol on safe, popped out the magazine, and racked the slide back, ejecting the nine-millimeter round from the chamber. He handed the pistol, magazine, and bullet to Luis Valencia, the senior agent, and walked back through the maze to the engineering division.

No one ever mentioned the tussle again. Billy McCarthy decided to request a transfer to the Phoenix, Arizona, office for his wife's health.

In the thirty years since that episode, Henry experienced hundreds of raging bouts, some violent, some loud, all hurtful to others and himself. His wife Sandy was the most frequent target of his outbursts. But as he aged the ferocity of his fits diminished, but the frequency increased.

Tobias decided he had bothered Henry enough for one night and returned to the angelic base. Michael said, "Tobias, Henry belongs to you. Respond to his every request."

Mrs. Devens offered Henry a full-time job in her department after one of her three engineers got promoted a few months before Henry graduated. Henry accepted her offer. Not only did it pay him enough to rent a small apartment in Danvers, own a used Honda, and have some discretionary income to eat out and support his fishing addiction, but he also enjoyed the luxury of not having to do any real work.

Then he met Sandy.

When the Massachusetts weather permitted, Henry's Saturday routine included a big breakfast at Candee's Kitchen in Gloucester after a morning of fishing from 4:00 to 7:00 a.m.

One May Saturday morning, Henry ordered his usual breakfast—a thick slab of ham, home-fried potatoes, buttered toast, four fried eggs, overeasy, and a bottomless cup of black coffee—listed on Candee's menu as the "Hungry Helmsman." Halfway through his pile of greasy food and halfway through a scathing article in the *Boston Herald* by sports writer Joe Gordon hotly criticizing Red Sox manager Ralph Houk for keeping Rainey in the game after allowing three runs in the fifth, Henry noticed this tall, striking brunette at the takeout counter. She wore a faded blue man's dress shirt, loose khaki pants, and a confident, unselfconscious attitude. Her smile and cheery conversation with Candee over the counter cast something pleasant and intense at Henry's heart. The careless outfit couldn't conceal what Henry saw—a gorgeous figure, a beautiful face, and a vivacious countenance.

For seven consecutive Saturdays, Henry studied this compelling woman dressed in the same indifferent clothes as she picked up her order at Candee's counter. Henry carried her image around in his memory all week from Saturday to Saturday. On the seventh Saturday, Henry finally felt noticed. Looking up over the top edge of his *Boston Herald*, he briefly met the gaze of the lovely brunette in the loose shirt and baggy khakis. Henry nodded. She held his gaze for a few meaningful seconds, enough to communicate interest. Then out she marched with a quick look back over her broad, square shoulder, a look that stirred Henry in the gut—a look that offered promise.

The next Saturday Henry decided to sit on the old wooden bench outside Candee's by the takeout counter. Sandy arrived on schedule in her beat-up El Camino and he said, "Hello."

"Hi," Sandy said. "Seen you around here. You a fisherman?"

That started it.

In the months that Henry got to know Sandy, he became more and more fascinated with her life. She lived with her ancient grandmother on a secluded stretch of cliff overlooking Magnolia Bay, a few miles south of Gloucester. When he drove there to meet her for their first date, he was struck, not by any display of extravagance because at Cielavista there was no such display, but by a deep stirring in his spirit. Never before had Henry been aware of such a sensation—couldn't figure out what was going on inside himself.

Henry arrived late at Cielavista, having missed Woodlawn Avenue, the hard-to-notice road from Gloucester to Magnolia—no signpost. Couldn't find Shore Drive, the unpaved lane off Woodlawn Avenue that swept through the thick woods along the coast—frustrating. Henry missed it twice because it was hidden by brush and overhanging branches. Eventually he found the narrow dirt road through the woods, dark even at high noon. He urged his Honda slowly over several miles of bumps and ruts.

The estate first announced its presence on the left side of the lane with a high wrought iron fence, interrupted by a series of fieldstone pillars every fifty feet. The fence ran for over a mile. Henry was thinking, *How big is this place? Talk about secluded from the outside world.*

Then the wide, unguarded gate, supported by huge fieldstone pillars on each side, gave way to a peastone driveway that wound through a manicured wood—still no view of any buildings. Henry's fears and uncertainties were somehow assuaged by a strange, calming spirit that hovered over the property.

Finally, after what seemed like miles, an imposing granite mansion appeared down the hill before him through the trees. Surrounded by meticulously pruned hedges and fastidiously trimmed gardens, the three-story colonial-style manse gave Henry the impression of a grand, yet comfortable castle. He stopped his car on the high ground overlooking the stately home to absorb the effect this property was having on him. Not a hint of intimidation—just safety and security.

Behind and to the right of the big house was a substantial stucco bungalow, then the Atlantic Ocean, then the distant horizon and then the sky. The grounds around the two buildings were laid out in a careful array of lawns, gardens, fruit orchards, and wispy fields of high grass.

The tires of Henry's Honda crunched to a stop near the portico of the mansion. Sandy skipped across the grass to Henry's car, pulled open the passenger-side door, and sat beside him. Evidently she decided to upgrade her wardrobe today from the familiar faded outfit to a light-green V-neck jersey and black cotton slacks.

"You look nice," Henry managed.

"Thanks. Pull around to our house in back. How are you, Henry?" She smiled at him.

"Sorry I'm late," Henry said. "I felt like I was on a scavenger hunt trying to find this place. You could have a war here and no one would even hear it."

She looked over at him and their eyes met. Henry noticed a touch of extra color on her lips and her dark hair was nicely arranged today. Having her seated so close to him made him pleasantly nervous.

"You look a bit flustered, Henry. You okay?" she asked.

He guided the Honda around the driveway toward the smaller house near the cliff.

"Heh, heh, heh," chuckled Henry. "This may not be the right way to say it, but you ever go fishing?"

"Yeah, sure."

"And that feeling right when you get a strike and you know the fish is hooked, that rush of excitement?"

"Henry, you're such a romantic. I'm getting some of that too," she said, laughing. "Which one of us is the fish?"

As they approached the bungalow, she said, "Yeah, pull in right here. Good." And she hopped out and waited for Henry at the foot of the steps leading up to the porch.

"Grandma and I live here. Come on in," she said and walked through the screen door ahead of Henry. He let the door clack behind him against the wood frame and he followed Sandy through the foyer into the living room.

"Grandma's praying out on her rock. We're alone so you can kiss me," she said, turning to him with a grin.

So he did.

On their next date, Henry took Sandy out on his thirty-foot fishing boat past the horizon and he dropped anchor in a calm, flat sea. He fired up the gas grill and put on the flounder he'd just caught and cleaned, unfolded a stainless steel table and spread a linen cloth over it, lit a candle in a hurricane lamp, set the table with silver, china, and crystal, poured champagne, and sat across from his girlfriend.

"Tell me about your life," he said.

Sandy sipped the champagne and nibbled on a cracker covered with caviar and said, "I suppose I should start with my grandmother, okay?"

Henry nodded. Twilight in the eastern sky was giving way to Vega, the evening star.

"My grandmother, Gabriella Quartarone, spent her first ten years in Aci Trezza, Sicily. She lived in one of the homes in the seaside villa of her great uncle, Don Giovanni Quartarone, the *padrino* of one of the most prosperous and influential families in Catania Province. Don Giovanni's father and uncles had built a wide network of enterprises from their small fishing fleet, to a pair of cargo vessels to an ever-expanding global merchant marine fleet, eventually adding several international banks and steel plants to their corporate empire."

Henry served the flounder a la Moutarde with home-fried red potatoes and onions, mixed vegetables, and baguettes. He refilled the champagne glasses and set water bottles on the table. "Hope you like flounder," he said.

"If you're trying to impress a girl, you might be getting there," said Sandy. "Mind if I say a quick blessing?"

"Fine."

"Lord, thank you for all you provide. Bless this meal with your grace. Amen."

"Okay," said Henry, "where were you?"

Sandy savored a bite of the fish and closed her eyes for a few seconds. "Man, this is really good. Let's see.

"When Gabriella was born there were thirty-six people living at the family villa in Sicily, all *famiglia estesa*. Her mother died of smallpox two years after Gabriella's birth, so her aunt Maria assumed responsibility for her upbringing.

"Some of Maria's family moved to the United States in the early nineteen hundreds and set up a trading company in Gloucester, and purchased what is now Cielavista, our villa on Magnolia Bay. They had amassed enough money to maintain the property into perpetuity. Gabriella became the sole owner of Cielavista by outliving the rest of her extended family. As you have noticed, Gabriella and I live in the cottage near the cliff. She gave the big stone house over to her landscaper, Carlos Santiago, and his extended family. So now it's just me and my grandma in the cottage and her adopted family in the mansion."

CHAPTER FIVE

A friendly shout from the driveway interrupted Henry's reverie. It was Carlos Santiago, the head groundskeeper and patriarch of the clan who lived in the stone mansion.

"*Hola, Senior Henri. Como se va?*" Carlos's body wasn't much bigger than a twelve-year-old boy's—tight, compact, and lithe. But his brown, leathery face and long, white mane of hair affirmed the great-grandfather's true age. He drove his golf cart to Henry and said, "Hop in, chief."

Henry smiled at his good friend. "Can't join you tonight, Carlos. I have to come up with a security scheme for Gabriella. She's concerned that there may be a threat against us. But hey, tomorrow night let's get together. I'm gonna need your help, okay?"

"Fine with me. See you *mañana*." Before he drove away he said, "How do you like your new body guard?"

Henry gave Carlos a curious scowl, "What're you talking about?"

"Oh, I guess you haven't met him yet. *No problemo,*" and he waved and drove into the pine grove beyond the herb garden.

Henry spent the next six hours on his home computer connected to the FBI database. First he reviewed the latest updates of his colleagues at *PEAR— Princeton Engineering Anomalies Research.* Then he combed the criminal database, locating the incident file on the North Little Rock explosion.

"There's gotta be a way," Henry said to his computer, "to block our enemy from getting a fix on our location here at Cielavista."

"Do you know who I am?" asked Frances O'Donnelly. She had driven directly without sleep from southern California to the Directorate's operations center in central Missouri.

"Yep," said Andrew Johansen as he remained riveted to the project on his computer.

Frances wavered between scolding Andrew like a naughty child or lording over him like the powerful boss that she was. Before she could decide, he got up and left the room.

Unsettled, Frances could only stand there in Andrew's operations center and wait for him to return. It was the first time that she or any of the directors had come to inspect this bunker, buried deep in the limestone caves of the Gasconade River. She looked around. It was a one-man control room with three huge HD screens on the back wall, two crescent-shaped terraces of computer screens, and at the center of the concentric arcs was Andrew's semicircular console with controls for every computer and screen.

Frances studied the screens on the upper terrace labeled Alpha through Foxtrot. She recognized the names of the Directorate's six operational squads. On the next lower level was an array of screens with spreadsheets, calendars, lists, diagrams, bank account balances, and maps. The sharp executive quickly comprehended the meaning of all the displays, but she couldn't grasp how to operate the control console on the first level. The longer she studied the content on all the screens, the more she understood the intellectual power this young man possessed.

After thirty minutes, Andrew returned from somewhere in the dark recesses of the cave with his face buried in a subway sandwich wrapped in paper. He looked up with mayonnaise all over his cheeks and he took his seat in the black carbon-fiber swivel chair—the only seat in the ops center.

"Look," Andrew started right in. "As you probably know, I'm a high functioning sociopath—certified if you want to see my medical records. Being so born has its advantages and disadvantages. One of the advantages is that I couldn't give half a crap about you and your pompous position. Another advantage is that, since I have nearly zero emotions, you can't really bother me with the authority you're going to try to impose here. One more is that if you have anything to offer that isn't totally worthless, I can quickly evaluate it and see if I can use it. So, Frances, what are you here for? Get on with it."

"What are the disadvantages?"

"Nobody likes me."

"Okay, Andrew, the board wants to know why you can't successfully accomplish a mission."

Without rancor or disrespect, the young operations officer replied, "Somebody or something has invaded my system, and they're pretty darn good at it."

"What do you know so far?" she asked, now that the lines of communication had been established.

"You know how this works, right? We use advanced psychokinesis to manipulate two groups of people: seers and operators. We instruct the seers to identify the location of our targets and perform deep reconnaissance, then we alert one of the operational squads to support and conduct the attack. We select an unsuspecting loner, manipulate his mind and, with the help of the squad, he follows our orders and accomplishes the pruning mission."

"Yeah, I understand the process, so what's going wrong?"

"Not sure, but I'm getting close. There's a computer somewhere that logged on to the same website at the exact same time I was logged on to it."

"What site?" Frances asked.

Andrew finished chomping on his sandwich and he wiped off his face with his sleeve. He reached in the pocket of his faded black tee shirt and pulled out a pack of Trident Gum. He unwrapped a stick and popped it in his mouth and dropped the wrapper on the floor.

"Want a piece?" he offered.

Frances took the pack and pulled out a piece of gum for herself. They sat there in silence for a few minutes chewing and staring at each other, engaged in some tribal ritual like smoking a peace pipe.

"What site?" she asked again.

Andrew clicked the space bar and the website for *PEAR—Princeton Engineering Anomalies Research—*appeared on screen. Frances quickly understood the essence of what she was reading.

She read aloud, "They study the interaction of human consciousness with sensitive physical devices, systems, and processes, and develop complementary theoretical models to enable better understanding of the role of consciousness in the establishment of physical reality."

"Yeah," said Andrew. "The forces of consciousness they've been studying are similar to our advanced psychokinesis powers that generate human motivations over long distances. My point is that someone somewhere is visiting the same site. I programed my computer number seven to conduct a search to locate this computer. It may take some time. I'm not one hundred percent sure on this, but I think whoever he is—that's the monkey wrench in the works."

"Akebe prefers 'fly in the ointment.' He thinks it's more biblical," Frances said.

No response from Andrew as he stared into the screen directly over his keyboard on the first elevated crescent. He kept clicking the keys, leaning closer and closer toward the screen. Frances' gaze alternated between the screen and the operations officer.

"Geez, this guy's good," Andrew said with a touch of the emotion he claimed he did not possess.

"Look at this," Andrew pointed with his greasy, unshaven chin to the big HD screen high up on the back wall. Frances looked up to the screen depicting a world map on Mercator projection. Hundreds of arching red lines connecting hundreds of red dots crisscrossed the world map.

"Our fly is very carefully covering his whereabouts," Andrew stated. "How many dots do you count?"

"Eight hundred, twenty-seven," Frances answered quickly.

Andrew turned to her with a look of fresh respect. "Yep," he affirmed.

Frances continued, "And these are the proxy servers our 'fly' is using to mask his location. How many layers of camouflage is he using?"

Andrew's fingers flew over his keyboard, his bulging eyes fixated on the big screen, his jaws jack-hammering on his gum. "Eleven. This is the outer layer, then his countermeasure program makes those locations look like they are linked to another matrix of locations, here, see?" And a maze of green lines replaced the red. "Four hundred-fifty-six dots on this layer. I'm gonna try something different, wait."

"Where you going now?" Frances asked. "How about the Little Rock, Arkansas, highway network?"

Without looking up from the screen in front of him, Andrew said, "Yup."

And again the big screen displayed the maze of red lines showing the "computer" that logged onto the same FBI highway site that Andrew had hacked into when planning the Sherwood, Arkansas, attack on Doctor Stone.

After another minute of seemingly random, frantic keystrokes and gum chomping, Andrew turned his swivel chair to face Frances who was squatting on her haunches next to him, watching the code he was typing with full comprehension. For the first time in his life he experienced a twinge of collegiality, but he didn't know what it was.

"You see what I see?" he asked.

"Yes," she said. "He didn't hack into the FBI system. He has official access. That will condense your algorithm. So we must wait for computer number seven to find this FBI agent, right?"

"Yup."

"What's our next target?" she asked.

Andrew considered the question. Why he would even think about including anyone in his plans was beyond him. Then he wondered if he himself was being manipulated by the same forces he used on his subjects.

Dismissing that notion, he replied, "A little community college in Rosemont, Oregon. Our seers have identified two mindful thinkers there that need to be pruned out, a teacher named Martha Freeman and an Army veteran named Chris Mintz. We have a shooter under our control, who will make it look like an anti-Christian rampage. He will ask the roomful of students what their religion is and shoot them.

"I'm also rescheduling Anna Stone for elimination. Probably next month."

Frances kept a mental notepad in her head. She recorded two items to track: 1. Locate and destroy the fly in the ointment, and 2. Increase offensive operations against targets.

"Sounds good, Andrew, keep me posted. I'm off to Sherwood, Arkansas, to visit your last failure." She turned into the dark passageway leading out to the daylight and over her shoulder she said, "You might think about getting another chair in there."

Andrew's head was burrowed back in his computer. "I told you I don't give a crap about you."

"Thanks for the gum," she said, smiling as she exited his tomblike ops center.

Frances climbed up the winding limestone stairs to the cave's opening on a remote ledge overlooking the Gasconade River. On the path to the parking lot by Highway 305, she called in her deciding vote to Chairman Cheron.

CHAPTER SIX

That evening, at the same time that Gabriella made her graceful leap across the crevice onto that one flat table of rock where her psychokinesis energy was magnified a thousandfold, Frances O'Donnelly drove a rented Chevy Impala from the executive air terminal in Little Rock, Arkansas, toward Sherwood where Doctor Anna Stone was finishing up her day at Abundant Health Chiropractic. Frances' Learjet had made the trip from the Kansas City Airport to Little Rock in less than an hour.

Frances listened to the audio recording the Directorate's background summary of Anna Stone. Andrew's computer model of Doctor Stone's future projected that she was to become an international leader of nontraditional healing methods. That projection puzzled Frances—how could a country chiropractor from a small town in Arkansas rise to a position of global influence? But the Directorate chose to trust the computer. So to protect America's future they had to kill Anna Stone. The Directorate must neutralize every one of these quacks who would attempt to derail modern medicine, supported by modern pharmaceuticals, funded by global chemical producers, all generating billions for the financial security of the international community.

Fifteen hundred miles away in the Eastern Time zone where the setting sun glimmered on the horizon, Gabriella Quartarone continued her watch over Frances O'Donnelly closing in on Anna Stone's office. Whereas Frances was unsure of her purpose for meeting with Anna, Gabriella was absolutely certain. The old sage figured out that Frances' mind had been placed under Andrew's operational control.

Gabriella closed her eyes, enabling her to "see" in the sky above the ocean something like a movie screen. On this evening, Gabriella observed the rays of energy emanating from Andrew's seers in Team Foxtrot, all terminating on Frances as she drove up Highway 167 in North Little Rock. Gabriella knew without a doubt that Frances was being used by Andrew as a detection device to uncover the source of the power that had warned Anna to avoid his ambush. Andrew had all his systems set up so he could track the energy emanating from Gabriella through Anna linked to Frances and back to his computers. Once he tracked down the "fly in the ointment," he would be able to eliminate Gabriella and her family at Cielavista.

A curious blend of amusement and concentration brought a smile to Gabriella's lips. The Spirit that engulfed Gabriella's body had created the appropriate countermeasure in Gabriella's heart, and it was flowing from there into her intellect. She was being instructed to take advantage of this opportunity to send Andrew and the Directorate on a wild goose chase.

Gabriella's heavenly video displayed all the screens in Andrew's underground operations center. She watched Andrew as he watched Anna Stone log off her computer, turn off the coffee maker, and set it up to brew the next morning.

Gabriella constructed a dummy energy-generating location in Cape Neddick, Maine, seventy miles north of her estate on the Massachusetts coast. The iron deposits in the granite cliff beneath her feet were connected directly to a thick vein of iron ore that travelled under a half mile of earth to a similar deposit in Neddick. Her wiry body trembled violently for several seconds as a lightning rod of spiritual power transmitted a flow of supernatural electricity to the dummy location. Once the connection was established, she could walk away and it would remain intact as a closed circuit, making Andrew and his delusional bosses think that her headquarters was located in Neddick, far enough away to keep her and her family safe.

Having established the decoy generator, Gabriella turned her attention back to her heavenly theater showing the back of Andrew's head as he watched in real time the video feed of Frances as she turned her rented Impala into the gravel driveway of Abundant Health Chiropractic.

Gabriella made sure that Anna was equipped with a kinetic energy connection that emanated from the generator in Neddick. The old prophetess closed her eyes and concentrated on the spiritual events taking place on her cosmic movie screen. From the dummy location in Neddick, she sent rays of protection that settled on Anna's mind and body. She had never before attempted such a complicated paranormal network. All she had to rely on was her trust in her God that He had arranged all this. She was an instrument in His hands.

When Gabriella opened her eyes again, the sky over the North Atlantic had lost all traces of sunset. A thick carpet of clouds obscured even a glimmer of starlight, remanding the night to absolute blackness. Facing southeast, Gabriella saw nothing as if "nothing" had a substance. No shoreline, no ocean, no sky, no horizon, just the tangible essence of emptiness. With no visible reference points representing distance or time, Gabriella sensed the pleasure of infinite vastness. No limits. No boundaries. Eternity.

Gabriella's screen opened up through the blackness like a movie theater. She saw Frances open the door to Anna's clinic and step into the waiting room. Her vision expanded from North Little Rock, Arkansas, to Andrew's cave in the cliff over the Gasconade River in Missouri. Nearly invisible blue rays of power radiated from Neddick, Maine, through Anna to Frances who unknowingly was being used by Andrew as a receiver-transmitter. The video in the night sky over Magnolia, Massachusetts—seen only by Gabriella—showed a map of the region that included Arkansas and Missouri. The blue lines being transmitted from

Frances straight up past the atmosphere to Directorate Satellite number 31, then three hundred miles due north to the receiver connected to Andrew's computer on the second row in his ops center.

Gabriella's vision snapped quickly to a close-up of Andrew's head as he shouted at the screen, "Gotcha, you fly in the ointment. You're in Neddick, Maine."

Anna turned off the light in the kitchenette and walked down the hall into the waiting room. The spirit within her flexed its muscles when she discovered Frances O'Donnelly standing in her foyer. An inner warmth swarmed through Anna's nervous system and spoke instructions to her consciousness from an unknown distance. Confidence, courage, strength, wisdom—all in quantities she had never seemed to possess—streamed into her heart and mind.

"Hello," Anna heard her own voice say. But the voice was more masculine, more commanding than it had ever been before. She wondered if her surprise showed on her face as she stepped toward the well-dressed, smart-looking woman in her waiting room. Anna offered her hand and Frances gripped it firmly.

"Hello, Doctor," Frances said, "I'm Sarah Perkins, in town on business, and I was hoping I could make an appointment with you. Air travel has really messed up my back."

Volumes of data streamed into Anna's subconscious. In three seconds she knew: 1. the lady was lying, 2. the lady was dangerous, 3. the lady was extremely brilliant, 4. Anna was being protected, and 5. Anna was more powerful than this phony "Sarah."

"My dear Ms. Perkins." Words radiated into Anna's head and out her mouth, "Please sit down. Here, take this chair." Anna sat next to her on the couch, an end table separating them. The gaze between the two women was like a track between two jousting knights charging at each other with lances leveled.

Frances, an experienced jouster, searched for the white knight's weak spot as she galloped toward her. Finding none, she decided to angle away from her adversary's lance. "Thank you, Doctor." Her eyelashes fluttered. "I'm sorry to barge in like this, but the pain is excruciating."

Anna, now enjoying the surge of power in her spirit and sensing her advantage, said, "And I'm sorry that I can't help you today, but I have an opening tomorrow at ten. Where are you staying?"

"You know," Frances said, "I drove directly here after my plane landed. My office in Hartford made all the arrangements for my trip here, and I'll have to text them to see what hotel they booked me in."

"Hartford! My husband's family is from Hartford. Where is your office, Sarah?" Anna asked, laying the trap for her foe. "Are you near the Sears building on Main Street?" she asked, knowing that there was never a Sears building in the city of Hartford, Connecticut.

Without hesitation, Frances responded, "You know, I've only been assigned there for just over a month and I'm not that familiar with downtown. We're in a small plaza on the west side. But enough about me. Ten o'clock sounds good. I'll arrange my schedule tomorrow to come see you. Thank you very much."

Slippery and smart, thought Anna. "Okay, Sarah. Drink plenty of water tonight and let me give you an old-fashioned ice bag for your back."

She went to the supply closet and came back to the waiting room with a black and white checked ice bag.

"Here, get some ice from the machine in your hotel, fill this bag two thirds full, add some water, and lie on your stomach and let this sit on your back.

"Stand up," Anna commanded.

Frances obeyed the young chiropractor. She had not sensed that level of obeisance since she lived under her father's command as a teenager. A wrestling match broke out in her mind between her own dominant self-possession and these strange feelings of girlish inferiority.

She stood up as directed.

Anna placed her left hand on Frances' left shoulder and placed her right hand in the small of her back. She murmured comfort through her lips like a mother quieting an excited child. Moments ticked by. Her hand kindled warmth in Frances' back. The corporate executive closed her eyes and groaned as the sweet, grace-filled power permeated her muscles and her spinal cord. Her mind relaxed.

———

Hours later Frances woke up from a dreamless trance, reclined in the nearly-dark waiting room of Abundant Health. Alone. Her eyes were drawn to the flickering flame of a eucalyptus candle on the end table. Next to the candle was a brief note: *"Sarah, you have received a wonderfully spiritual experience. You will be fine. Have a nice evening. Don't forget the ice bag for your back. I look forward to treating you tomorrow at ten. Love and Peace, Anna."*

———

Andrew drummed his fingers on the edge of his desk. As usual he was controlling a dozen murderous operations simultaneously across the nation. But tonight, having located the enemy's headquarters, he concentrated his focus on that most urgent operation, letting his computers control the lower priorities. Andrew gave a name to the operation that would destroy the FLY IN THE OINTMENT: "Operation FITO."

After forty-five minutes of designing several courses of action for the destruction of the FITO's headquarters, he paused to monitor the other operations.

On screen number twelve, Andrew watched the recording of Frances entering Abundant Life. Anna Stone got in her car and drove away. Frances' rented Impala sat by itself in the gravel parking lot between the office building and the street as the night grew dark in Arkansas. He was getting hungry but he was glued to his chair, wondering what happened to Frances.

No matter. He got what he was after—the location of his enemy, now named FITO. His ingenious system of reverse tracking located the enemy's position in the coastal town of Neddick, Maine.

Eventually Andrew's eye swept over to screen twelve showing Frances in the dark gravel parking lot gazing around for an unusually long time. She walked shakily to the car, squeezed the remote to unlock the door, and slid into the driver's seat. He dialed her cell phone. It rang six times and went to voicemail.

"What the heck happened to you, you dumb broad?" he shouted. "What were you doing in there? Why did she leave you in there alone? What the heck's going on? You better call me now. Now." He hung up knowing he wouldn't hear from her.

———

Gabriella had switched channels on her metaphysical screen when Anna laid her hand on Frances' back and prayed for her. The ancient prophetess had other critical incidents to observe and others to protect, like Supreme Court Justice Allen Scales.

She prayed, "You know, Father, I admit I was a bit skeptical about this business of bouncing energy streams off one lady to the next, but I trusted you. I rest in your grace, dear Father, knowing that Anna is in your control, and that you have directed the forces of the Directorate away from my home and my family."

Then she added, "At least for now."

———

Randal Sanford had made his way from Akebe Cheron's yacht back to his home in Salem, Massachusetts–the Witch City. He was not used to being confused. But now he was. Sanford's seers had the capacity to perceive spiritual and kinetic energy out to a range of over two-hundred miles. For two months his team had been receiving signals that a force field was emanating from somewhere on Boston's north shore.

But now Directorate Headquarters, DHQ, was ordering him to concentrate on Cape Neddick, Maine. *Where the heck were they getting their intel?*

Randal called one of his operators, Firdos Gaffardi, and arranged to meet him at Coffee Time Bakery in Salem, "Home of the Real Cream Bismark," at 5:30 a.m.. They were both insomniacs and Coffee Time opened at four, and offered the best quality and variety of pastries in greater Boston, maybe the world.

Randal was passionate about the Real Cream Bismark. Randal, seated at a corner table with his favorite pastry poised in front of his open mouth, shoved it into his dumpsterlike stomach. He looked up as Firdos pushed open the glass door at Coffee Time and surveyed the clientele.

"Hi," Firdos greeted Randal.

Randal harbored a respectful distain for Firdos, but restrained his anger at the young operator's attempt to ruin Randal's indulgent moment. The Executive knew that Firdos pursued a Spartan lifestyle. He also knew that Firdos was unaware that his thoughts and motives were all being programed by one obsessed computer geek in a cave in Missouri. Firdos had taken on the persona of an arrogant outsider who viewed American consumption with self-satisfying contempt. Randal had instructed the young recruit to bank three fourths of his now-substantial income from the Directorate. He told him to choose a modest one-bedroom apartment, a six-year-old Toyota Corolla, and a blue-collar wardrobe. Firdos' only vice was smoking, which he justified because he felt smoking made him look more sinister.

Randal, on the other hand, was addicted to all junk foods, television, heavy metal rock concerts, and vodka. Addicted equally to all four.

"You having anything, Firdos?" muffled Randal through a mouthful of "real" whipped cream and sweet pastry.

"I may indulge in a bottle of water," Firdos said. "What are we here for, Randal, besides face-stuffing?"

"You have to have one of these cream Bismarks. This is the only place on the planet that makes them with real whipped cream, and the pastry—it's like a cream puff that dissolves on your tongue. A morsel of heaven in your mouth."

Flaky crumbs of the heavenly morsel were decorating Randal's fleece vest and a ring of whipped cream surrounded his lips.

Again, "What are we here for, Randal?" repeated Firdos, making no effort to conceal his impatience.

"DHQ says we're barking up the wrong tree."

"Imposs...." *Impossible* was the word Firdos tried to say. Randal observed the young man try to manage his anger and frustration, fully aware that Firdos' words and the emotions were being controlled by one of Andrew's algorithms half a continent away.

Randal recognized the change in Firdos' demeanor as the trigger word, "DHQ," immobilized his cognitive abilities, rendering Firdos directionless and totally dependent on him. Randal tried unsuccessfully to suppress a grin on his fleshy mouth.

"They got some hard intel that our target is located on the Maine coast about an hour north of us on I-95," Randal said.

Firdos' ability to be curious was failing him. "Okay, so what am I supposed to do, move up there?"

"You got a problem with making a change in location, Firdos? You building a big career here in the Pizza delivery industry? Starting a family? Putting down roots? Joining the Rotary Club, the Country Club?" Randal carefully observed Firdos' reaction to his scoffing. He could read no anger, no humiliation, not even a giggle. So the key word "DHQ" was still an effective prompt. Firdos was his marionette once again.

"No, Firdos, you don't move. You just have to commute to your new job in Neddick, Maine—nice beach town. We don't want to have to go through the hassle of getting you a new driver's license and filing taxes in a new state. You keep your lovely home here in Salem and you find a motel or a B&B or whatever's up there and commute, understand?"

CHAPTER SEVEN

Firdos Gaffardi never fit in. He blamed his perpetual state of exclusion on his new country, America. But if he were honest (a virtue he never completely grasped), he would have remembered that even in his native Iran, for sixteen years he never fit in there either.

He could not engage customers at STOP QUIK, his father's convenience store in Lynn, Massachusetts. Firdos' face always remained blank as he rang up the orders for coffee, candy, magazines, or cigarettes. His gaze would rest on their chests, not their eyes. He was too obtuse to pick up on the self-conscious fidgeting of the females when they felt him staring at their breasts. His father gave up on trying to coach Firdos into being more friendly to their customers. The young man simply did not fit in.

"He keeps doing it, Dad," Firdos' older brother, Zahed, complained to their father.

"Doing what?" the exasperated store proprietor asked.

"The moron drives away customers. He's like a robot, Dad. After he waits on them, they stare at him with this disgusted look on their faces and walk out all angry and disturbed."

"Firdos does all that?" asked the father, not wanting to waste his dwindling supply of energy on such a trivial matter. "How many times have I told you, son. You boys work for me as I worked for my father and as his father worked for his and on back into ancient Persia. Whether

Firdos is suited for this work or not is irrelevant. Life's not perfect, Zahed. Make the best of it."

Firdos' unusually sharp mind and extraordinary powers of observation allowed him to describe every customer who entered the store in the exact order they arrived as far back as two weeks. He was like a human security camera, but no one else knew about the data in his head. And when the nice-smelling woman approached him as he left the store after his shift was done, he sensed a weird familiarity with her. She had been in the store eleven times over the last month. In the last week she only came to the store around Firdos' quitting time.

"Could I bother you for just a sec, please?" She caught Firdos in the parking lot as he exited the store.

Firdos said, "What do you want?"

"I swear I bought two of these Red Sox hats, but here in my bag there's only one." She looked at his face.

His eyes went right to her tank top and he said, "Do you have a receipt?"

"Yeah, let me dig it out of the bag." But before she reached into the bag, she nervously grasped the sunglasses hanging on the neck of her shirt and removed them.

"Here." She pulled the slip of paper from the bag and handed it to Firdos.

"This says you only bought one," he stated, and handed it back to her.

"Oh, thanks. I'm such an airhead. I'll have to get another hat. If I give something to one nephew, I have to give the same thing to his brother." She attempted to connect with him, but his gaze remained fixed on her shirt.

As she went back into the convenience store, Firdos lit a cigarette and began his walk to his family's apartment on Essex Street. His mind fogged over and the voice of the woman seeped into his subconscious.

"*My name is Carlene. A mighty power has sent me to you. You will come with me and you will experience a new fulfilling life as a soldier in the Directorate's army.*"

A silver Civic pulled up to the curb just ahead of Firdos, and the woman with the Red Sox hats opened the passenger side window and shouted, "Can I give you a lift? Hop in."

The sweet vanilla fragrance of Carlene Wood's perfume swirled out from the Honda's window and penetrated Firdos' mind. He got into her car and never saw his family again. But now, finally, Firdos would fit in.

Frances O'Donnell woke up smiling. She had found the Riverfront Hotel in North Little Rock, checked in, removed her business suit, pulled back the covers, lay down, and slept the sleep of the righteous. The drapes covering the south-facing window on her eighth floor room left a sliver of space where they came together, and a sharp blade of sunlight beamed through, painting a bright stripe across the width of her king-size bed. She sat up and studied it, kicking at the sheets, causing the line of light to ripple like a clothesline in the wind. Frances laughed at it, and then tried to remember the last time she laughed other than at someone's demise.

For ten years Frances woke up to pain, stiffness, nausea, and feeling like she hadn't slept at all. In fact she had not slept through the night for ten years. The doctors called her condition fibromyalgia. They prescribed at various times Cymbalta, Lyrica, Savella, physical therapy, and medical marijuana. Nothing helped. They only made her sicker.

Frances was coming to grips with the fact that last night, after meeting with Anna Stone and passing out in her waiting room, she had slept for—what time was it, ten-thirty, she missed her appointment with Anna, and now she laughed out loud—twelve hours.

She stood up from the bed gingerly, expecting to feel the aches and stiffness that had become part of who she was. She took a step on the thick beige carpet. She walked over to where the thin line of sunlight fell on the floor and walked it like a tightrope walker. She grabbed the drapes and flung them open and let the blazing Arkansas sun radiate into her body. No pain. No discomfort. What did Anna Stone do to her while she was out? What drug did she give her? She walked back away from the big bed, took two running steps, and dove onto the sheets like a fourth-grader. Something fabulous had happened to her.

Frances showered, ran her fingers through the snarls in her hair, and got dressed and ordered breakfast up to her room. She went to the window again and looked out on the Arkansas River with its six bridges. Traffic was flowing over the I-30 bridge from North Little Rock into Little Rock. Just to the east of the interstate was the Junction Bridge, a pedestrian walkway. Frances' face went dark.

On the south shore the Junction Bridge terminated at the William J. Clinton Presidential Library and Clinton Foundation.

Her breath came in quick bursts as her mind went back to 1992. Frances was sixteen, waiting for her dad to drive her to school. The *Time Magazine* lay on the little maple table in the foyer of her parents' home a few miles from the front gate of Fort McPherson, Georgia. Her dad, Sergeant Major Kenneth O'Donnell, had just returned from Kuwait, where he led Infantry troops against Saddam's Republican Guards in the Gulf War.

The sergeant-major's battle gear stood against the wall in the foyer waiting for him to take it back to the post. His Kabar knife lay on top of his rucksack. The sheath was made of a coarse brown leather stitched around the edges with nylon thread, and there was a little rectangular pocket for a sharpening stone. Frances knew that the dark stain on the leather was from the blood of an enemy soldier.

Her dad walked down the hall from his bedroom into the foyer in his sand-colored camouflage uniform and glanced at the cover of the *Time Magazine*—a portrait of then-governor Bill Clinton, announcing his candidacy for US president. Her dad, in a set of smooth, quick, unemotional moves, slipped the vicious-looking knife from its sheath, raised it to his shoulder, and rammed the point through the magazine, impaling it to the maple tabletop—right through candidate Clinton's right eye. The sergeant-major then went to the coffee pot in the kitchen and poured himself a cup—black.

Frances jerked the handle back and forth, left and right, finally dislodging it from the table and Clinton's face. She returned it to its sheath and snapped the strap in place. The gash in the table remained.

Staring out over the Arkansas River at the expansive edifice built to honor the man reviled by Frances and her father caused a dark curtain to fall over her joyous mood.

A knock at her door announced the arrival of her breakfast. "Room service."

Frances opened the door. The woman pushing the stainless steel serving cart loaded down with two breakfast services was not a member of the hotel staff. It was Anna Stone.

"Good morning, Sarah, how did you sleep?" asked Anna.

A faint smile suggested itself onto Frances' lips. "Well, good morning, Anna," Frances replied, trying to conceal her amazement—and her delight. Her surprise at Anna Stone's presence in her room was somehow mitigated by the surreal events she had experienced the day before.

"I assure you I am as surprised as you are," said Anna. "And I'm as interested in how all these events are going to play out as you are. So how I came to know where you are staying, how I found myself in the hotel kitchen when they got your call for room service, and how I convinced them to let me deliver it to your room—all beyond me, but here we are, sister, so let's see what we know."

Anna and Frances sat at the round hotel table with two orders of scrambled eggs, toast, sausage, home-fried potatoes, grits, pancakes, fruit, and coffee. The two women surveyed the morning feast like commandos reconnoitering an enemy objective. Frances looked up at Anna and said, "Attack."

Henry heard his wife call, "Hey, babe, come in here. I'm getting something."

He reluctantly tore himself away from his unfinished security plan on the computer. Twenty-five years of marriage taught him to control his angry outbursts.

"What?" he snarled.

"Okay, I have to keep both my hands on my head to get what's coming to me, and I need you to write down what I'm getting here. Would you?"

Henry pulled his notebook from his breast pocket and unclipped the pen from the cover. "Shoot," he said.

"Right, here we go: Riverside Hotel, North Little Rock, Arkansas, countermeasures. Scramble the color coding of the signals radiating from woman in room 562. Move color spectrum five shades to the right," Sandy dictated. "Add the time and date, hon.

"Okay," she continued. "Now sending information to Anna Stone: 'Frances works for the Directorate whose diabolical mission is to control every established institution in the US. Tell her you know that and the chairman's name is Akebe Cheron and the name of his yacht is *Medusa*.'"

"Where you getting this stuff?" asked Henry.

"No idea," she said, "but we just messed up somebody's plans."

Andrew watched on screen number 4 the image of the roof of the Riverside Hotel in North Little Rock. His satellite imaging device picked up telekinetic radiation that he had programmed into Frances when she was in his ops center.

Andrew decoded the colors from the hotel roof and read the message, "Frances is following Directorate orders, accomplishing mission."

Having no longer any need to monitor Frances, Andrew clicked over to monitors three, seven, and eight, and directed the actions of his six squads of seers and operators. Squad Alpha in Phoenix, Bravo in Burlington, Vermont, Charlie and Echo in Washington DC, Delta in Boston, and Foxtrot held in strategic reserve.

Chapter Eight

Anna Stone paused and watched the veil of astonishment fall over Frances' face. Frances took a sip of coffee and said, "How do you know Akebe Cheron?"

"And he has a lovely, luxurious yacht named *Medusa*," Anna added. She tried the grits with butter.

Frances dropped her utensils, sat back against the back of her chair, folded her arms across her chest, and asked, "Just what is going on here, Anna?"

Anna Stone's eyelashes draped down over her eyes and she concentrated on the instructions filtering into her mind. She took a deep breath and let it out slowly through pursed lips.

"It seems, Frances, your chairman has hypnotized and brainwashed you. Your brilliant mind and your intense patriotic drive made you very attractive to the Directorate and they assimilated you into their organization through a very sophisticated system of mind control. However, the Directorate has a tenacious enemy that protects those courageous, mindful professionals that your board of billionaires target for assassination. Somehow, they recruited me and assigned me the mission to set you free. And there's more."

Anna admired Frances' stately figure as the wealthy executive stood and marched to the window overlooking the Arkansas River. Minimal makeup, streaks of grey in the auburn hair, and an understated wardrobe showcased her natural handsomeness. The late-morning sun arched higher over the urban valley below. Traffic streamed east and west on I-40 and flowed ambitiously on the surface roads in and out of Little Rock.

"My dad and I were very close," Frances began. "He was a warrior in the US Army Special Forces. They wanted him to go to college and become an officer, but he knew precisely what he was cut out for—leading small teams in close combat, not directing the fight from a distant command post. He was brilliant. Often much smarter than his commanding officers, but he never flaunted it. When he was deployed he sent me long letters. I could publish them as a tome to integrity, courage, and strong moral character. But I never would.

"Our political leadership devolved deeper and deeper into the collection of bought-and-paid-for cartoon characters that we now have in our government, and my dad became more and more incensed. As a perfect soldier he never expressed or displayed his discontent, but in his letters to me he raged hot and angry about the decline of the nation for which he constantly offered his life. He wrote, 'A man can justify giving his life for his country only if it's a good country. And a country is only good when the people are good.'

"He pulled the plug at his twenty-third year, and he lost his identity. His spirit shriveled up as his body bloated up with binges of crappy food, beer, and bourbon. I watched him slowly crumble from the strongest, bravest man in the world to a pitiful, sloppy pensioner, and then to the grave in two short years. The way his life ended devastated me, and I focused my visceral hatred at the White House gang from this city and their left-wing coconspirators."

"My hatred for our government, our education system, our health care institutions, our so-called entertainment industry, and every business enterprise, even the shallow, self-indulgent values that Americans have adopted, swelled up inside me until I felt I would explode under the emotional stress. My own overeducated, overachieved life tasted rotten to me when I looked in the mirror. The Directorate offered me the opportunity to fix it. They seemed to have the power, Anna, to cleanse the country of all the individuals that obstruct the natural flow of intelligent control."

The young woman silently watched Frances gaze alternately out the window then down to the carpet, as if she were reading her reveries from the carpet and clarifying them from the sky. She stopped, poured herself a second cup of coffee, and sat down across from Anna at the table. She cocked her head to the left and looked at Anna.

"Somehow, someone connected me with you. It seems this other force, this enemy of the Directorate, has some kind of paranormal power to thwart their plans."

"Hmmm. That may explain some of my recent phenomena," said Anna.

"What do you mean?"

"Well," Anna said, "You must know that I stopped driving on Route 167 the other day and avoided a bridge explosion that would have killed me. I had this notion that a voice—no, not a voice—an impression, I guess told me to stop and help this lady and child sitting on the guardrail. But they disappeared. None of the other people even saw them. Made me wonder if they were just some figment of my imagination. Or something else.

"Then, when you showed up in my office yesterday," Anna was recalling the sensations she felt the day before, "I know I was operating under the influence of a spiritual power way beyond my understanding. Even the words coming out of my mouth weren't mine."

"So," interrupted Frances, "What was going on when you put your hand on my back?"

"Oh, that. Well, I guess under the power of this Spirit I must have possessed the ability to heal you. It's in the Bible—the gift of healing. How do you feel?"

"I feel totally pain-free." Frances put her elbows on the table, her head in her hands. Her tears flowed and her voice cried out. Anna watched

Frances' hidden misery rise off her like the fog lifting off the Arkansas River down below.

Frances took several deep breaths.

"I think I'll try these grits," she said with a new voice.

"Just put a little butter on 'em," Anna advised. "Some people use the maple syrup."

Frances took a small bite and scowled. "Not a fan," she said, and drank some coffee.

"So now what?" Anna asked.

"Well, neither of us knows much," Frances said, "but I know this: if the operations officer of the Directorate—a very smart, very gross young man named Andrew—could effectively monitor our meeting this morning, we would have had some very violent visitors by now. I know he has the capability to monitor us, but there must be someone with the power to mask our words and actions so he can't see or hear us. You know anything about that?"

"Nope," said Anna, working on her eggs and toast. Then Anna asked, "Why go after me?"

"Look," Frances said, "I realize that you have been instrumental in opening up my eyes and relieving me of a very painful disease. I have the utmost respect for you. I need to take some time to process all this and see what I'm supposed to do. I'm not ready to go into detail about how you were targeted or all the insane plans this organization has on the table. I know we will be seeing each other again. But for now, let's just finish this pile of unholy food and go about our separate lives. Okay?"

Anna received a notion deep in her subconscious that she was done here.

"Okay. Let's eat."

Henry was amazed. He wondered aloud, "What just happened here, babe?"

Henry looked out the east-facing window of the tower that topped a silo-looking addition on the corner of the house. It was designed to emulate a lighthouse, but it didn't quite make it.

He could see old Gabriella sitting on one of the stone cubes out on her granite outcropping below the cliff. The aged woman, rigid, unmoving, could have been a statue carved out of the same stone on which she sat.

Sandy turned to her husband and said, "It appears that God is imparting to me some of the power that Nonina possesses."

Henry looked at Sandy with a glazed stare. *Here it comes again. I know she can see it. I can't control what it does to my insides, but I can control how I react. Sandy is getting involved in a very dangerous game here, and I'm being dragged in too. Sit tight, boy. Be still and listen to your wife.*

"And, apparently you don't have to sit out there in all kinds of weather," Henry said, trying to lighten this profoundly disturbing revelation about his wife.

"I get it up here in the tower, she gets it out there on the rock."

"So what are you 'getting,' my dearest darling weirdo?" *So far, I'm doing all right. Hope I can hold it.*

"Yeah," she laughed, "I'm weird, all right. And mighty proud of it.

"What I'm getting, Henry, is this ability to perceive activity in distant places. And I'm getting a supernatural power to transmit some kind of impulses that influences the action in those places.

"See, in this case, Anna Stone, the young chiropractor whose life Nonina saved last week, has made a connection with one of the chief leaders of the enemy's power structure, this Frances O'Donnelly. Evidently Anna has a gift of divine healing, and she prayed for Frances' fibromyalgia to be healed and God did it. As a result, Frances was open to having a conversation with Anna, and possibly having a relationship with her. So I guess Nonina arranged a meeting with the two women and it appears that Frances may be coming out from under the insidious brain-washing of the enemy. I suspect Nonina will be using her as a spy in the enemy's camp."

"So what's your next move, thy awesome prophetess?" and Henry bowed deeply at the waist in not-so-mock adoration.

Sandy gave him a smack on the head. "Rise, you unclean serf," she commanded. "I don't think I have any control over what I'm supposed to do. I'm just going to be open to these paranormal signals and respond and react. Does that seem reasonable to you?"

Henry looked at his wife. Like her grandmother, Sandy barely showed any signs of aging, except for her hair, still thick and lustrous, worn in the same style as when he met her, in a short bob like Paul McCartney's in the Beatles' early years. It had turned from pure black to pure white in less than a year. Somehow the snowy moptop made her look even more startlingly attractive than when she was younger. Henry was aware of the looks she got from just about every man—and some women. Despite the constant undercurrent of discontent in Henry's gut, he was still wildly attracted to Sandy's physical beauty.

She was a marvelous swimmer. Henry and Sandy would walk down to the little cove below Gabriella's rock nearly every day when the weather was nice. Sandy would modestly let her robe drop to the pebbly beach, revealing her striking figure in a black competition swimsuit, and she'd charge headlong into the surf. She would swim long elliptical laps for over an hour. While she was swimming, Henry climbed up and down the natural stairway created by the stones that have been tumbling from the cliff over the millennia. When Sandy was done, she would stride to the beach through the breaking waves and into her robe and Henry's arms. Each of them, in that state of intoxicating exhaustion, would climb back to their room arm-in-arm.

Henry's mind came back to Sandy's question. *Okay, the storm in my gut has passed. But I'm still terrified. Sandy and I are entering a new paradigm. We are becoming partners in a deadly battle. We are becoming comrades-in-arms.*

"Reasonable?" he asked. "Well, I suppose if you accept the entirely insane bubble we all live in here, I would have to say yes, your explanation is totally reasonable. It is also reasonable that all this adoration I am feeling for you and your newfound supernatural powers is causing an uncontrollable lust in my innermost being, if you get my drift. So if I may be so bold as to ask your loveliness, wanna make out?"

"You got it, buster."

CHAPTER NINE

Andrew swiveled his chair and rolled it across the cave floor to get a closer view of monitor number four and the meeting between Randal Sanford and Firdos Gaffardi in the Boston sector.

"Let's see your journal there, Firdos," said Randal Sanford after wiping his mouth with the back of his sleeve. "Geeze, you've had your share of bad luck since you've been here in Witch City, haven't you? You've totaled four automobiles! What the heck?"

"Not exactly," Firdos corrected. "None of these accidents were my fault. I have the police reports in my file, and the insurance claims."

"Okay, swell, but you also have run into all these road blocks and detours."

"Yep," Firdos replied. Despite his revulsion at the gross habits of this ogre of a man, Firdos, for the first time in his life, was experiencing something that he observed others had—a relationship. Even though the interest that Sanford showed in him was all wrapped up in his position with the Directorate, still it was *interest*. In him.

Randal grunted up from his seat behind the table with some difficulty and squeezed his girth out of the booth. "Get me another cup of coffee, would you, son? I've got to get something from my car."

Firdos went to the counter and ordered a coffee for Randal and a hot tea for himself. Randal came back from his car with a roadmap and he squeezed back into his seat. Firdos sat down and placed Randal's coffee on the table. He studied what Randal was doing—comparing Firdos' journal and the map laid out on the table. Randal plotted the locations of all the incidents in the journal on the road map of North Shore Boston. The car accidents, the road blocks, the detours, and the breakdowns:

A fender-bender on Route 128 near the exit to the North Shore Mall.
A mail truck sideswiped Firdos' car on Route 1A in Beverly.
Getting rear-ended on Route 133 in Hamilton.
Getting a speeding ticket on Topsfield Road in Ipswich.
The clutch going out on Arbor Street in Wenham.
Bridge Street in Salem getting flooded out in a violent rainstorm,
blocking Firdos' route.

"Hey, that last item happened just down the street here. Does this street get flooded often?"

"How should I know," replied Firdos, "I just moved here a few months ago."

"Ask a native. That girl over there. She looks like she was born here."

"How can you tell that?" asked Firdos.

"Just ask her. She won't bite," ordered Randal.

Firdos never approached a female unless he was buying something across a counter. He turned in his seat in the booth and leaned toward the young lady at the next table. Awkward, eyes downcast, he asked, "Excuse me. Do you know if this street gets flooded often?"

The woman sporting a Salem State tee shirt knit her eyebrows together and peered over the top of her Wayfarer sunglasses. She said, "This street is raised up from the tideline by over fifty feet. It's called Bridge Street because it's a natural bridge between Salem and Beverly. It never gets flooded, except for one time a few weeks ago, and that was strange. I think it was a water main break during a downpour."

"Uh, thanks. Miss. Thanks," Firdos kept his gaze focused on the floor and he spun back to Randal. "You got that?"

"Yeah. You're a regular Romeo, ain't ya?" said Randal. "The flood here on Bridge Street was a fluke—a water main break just coincidently occurred the same time as a major rainfall. So, Firdos, all these incidents, see them on the map? What do you think is going on here?"

"I know exactly what's going on here, and I have known it for several weeks now. Something weird is messing me up."

"Right, son, but there's a pattern. See what I see with all these dots on my map?" Randal asked.

Firdos felt a faint positive buzz in his gut at the word "son." "Umm, it looks like, if you connect the dots, they're forming sort of an L shape around Cape Ann."

"Bingo. You're not as dumb as you look. Someone or something is trying to keep you from getting close to that area."

"Right," said Firdos, "but why is the operations center sending me to Maine?"

"The only logical explanation is that our geniuses at DHQ have determined that our enemy, FITO, has moved because they have figured out that you are getting too close."

"FITO?" asked Firdos. "What' that?"

"Our bosses call our enemy the fly in the ointment, FITO, get it?"

"Okay," said Firdos. "Either the geniuses at DHQ have access to some information that we don't have, or the geniuses at DHQ are stupid fools."

"Well, there's that." Pastry crumbs decorated Randal's vest and face.

Andrew concentrated on the two men—one a fifty-ish Caucasian old-school executive, and one a young Persian immigrant. They looked out the window next to their booth. The colonial Salem Street, first paved in the 1600s, was busy with moderate commuter traffic. Firdos' rental car, a compact black Toyota, was parked right behind Randal's super luxury Mercedes Maybach S600. Andrew's computer calculated the price difference of these vehicles was well over $100,000. The men in the cafe sipped their drinks in silence, apparently ruminating on the conflicting sets of intelligence before them.

Andrew watched as a roll-off dumpster truck backed out of the driveway directly across the street, where a building demolition was in progress. The truck's forty-foot container was full of construction waste from the work site. The truck backed up beeping that annoying warning signal. The driver inserted the truck's rear end into traffic, blocking the flow of cars in both directions. The loaded dumpster astonishingly slipped its moorings and gently rolled off the truck onto the hood of the $17,000 Toyota and the trunk of the $195,000 Mercedes-Maybach and crushed them. Andrew studied Randal's reaction. The portly billionaire calmly took out his pen and marked yet another dot on his map. Firdos nodded.

Andrew entered Randal Sanford's map of Boston's North Shore into his database. He and his best friends, the computers in his operations center, were busy developing courses of action for Operation FITO.

Computer number sixteen spoke first, "All the interruptions of Firdos' activities were deliberate. The chances of one man having that many accidents—not-his-fault—and that many other incidents, including a flooded road that never flooded, were one in three-hundred-thousand. When the dumpster crushed both Randal's and Firdos' cars, my calculation spiked. The line connecting their locations indicates that they are related to a specific location on the Atlantic coast near Gloucester, Massachusetts."

"Now what about these indicators that plot FITO's location in Neddick, Maine?" Andrew said. "These are unambiguous signals from Neddick sent from FITO's operations center to Anna Stone through Frances O'Donnelly and by satellite to my receiver here in Missouri."

From the speaker on computer number eleven, "The energy emitting from Director Randal Sanford and Operator Firdos Gaffardi during their conversation in the Coffee Time Bakery reaffirms the theory that there is an unresolved conflict between our two sources of intelligence. Our analysis shows a high degree of confidence in Sanford and Gifardi. They both displayed confusion over FITO's new location in Neddick. We give that factor a high rating."

Andrew said, "I see three possible conclusions: one, FITO now operates out of two locations; two, FITO moved its base of operations in Massachusetts to Neddick, Maine; or three, FITO devised a way to set up a decoy location in Neddick to divert our attention away from Massachusetts."

Andrew decided to call Randal—as repulsive as that conversation would be.

Randal Sanford was heading west in the backseat of one of his company's Cadillac Escalades. He always enjoyed the way the scenery on the Massachusetts Turnpike evolved from urban to suburban, and by the time they crossed I-495 it was all trees, hills, and country. He puffed on a high-quality reefer and zoned out as the big, comfortable vehicle sailed westward.

Randal's cell phone vibrated in his pocket. He pulled it out and the phone's screen told him it was a secure call from the Directorate's Operations Center.

"What, Andrew?" Randal didn't hate the guy, he just liked to make him think he did.

"Too bad about your Mercedes, Randal. I am so sorry your lovely car was wounded," Andrew said.

"Okay, meathead, what are you calling about?"

"Well, Randal, believe it or not you and I may agree on something, and it's going to make us waste some time."

"What's that?"

"You and your little buddy there in the Northeast, that Firdos Gaffardi thug we hypnotized and hired—you both think my new intelligence on FITO's location is faulty. Right?"

Randal sat back in his seat and watched the landscape of central Massachusetts flow by in the windshield. "Firdos isn't quite the thug you may think he is," Randal said. "I realize you consider yourself as omniscient as God there in your sanctuary command post, but you don't know jack. But, yeah, we think you're out-to-lunch with that idea that FITO moved to Maine. Where'd you get that, anyway?"

"Too complicated to explain to you, Randal, but that's where we agree. I have some doubts about FITO's setting up a new location. I think they may be still in the Gloucester area, or they may be up there in Maine, maybe both.

"Now we have Firdos headed up there to conduct seer operations," Andrew continued. "And you know he will continue to keep an eye on the Gloucester area, even though we have ordered him not to, right?"

"Yeah. That's what his profile tells us. He doesn't trust anything coming out of higher headquarters. I could have programmed his brain to concentrate on Neddick and forget the Massachusetts location, but I saw the value of letting him think he's disobeying orders by watching both," Randal said.

"Right," agreed Andrew. "I'm dispatching Golf Squad to New England to support Firdos' seer activities. You think we should tell him or keep him unaware?"

"You can afford to send a squad here? With all the pruning we have lined up this month, how can you justify that?" Randal said.

"Locating our enemy has taken a higher priority since your little pow-wow on Akebe's yacht. You directors have figured out that this FITO is more than just a fly in the ointment. They disrupt our pruning efforts with increasing effectiveness. If we are going to reduce the number of freethinkers in America at the rate we need to prune them, we have to wipe out FITO. Now my question: tell Firdos or not?"

"Keep him in the dark about Golf Squad," Randal said. "But I want to know every move that squad makes, you got it? I took leave from my day job and I'm setting up my command post here in New England. I'll be calling Akebe this afternoon."

"Okay. I want to settle this FITO location question in less than three weeks."

"We'll see," said Randal. "And I'm sending the bill for the damages on my car to Akebe." Randal punched the "end call" button on his cell phone.

To Beatrice in the driver's seat he said, "Hey, girl, pull over here at the Palmer exit. There's a great barbecue place a few miles down Route 20. We'll stop for lunch. Then we turn around, head back east to my summer house in Salem. You're coming with me."

"Mind if I make a few calls?" Beatrice asked.

Randal grunted his approval and closed his eyes.

The grey mood of the overcast sky sped into the dining room at the cottage at Cielavista. The rain had stopped, but the quilt of clouds outside the tall bay window behind Gabriella's chair at the head of the table darkened the atmosphere at the table. Henry slouched in his chair.

On most nights the order of their supper meal gave Henry a glimmer of sanity—in Henry's mind dinner was the only consistent routine that the trio observed in this moment-by-moment existence. Sandy always finished up the preparation of the meal in the kitchen. Gabriella stood in the bay window prayerfully meditating on the horizon. Henry always selected a bottle of wine and poured three glasses—after he took a couple extra sips from his glass and refilled it. Tonight, though, even the dinner routine would not console Henry's dolefulness.

Sandy entered the dining room with a baking pan of lasagna in her oven mitts. "Henry, would you get a couple trivets from the kitchen so I can put this down on the table? It's hot."

Henry thought, *No problem. Minor blip in tonight's routine. No problem.*

"Okay, hon. What's a trivet?"

"Hanging on the wall there above the toaster. Black metal thingies with handles. We need two of them," she said, holding the pan by the dining room table.

Henry rose from his seat, stepped into the kitchen, and spied the four black cast iron fish-shaped figures on the wall. "I thought these were decorations," he said.

"Knucklehead," teased Sandy. "Bring them in here. Set them on the table.

"No, not there; put them down in the center. Not like that, Henry, I have to set this pan down on them. Okay, that's good."

Control, control, control, Henry told himself. *You can do this. Just let it go, do what the bossy wife says and sit down. Do. Not. React. Sit. Down.*

"There you go—thanks," said Sandy, her irritation to creep into her tone as she set the baking pan down on the trivets. "Didn't realize that was going to be so complicated. Oh, well, no problem."

Gabriella turned from her stance by the window and took her seat. Henry and Sandy both knew that nothing got by the old lady. Nothing said or even felt escaped her radar. She put her arm out in front of her, palm down, and lowered it slowly toward the tabletop, looking once at Henry, then Sandy and back. Henry felt his rage gradually subside like a whistling teapot lifted from its burner. On one hand Henry did not like being controlled like that; on the other hand, he knew Gabriella saved him again from another unnecessary painful episode that he would regret. Over the twenty-eight years of marriage to Sandy, his unbridled anger had been the source of so much acrimony between them that he was amazed his wife could still live with him.

"My dear son," Gabriella began, "I know you have been so patient with us and the way we conduct our lives. I would be annoyed, too, being married into this nuthouse."

Henry was surprised at her admission and, in a strange way, comforted.

"But since I have been involved with these spiritual forces for over ninety years, I have become accustomed to submitting to them and letting my own desires slip away. It is my life, dear son, and by God's intentions, it is Sandy's life and yours, too.

"We don't get to choose our futures, make plans, and execute our plans. We are slaves to His plans and you must admit it's been rather adventuresome, no?"

Henry was thinking, *That's one way to put it. Not knowing what's going to come your way from one minute to the next, yeah, that could be an adventure. Or a pain in the butt.*

"I suppose you have a point, Gabriella," he lied.

"Well, later tonight I have a strong premonition we will be getting instructions for our future that will require some changes. Meanwhile, let's eat and drink, shall we? The lasagna looks delightful, Sandy, and the wine is just right."

CHAPTER TEN

Henry's anger simmered during supper—deepened by the sunless sky, triggered by the change in routine, then exacerbated by the prospect of some unknown major "changes" in the future. He left the table agitated.

Henry filled his wineglass and walked out into the semidarkness of the evening. He went straight to the barn, entered the stall where the heavy bag awaited its punishment. Henry set his wineglass on the shelf, removed his shirt, shoes and socks. He laced up his punching gloves and stepped up to the bag. His feet found the indentations he had worn in the hard dirt floor over the last quarter century. Here in this one spot on Cielavista, Henry was in complete control.

He leaned his forehead against the leather, placed his gloves on each side of the bag, and repeated his mantra: "Blessed be the Lord my rock, who trains my hands for war, my fingers for battle."

The "whomp" of his left fist on the bag filled the entire barn. The two horses in their stalls on the opposite side of the barn shifted their hooves and snorted.

"My loving kindness and my fortress," whomp, whomp, "My shield," whomp, "and He in whom I take refuge," bamp, bamp, bamp, bamp, "who subdues my people under me."

The four dogs took their usual places at the open end of the stall where they watched the nightly performance—the male human banging his fists against a defenseless, useless bag covered in the skin of a cow, and reciting the same scripture passage over and over again.

Lucille, the only female in the quartet, lay on her stomach with her paws pointing forward into the boxing stall. She and Mark, the other Irish Wolfhound, were reputed to be lovers but no, she only used him for breeding purposes when she was young. Sure, now they enjoyed each other's company, but there was no passion anymore. Mark would not take his eyes off the human. It was Lucille's belief that he wished he could punch like that, and maybe recite scripture too.

The two horses, Cinnamon and Sadie, hung their heads over the half wall, pawed their hooves, and snorted at the human.

Matt, the Bull Terrier, turned his eyes back to the horses and told them quit fussing around. "This happens every night, guys, so why do you insist on getting so worked up over it? He's just doing what humans do, wasting their energy on foolish things." Matt had that big black spot over his left eye that people thought was cute. He shook his oversized, egg-shaped head, turned to his friends, and said, "Stupid horses. They have absolutely no memory."

"I'll remember that remark, pooch," said Sadie, the chestnut mare with the white diamond on her forehead.

John had to resist the impulse to bump Henry away from the poor victim he was pummeling. His Australian Shepherd genes told him to protect the prey from the predator, but his training told him if he did that he would get punished. So he sat there all tensed up, eyes ablaze, conflicted.

"It's just a bag, John," said Lucille gently, "Henry's not really causing it any pain. He's playing around."

John wasn't sure. "He's pretty steamed up for someone who's just playing."

Whomp, whomp, whomp, whomp, "My stronghold, my deliver, my shield," Henry's voice wasn't loud, just hot. The dogs watched without fascination. Their friend, Carlos, came into the barn.

"I hate your guts, dirtbag. You're in for some real pain tonight." Henry kept slamming jabs right and left into the lower part of the leather EverLast bag, then he sent a hard right hook into the upper quadrant where "his" face would be. Jab, jab, hook. The slamming noise of the gloves against the leather bag resounded against the walls of the big barn. Thirty minutes of unrelenting pounding worked the excess adrenaline from Henry's system and left him panting, sweating, and leaning on the fourteen-inch post at the opening of the stall.

"Who you punching tonight?" asked Carlos from his perch on a hay bale across the barn floor. He scratched John's head behind the ears. "You like it there, don't you, John?" The shepherd closed his eyes to contain his pleasure.

Without looking up, Henry smiled as he toweled himself off and put on his shirt and shoes. "The list is long and still incomplete," said Henry.

"As long as I'm not on it," Carlos said. "I been thinking about what you said last night, about increased security."

"Yeah, and I been thinking about what you said last night, about my new bodyguard. What were you talking about?"

Carlos checked the fuel level in his golf cart. All four dogs scampered around the caretaker.

Henry took the passenger side of the vinyl bench seat next to Carlos. "You got a license for this thing, old man?"

"When did you become the state police?"

"Hey, Carlos, did the old lady talk to you about security? I can never figure her out."

"*Yo no se nada*," he said. He drove slowly down the gravel path that wound through the gardens and woods of Cielavista.

Carlos traced Cielavista's rocky coastline. The cart path took them sixty feet above the tide line and then dipped down to the beaches. Carlos steered the cart through the woods on the north path, the three tall dogs ranging in front of him and to each flank. Matt stayed close to the cart, his short legs not designed for sweeping runs through the woods.

Henry took the last sip from his wineglass and placed it upside-down in the cup holder on the dash.

"Gabriella's enemy in her heavenly war is getting closer to our location. She gave me the mission of force protection. She says eventually she'll give me further instructions about our spiritual countermeasures. I need you to take care of physical security here. What do you think?"

Carlos slammed on the breaks and the cart skidded to a stop.

"¿Qué estás haciendo? Casi te pego!" Carlos yelled at the air in front of the cart.

Henry turned to Carlos, "What the heck are you doing? Who you yelling at?" All four dogs assembled on the road in front of the little vehicle and stared up at the same point in the sky. Carlos got off his seat in the cart and squatted down next to Lucille.

"What is he doing here?" he asked the dog. Then he waited, looking from Lucille's eyes then up into the sky, then back to her.

"Ho boy, I guess I gotta explain it to Henry, eh?"

Henry watched Carlos communicate with Lucille. He tasted the rusty metal anger in the back of his throat. He made himself sit still, knowing that Carlos could tell when his blood was boiling—it was in the way his eyes strained open, unblinking. He tried to blink, but he couldn't.

Carlos sat back next to Henry and looked straight ahead over the front of the cart.

Tobias said to Carlos, "Not everyone can see and hear angels. You, Carlos and Lucille, have this spiritual vision. I would like you to inform Henry about me and the platoon of angels assigned to Cielavista, okay?"

Henry repeated his question to Carlos in an almost-normal tone, "Hey, old man, what the heck are you doing? Have you gone nuts like those two women I live with? You speak to the sky. You speak to the dog. You expect me to just stay calm like nothing weird is happening?" Henry's hands clinched and unclinched.

"Well," said Carlos, watching Henry's hands, "I'm glad you got all that violence out of your system, because you're not going to like this. At first you're not going to like it but pretty soon you'll be very grateful for what I have to tell you."

"What?" The veins in his neck were bulging and his forehead was scarlet.

Carlos considered where to start. He packed his pipe—took his time pinching little portions of tobacco from his pouch into the bowl of his father's pipe, tamping it down gently and pinching another portion. Then when he had it loaded just right, he struck a kitchen match with his thumbnail and set the flame over the bowl of tobacco and puffed in just the right amount of air until the pipe was well lit. The dogs were still peering into the air, their necks stretched upward.

"Okay, boss, here it goes. From when I was a little kid, I have this gift. I see some of what goes on in the spirit world around us." He looked at Henry.

"Yeah?" prodded Henry. He had been aware that Carlos was into a wild sort of religion where they seemed to consort with spiritual beings during the prayer meetings they held in the mansion. It was Henry's position that the best thing for him to do was just stay away, which he continued to do for over twenty-five years.

"Yeah, so occasionally, once in a while, over the years I will encounter an angel or two." Carlos paused again, pulled a mouthful of the savory smoke from the pipe into his mouth, and let it flow out through his lips without blowing it.

"You notice last night anything out of the ordinary when you were walking your rounds?"

Henry thought. "I do remember the tops of a spruce tree waving around for no good reason." Henry brought the scene into focus now, remembering his walk around Cielavista last night. "Oh, then I thought I heard a song, one of my favorites, 'Up Where We Belong,' but didn't think much of it. Why?"

"You got an angel. His name is Tobias," and Carlos looked again at Tobias still hovering there near the front of the golf cart with a big grin on his face. "He's not a big-shot angel like Michael or Gabriel, more of a water-boy type angel."

With that, Tobias whirled in the air above the cart and the wind from his move gave it a violent shake. Henry grabbed the golf cart's handle with his right hand and the dashboard with his left. "What the heck?"

"I guess he don't like me calling him a water-boy type angel." Then to Tobias, "I was just teasing, man," he said with a nervous laugh.

"Anyways, that's that," said Carlos. "You got an angel. You can tell him to do stuff, as long as it has to do with this battle that Gabriella is waging. That's what they're here for."

"They?" asked Henry. "How many are there?"

Carlos to Tobias now, "How many are with you, man?"

"Thirty five. And don't call me 'man.' I'm an angel, *man*."

"There're thirty-five of them. And he don't like being called 'man.' On account of he's an angel I guess."

"Whatever," said Henry. "So where does the dog come in?"

Carlos stalled. He relit his pipe, sucked in puffs of smoke, and blew them out. He blurted out. "Lucille sees angels, talks to them, and she communicates with me. That's it. Deal with it."

"Lord, make it stop," said Henry to no one. He leaned over with his elbows on his knees and put his head in his hands. "I'm going to get me one of those pipes.

"Hey, Tobias," Henry said, "we're taking a drive around the place. You just hover up there and stay out of our way, got it?"

A faint whoosh of air swept up in front of them. "He's going to be right up there," said Carlos.

CHAPTER ELEVEN

The golf cart brought the two men to the eastern edge of the estate that overlooked the ledges below and the horizon at the far edge of the sea. Henry was trying to process all this strange, mystical input. Carlos talked about angels like he talked about plants and fertilizer, no big thing. And his connection to the animals was really disturbing. Gabriella and Sandy were able to watch people thousands of miles away. And they exerted this power across thousands of miles that could alter the course of those lives. *I'm not like them!! But I can't escape.*

Henry watched as Vega strained hard to push some starlight through the cloud cover above the horizon. The bright evening star brought Henry back to that night over thirty years ago on his boat with Sandy. *God, we were young then.*

Carlos crunched down on the footbrake and walked slowly toward the high cliff. The two men stood side-by-side, Henry almost a foot taller than his wiry friend.

"How long you been married to Yolanda, Carlos?" Henry asked.

"Let's see…I think I was twenty…so what…that's fifty-two years, give or take I guess," the bantamweight caretaker answered. "Why you ask, Henry?"

"I don't know. Sometimes it's been such a struggle. Like God has this bait-and-switch scam he runs on us."

Carlos chuckled. "I think I know what you mean, amigo." He kneeled down next to Matt and scratched his back. "You one ugly mutt, bone-head." The dog seemed to enjoy what he was hearing.

Henry continued, "I mean the beginning, you know? I see Sandy at the coffee place there in Gloucester in her loose shirt and baggy slacks, like she's trying to hide herself under the clothes. But I can see, you know, I can see how great she looks. That was eighty-five, we were twenty-two years old. Stupid kids. Each of us lonely I guess."

Lucille nuzzled Henry's calf. She seemed to sympathize. Unconsciously Henry ran his fingers through the wolfhound's long, scraggly grey hair.

"So we meet. We date. Sparks fly. I can't get her out of my mind. Songs I never heard before become real to me. All these useless emotions become so large and unmanageable."

"Yes," Carlos was remembering too. "You can't get enough of her. Obsessed."

"There was a song from the movie *An Officer and a Gentleman,* 'Up Where We Belong,' something like that. I had a boom box in the boat with a cassette player, and we'd put that on and dance out there on the water."

"That's the bait," said Carlos.

"That's the bait. Then it doesn't take long, does it? Everything switches. The promise goes unkept."

Henry knew it wasn't Sandy's fault. If there was blame to be attributed, he knew it belonged to him. But she had changed too. As she matured she became less interested in the romance, in the touch, in the affection; all the things that attracted Henry to her, or even to the idea of having a relationship at all. Once the baby came along, all the practical requirements of parenting took over, pushing aside the physical pleasures. Henry never grew out of his need for that.

"The libido gap," Carlos said, reading Henry's thoughts.

"The what?" asked Henry.

"I read about it in a women's magazine. One of the hundreds that get delivered to my house. You know there's twenty females in that big house? They all study this thing. We don't study it, amigo, we just react to it. Anyways, I pick up one of the magazines and read this article about the libido gap. It's where one side of the couple needs more sex than the other side."

"Okay, so what does the article say about how to close this gap?"

"It doesn't matter," said Carlos. "No matter what they write nobody does it. They have all these solutions, but all they're doing is filling up space in the magazine with words so all the females in my house have something to do between work and chores."

"Speaking of kids, what do you hear from Hank Junior?" asked Carlos.

"Well, I called him a couple weeks ago. You know he's at that special facility in Washington State. Not much change," was all Henry wanted to say about his son—a former Army Ranger and Special Forces soldier.

From their vantage point they could make out Gabriella down on the ledge below where she stood, rock-steady facing the wind, her black hair flagging behind her. The sky around her shimmered like heat rising off a fire—transparent, but still visible for miles into the air—a vibrating radiation of energy occasionally emitting a faint ray of colored light, sometimes a pale blue-green, sometimes a pale yellow-orange.

"*Que pasa?*" Carlos asked Lucille. The dog peered into the shimmering pillar of air over Gabriella.

Carlos said, "Something about an enemy attack on a little community college in Oregon. She doesn't ever know exactly what's going on until it's over. She just knows she's supposed to send fire down on the attackers and let the power do its work. She is often surprised at the outcomes.

"God uses us all in some very strange ways, huh, amigo?"

"Yeah, 'strange' is one way to put it," Henry said. "And then there's this hurricane developing in the Atlantic somewhere off the coast of West Africa. His name is Joachim. The way Gabriella describes it, he doesn't know what his purpose is, so he isn't sure what direction he is supposed to take. Gabriella says she's supposed to help Joachim find out what his purpose is so he can travel the right path."

"What's his purpose?" asked Carlos.

"See, that's just it. Gabriella doesn't need to know that. She only knows that the pathway in his consciousness is blocked and her job is to unblock it."

The men looked at each other. "I know," said Henry, "I don't get it either."

"So, she knows that there is a threat to our security here at Cielavista?" asked Carlos.

"Yeah, all she said was, 'They're getting closer.' So she's developing a strategy in the heavens to throw them off track, and we have to come up with a strong defensive plan here in case they actually try to infiltrate the grounds."

Carlos repacked his pipe and lit it.

Henry said, "Not too many pipe smokers these days, Carlos."

"My dad gave me this old pipe. I always loved the aroma of pipe tobacco. Did I ever tell you the story of how my family got connected to Cielavista?"

The silent pause from Henry gave Carlos his cue to tell it.

"Gabriella's brother, Antonio Quartarone, bought this place some-where around 1920. The mansion was almost completed and the building site needed to be transformed into a beautiful estate. My father, Carlos Senior, was a day laborer on the project. He always got to the site before anyone else and was still working when the crew was dismissed in the evening. Antonio took notice. He told the project manager to have Carlos meet him in his car. It was a deep-brown 1929 Cadillac Phaeton. My dad would describe its lines, 'A sweeping running board curved upward to form the front fender, elegantly shaped across the long vented hood, over the front spoked wheel. The tan canvas convertible top was always in the up position, shading the elder Italian businessman.'

"My dad told me how he stepped up on the running board, opened the rear door, and settled in on the brown leather seat. Mr. Quartarone was smoking a pipe, looking out the open window on his side of the Cadillac observing the progress of the construction. The car was filled with the aromatic fragrance of the smoke.

"'I would like to offer you a position here at my new home, Carlos.

Will you consider working for me on a permanent basis?' the old gentleman said to Carlos Senior. According to my father, Mr. Quartarone always showed him the highest respect.

"Carlos was not expecting this kind of offer, so he said, 'Mr. Quartarone, thank you. What kind of work do you want me to do?'

"'I need someone like you who's smart and likes to work hard. I am looking for a man to take charge of landscaping this beautiful place and turning it into a garden that my sister and I and our family can enjoy. It's over a hundred acres,'" Carlos continued his story.

Now standing on the edge of the cliff that his family had managed for over eight decades he puffed on his father's pipe, filled with the same mix of tobacco that Gabriella's brother procured from a tobacconist in Boston.

"Even then when I was just a kid, that Gabriella would go out there to pray," the elderly landscaper said.

Henry asked, "So when did she decide to move into the small house?"

"I don't remember exactly," answered Carlos, "but at some point after Gabriella's brother and her husband died and it was just her and her son living in the big stone house and all of us living in the cottage, she said to me, 'Let's trade houses.' Just like that. So we did."

"Carlos, how many people live there with you?"

"I think it's over thirty now with my kids and their kids."

CHAPTER TWELVE

Gabriella turned and pointed her boney finger up at Henry and Carlos. They froze in place. The shimmering air around Gabriella suddenly arced over the cliff and embraced the men.

"What just happened?" asked Henry.

"Yo no se."

The old woman jumped from her flat table of rock across the wide crevice and she skipped up the rocks like a mountain goat.

She met the men on the lawn on the highest point of the bluff. Barely out of breath from her climb, she hooked her arms into each man's arms and walked with them to the cottage, leaving the golf cart parked on the grass. The dogs decided to trot back to the barn.

"My Lord has revealed our enemy's name to me. They call themselves the 'Directorate.'"

They took seats in the cottage's sun porch overlooking the ocean. Sandy joined them. She carried a tray from the kitchen with a coffee service for four.

Gabriella continued. "Tonight, God was showing me what happened at the Umpqua Community College shooting rampage yesterday."

"Yes," said Sandy. "I don't understand, when God has you defend people in a situation like that why He lets people get killed and wounded."

"I know," said Gabriella slowly, "it's a mystery to me too. All I know is what I know. No more." The old sage poured coffee for the four of them and put her cup to her thin lips and took a deep sip. "Excellent coffee, dear," she said. "Would you please get your laptop, honey?"

"The boy, the army veteran who charged the shooter, I think his name is Chris," Gabriella said. "He and one of the teachers there were the only real targets of the Directorate."

"But I thought the shooter was some kind of Antichrist, asking who believed in God and then shooting them," Henry said.

"Well," Gabriella continued as Sandy came back, "this is how the Directorate operates. First, let me show you something on the computer. Sandy, pull up a random sample of US citizens. Adults. About ten thousand."

Sandy keyboarded and her screen showed a chart covered with black dots.

"Now," said Gabriella, "tell it to differentiate between thinkers and reactors."

The screen now color-coded the dots, mostly red, a few green.

"See," said Gabriella, "the green dots, about eight percent of this sample, are thinkers. The red are people who are just reactors. The Directorate is a network of people more powerful than any government or institution, and their goal is to control the world through telekinetic brainwashing. Thinkers can't be mentally manipulated like the reactors. Reactors simply accept any influences that come into their brain and sheeplike, well, they just react."

"That's why advertising is so effective," said Henry. "I always wondered why retailers spend so much money telling people what to do. It just didn't make sense. But I guess if people just fall for a sales pitch without thinking, it must pay off."

"Yes, Henry, exactly," said Gabriella. "You see, you are one of the thinkers, the green dots. Advertising makes no sense to you because you come to your buying decisions mindfully, even though I can't understand why you spend so much on fishing tackle, but that's your choice." And she gave him one of her sweet smiles that crinkled her eyes.

"Who was it," Carlos chimed in, "said, 'There's a sucker born every minute"?

"Phineas Taylor Barnum," said Henry. "And if you look at how he made his fortune—in what, the 1840s—that notion formed the foundation for his business model. He created hoaxes and sold tickets to thousands of suckers who couldn't constrain their curiosity. Perfect example of what you're talking about, Gabriella. And according to Sandy's chart with over ninety-two percent of the population being red dots, reactors, Barnum may have been conservative in his estimate."

Sandy asked, getting back to the shooting in Oregon, "But why, if God instructed you to protect this Chris Mintz, did he get so badly wounded, and the professor, Larry Levine, was killed?"

"As I said, dear, I only know what I know, and I can only do what I can do," Gabriella said.

"I have a theory about that," said Carlos. "What I'm reading today in the papers, this Chris Mintz is being elevated to hero status, maybe justifiably so. His cousin set up a web site asking for donations to help Chris pay for medical expenses and compensate for lost income. They were trying to collect ten thousand dollars. As of today, the fund reached a million.

"Now his son, the one he talked about to the shooter—that it was his sixth birthday—his son is autistic. It could be, I'm not sure, but it could be that God's plan was to use Chris' injuries to raise money for the son and others."

"Okay," said Gabriella, "Perhaps. But I am not allowed to theorize. You may be correct, Carlos, but we really don't know.

"But," Gabriella continued, "getting back to the tactics of the Directorate. They trained a network of seers and operators. The seers can discern who the most threatening thinkers are. Once they identify the targets, they send the names back to an operations center where the operations officer prioritizes the target list."

"What kind of people make this death list?" asked Sandy.

"The common characteristic of all these targets is that they are thinkers. Many are nontraditional health practitioners like Anna Stone. Some in the military—the type of warriors who respectfully question their commander's decisions."

"Hmmm," Henry said. "You know that's our boy, Hank Junior. He always followed orders, but he would take the time to chat with his commanders about their senior leadership."

"Yes," said Gabriella, "perfect example of the type of person the Directorate would target. Some professors, some ministers, just about any professional who instinctively challenges mainstream thought.

"This Directorate, a powerful league of very wealthy men and women who operate under the delusion that they are the last bastion of true American patriotism, sends out the target list to their six squads of operators. To carry out their murderous plan, they'll select a poor dissociated weakling and hypnotize him. They'll manipulate their subjects into thinking they kill in the name of the Jihad, or Satan, and make the shooting look like fanatical violence, but that's just camouflage. Most of these incidents that the foolish journalists report as Islamic violence are orchestrated by the Directorate. They will kill hundreds in a crowd but they target only a certain few just to conceal their schemes."

In unison Henry and Sandy uttered, "These people are evil."

"Yes," said Gabriella, "and they're delusional. They're convinced that they're patriots, pruning out undesirable obstacles to their righteous master plan to shape America into a herd of mindless sheep."

"Are you the only one that God has chosen to combat these devils?" asked Carlos.

"I don't know," smiled Gabriella. "That's my favorite answer, because it's the truth. I only know what I know...."

"And you can only do what you can do," Carlos finished the sentence for the ancient sage.

Henry spoke, "So, Gabriella, let me get this straight: the Lord has chosen you to fight an organization with unlimited resources that can brainwash people from a distance, manipulate their minds to carry out horrific crimes, and now they target us. Yet you don't even know if we have any allies in this battle. Have you any idea how insane this all would sound to any rational person outside of this lunatic ranch of ours?"

Gabriella looked deeply at her grandson-in-law with what seemed to be centuries of angry power all focused on him. She was casting no threat, just an unambiguous reminder that she deserved the respect of a field marshal in a vast corps of divine legions.

"I apologize, Gabriella. You just worry the daylights out of me."

"So here is what we are going to do," said Gabriella. And she laid out her plan.

Frances O'Donnelly harbored heavy doubts about the Directorate's purchase of the exclusive use of the entire Bellefontaine Mansion, the "world's leader among luxury spas," for four days at a cost of nearly three hundred thousand dollars.

She frowned at Akebe Cheron's entrance into the sumptuous ballroom at the Canyon Ranch Resort in the Berkshires of western Massachusetts. He wore a serenely composed look, having just come from a steam bath and deep therapeutic massage.

The rest of the Executive Board huddled around the appetizer bar— Donald Snow sipping a glass of chardonnay, Romano Goldstein picking over the cheese selections. Frances chatted with Olivia Kingston, and Randal Sanford heaped as much food as possible onto a much-too-small plate.

In the past ten years this secret band of billionaires had only met together four times. The chairman inexplicably called a second meeting in a month. Apparently the operational tempo was ramping up.

Frances kept her skepticism under wraps. She noticed Akebe pushing a button on the credenza behind the serving table and two waiters appeared—well-muscled young men, too dangerous-looking for a career in food-service work. She knew they were employees of the Directorate, not the Canyon Ranch. Akebe gave them instructions for serving the afternoon meal, and for security precautions. The men left the room.

"Well, folks," Akebe said, "I'm ever so grateful that you all could make time in your busy schedules to attend this meeting on such short notice. Thank you very much." Neither his tone nor his demeanor communicated the slightest hint of distress—curious because on the notification Frances received, Akebe used the heading: *Urgent Emergency Meeting.*

"What a wonderful place, don't you think? Who would believe such a treasure would be tucked away back here in the New England woods, far away from the public's prying eyes? Let's take some time to enjoy each other's company before we get down to business. What do you say?"

Frances glanced around at her fellow board members and noted the same suspicious looks on their faces. Randal was compelled to give voice to what they all were wondering, "I want some of what Akebe's been smoking."

Akebe joined Frances and the clutch of colleagues near the wine and cheese bar and offered a sketchy agenda for the long weekend, "We won't sit down for our first session until tomorrow afternoon, folks, so take some time to enjoy the grounds and the spa. We have exclusive use of the Bellefontaine Mansion, but you might run across a few other guests staying in one of the out buildings. I'd like you all to find some time to relax and refresh before we gather, okay?"

The group's skepticism changed to angry apprehension and no one tried to conceal it.

Romano Goldstein said, "Akebe, I have to say, and I think I speak for the rest of us, the tone you are setting for this conference does not match the urgency of our situation. We did not leave our business concerns to waste time on our personal wellness. The Directorate does not gather to play, we gather to accomplish the serious business of transforming America. You owe us an explanation."

"You don't speak for me, Romano," Randal Sanford mumbled through a mouthful of shrimp popover, washing it down with a cabernet at twenty dollars a gulp. "See, I get where Akebe is coming from for once.

He knows the importance of creating a climate conducive to intellectual collaboration."

Four pairs of stunned eyes stared at Randal Sanford as he flicked flakes of Chinese dumplings off his bulging sweatshirt. It occurred to Frances that Akebe has hypnotized the board members, using the same telekinetic power they use to manipulate their targets.

Frances strode from the room, heels clicking on the polished hardwood floor. She pulled her mobile phone out of the pocket of her pleated slacks and tapped the application she had Andrew design for her. The screen came up green, meaning that no telekinetic energy was influencing her mind. She had become hypervigilant after her meeting with Anna Stone. A puzzling apprehension gnawed at her gut.

Frances took the stairs to her suite of rooms in the mansion and quickly changed into white tennis shorts and a light-green tee shirt. She hurried back down to the boardroom.

"Guys," Frances said to the group, "I don't know what Akebe is up to, but you know, I have to agree with our bohemian brother here," indicating Randal, busy building himself a plate full of bacon wrapped dates stuffed with blue cheese. "We've all been through plenty of stressful months keeping up with our day jobs at the heads of international organizations while playing a pivotal role in our heroic efforts to make America great."

The three remaining dissenters were warming up to Frances's speech.

"I'm going to take this opportunity to relax in these luxurious surroundings, have some fine wine, gourmet food, and try out the spa. See you all around the table tomorrow afternoon. Ciao."

With that she sidled up next to Randal and piled Filipino lumpia, stuffed mushrooms, and shrimp with remoulade sauce on her plate. She poured herself a glass of champagne and went out to the patio to soak up some New England sun before it dipped down past the Berkshire Hills.

Frances heard Akebe reassure his team, "Well, folks, I guess there are three of us who agree on the need to relax. I suggest, Romano, Olivia, and Don that you let your concerns wash away in the steam bath and enjoy a relaxing evening. Perhaps we could take a drive to Jacob's Pillow Dance

Theater a few miles away. Their program tonight features a troupe from Cuba. I have tickets."

The room became a buzz of social conversation.

Frances called Andrew. When he answered she asked, "Have you been invited to this meeting in Massachusetts?"

"Yeah," Andrew's sullen voice responded, "why?"

"Okay, Andrew listen to me," Frances commanded. "Your job is on the line. You know what that means, right? I realize you don't give a crap, but you might consider your future just for a second. If you're supposed to be here, that means *you* are on the agenda, and that's not a good thing for you. You need to be prepared."

"Okay," Andrew responded, suspicious. "Why do you care?"

"I don't," and Frances hung up.

She decided to call her new friend Anna Stone.

"Is it possible for you to get away from your practice for a few days?" Frances asked her.

Anna thought, "Yes, I suppose so, why?"

"I'm at a beautiful exclusive resort in Massachusetts and I would love to spend a few days with you. Just a whim," Frances said.

"Well, I can afford the time, but I certainly can't afford the money for such a trip on such short notice, I'm sorry."

"Anna, I'll take care of everything. Just say yes, pack a bag, and a driver will pick you up at your house. You don't have to arrange a thing. I want to say, Anna, I feel that I need to have you here for some very important reasons I can't explain on the phone."

"I think I understand, Frances. Okay, my answer is yes. I'll tell my husband and I will be ready in two hours."

Chapter Thirteen

Paul Stone glared at his wife and tried to restrain his rage. But Anna explained her need to get away for a free spa weekend. Paul was amazed when an unexpected peace soaked into his heart and he helped her pack. He stood at the door looking out as a black Lincoln limousine pulled into the driveway and a young lady in a suit came to the door and carried Anna's suitcase to the car. Anna turned around as she followed the driver down the driveway and gave Paul a shrug and a grin. He just shook his head.

All Henry's basic needs for a comfortable life were satisfied in the cottage he shared with his wife and her grandmother. Henry and Sandy lived on the second floor, which included their large bedroom with a balcony that looked out to the ocean, two extra bedrooms now set up as offices and a bath. But at age fifty-three the beauty of this seaside home could not resolve Henry's persistent rage. He was packing.

Sandy said, "Can you tell me where you're going?"

"Fishing," Henry said. "I have four weeks of leave coming, and in our department if you don't take them before the fiscal year ends, your boss gets in trouble. So I have been ordered to take my four weeks leave from the Bureau, and I'm going fishing." Henry thought he was doing pretty well.

"Sure, well I'm glad for you honey," Sandy said. "Any idea how long this trip will be?" She sounded frightened.

Henry turned to her. "Do you have an angel?"

Sandy managed a smile. "Yes, why?"

"Well," said Henry, "it seems our Lord and Savior has deemed it necessary to assign me my own personal angel. Apparently there are over thirty of these heavenly creatures swarming around the sky over Cielavista and I simply assumed that if I deserved to have one tailing me around, then you deserved at least one. Mine is kind of a water-boy level angel. Not real high ranking."

"What's his name?"

"Tobias," answered Henry. "And I'm not a big fan of having a divine spy hovering over me all the time, not knowing where he is and what he's up to. In fact, this whole scenario is so ludicrous I can't stand it."

Henry needed to control every detail of his life. He longed for a place where he could set everything up in perfect rows and columns, where he could fix anything that broke, direct anything that went out of line, and put everything within his reach in perfect order. Even now, at middle age, he still operated under the delusion that perfection was attainable.

Sandy said, "Return to a stronghold, you prisoners of hope; today I declare that I will restore double to you. That's from Zechariah I think."

"What?" said Henry. He meticulously folded his underwear into his duffle bag.

"I don't know," said Sandy. "Just a scripture verse popped into my head. I'm going to bed. I'll see you whenever."

Henry could sense Sandy's anxiety. She lay on her side with her face to the wall. He knew she was listening to his constant rustling of clothing, opening and closing drawers, his footsteps on the floor, the zipper of his duffle bags opening and closing, and the clack of his clipboard on the dresser every time he checked off an item on his packing list. Just last year as they were preparing for a trip to the Cape, she shouted at him, "Just cram the stuff in the bag and get out of here. What you forget we can just buy when we get there!"

Henry finished wrapping his extra running shoes in separate towels and tucking them in their proper places in the duffle. He checked each item off his list on his clipboard as he packed it. When he was done he put the clipboard in the bag, zipped it up, and locked the zipper tabs together with a padlock.

Henry was at the threshold of their bedroom. He wondered if Sandy could sense the possibility that he was leaving for good.

She said, "I can live without you, you know."

"We'll see." Henry left.

Sandy lay awake all night and watched the sun slowly tease the morning darkness with hints of light. Then like a fireball bobbing up out of the water the sun popped up over the horizon, orange-red and angry. Paralyzed under the weight of the vacancy in her bedroom, Sandy wondered how she could function without Henry loving her and annoying her.

In the thirty years that she knew Henry—two dating and twenty-eight married—she could remember only a few really happy ones. Like their first year.

Sandy had just come home from a year of rehabilitation feeling almost human when she saw the lanky fisherman sitting in Candee's Kitchen reading the *Boston Herald*. Of all the papers he could have chosen, why, she wondered, would anyone read that brainless propaganda rag? And he looked ridiculous in his cutoff blue jeans, rubber boots, and ragged sweatshirt. His shapeless, light-brown hair lay every which way.

Weeks later, in her therapy session, she asked Dr. Dorothy Hanson, "What unfathomable notion caused me to have any interest in 'Herald Reader'?"

"What emotions did you feel when you encountered this man?" Dr. Hanson asked her.

"Oh, boy, here we go again," Sandy tried to seem upbeat. "Where's that list again? You know I can never pinpoint the name of any of my feelings."

Even the simple motion—reaching her long arm across the desk, extending her wrist, and holding open her fingers to receive the sheet of paper from Doctor Hanson—attested to Sandy's natural grace. Sandy sat back in the leather wingback chair, crossed her long legs, and studied the list of feelings.

"Picture in your mind what you were doing when you noticed him. How many times have you seen this 'Herald Reader'?" Dorothy Hanson couldn't help grinning at the name Sandy had given the object of her favorite client's current obsession.

"I guess three or four. Every Saturday lately when I go to Candee's to pick up breakfast for my Nonina, he's sitting there at the same table by himself reading that vile excuse for a newspaper and eating this huge pile of breakfast. He never looks up. I think he's tall because his rubber boots stick way out from under the table."

"Okay," the matronly doctor said, "so, keep that scene in mind and scan over the list of feelings there." And she waited. Silence here was their friend.

Sandy's mind percolated. She focused on the visual scene that her memory provided. *She's standing at the counter, waiting for her order. The tables in the dining area bustled with breakfast customers. She looks casually at the crowd and at the far end of the room, with his back to the knotty pine wall, sits this man about her age, all neck, elbows, and legs topped with a bush of scraggly light-brown hair.*

"'Intrigued,'" Sandy pointed to a word, "'tense,' and maybe 'drawn.' Is that an emotion?"

"For you, Sandy, that's pretty good," said Dorothy. "Intrigued, tense, and drawn."

"Yeah. *Maybe* drawn," Sandy clarified. "I don't know." And she looked down at her long knuckly fingers.

"What?" asked the therapist.

"You know exactly what. As soon as I go there I have to confront all my baggage. I'd just as soon avoid the 'feelings stuff' and stay away from that pain we've been talking about for the last year."

Dorothy waited, just looking at Sandy for a few minutes.

Sandy continued, "You know, I guess I'm not quite as crazy as I was when it happened, but it's still there. Is it always going to be there?"

"It's part of you, Sandy. Whenever a person experiences as much violence as you have, especially when it involves people they are close to, they respond with crazy behaviors. You, my dear, reacted to the deaths of your parents in a way that most healthy people would react. And the fact that you sought help and now are getting better is all very positive."

"I'm going to run it by you one more time just to see if I can, okay?"

"Sure. And let me remind you, try to tell me how you felt, not just what you experienced."

One more time Sandy verbalize the events that brought her to the edge. Her mother's slow painful battle with stomach cancer. How, as a teenager, she witnessed the pain, the cries, moans, and screams. And that day when Sandy skipped school to help the home health aide give her mother a bath, how she stayed in her bedroom just staring at the ceiling, after the physically and emotionally draining work with her mother. How she heard her father's pickup truck pull into the driveway. How she heard his footsteps across the dining room into the spare room that had become her mother's bedroom. How she heard the two sentences her father spoke.

Sandy looked into Dr. Hanson's eyes for a long moment, pushing herself to dig out the words that were stuck in her head. The words she had never said out loud before. She felt the tears pooling in her eyes and she hated them. "I'm going to do this, Dorothy," she said.

The doctor just nodded and waited.

"At my mother's bedside, my father said, 'You have ruined my life with all your suffering. Deal with this.' Then the gunshot and the thump of his body on the floor. The smell of the gun smoke and medicine in the room when I ran in there. And the screams—mine and my mother's."

Dorothy rose from her chair and put her arms around Sandy.

"We'll get back to this intriguing young man later, okay?"

The Saturday after that session, Sandy stood again at the takeout counter at Candee's Kitchen waiting for her breakfast order. She found herself candidly staring at 'Herald.'

Candee had to wake her up out of her trance, "Hey, Sandy girl. Your food."

"Oh, thanks, Candee. I was thinking of something, kinda zoned out there," said Sandy vaguely.

"No. You were staring at Henry," Candee said, smiling.

"No, I don't think so," said Sandy.

"You wanna meet the guy?" Candee offered.

"Oh, no, no, no. Don't be silly. Here." Sandy gave Candee the ten-dollar bill that covered the meals and the tip. Candee pretended to figure out the change as she did every Saturday and Sandy waved toward the tip jar and walked across the street to her car.

The next Saturday, Sandy stood again at the takeout counter. Henry sat right there on the bench, smiling at her.

"Hi," Sandy said. "Seen you around here. You a fisherman?"

"Yep."

Sandy said, "I suppose Candee made some kind of remark to you about me, didn't she?"

"I suppose," Henry replied.

"Well, she's wrong. I wasn't looking at you. I never even noticed you."

"I noticed you," he said.

Neither of them knew what to say or do next. He watched her receive her order, pay Candee, and turn toward him.

Candee leaned out of her window and said, "Henry, ask her if she wants to go for a boat ride."

"You wanna go for a boat ride?"

"I have to bring this breakfast home for my grandmother," Sandy said.

"I didn't mean right now," Henry said, smiling.

"I didn't mean right now either," Sandy said.

Candee interrupted, "Hey, you two get out of the window. I got other customers, you know."

Sandy and Henry turned to the line of people behind them. None of them seemed the least bit bothered at having to wait as they watched the live comedy unfold in front of them.

So began that first happy year, neither of them allowing the veneer covering their true selves to crack. Sandy kept her depression hidden and Henry did the same with his fits of rage. But the deception couldn't last forever.

Chapter Fourteen

Sandy heard Gabriella's quick, assertive steps on the stairs. Sandy tried to move, but she could not. The wiry little woman appeared in the doorway and she stepped over to Sandy's bedside and set two cups on the marble surface of the night table. She sat on the edge of the bed and placed her hand on Sandy's face.

"I made us some cappuccino. Here."

Sandy opened her eyes, tried to focus.

"You have to sit up, dear girl." Gabriella stood up from the edge of the bed. Sandy lifted her heavy legs over the edge and sat slumping.

"Apparently, Sandy, you have been promoted," Gabriella said.

Sandy's nightgown slipped off her shoulder. "What the heck is that supposed to mean?"

POP! Sandy's cheek stung. Gabriella's tiny palm flashed from her side to Sandy's unsuspecting face and back down to her dress in less than a second.

Sandy fingered her stinging cheek. Tears welled up in her eyes. "What was that for?"

"That, my dear, was for two things: to curb your disrespectful tone toward me, and to wake you up out of your self-pity. Now have some of this coffee. I sprinkled cinnamon on the foam the way you like it."

Sandy struggled through her resentment. She wiped the tears from each eye with her thumb. The hot cappuccino roused her from her funk. She glared at her Nonina over the rim of the cup.

"With all due respect," Sandy said, disrespectfully, "my dear Nonina, what in the name of God are you talking about?"

Gabriella smiled. "Welcome back to the land of the living, dear girl. Our Lord and Commander does not dispatch a squad of angels to guard just anyone."

Sandy sipped deep the warm coffee. The caffeine began to arouse her fuzzy brain. "Please elaborate, Nonina."

"You have five angel warriors surrounding you at all times. Eventually you will be able to give them commands, and they will comply as long as your orders are in line with God's mission. Carlos has the gift of communicating with them, too. And Lucille."

Sandy pondered that one. She stood. The hem of her gown unfolded over her knees. She took several deep breaths and forced her eyes wide open.

"You know, Nonina, there's no end to the absurdities that surround you. So let me get this straight: Carlos can see, hear, and talk to the angels. That's within my range. That the wolfhound can do the same is just a touch beyond me."

"I have to agree with you. But long ago, I have managed to avoid trying to fit the absurdities of the divine realm into the limits of my own understanding. Being able to 'see' things that are outside our natural vision expands our universe, don't you think?"

"I have to shower and get dressed. I'll be down for breakfast in a few minutes. I suppose you know about Henry, right?"

"Yes. I had young Beto accompany him," said Gabriella.

Sandy turned around to face her grandmother. "What do you mean you had Beto accompany him? You knew he was going to leave me?"

"No, dear, and watch that tone. Henry left under what he thinks is his own accord, in one of his fits of rage. Weeks ago I instructed Beto, one of Carlos's nephews, I believe—I can't keep that family straight; there are so many of them—to keep an eye on Henry. I told him if he sees Henry preparing to go off on one of his escapades, to catch him and go with him."

"I hate that man," stated Sandy. "He's abandoned us. This threat to our security from the Directorate must be getting more imminent. How selfish can a man be?"

"A man's heart plans his way, but the Lord determines his steps," said Gabriella.

"What?" said Sandy from the bathroom. "I know it's a proverb, but what does it have to do with what we're talking about?"

No answer from Gabriella.

Sandy thought about it while she tested the temperature of the water in the shower. "You mean Henry's tantrum and his leaving us when we need him here more than ever is what God wants him to do? That makes no sense."

Gabriella shook her head as she walked down the stairs with the two empty cups in her hands. Out loud she said to herself, "When it makes no sense, that's when it makes sense."

Loud from the bathroom Sandy called, "Can these angels see me in here?"

"You know where you want to hang out, Henry?" asked young Beto as they sped north up the Atlantic coast on Interstate 95.

"Not sure, Beto. I want to find a good fishing spot."

"I have an idea, Henry," he said.

"I'm open, Beto. What'd you have in mind?" Henry leaned back into the Chevy Tahoe's leather seat.

"I have a cousin. Has a nice fishing boat up in Maine. He's recovering from knee surgery, so he's laid up. I'm sure he'll let us use his boat."

"You guys have cousins all over the place, don't you? So where is this cousin and more important, where is his boat?"

"Cape Neddick Harbor. He has a private slip up the Neddick River about a half mile from the ocean."

"Sounds good to me. You know how to get there?"

"Sure, stay on ninety-five until we get into Maine," said Beto. "So you haven't really planned out this trip, huh? Not like you, Henry"

"I had to get out of there."

"I hear you," said Beto. "Sometimes those ladies come up with some crazy stuff."

They crossed the state line into New Hampshire and Beto read the sign out loud, "Welcome to New Hampshire, 'Live Free or Die.' What's that supposed to mean anyway?"

Henry considered the state motto of New Hampshire. "Yeah, that's a good question. 'Live free or die,' like in New Hampshire those are the only two options. No wiggle room in the middle. I wonder how it's supposed to play out.

"Hey, you don't mind we take exit two into Hampton?" Beto said. "They got a Chic-fil-A place there. Just opened up. Best chicken."

"Sounds good, Beto," said Henry. The rhythm of the tires on the highway lent a soundtrack to his thoughts.

After a few miles of ruminating he said, "I mean who is making the statement, anyway?"

"Huh?" asked Beto, "What statement you talking about?"

"The 'live free or die' statement. "Is it like someone in New Hampshire is giving an order to someone, or is it like me making some kind of proclamation about my own belief?"

Beto looked over at Henry behind the wheel. "I think you might be overthinking it, Henry. It's just a motto, like a historical thing."

"So why keep it? I mean it's on all their license plates, and there it was in our face as we crossed the state line. Stay with me on this, will ya?"

"Sure, okay," said Beto, "Let's say New Hampshire has this freedom police, right? And they go around to every new resident and command them, 'Hey, you: live free or die.' So the guy says, 'I'm living free, I promise. See how free I am?' And then the police guy says, 'What if your wife tells you to do something you don't want to do?' And the new resident says, 'Well, sometimes I go along with her I suppose.' And the police guy says, 'You call that freedom? Off with your head.'"

Henry picked up on Beto's scenario. "Yeah, see? No alternatives, just freedom or death here in New Hampshire. Another guy drives into the state from Massachusetts with his wife, mother-in-law, and his daughter in the car. At the toll booth the attendant goes, 'Live free or die?' The motorist looks at the three females in his car, what's he going to say? 'You call this freedom? Just kill me!'" And the men laughed.

Henry's face turned serious. "See, Beto, welcome to my world at Cielavista. I'm a planner, an organizer, a control freak, I admit it. And with Gabriella and Sandy all these spiritual mysteries and secret plots sail around the place and you never know what to expect. Too many surprises. I can't breathe."

Henry eased to Tahoe down the off ramp on exit two onto Route 101.

"I mean what's wrong with living a normal day-to-day life where you know pretty much what's going to happen next and you're prepared to deal with it? At our place it seems the sky is full of supernatural electricity and you never know when you're going to get struck by divine lightning,"

Henry guided the big Tahoe into the parking lot of the Chick-fil-A. "You want to eat in or go through the drive through?"

"If you don't mind I'd rather eat in. I like to concentrate on my food when I'm eating it," Beto said. "How long have you been living at Cielavista?"

"Let's see…we got married in 1987." Henry opened the driver's door and slid off his seat onto the asphalt parking lot. "So that's what…twenty-eight years now?"

Henry removed the floor mat from underneath the dashboard and swept it off over the pavement with his hand. He went around the vehicle and swept off Beto's floor mat. Then he locked the SUV and walked into the restaurant.

"You do that all the time, Henry?" Beto said.

"What?"

"With the floor mats in the car? Wipe them off?"

"Oh, did I do that?" said Henry.

Inside the restaurant Beto said, "Twenty-eight years married and living at the estate. Man, you were there six years before I was even born."

"Gee, they got quite a selection here," said Henry. "What're you having?"

Beto told the girl at the register, "I'll have the chargrilled chicken sandwich, the waffle potato fries, and a medium Coke, please."

"I got these," said Henry to the girl as he pulled out his wallet. "I'll have the chicken Caesar cool wrap with the fries and a medium Coke. No dressing on the wrap; put it in a cup on the side."

Beto followed Henry to a table. Henry wiped off the table with a napkin.

"Yeah, it's been good mostly, but sometimes really difficult, you know?" Henry said. "I guess I'm what they call obsessive-compulsive. I like everything in order, nice and neat. I hate chaos. And everything at Cielavista is one surprise after another. It's like a real-world fun house. So I need some time away, you know, without all that supernatural drama.

"Man this wrap is great, and these fries. Good choice, Beto."

They finished their meal and got back on the interstate.

"Beto, I feel like that place is a high-security prison, and you know what's the really sad part?"

"No, what's that?" Beto sipped his Coke through the straw and gazed out the windshield.

"I'm my own warden."

"How's that?" Beto said.

"I have accepted all the constraining conditions Gabriella and Sandy put on me. Then instead of just turning the key and changing the conditions, I keep myself locked up."

"Good thing you're not living in New Hampshire."

"Why's that?" said Henry.

"You ain't living free, man, you'd be dead." Beto snorted Coke through his nose when he laughed.

"I was gonna ask you something, and I hope it doesn't make you angry, Henry," Beto said cautiously.

"What?" Henry looked over at Beto.

"How long've you had this angel hanging around?"

"What did you say?" Henry pulled over onto the shoulder of the interstate and stopped the SUV.

"The angel. He's been following us the whole way. How long have you had him?"

Henry put the vehicle in park and turned in the driver's seat to face the young Hispanic gardener. He stared accusingly into Beto's eyes for several minutes.

"What angel?" Henry asked through his growing rage.

"Hey, I'm sorry, but I was kinda curious. Not everyone I know has special forces angel like this one that's flying around the car all the time. He's not mine, so he must be yours."

"See," Henry's voice heated up, "that's exactly what I'm talking about: all this mysterious insanity going on that I can't see but everyone else can. How can you see this angel, Beto?"

"Look, I have the same vision that my Uncle Carlos has. I can't help it. Don't blame me, man. I won't mention it again, trust me."

Henry peered through the windshield into the sky over the interstate. "His name is supposed to be Tobias, kind of a second-string type angel, not as powerful as the big guys, I guess. I'm told that I can order him around, get him to help me out. Where is he?"

"I think he's still back there at Chic-fil-A talking to that counter girl. Apparently she can see angels too."

"Great, my angel's a flirt," said Henry and he put the Tahoe in drive, spun the tires in the gravel, and fishtailed onto the driving lane, causing a BMW to honk and swerve around him.

They crossed the bridge over the Piscataqua River into Maine. Beto pointed to the "Welcome to Maine" sign.

"Now there's a motto we can live with," he said. "'Welcome to Maine, the way life should be.'"

Chapter Fifteen

Frances O'Donnelly pulled the lever on the leather recliner in her suite. The view out her balcony—autumn hills layered beyond the valley splashing gold, red, orange, and green against an amber sky—offered Frances a temporary sense of luxurious ease. She was well aware that tomorrow augured violence and trauma. She hoped that Anna Stone's presence could somehow assuage her anxiety about the impending conflict.

There was a knock on her door. "Come on in," she called.

Frances' administrative assistant, Monica Browers, opened the door for Anna.

"Anna, come over here," said Frances. "I'd get up, but I'm slightly buzzed by some wonderful wine, and I had a long, luxurious massage and a steam bath. I have all the strength of overcooked macaroni. How was your trip from Arkansas?"

"Oh, you know, just the normal routine—got picked up at the house by a private limo, driven to an executive airport in Little Rock I had no idea existed, then the flight in your jet with Monica, who is lovely by the way. Enjoyed a nice cocktail and appetizers on the flight and then a comfortable ride in a private car here to the Canyon Ranch—nothing out of the ordinary for this country girl."

Anna's sweet laugh swept through the suite.

"Well, Anna, your rooms are across the hall, so get settled in, put on some sweats, and come on over. Would you like me to order anything? Are you hungry?"

"I'd love some kind of dessert," Anna said. "Do you suppose they could put together some pie and ice cream?"

Frances ordered Anna's dessert from room service. As soon as she hung up the phone it rang. She picked up the receiver again, "Hello, this is Frances," she said.

"It's Romano Goldstein. We have to talk. It's about Akebe. It's bad." Frances detected both fear and assertiveness in Romano's tone.

"I'll meet you in your suite in half an hour, okay?" answered Frances, forming a quick action plan in her mind.

"Good. Number 15A. See you at seven." He hung up.

Frances asked Anna to sit on the couch next to her. They took their time with the tea and pie à la mode.

"This is even better than my mother's apple pie, and she makes the best," said Anna. "So what am I doing here?"

"Anna, I'm attending an important board meeting. I was hoping I could talk with you and get your moral support because the fireworks will be overwhelming. You and I have formed some kind of bond, and I find a tremendous amount of strength from our friendship. I hope I haven't inconvenienced you. I'm so grateful that you could give me this time. You may have to sit around and just chill out, not knowing when I'll be needing you."

"Are you in trouble, Frances?"

"Not really. Just conflicted. The work of this executive board will improve life in American forever. Our operations are highly classified, but I can tell you that we control thousands of prominent American leaders. We are a small group of highly enlightened, powerful people. For years I have been convinced that we were on the right track, but after meeting you and having those powerful experiences with you, my mind has been in turmoil."

"Sure, Frances. I'll be able to occupy myself while you are busy in your meetings. If you don't mind, I'll be praying for you."

"Pray? Well, if I did mind, what could I do about it?" Frances smiled. "I have a meeting. See you later."

Frances got up and gave Anna a kiss on the forehead and left her there in her suite.

Anna rested her head back on the couch. Strange, untapped mental powers flowed from some divine source into her soul like waves of cosmic rivers. She felt exhilarated that her humanity was being expanded beyond her body, beyond the visible realm, enabling her to see the unseeable and understand the unfathomable.

Anna felt like a radio—receiving transmissions, processing them, and transmitting them. Now she was receiving supernatural wisdom, not for her but for Frances. She felt the waves passing into her that transformed into specific thoughts for Frances to use in her conversations. Anna shut her eyes and realized that Frances was unaware of the spiritual forces acting in and around her.

Frances knew Romano's background. His parents—German Jews hidden in Amsterdam when the Nazis occupied Holland—smuggled the two-year-old Romano out of the country in a crate bound for America. A friendly Dutch merchant arranged the trip and once out of port, he recovered the baby and found a place for him to live in New York. The parents eventually died in Auschwitz. Romano employed his superior intellect, his drive, and his diverse skills to become one of America's leading psychologists. Although he focused most of his time researching treatments of posttraumatic stress disorder, he still saw a few selected patients, all young combat veterans.

Frances knocked on the door of room 15A. Romano held out his hand toward the inner room for her to come in. He was short and chubby, always a meticulous dresser, his white hair combed back from a narrow forehead. His intelligent eyes were almost black. Tonight he was wearing a dark blue dress shirt with topaz cufflinks, tan worsted slacks, and light tan alligator slippers.

"Oh, my," the calm doctor sighed, "my dear Frances, we have a sticky problem on our hands and I know the two of us are more than capable of solving it. Would you like some wine, dear?"

"Sure, Romano—thanks," said Frances, taking a seat on the couch near the window that looked out over the deck. She felt her body shutter. She received a flash of a vision in her head. Whispers of disturbing secrets swirled through her subconscious. She grasped the stem of the wineglass Romano was handing her.

Romano sipped from his glass and seemed to savor the taste and feel of the Chablis. "They really know how to treat their guests here, don't they, dear? I will certainly return to this ranch with my wife when I have some time. If I ever have some time," he said.

"Romano, did you know Andrew would be coming here tomorrow?" Frances imparted a bit of the new knowledge she was receiving to Romano. "Akebe never calls Andrew to board meetings. It's a terrible breach of operational security. Akebe must have something demonic in mind."

"You know, my dear, the kind of research I do?" Romano asked.

"Yes, you are a psychologist, and a world renowned psychologist at that. You do a lot of work with PTSD patients, right?"

"Well, yes, and Akebe is showing classic symptoms."

Frances was surprised. "Akebe? Symptoms of what, Doctor?"

"When a man demonstrates such drastic change in behavior, as we are witnessing here today, that's a sign that he has cracked under stress. We know Akebe, always aggressive and acerbic in his actions and his speech. For him that's normal. This pleasant composure, this relaxed attitude, is a symptom. In all my years with the Directorate, I performed an extensive psychological profile on Akebe. I know that his life story is infested with hundreds of traumatic episodes. He manages to function, but he can only suppress those emotional injuries so long. He has never sought treatment. He has never dealt with any of his past trauma and now the effects of all his emotional wounds have surfaced. He is operating in a state of volatile agitation. He's a time bomb ready to explode, and I believe he will be exploding tomorrow."

"I have complete faith in your assessment, Doctor. And I have a strong intuition that Andrew's presence at this conference is connected to Akebe's unstable frame of mind," said Frances. "So what are we to do?"

"That's why I asked you to meet with me," said Doctor Romano Goldstein.

Firdos leaned against the front fender of the Ford 250 truck that his boss was repairing. He wiped his greasy hands on the new green overalls with his name stitched over the right breast pocket.

"Hand me that three-eight socket with the extension, Firdos." The voice came from under the wheel well of the truck where Dick was draining the brake fluid.

Firdos turned to the rolling toolbox, opened the drawer, and found the three-eight socket and the extension for the wrench Dick was using under the vehicle and he handed it to him.

The Directorate had arranged for Firdos' job at Dick's Auto Repair in Neddick, Maine. Carlene Wood and Randal Sanford managed every detail of his new life. He quit questioning.

Randal told him that Carlene's Delta Squad would be located nearby and she would be contacting him. Firdos thought of her as the vanilla lady. Her sweet aroma lingered in his olfactory gland and his mind.

Firdos liked this job. It gave him plenty of time off to observe the comings and goings of the folks around Cape Neddick. His magnet of a brain had recorded and catalogued hundreds of faces, cars, boats, and places in his new place of work. As he stood by the Ford's fender, he watched Route 1A and the occasional vehicle that passed by. In October all the summer tourists in this beach town were long gone and over half of the businesses were boarded up, waiting for spring.

There's a new one. A black Chevy Tahoe with two guys in the front seat. Firdos's mental video camera recorded the SUV and the faces. He was transfixed by a swirl of wind making the leaves dance across the yard chasing the starlings out of the oak tree. The gentle whirlwind followed the Tahoe north on Route 1A toward Neddick Harbor. For some reason Firdos detected a peculiar significance about these two men. The hair on the back of Firdos's neck stood up and he felt a pang of fear in his gut. He had to call Carlene.

It took Andrew Johansen less than a day-and-a-half to outfit the Ford Transit van as a mobile operations center—tall enough to stand up in and roomy enough for all his equipment. On one side he bolted a swivel chair and a narrow counter where he secured five laptop computers, and on the opposite wall he built a shelf for satcom receivers and radio transmitters. Above that he mounted a large flat screen. In this command-center-on-wheels he drove from Missouri to Massachusetts in three days, maintaining his supervision of the operations of his six squads in the field.

As he rolled down the long driveway off Route 7 in Lenox, Massachusetts, toward the Canyon Ranch Resort, he listened to his squad leader on the East Coast, Carlene Wood. She had just held a meeting with her squad. Andrew read her Situation Report, pleased that she followed his precise format. The Directorate's communications network was secure. Anyone trying to listen in on the conversation would hear only static and garbled noise.

Carlene's voice in Andrew's earpiece: "SITREP. Paragraph one: All friendly forces in place and operational. Five seers, three operators. Paragraph two: Current operations ongoing, seers one and two have identified four new targets, profiles in annex 1, seer three reconnoitering southern New Hampshire, no new targets thus far, seer four reports that target number 0925 is isolated for elimination.

"Paragraph three: Operator Green Arrow and Blue Wolf are staging to remove target 0925 at your command. Operator Red Falcon is in direct support of seer five, see annex 2.

Paragraph four: Request one-on-one meeting to discuss our need for reinforcements.

End of SITREP, date stamp: 10OCT2015."

"SITREP received, Carlene," said Andrew. "I will review the recorded version immediately. I will respond within the hour. Out." And he clicked off the radio, terminating the connection.

Andrew pulled into the lot at the east end of Bellefontaine Mansion and parked the van so he could give his full attention to his squad leader's report. Oblivious to the beauty and luxury that surrounded him at the Canyon Ranch, he toggled his control switch to computer number four. The computer decrypted and recorded Carlene's report. Andrew gave a voice command into the audio reader, "Start with annex 2." The computer's voice read the document into Andrew's earpiece.

"Firdos Gaffardi, seer number five, Delta Squad, is observing the new location of FITO in Neddick, Maine. He reports human enemy activity in that location but has not determined their identity. He also reports telekinetic activity streaming from that location. BREAK.

"Director Randal Sanford has met with Firdos, against my instructions. Randal reports that FITO may be attempting to divert attention away from their previous location in the vicinity of Gloucester, Massachusetts. Thus raising the question: is FITO operating from two locations, have they moved, or are they using the Neddick location as a decoy?

"Request you attach two squads to my operational control to gain more accurate intelligence about this high-priority target. End of Annex 2. BREAK."

Andrew sat back in his chair and studied his map of the Atlantic coast north of Boston that included Cape Ann in Massachusetts and Cape

Neddick in Maine. Carlene's report confirmed his own conclusions about FITO's location or locations: either they moved or they are operating in two locations, or the new location is a decoy. His next course of action took shape in his mind. All-out-war against FITO.

CHAPTER SIXTEEN

Henry and Beto reached the home of Beto's cousin at 9:00 p.m. They had turned off Route 1A onto Agamenticus Avenue and followed the narrow road up the hill overlooking Neddick Harbor. They passed large stately homes with spacious lawns on both sides of the road.

"Up there on the right," Beto said. "That's the driveway."

Henry pulled into the cobblestone driveway that ended in a large circular parking lot between a three-car garage and the side of a Dutch colonial house. He turned off the engine and they got out and walked up the stairs to the wraparound porch at the rear of the home. Beto rapped on the door. As they waited on the porch, Henry looked down the hill to the boathouse and the slip where the fishing boat was moored.

"That looks like a nice boat, Beto. Are we taking that one?"

Beto looked down where Henry was looking. "Yep, that's it. '*Water Walker*.'"

"Hi guys," the voice from the house greeted them through the screen door. "Come on in."

"Hola, my brother," said Beto, and he gave their host a bear hug. "How are you?"

"Good to see you, Beto. And this must be Henry—hello and welcome. I hope you will enjoy the boat. I'm sorry I can't join you. I'll be taking off in the morning for business in New York."

Beto said, "Henry, this is my cousin, Luis Santiago. Luis, my friend, Henry."

Henry said, "Hello, Luis," and shook his hand. "Well, we are very grateful for your generosity, Luis. You have quite a place here."

"Yes. And about that," Luis said, "unfortunately you won't have use of the house. Too complicated to get into. Family stuff. My son and his friend need their privacy. We have a mobile home just a few miles away that you can use. And when you come here for the boat, just drive right down to the boathouse and you can launch from there. I hope that's okay."

"Sounds fine to us," said Beto. "We will stay out of Luis Junior's way, for sure. Thank you."

"Here is the key to the trailer in the View Point Campground, right off Route 1A about a mile from where our avenue intersects."

"Yes," said Henry. "I remember seeing it on the way in. No problem. Thanks. I guess we should make our way over there now, if that's all right."

"Sure," said Luis. "You need to get bedded down so you can get up before the fish. Good seeing you, Beto. Next time we can spend more time catching up."

In a few minutes they were driving into the View Point Campground looking for lot number 19. They pulled into the gravel space next to the trailer and carried their bags inside, leaving the fishing gear in the SUV.

As Beto took the last of their luggage out of the car, he turned around on the little porch under the trailer's awning and noticed the guy across the street sitting on a lawn chair outside his trailer smoking a cigarette. It seemed to Beto that the man was watching him maybe just a little more intently than a temporary neighbor would watch. He also noticed Tobias hovering over the man's trailer with a concerned look on his angelic face.

"What are you grinning about?" Gabriella asked her granddaughter. Sandy walked into the kitchen of their cottage at Cielavista.

"Nothing, really. I shouldn't be feeling this way. I mean, I have serious concerns about us here without Henry, but I thought it was humorous, that's all."

"What's humorous?"

"The bed's unmade," Sandy said, smiling.

Gabriella chuckled. "And when's the last time that happened?"

"And my nightgown's lying on top of the unmade bed. And the towel in the bathroom is lying on the floor. I guess I miss him, but the mess is very liberating." Sandy laughed again.

"Okay, my little piggy, get over here, have some breakfast. We have to talk."

Sandy made herself a bowl of oatmeal with honey, almonds, and milk, poured another cup of coffee, and sat at the dining table by the big bay window.

Gabriella sat down next to her with a cup of tea.

"I have seen the storm clouds of war looming on the horizon," Gabriella started.

Sandy ate and listened. "Storm clouds," she repeated.

"I have stymied the Directorate's attempts at eliminating the people on their hit list. Did you know that since 2006, there have been more than 200 mass killings in the United States? Everyone has heard of the most famous incidents. Newtown, Aurora, and Virginia Tech captured the nation's attention, but many more have happened at an alarming frequency and much less scrutiny.

"Henry has examined FBI data. The Bureau defines a mass killing as four or more victims. He has combed local police records that record mass killings in America. They happen far more often than the government reports, and only a select few investigators know the circumstances of those killings—the people who commit them, the weapons they use, and the forces that motivate them.

"There is a mass killing in America about every two weeks."

Sandy stopped eating and put down her spoon. She looked out the bay window into the afternoon sky, where high white clouds chased each other through the stratosphere.

Gabriella was citing numbers from memory. "The FBI counted 172 cases of mass killings between 2006 and 2011. That does not include some large states such as Florida, for example. Poor reporting by police agencies to the FBI also means they left out a fair number of mass killings.

"In March and April of 2009 mass murderers killed thirteen times, but the press reported only. Most mass killings are family oriented."

"Family mass shooting? What do you mean?" asked Sandy.

"Breakups, estrangements, and family arguments make up the majority of family shootings. Sometimes innocent victims get caught in the crossfire."

"So how does all this relate to us? Our mission? How did God select you—and now all of us here at Cielavista—to combat these people?"

"What the FBI and all our law enforcement people do not know is that the Directorate is behind all of these shootings, public, private, and whatever. Since the powers being used by the Directorate are paranormal, the government cannot understand it. They have to deal with what they can see and what they can evaluate.

"Apparently God designed my mind to operate differently than other peoples'. Since I was a little girl everyone thought I was strange. I horrified most of the people I grew up with, so they made fun of me. Then God opened my eyes. He showed me that this weird little girl was his specialized instrument. And now he wants to use you, Sandy."

"So this is genetic?" asked Sandy.

"Yes and no," Gabriella said. "Your father—God rest his soul—couldn't seem to acknowledge the gift. He possessed it. I could tell because he had flashes of prophetic wisdom, but he lived his own busy, earthly life, so he could not experience his spiritual life. But I must admit he was a joyful guy, and he kept us all in stitches with his antics and his jokes."

"Okay, so now it appears that your granddaughter has the weird gene," Sandy said. "A few days ago I saw Anna Stone heal Frances O'Donnelly's fibromyalgia."

"I thought so," Gabriella said. "Now we have to synergize our powers. Put some good walking shoes on and come with me."

Sandy followed Gabriella across the wide lawn and down the rocky steps. "I get the power up in the tower," she tried to explain, but Gabriella ignored her.

The two women—one tall and angular with short, white hair and the other tiny and petite with a mane of long black hair—stood at the near side of the wide crevice. The tide swelled high and the wind blew hard from the northeast. The waves crashed into the deep space between the rock where they stood and Gabriella's praying rock. Sandy never realized the immense power emanating from this place. She was surprised at the width of the crevice and how deep and dangerous it looked. The crashing waves sent sprays of white foam into their faces.

Without a word Gabriella took two steps back, then two quick, powerful running steps toward the edge and sailed over the crevice and landed on her flat granite outcropping.

Sandy's heart pounded.

"Your angel's name is Naomi. Tell her to sail under you," Gabriella ordered.

Sandy closed her eyes. The panic she felt was triggering her past traumas, paralyzing her.

"Look at me," Gabriella shouted over the roar of the churning water between them. "Hold your hand out toward me."

Sandy stretched her arm toward her grandmother. Gabriella pointed her extended fingers toward Sandy. "Listen to me. You have to agree with me as I say this. Tell me you agree."

Sandy's feet were stuck as if locked in hardened concrete. She looked at Gabriella. A spit of salt foam from the chasm soaked Sandy's shirt. It woke her up out of her panic-driven trance. "I am listening, Nonina. I will agree with you," she said.

Gabriella stretched out her hand at Sandy's face and proclaimed, "God is reprograming the defective DNA in your mind. I speak wholeness, healing, and wellness to your soul. All the pathways that have been blocking your mental immune system from operating at peak performance,

open wide! Open wide you pathways and allow the flow of healing stim-
ulants to restore Sandy's mind in accordance with God's original design."

Sandy's body shook, her arms flew involuntarily up into the air, and
she shouted something unintelligible into the foam and mist. "Naomi, sail
under my feet as I jump across this chasm," she ordered.

Sandy took two steps back and two running steps toward the edge.
She felt her right leg flex and push away from the rock like a steel spring.
Her left leg extended outward and she seemed to hold there above the
deep raging crevice, exhilarated, laughing, sailing in the air on an invisible pillow of energy. She felt the folds of her loose shirt flutter in the
wind and her pants stretch out against her thighs. She felt the ball of her
left foot fall soft on the far side of the crevice as if she were weightless.
Her momentum carried her two more steps as she landed on Gabriella's
praying rock.

Sandy stood amazed next to Gabriella. They didn't say anything for
several minutes—just looked at each other and at the ocean and the horizon beyond. Sandy's mind finally came down to earth, catching up to
her body.

"So that's how it's done," she said.

Gabriella took Sandy's hand and they stood side-by-side looking at
the sky. "It's called a leap of faith," the old woman said. Sandy squeezed
her hand.

"The wind is warm for October," Sandy observed.

"Here the wind is always warm, no matter what month it is," explained
Gabriella. "Watch the sky with me."

Time slipped by unnoticed. Sandy did not know what to call this
experience. As strange as the sensation of timelessness was, as surreal as
the swirling atmosphere around them was, it all seemed warm and comfortable. She realized that she had just crossed some kind of supernatural
threshold that would change the course of her future.

Then it appeared. In the sky. As real as a movie screen in the cinema,
a scene projected onto the sky above the ocean played out before them.
An overhead shot of a beautiful resort in the Berkshires came into focus.

Then as if floating through the roof of a huge mansion, the scene became a suite where a woman sat alone.

"Nonina, that's Anna Stone. I've seen her before," said Sandy.

"Yes. She has opened her mind to receive information and energy from us," said Gabriella. "I led her to accept Frances O'Donnelly's invitation to join her at the Canyon Ranch where the Directorate is meeting. I have sent two of our angels to protect her. There is danger coming to that place."

Sandy turned to her grandmother. She said, "There is danger coming to this place too."

CHAPTER SEVENTEEN

Anna Stone woke up before dawn, ordered coffee, and called her husband in Cabot, Arkansas. She padded out to the balcony off her bedroom and watched the morning star fade into the dawn light. She greeted the new forces at work in her spirit. They welled up somewhere in her mind—her soul? She was certain these forces took the form of information and strength.

She concentrated on her morning meditations, finding comfort in familiar routines in these unfamiliar surroundings. She pushed the hassock out onto the balcony and took up the Burmese position—hands resting on her thighs, palms up. She closed her eyes, then opened them as the eastern sky made way for the rising sun. A thin layer of white clouds drifted nonchalantly from north to south.

"What is that?" Anna heard herself say out loud. She watched unafraid, but curious as two shimmering shapes of air raced toward her from the east.

An inner voice said, "Angels."

Anna smiled. She had heard of such visitations. She watched the transparent visible forms take humanlike form, hanging there in the air. She smiled.

"You guys have names?" Anna asked, half expecting the whole hallucination to disappear.

The voice of one said, "I'm Thomas. This is Joe. You can call for us to help you. We are here for Frances, too."

Anna closed her eyes and shook her head. Silently she prayed, *God, I am fine believing in you and your son and the Holy Spirit, but I really need to know if this angel thing is real.*

The angel, Thomas said, "Yeah, we're real. The Master sent several detachments of us creatures to combat this evil Directorate. Most of us are at FITO's headquarters on the coast about one hundred fifty miles from here."

"More like one hundred sixty miles," said Joe.

"You clocked it?" asked Thomas.

"I'm just very good at estimating these earthly measurements. Took us about four minutes to get here, so that means one hundred sixty miles. Trust me," said Joe.

Anna said, "So you heard me praying in my head? And what is FITO?"

Thomas and Joe swooped down and stood on Anna's balcony, human now, no wings. Thomas explained, "When you pray to the Master, we can hear all of it. Obviously you aren't really part of this evil society called the Directorate. They've been orchestrating all these mass murders you've been reading and hearing about in the media. There's a small cell of powerful prophets and spirit-warriors that have messed up the Directorate's plans. The board of directors calls them FITO, for fly-in-the-ointment."

"'Dead flies putrefy the perfumer's ointment and cause it to give off a foul odor; so does a little folly to one respected for wisdom and honor,'" recited Anna from the Book of Ecclesiastes.

"So this Directorate thinks they are morally superior to everyone, and they consider FITO some kind of dirty contamination. Man, are these people deluded."

"The people at FITO now understand about all the activities that the Directorate is involved with," said Thomas who seemed to be the more senior angel. Joe busied himself exploring the hallways and rooms in the Bellefontaine Mansion.

"You need to tell Frances that Akebe is planning to murder Andrew in plain sight of all the other board members during the first session this morning. Frances has to stop him."

A chill ran up Anna's spine. "Murder! My God, what have I gotten into?"

"Actually you haven't gotten yourself into this. The master called you, and you answered the call," explained Thomas.

"So what is Frances' role in all this? She seems to be a decent person. I can't imagine her involved in arranging mass murders. That's horrible."

"Well, here's the way their twisted logic goes: America is being led by people who don't know what they are doing, so the members of the Directorate have to take control. They use a combination of long-distance telekinesis, hypnosis, and brainwashing to manipulate the minds of key leaders in every area of American culture. They use this same paranormal power, enhanced with high-tech energy-producing equipment, to mentally coerce unsuspecting people to murder those whom they can't brainwash. They lay down smokescreens, making the mass killings look like crimes of passion, accidents, the work of religious fanatics or mentally impaired people, or disgruntled employees. But the Directorate masterminds all of them. Their perverted logic stems from a delusional form of patriotism that trumps any kind of moral discernment. Their definition of the ends—an improved America under their control—justifies the means—killing off anyone who doesn't accept the inducements of American consumerism and liberal education and the institutions that control them."

"Wow," said Anna. "I suppose Frances could be seduced by such logic. Her father's decline and death fractured her soul. To assuage her emotional pain, she envisioned herself rescuing America and extinguishing those who want to bring the country down."

"You might be right," replied Thomas. "Something happened to Frances O'Donnelly when she went to see you in Arkansas. Your love for her in the form of healing opened up a seam in her psychological defenses that allowed the power from FITO to enter her soul. You may recall that you were led by some mysterious force to access her hotel room with that room service cart, and she accepted your friendship. Well, the folks at FITO influenced you and Frances to make all that happen. Their power is stronger than the Directorate's. It's different than theirs because the source of it comes from the Master through his Spirit."

"Okay, my brain is busting right now. Any more information and I'll have to wrap my head in duct tape.

"My job right now is to tell Frances that Akebe—whoever he is—is planning to murder Andrew—whoever he is—at the first session today. And she is supposed to stop him. See you guys around."

"That's one nice big boat," said Henry as they walked through the boathouse to the slip on Neddick Harbor. "I mean you have your nice boats, not necessarily big. And you have your big boats, not necessarily nice. But this is a nice big boat."

"It's a sixty-two-foot Cape Dory trawler," said Beto. "I knew you'd love it because Luis obsesses over neatness like you. By the way, thanks for making my bed this morning."

"Luis is my kind of guy," said Henry. "This trawler shines." Henry ran his hand over the fiberglass surfaces on the rear deck and the aluminum steps to the cabin.

"Have you been down here in the cabin?" he shouted up to Beto. "The interior is all mahogany. It's spotless." Henry ran his fingers over the shelves and dining table like a drill instructor in boot camp.

"Let's cast off and fire this baby up," said Beto. "Luis keeps all the fishing tackle we'll ever need onboard. "I'll stow our food in the refrigerator in the galley below."

They chugged the *Water Walker* slowly out of Neddick. The twin 490-horsepower John Deer diesel engines hummed smoothly in the boat's belly. Henry and Beto sat in the comfortable seats in the helm above the main deck. The sweet morning air charmed Henry's heavy heart.

"We're living free now, brother," said Beto. He poured two cups of hot black coffee from his Thermos.

"Thanks, Beto," said Henry. He took a sip. "Hey, something just occurred to me." They had cleared the mouth of Neddick Harbor and he gave the engines more gas, taking the boat up to twenty knots.

"What's that, Skipper?"

"This angel of mine—your uncle Carlos said his name is Tobias. And you can see him, right?"

"Yeah."

"I don't suppose he can find a nice big school of stripers for us," Henry said, smiling.

"Why don't you just ask him?"

A rush of excitement sliced open his veil of skepticism. "Hey, Tobias, are you there?"

A spout of water flushed up from the surface of the ocean off their starboard side. "That's him," said Beto.

"Tobias," Henry said, "find us some fish."

The *Water Walker* pushed out into the calm, lazy water before them under a flat, blue-grey sky.

"Henry, I hate to bring up negative vibes here on this nice relaxing day, but something bothered me last night when we were moving into the trailer."

"What?" Henry checked the instruments on the mahogany dash in front of him. He gently rolled the wheel a few degrees starboard.

"Across the street from our trailer, this guy sat there watching us. Did you notice him?"

"I guess so. Dark guy, smoking a cigarette in a lawn chair?" asked Henry.

"Yeah," Beto said. "I wouldn't have cared much about him, but your angel, Tobias, was paying him a lot of attention. I got the feeling Tobias didn't feel very comfortable around him."

"Okay. Noted. We'll have to watch out for him, I guess." Henry was distracted by what was going on a quarter mile to their front. Several spouts of water were churning up out there as if tiny tornados were forming, but there were no funnel clouds around. As they pulled closer to the spouts, they noticed that they were full of fish being flung up out of the water.

"No more talk, buddy. Tobias has finally done something worthwhile. Let's go fishing."

Carlos set up a war room in the barn at Gabriella's instruction. She insisted that they use the barn so the animals could attend the operational briefings. He installed a bank of fluorescent lights over the space where they stored hay and feed. He constructed half walls with plywood over two-by-four frames. He purchased eight plastic folding tables and forty chairs and set them up as a meeting room. At the end of the room he built a tall wall with a screen for the digital projector that he hung from one of the beams overhead. His wife and two nephews helped him with the final setup. She brought in a coffee urn, cups, sugar and cream.

"Gabriella wants us all in the barn at eight o'clock. Pass the word," he said to those of his family who gathered for lunch in the kitchen of the big house. "We will defend our home against some dangerous people who seek to destroy us."

Carlos watched his family's various reactions. His announcement angered some, challenged others, and worried the rest. Some of the women responded with the same bravado as those men who looked forward to a battle. All the elders, both men and women, silently pondered their future.

At eight o'clock Carlos cast a concerned look over the assemblage. All the residents of Cielavista over the age of twelve and all of Carlos' extended family living nearby found a seat or a place to stand along the walls of his war room. Carlos joined Gabriella, Sandy, and his two eldest sons, Frederick and Roberto, at the head table facing the group. The sharp old caretaker glanced over the edge of the half wall where his two horses,

Sadie and Cinnamon, joined the audience. He gave a quick whistle and all four dogs took up places near the front where they could view the screen.

Carlos took attendance, reading from a list of all the members of his family:

The three elders, Carlos, Roberto Sr., and Fredrick and their wives: six;

Roberto's six adult children and their spouses: twelve (Beto—detached);

Carlos's four adult children and their spouses: eight;

Frederick's six adult children and their spouses: twelve;

Roberto's teenage grandchildren: twelve;

Carlos's teenage grandchildren: eight;

Frederick's teenage grandchildren: twelve.

"That's seventy from my house who can bear a sword," said Carlos. "Then there are four canine and two equine who can take orders and fight. And of course you, Sandy, Gabriella, and I suppose Henry and Beto when they return."

Sandy spoke. "We are at war." She let that statement sink in with the assembled force. "I am going to ask my Nonina to offer a prayer."

Gabriella stood at her place at the table and recited from the Book of Psalms, "'Blessed be the Lord my Rock, who trains my hands for war, my fingers for battle,'" she paused and each of the animals perked up their ears at the familiar passage they'd heard Henry shout night after night as he pounded his heavy bag in the stall behind them. "'My lovingkindness, and my fortress, my stronghold and my deliverer, My shield and He in whom I make refuge.' Lord, be with us. The victory is yours. Amen."

"Amen," the war council repeated in one voice.

Carlos was impressed with the dramatic change in Sandy's countenance. A commanding spirit inhabited her. He carefully digested every word of her briefing.

"Before I begin the operational briefing, I will take a moment to offer the opportunity to anyone who does not feel fit for the fight to leave the room and make plans to find a safe place to live until our victory is won.

No one will judge you for your decision to detach yourselves from the warrior force defending Cielavista. In the same way that Gideon reduced the size of his fighting force when faced with overwhelming odds, we will do the same."

Frederick's wife stood up, "I must go and attend to our elderly parents who are living in a home in Gloucester. I am behind you in your decision. God be with you."

One of the married couples in Roberto's family stood down, offering to care for all the small children who were too young to be among the war fighters. Three teenage girls joined them. Carlos stood at the door of the barn to bless them as they exited the briefing. The remaining force of seventy two humans and four animals focused their attention on Sandy's operations order.

CHAPTER EIGHTEEN

Carlene lost her argument with Director Randal Sanford. He insisted that she assemble her team of seers and operators somewhere in the vicinity of York, Maine. He told her that the Directorate issued a new set of orders for her squad. She argued with Director Sanford that her standing operating procedures required that all members of her squad must remain separated, keeping their identities secret even from each other. She tried to get this fat civilian to understand what she knew from her experience in the CIA—compartmentalization. The members of her squad had contact only with her, and if any of them became compromised, she would extract herself from the area of operations and disappear into the atmosphere like smoke.

Randal overruled his subordinate so Carlene scheduled a squad meeting, but she still made every attempt to keep her people apart. She had all her seers and her two operators check in to the Atlantic Inn, each in separate rooms far apart from each other. She made a strict schedule of check-in times so they would not see one another at the registration desk. She delivered a package to each room, a box of theater makeup with instructions how to disguise their faces, and large clothing to conceal the shape of their bodies. Then to assemble them for the meeting, she set up an elaborate plan where each person was picked up in a separate hired car and taken by different routes to the meeting place, a cottage she had rented for her temporary lodging near the objective: Cape Neddick, Maine.

The cottage smelled like vanilla to Firdos, a fragrance he associated with his controller, Carlene Wood. Back in his trailer at View Point, he kept a vanilla-scented candle lit all the time. He always drank vanilla-flavored coffee and at most of his meals he ordered vanilla ice cream for dessert.

Firdos' feelings for Carlene affected him in a strange and powerful way. He never felt a thing for his parents. His school teachers in Baghdad scolded him for having no respect for them or his classmates. They brutally punished him for his selfish and uncaring attitude. At home his family gave up on him after he turned six. To them he would simply be the one son who had no future. But now under the seductive influence of Carlene, something new and frightening and exciting came alive in him. He craved her dominance.

The hired limousine dropped Firdos off at the side of the cottage. It was a large seaside rental property with six rooms on the first floor and four on the second. He wandered through the rooms, following Carlene's hypnotic fragrance into the kitchen.

"You're the first one here, Firdos," she said. "Have a seat there at the counter. Nice job with the makeup. I wouldn't have recognize you if I didn't know who you were. The overalls make you look fat, and I know you're in good physical shape."

Firdos sat on one of the stools at the counter. Carlene put a cup of black coffee in front of him. He looked at her chest. She was wearing a loose-fitting sweatshirt with the words, "Welcome to Maine, the way life should be" stenciled on it.

"How you doing, Firdos?" she asked.

"I have no problems," he stated flatly.

"I noticed that Dick lets you use the shop car. Do you drive that to

Salem and back?" Firdos was growing more comfortable talking with her, unconsciously falling under her mind-controlling power, unaware that Carlene was probing his brain for the essential elements of information she needed for her report.

"I got a place here in a trailer park—View Point," Firdos said. "I kept my apartment in Salem so I don't have to change residence from Massachusetts to Maine. Randal suggested it that way."

"So is the work at the shop going okay?"

"I don't care much about it."

"What's the trailer park like?" she asked.

"My rooms in the trailer are fine. No smoking allowed. I have to smoke outside," answered Firdos. The voice of this woman was having a warming effect on his insides. He focused his eyes on her back as she moved around the kitchen preparing some rolls and pastries for the gathering. The sweatshirt concealed her form, and her slacks hung loosely from her hips, keeping the shape of her lower body a mystery.

Carlene looked over her shoulder and asked, "Any neighbors there?"

"Uh, at the trailer park—no. It's empty after the summer season," he said.

Then he thought a second. "Umm, a couple fishermen came in the other night, across the street. I saw them unpacking their car."

"What did you say to them?"

"Nothing."

"Firdos, would you tell me a little more about these two fishermen? What were they like?"

He let his gaze drop from looking at Carlene to the countertop in front of him. This type of question always made him stumble. He wanted to answer correctly. He wanted to impress Carlene.

"What do you mean 'what were they like'?"

Firdos froze as Carlene leaned toward him from her side of the counter. He stared at the smile she implanted on her face. He followed her hand as it brushed back a strand of hair.

"Anything, Firdos, you remember about these two men who entered the trailer across from you in the View Point Trailer Park? You were outside your unit having a cigarette, right?"

Speaking from a half-trance, Firdos's brain strained to please his supervisor. "There were two guys," he began. "One tall with light skin, one short guy, darker, black hair. The little one seemed to be helping the bigger one. They got out of a black SUV with Massachusetts plates. The tall one concentrated on the luggage and their fishing tackle, the small one was more observant of the trailer, the yard, the street and…."

Carlene crossed her arms, rested her forearms on the counter, and leaned close to Firdos' face. She locked eyes with him. "And what, dear?"

The "dear" fell on Firdos's heart like a silk scarf. He belonged to her. This moment was the first time in his life that he actually looked someone in the eyes. It took him a minute to reengage his brain so he could speak.

"And there was a feeling I had," Firdos found himself continuing from a place in his mind he'd never used before. "I can't explain it, but the best I can say is these men shined. Not with light but with something, they shined. Some kind of power came off them, I don't know how to say it. I'm sorry. I don't have the words. I'm sorry, Carlene."

"That's okay," Carlene said softly and placed her hand on his arm. "You are doing phenomenal, Firdos. Anything else?"

"This is very strange," Firdos said. "Another thing I saw last night."

"Start by telling me where you were and what you were doing, my dear," coaxed Carlene.

"I was sitting in the yard in front of my trailer. I was sitting in a lawn chair. Smoking. I was on my second cigarette. Then the black SUV pulled up."

"Good, go on," she said.

"As the two guys unloaded their bags from the car, a wind swirled around in the street between where I was sitting and where they were unpacking."

"Yes, dear, a wind," said Carlene. "Tell me more about this wind."

Firdos was exploring the depths of a hidden cavern deep inside himself. Carlene was with him on the expedition, her hand on his arm, mothering him. He was having difficulty expressing the effect the wind had on him and on the climate around him.

From a memory of a hot, sparsely furnished classroom in Baghdad, a childhood scene flashed into Firdos's mind. His tongue came alive with a verse from the Quran, *"And We shall remove from their breasts any hatred or sense of injury. Gardens of perpetual bliss: they shall enter there, as well as the righteous among their fathers, their spouses, and their offspring. Angels shall enter from every gate (with the salutation): 'Peace be with you, that you persevered in patience! Now how excellent is the final home!'* From the Quran 7:43 and 13:23–24."

Firdos was trembling and tears were coursing down his cheeks. Carlene leaned back and nodded.

"Firdos, you have done very well. Your report is extremely important," Carlene said. "You see, our organization has been confused about the location of our enemy. They have been under the impression that our enemy was located on the shoreline on Cape Ann down in Massachusetts, and recently they have some indications that they may be located on Cape Neddick, Maine. With your incredible talent for seeing into the spiritual realm, you have determined that there are enemy agents on Cape Neddick."

Firdos sniffed and wiped away his tears. He was overjoyed with the praise Carlene was heaping on him.

"This report of human and angelic activity on Cape Neddick confirms that our enemy is in fact located there," said Carlene.

He watched her go to her briefcase and take out a spiral notebook and pen. She put it in front of Firdos and told him to record the Quran verses and everything else he could remember from what he just told her about his experience in the trailer park.

"Stay here, Firdos. I'll be back in a few," Carlene told him as he started writing. "One of my other squad members is arriving."

CHAPTER NINETEEN

An unexplained calm settled over Anna as she walked from her balcony, through her bedroom to the living room of her suite, and picked up the hotel phone.

"Frances O'Donnelly's room, please," she spoke into the receiver.

"Good morning, Frances. It's Anna. How are you this morning?" Anna greeted Frances.

"Fine, my friend. You're up early."

"And so are you. If it's all right, I'd like to come over to see you. Okay?"

"Sure, come on over. I'll order up some breakfast," Frances said.

Anna sat across from Frances in the breakfast nook in Frances' suite. "I suppose neither of us are really aware of exactly why you invited me here, but it's becoming clearer and clearer to me."

"Okay, Anna, I'm all ears. I ordered eggs, toast, home fries, orange juice, and coffee from room service. What have you discovered about your purpose for being here other than moral support for me?" Frances was smiling.

"Apparently I can see angels," stated Anna.

Frances seemed receptive, "Okay."

"Two of them appeared to me a little while ago while I was meditating on my balcony. If you can imagine a clear glass bottle, shaped like a man filled with water, that's kind of like what they looked like. Transparent but still visible. Each of them a little larger than a typical man. They hovered in the air outside my balcony." She waited to see how Frances took this description.

"Two angels. Did they speak?"

"Oh, yeah. They spoke. Look, I don't really get what you are into here, but from our conversation there in North Little Rock, I'm certain that this Directorate is controlling all or most of the mass killings in the news. You assert that your board is morally superior to everyone else and that justifies the killings. You, my dear Frances, have had your eyes opened. God chose me as the instrument of your revelation. Akebe Cheron called this meeting here at the Canyon Ranch Resort to solidify his authority over the activities of the Directorate and over all of you."

"So what did these angelic messengers say?"

Anna looked up to the ceiling and noticed the waves of barely discernible blue air. "Is that you, Thomas?"

His voice in her mind said, *Yes.* Frances watched all this, wondering.

Anna said, "I'm quoting the angel: 'Tell Frances that Akebe is planning to murder Andrew in plain sight of all the other board members during the first session this morning. Frances has to stop him.'"

Frances coolly put her fingertips together and touched her index fingers to her lips as in prayer.

Room service arrived with the breakfast order. The waiter was one of the servers from the reception, a security specialist hired by Akebe.

"Thank you, sir," said Frances. "Would you please stay here for just a few minutes? I'd like to have a quick word with you."

"Yes, ma'am," the server—too muscular to be a waiter—said.

"Anna, I'm going to ask you to remain in your room this morning. I'll take care of this situation," said Frances as she removed her portion of the breakfast.

Anna gave Frances a pat on the shoulder and exited her suite, pushing the serving cart across the hall to her room.

Andrew stepped out of his van into the New England morning and urinated in the parking lot. Once again he had not needed any sleep. He walked around his vehicle scratching himself and dialing his cell phone. Frances' voice came into his headphone.

"Good morning," she said.

"I got here last night. I have the op-plan completed. You wanna see it before the meeting or what?" Andrew said.

"Send it to my phone."

"What time's the meeting?"

"Two. Meet me in my suite at noon—23B," and Frances clicked off her phone.

Romano Goldstein stood up from his lotus meditation position and stretched his body in every direction. The house phone rang in the living room of his suite. It was still early, 7:00 a.m. Frances wanted to meet him in her room.

Romano entered Frances' suite almost immediately. One of the waiters from the reception was standing in her living room talking to Frances.

"Romano, I believe you remember this gentleman from our reception yesterday," Frances started.

"Yes, hello," Romano said.

"Please, sit down," Frances said. To the young waiter she said, "Be kind enough to tell us your background and how you were hired to assist in this meeting. It's clear to me that you are trained in some other areas of expertise besides food service."

"Sure," said the waiter. "My name is Stephen Walters. I work for a security agency out of Arlington, Virginia. We specialize in personal security for VIPs, usually foreign nationals visiting the US, or US dignitaries in foreign countries. We also have security units that advise police and military forces in underdeveloped countries."

"Education?" asked Frances.

Stephen went down the list, "Army Special Forces Operations, Command and General Staff Course, Bachelors in Engineering from University of Ohio, Masters in Organizational Leadership from Lewis University, and I have a doctorate in how-to-get-things-done from the school of hard knocks," he finished with a slight humorless smile.

"Thanks," said Frances. "And how did you get hired to be our caterer?"

"Our agency got a call from Cheron asking for four guys. I was just off a job in Kuwait, so I got the call. Me, Ralph, Jeff, and Don."

"Stephen, thank you. Mr. Cheron will be leaving our organization today, so we need to make a few changes in your orders for this job. How much are we paying you?"

Romano was puzzled and more than a little shocked, but he hid his feelings and kept quiet. He knew he was being included in a plan that would have serious consequences.

"We're getting six grand apiece for the three-day gig," Stephen answered.

"Okay, I just upped it to eight thousand each. You will be taking your orders from me and Mr. Goldstein here, got it?"

"Loud and clear."

"You will continue your cover jobs as caterers. There will be an incident at our fourteen-hundred hours session in the boardroom of this building. You will have to be available for immediate cleanup, understand?"

"Right. Large plastic bags, cleaning materials. Stretcher, ambulance. That sort of cleanup?"

"Very good, Stephen," said Frances. "Thank you. We'll see you at the meeting."

"Good day, ma'am. Sir." Stephen left the suite.

"What the devil's going on?" asked an agitated Romano Goldstein.

"Romano, you know how our instruments are able to monitor telekinesis energy and information from distant sources?"

"Of course. So?"

"So, through a similar system—off line from the Directorate's network in a dramatic fashion in front of all us directors. He plans to do so at our two o'clock board meeting. I need to stop him. I'm asking you for your assistance."

"The vote," Goldstein said, "back at our meeting on Akebe's yacht. We were deadlocked awaiting your decision. You visited Andrew at the ops center, and you phoned in your vote. Which way did you vote, Frances?"

"I voted to keep Andrew in his position, not to kill him."

Doctor Goldstein reacted to this information on two levels. Consciously, he came to a logical agreement with what she told him.

"All right, Frances," he said. "So Akebe is acting contrary to the board's direction, and only you and he know it. I can see the necessity of removing Akebe. And I must say I'm not surprised that he intends to murder Andrew after his series of failures."

Subconsciously, Romano's mind was racing through layers of his own traumas, sorting them out and organizing his emotions so as to stack them in such a way that would enable him to think and act courageously in this new situation.

"Give me a second here, Frances, to think this through. Is the coffee still hot?"

Romano made a pretense of thoughtful contemplation, pouring coffee, stirring in cream and sugar, walking to the balcony. All the time he was silently following the mental protocol he had created for himself and many of his patients. Over the years he reinforced his inner discipline, preventing himself from reacting to his emotions and instead arranging them into a pyramid so that only the most positive feelings would emerge at the top through the surface.

His brain raked up his terror as an infant in a dark crate with frightening noises pounding against the sides, his fear at being handed over to a strange Jewish family in a tiny apartment in Brooklyn, his isolation and dissociation as an orphan in a home with six siblings who belonged there, his desperate loneliness and hopelessness as the victim of schoolyard bullies and sexual predators, and finally his courage and discipline after escaping the neighborhood through his acceptance at Harvard University.

The process lasted only seconds, and the emotions that emerged were anger, revenge, and a call to duty.

"Frances, you have teamed up with the right ally in your cause to overcome Akebe and eliminate him as the chairman. You have my complete support. What do you plan to do?"

Sandy opened Hank's *Ranger Handbook* to page 3.01, titled, "Operations Order for a Patrol." She checked the screen behind her where the projector displayed the operations order line-by-line. She looked out over the faces before her and she smiled the smile of Joan of Arc. She exuded confidence, honor, and victory.

"My dear family," Sandy began her mission briefing, "we will prevail over the evil, inhuman enemy that would dare to come against America and Cielavista. God gave me this name for our defensive force: 'Task Force Saber.'"

Sandy saw Gabriella's eyes widen at the name. In her meditation that morning, Sandy had heard this title for the combat force that would evolve out of the family of people and animals at Cielavista. She and Gabriella had been preparing for this mission briefing since 3:00 a.m. out on the granite outcropping. They'd scanned the nation for potential mass murders and saw none. That signaled to them that the Directorate was consolidating their forces for one mission, and it was clear to them that Cielavista was the primary objective of that mission. After the two women monitored the Directorate's on the supernatural screen in the sky over the ocean, the VOICE came through to Sandy.

At first Sandy thought it was a storm raking over the water churning up the surf, but there were no waves on the water, no wind in the air. It was *His* voice, the King. Sandy knew it was *Him*, the one John the apostle was trying to describe in the Book of Revelation in the New Testament. She remembered clearly now reading that description of *His* voice. "His voice like the sound of cascading waters." That was it exactly, like roar and power she had felt standing under Niagara Falls.

"*Sandy, do not be afraid. I am your shield. I will protect your family. My saber will destroy your enemy. Take courage. I am with you.*"

Sandy was stunned, rigid as a statue. She found the strength to utter, "Nonina, did you hear that?"

"I heard nothing, dear," Gabriella said. "Sandy, you have heard a message that was meant for you alone. You are being called to go where one cannot go, to see what one cannot see, to know what one cannot know and to be what one cannot be."

Sandy understood. "Yes."

In the war room, Sandy continued her operations order.

"The first element of information you will hear is about the nature of the enemy force. My grandmother will give that portion of the briefing."

Gabriella took her place at the head of the table. "The name of our enemy is the Directorate," Gabriella said. "Let me describe them to you in as much detail as you need to know for this operation.

"The Directorate consists of a board of directors, six very wealthy, very powerful people who live under the delusion that they have a monopoly on true American patriotism. In their perverted view of nationalism, they think that the nation's biggest problem is those of us who think for ourselves and do not fall in line with the mainstream of modern American culture."

She paused to allow this monstrous statement to soak in.

"This board of directors has contrived a system of highly sophisticated devices that collects brain waves and analyzes them. With this system they can identify the thinkers from the sheep. Then they compile a list of thinkers, prioritize all the names, and systematically murder them.

"The way they carry out these murders is through a network of seers and operators. These people are organized into six squads located strategically throughout the country."

Sandy was standing to the side of the briefing room watching the faces of the men and women who remained with the fighting force. She perceived no fear or anxiety in their eyes. Even on the faces of the young girls and boys, she saw a growing sense of purpose and resolve.

Gabriella continued, "The Directorate's transmitting equipment uses satellite technology to send hypnoticlike radiation onto unsuspecting pawns who carry out their assassinations as directed. When they are confronted by law enforcement personnel, they either take their own lives or get killed in a gunfight.

"Every one of these pitiful patsies appears to have some insane agenda for their mass murder attacks. Additionally the Directorate manipulates the minds of the news media and they report the mass killings as the work of religious fanatics or deranged maniacs. That way, none of our law enforcement agencies make any connection between the murderers and the ultimate masterminds of these horrific attacks.

"All of the mass killings in America over the past three years have been the work of the Directorate. What the media has not reported are those incidents where the murderer has been prevented from carrying out his mission. I have been able to stop more than seventy-five percent of the mass murders."

A hand went up in the middle of the room. "Yes, Sebastian," Gabriella said to one of Carlos's grandsons, a twenty-year-old carpenter.

"How do you stop them, Nonina?"

"Since I was a child, Sebastian, I have had these supernatural powers given to me by the Spirit. I see all kinds of human activity over a long range of distance when I stand out on the rock outcropping where I go to pray. Not only can I see things, I also have the power to exert forces onto peoples' minds and bodies. With this power I have been able to save thousands of people from being killed. But this information comes in another section of Sandy's briefing. I am concentrating on the enemy forces."

"Can you give us an example, Nonina?" asked Sebastian.

"The Directorate has been trying to take out a Supreme Court justice and a conservative presidential candidate. I intervened with energy fields that disrupted the attackers and caused them to lose their way when they tried to assassinate these two essential Americans."

"Thank you, Nonina," said Sebastian.

"Currently, the Directorate operates in chaos because of all their recent failed attacks. Today they will hold a council of war that will divert all their assets from their primary missions of murdering thinkers to a concentrated ground attack on Cielavista." She paused and looked over at Sandy to see if she wanted her to continue.

Sandy monitored the mood of the room. She was prepared to offer encouragement at this point if she thought she needed it. She perceived some concern in the eyes of some of the family, but no anxiety or agitation. She nodded at Gabriella to continue.

"I will now list our allies," Gabriella said. "We have been assigned a platoon of angels from the throne room. They hover in the air overhead. Carlos, young Beto, myself, and the dog, Lucille, have the visionary power to see them, hear their voices, and talk to them. Five angels directly support our commander, Sandy. One protects and responds to Henry. The Master sent two on special assignment to the Directorate's meeting in the Berkshires.

"Henry and Beto have relocated to Cape Neddick, Maine. I have established a decoy headquarters location there to confuse the enemy."

At that, Sandy said, "What? What did you just say?" She approached Gabriella at the front of the briefing room under the screen.

"Yes, my love. Henry thinks he has abandoned us in a huff. In his mind that may be true, but I arranged for him go spend his vacation at Cape Neddick after I programmed an energy source there that duplicated the energy source here at Cielavista."

"You should have told me, Nonina!"

"I just did, dear." And the briefing room rippled with chuckles.

Sandy looked around at the soldiers in their seats. Her anger drained away.

"Proceed with your portion of the briefing," she said.

Gabriella proceeded with a smile. "In order to complete the deception that our location had moved from here to Cape Neddick, we needed to have boots on the ground there. One of their seers observed Beto and

Henry and he reported their presence to his higher headquarters. The ruse has convinced them that we now occupy Cape Neddick.

"However we cannot depend on that deception holding forever. Eventually they will discover that we still reside here at Cielavista. But they will spend valuable time and resources attacking our decoy location.

"We may have a spy in the enemy's camp. Her name is Frances O'Donnelly. She has served on the executive board of the Directorate for many years. By using one of their former targets, Anna Stone, I have reprogramed Frances' mind without her knowledge. She still thinks she is working for the Directorate, but if my efforts are successful, she will actually be working for us.

"That's it for my part of this battle briefing. Warriors, know these two important truths: we are Task Force Saber, and in the words of the prophet, 'no weapon formed against us will succeed.'" Gabriella took her seat.

Chapter Twenty

"**Y**ou doing all right, amigo?" Beto said, leaning back in the fishing chair on *Water Walker*. "I'm glad we're not in a sailboat. There's not a puff of breeze out here today."

"Yes, I'm fine," said Henry. "I got to feeling guilty using Tobias to scare up fish for us. Way too much work hauling in all those stripers anyway."

Beto took his pipe and tobacco out of his pocket. He began meticulously packing the bowl. "Guilty?" he said, "You mean about telling Tobias to find fish for us?"

"You smoke a pipe, too? Like your Uncle Carlos?" Henry said. "Yeah, that. But more about taking off from Cielavista. The way I did it, I guess."

"You mean taking off like a raging maniac?"

"What do you know about why I left?"

"Not sure, but that old lady told me to keep an eye on you and if you started packing I was supposed to go along with you," Beto said through puffs on the stem of his pipe as he held his lighter over the packed tobacco.

"Not surprised; always ten steps ahead of everybody. Yeah, I have a problem living there. You can't predict what's going to happen from one day to the next, heck from one minute to the next. How's a guy supposed to make plans? How can you get ready for the next day? I was boiling mad when I left. I had to get away. I packed in a fuming rage. The last thing she said was she could live without me."

Henry leaned back in the captain's chair and gazed at the sky, breathing in the sweet aroma of Beto's pipe smoke.

"Beto, I'm not sure I want to go back to Sandy."

Carlene led Firdos to the basement of the cottage.

"Set up these office partitions so each squad member has their own separate cubicle. None of you will make contact with any other member of my squad."

After leading each of her eight soldiers separately to his cubicle and placing the one-page operations order on their tables, she began her briefing.

"One of our directors has ordered this meeting. He will be connecting with us via the internet in a few moments." Carlene checked her watch.

"Here's where we are: seers one and two are working the same sector and they have developed a list of four targets. Seer three has no targets. Seer four has an attack plan for target number 0925, and is awaiting the order to execute. Green Arrow and Blue Wolf are prepared to complete that mission on order.

"Seer number five has been given a special recon mission," Carlene said. When she paused to look over the SITREP she had sent to Andrew, Firdos flushed with pride, knowing he had the most important mission in Carlene's squad.

"Listen carefully, people. Seer five is watching a target, code name FITO. That's foxtrot, india, tango, oscar. It's an acronym for 'fly in the ointment.' Too many missions have failed here in our sector and across the country. According to higher headquarters, this FITO keeps disrupting our operations.

"None of you soldiers hold a high enough security clearance to know the details of any operations except your own, but all of you have botched assignments. And in each case, no one has been able to explain the reason for these failures. So on one hand you may take some small comfort that our leaders are no longer placing blame on us. But do not get too comfortable.

"The objective of seer five's reconnaissance is FITO. Their command post sits somewhere here in our area of operations.

"The director will be giving us our new mission briefing for Operation FITO. He will explain our coordinated attack on their base of operations. FITO must be eliminated before we can effectively proceed with our normal routine.

"The only scheduled operation prior to Operation FITO will be the elimination of target 0925.

"In three minutes you will give your undivided attention to the voice of our director over the speakers."

Carlene adjusted the volume on the amplifier. She checked to ensure that each squad member was properly compartmentalized. A faint crackle of static came through the speakers.

"Greetings, Delta Squad," the amplified voice of Randal Sanford radiated into the room. "I greet you in the name of a new and better America. Please stand as we recite our pledge."

Chairs scraped against the concrete floor and each squad member stood and recited with Carlene and Randal, "We are the Directorate. We humbly accept our role as the overseers of the free world's institutions, and where necessary we will carry out our duty to prune out those branches that hinder the healthy advancement of the American culture. Duty. Honor. Oversight. Always loyal to the Directorate."

"Take seats," said Randal.

"Mission statement," said Sandy. She looked down at her notes, amazed at how her mind had uploaded the equivalent of four years of military tactical training in a matter of a few hours. *You will know that which you cannot know.*

"The mission of Task Force Saber is to defend Cielavista against an attacking force of natural and paranormal elements. If necessary, Task Force Saber will execute an orderly evacuation of Cielavista."

She looked at the outline in the *Ranger Handbook*. The next paragraph titled "Execution" detailed every step of the operation. Sandy could barely sense anyone breathing. The people facing her and the animals listened, calm and courageous waiting for the next instruction from their field commander. Sandy realized that everyone in this band of guerrilla fighters rested under the anointing of the Spirit for war.

"I have organized us into two companies of about thirty in each. Each company has three squads of ten fighters. I will command a headquarters element with five personnel consisting of me, Gabriella, Carlos, Frederick's son Peter, and my intrepid wolfhound, Lucille. We will have five angels attached. So Carlos, Lucille, and Peter, would you please join Nonina and me here in the front?

"Frederick, you will command Company Striker. Here is the list of warriors in your company."

Frederick rose from his place and walked to the front and received the list from Sandy, looked it over, and ordered his warriors to stand on the left side of the briefing room.

"Roberto, you will command Company Anvil." Roberto Sr. came to the front and assembled his unit on the other side of the room.

"Gentlemen," said Sandy, "please stand at attention and I will commission you as captains of your companies.

"Frederick Sanchez, by the power vested in me by Our Lord the Christ, I commission you Captain of Company Striker in Task Force Saber." Then she turned to Roberto Senior and said, "Roberto Ramos, by the power vested in me by Our Lord the Christ, I commission you Captain of Company Anvil in Task Force Saber."

Carlos came forward, "Commander Sandy, if I may."

"Yes, Carlos?"

"I have a strong impression that I have received a Word in my spirit. Let me try to explain," Carlos said.

"Captains, please have your companies be seated."

"Sandy, this prophetic word supports the operations order, but it doesn't fit into any of the subparagraphs of the order in the *Ranger Handbook*."

"Go ahead, Carlos," said Sandy.

"In the Bible, the Book of Judges, the Lord instructed Gideon, with a band of 300 irregulars against 135,000 trained soldiers, to give a shout of victory at the beginning of their battle against the Midianites and their allies. Their battle cry was 'A sword for the Lord and for Gideon.'"

At this, Carlos unsheathed a wide gleaming sword and brandished it over his head. "Here's what the Lord is saying, 'The power of victory came from God Almighty through the man, Gideon. Today the power of victory in battle over this barbaric enemy comes from the same God Almighty through the woman, Gabriella. So I declare that when I raise this sword over my head we will shout, 'A sword for the Lord and for Gabriella.'"

His words stirred the assembled battalion in the briefing room. They all stood up and roared a growling scream and a terrifying yell that shook the barn's walls and ceiling.

Romano Goldstein sat with Frances O'Donnelly and the four caterers in the basement of the mansion among canned goods and kitchen supplies. A familiar calm came over him.

Operator Stephen Walters explained the change of personnel in the security force. "These things happen. Ralph and Jeff got the call to report to another assignment. They're both Farsi linguists now deployed in the Mideast. Our company sent these replacements, Thomas Danforth and Joe Hankley. Both good operators. So no change to your plans, just different faces."

Frances looked at the text on her phone.

"Okay, thanks," Romano said. "I'll make it brief and simple. At some point near the beginning of our two o'clock board meeting, our chairman,

Akebe Cheron, will make a move to murder a young man in our organization named Andrew Johansen. These guys are easily identifiable. Akebe is black. He'll be doing the talking. Andrew is twenty-seven, wears a grubby tee shirt, longish brown hair, and black jeans and running shoes. Got it so far?"

Four men: "Yes, sir."

"We suspect the method of attack will be some kind of blade: sword, knife, machete, something like that. Akebe wants to leave a horrific impression, lots of blood, that sort of thing."

Romano noticed the odd grin on Frances' face when she looked up from her text. She gave Thomas and Joe a curious gaze as Romano continued his talk.

"We want Andrew protected from harm and we want Akebe killed. It has to be done with these conditions: the rest of the board must witness Akebe's attempt on Andrew's life. You will have to grab him in the act. It is necessary for our future plans that the board sees all this action take place. No one can know that Frances and I have any foreknowledge of the incident. Clear?"

"Very clear, sir," said Stephen and he looked at his associates. They nodded. "Just another day at the office."

"Good. We will leave the details to you. You're the professionals," said Romano. "You will receive payment as soon as you complete the cleanup. I suppose you prefer cash?"

"Correct, sir," said Stephen.

"All right then, we'll see you at the two o'clock board meeting," Romano said.

The four operators posing as caterers left the storage room.

"What was the text about, Frances?" asked Romano.

"Oh, just a confirmation about the change in personnel. No change in plans. Looks like we are all set," said Frances. "Romano, I am grateful to have a trusted ally in this matter, and I appreciate your vote of support to stand behind me as I take the chair of the Directorate."

Akebe heard the knock on his suite door and he opened it for Stephen.

"I trust no one saw you come up to my room," said Akebe.

Stephen shrugged off the suggestion. "Sir, please, don't insult my professionalism."

"So, what do you have?"

"Frances and Romano have found out that you plan to kill Andrew at the meeting. We are all set with your plan. We will ensure that you have a clear shot at Andrew."

"Splendid, my good man. Here is your bonus. Your associates will receive their ten thousand when the job is complete."

Stephen took a minute to count the cash in the envelope. "Twenty grand; got it, sir."

"After the meeting, you will terminate Frances O'Donnelly neatly and quietly. Then you will secure Goldstein and prepare him for torture and interrogation. I need to find out how they got wind of my plans."

"Sounds good, sir," said Stephen.

Romano will be a pushover. Akebe smiled.

CHAPTER TWENTY-ONE

"I want you all to know, Delta Squad, that your fine leader, Carlene Wood, objected to this meeting. However, I knew she would create security measures that will keep you all compartmentalized. Am I correct?"

Carlene responded, "Yes, Director. They cannot see or communicate with each other, and if by chance they do come into visual contact, they are all in disguise."

"Well done, Carlene."

Was she imagining it, or was she hearing a more sinister ring to Sanford's voice than usual? She sensed that a new violent kind of evil had inhabited Randal Sanford.

"I will get right to it, you warriors for a better America. We have an enemy. And in the words of Sun Tzu, 'He who exercises no forethought but makes light of his opponents is sure to be captured by them.' So we will not underestimate our enemy. He has been successful in foiling a significant number of our pruning efforts. He has protected or rescued these vermin. So we are marshaling maximum resources to destroy his headquarters.

"His location, while we have not ascertained exact coordinates, exists in your area of operations. So you, my New England warriors, form the tip of the spear in our attack against our enemy."

Carlene had arranged her position on a high platform from which she could see the faces of all her people in their cubicles. Their eyes were vacant, as if they were staring into a campfire—just the way she wanted them.

"With the exception of one remaining operation, you will suspend all actions on your current target list. Soon I will order you to form a commando attack team along with allies to destroy our enemy whose code name is FITO, a fly in the ointment. It's a fitting code name as it comes from the bible, 'Dead flies make a perfumer's oil ferment and stink; so a little folly outweighs wisdom and honor.'"

"There remains one target on your list," Randal said. "That's the reason I took this unprecedented measure of gathering you in one place. The target is number 0925. Who will take out that target, Carlene?"

Carlene could taste the acrid tension in her sinuses. Her gut tightened up. "Green Arrow has primary, with Operator Blue Wolf in direct support."

"Thank you," Randal said. "Seer number three, would you give me a brief progress report of your activity?"

"Yes, sir," the middle-aged, librarian-looking woman said. "I have been watchful in my sector for six weeks now since identifying my last target in late July."

Carlene had stepped down from her perch and took her place behind Green Arrow's chair. She dropped the garrote on Green Arrow's lap. He picked up the wooden handles on each end of the eighteen-inch telephone wire. Carlene chose the materials for this mission. Knowing the strength of Green Arrow's arms, she wanted a cord strong enough to accept his three hundred pounds of pull. She also wanted a wire with enough thick insulation so it would not cut Seer Three's skin and make a bloody mess here in the rented basement.

She placed her right hand on his shoulder, his signal to stand up. She led him to the cubicle next to his where he stood behind Seer Three, a divorcee named Marla Benda, who had been homeless when Carlene recruited her two years ago. Until recently she was quite effective utilizing her gift of telekinesis to identify thinkers for the target list. But six weeks without a target in this stressful environment spelled termination for her.

Randal spoke again through the speakers. Carlene could smell the revolting odor of a dark spirit.

"Seer Three, the Directorate has tightened our corporate personnel policies recently in light of the threat that faces us. We have to thin out our ranks. We don't hand out pink slips like a lot of overindulgent American companies. When we determine that one of our employees can't operate up to standards, we terminate them. Okay, Carlene, you know what to do."

Carlene said, "Now," into Green Arrow's ear.

In an instant the assassin wrapped the telephone wire around Marla Benda's fleshy neck and tightened. Marla stiffened, kicked, evacuated her bowl and bladder, gurgled and became still. Carlene tapped Blue Wolf's shoulder. He used bottled water, a spray bottle of bleach, towels, and two plastic trash bags to clean up the mess.

The men returned to their seats and Carlene stood on her platform watching for a reaction of her squad members—dead-eyed stares. Good.

"Sir, we're all set here," she reported.

Randal continued his briefing. "Fine, Carlene, you are a professional. There will be a bonus in your next pay envelope. And for the rest of you, I am sure you will operate at even higher levels of competence and loyalty as we embark on the largest scale mission in our history. I will soon join you on the ground in your location to lead you from the front. Victory is ours, men and women. Victory for a greater America."

Carlene barked out an order from her platform, "At my command: when you hear your code name, return to your rooms. Seer One." She continued down the roster until the basement was vacant.

She returned to her bedroom on the first floor of the cottage and took a long pull of vodka from the bottle. She looked up at the ceiling and said, "Andrew, if you can see this from where you are, so be it. Here's to a greater America." And she took another long drink.

Firdos forgot. After Delta Squad left the cottage, he got in his car and returned to his trailer, still in disguise. He had been involved, directly or indirectly, in seven executions since his enlistment in Delta Squad, but Marla's murder rattled him at the core.

All the turmoil in his head over Carlene's touch and the sound of Randal's lizardlike voice and their heartless execution of a fellow squad member made him forget to remove his disguise when he returned to his trailer.

Firdos sat on his lawn chair at View Point Trailer Park dressed in his fat-man costume with stage makeup on his face, and he lit up a cigarette. Firdos noticed Carlene pass behind him and he savored that intoxicating fragrance in her wake. He knew she was standing behind the operator in the cubicle next to him.

The voice of the man who had given him attention and respect when they met at the bakery in Salem and the aroma of the woman who gave Firdos a new life captured the young Iranian's soul. Caught up in this strange bubble of warm feelings, Firdos heard Carlene's order, "Green Arrow has primary, with Operator Blue Wolf in direct support."

Something about target 0925 Firdos recalled as his cigarette burned down to his fingers. The black SUV pulled into the gravel driveway across the street, but his mind remained back in the meeting.

Carlene said, "Now." Then a violent thumping, rustling, shoes kicking against the floor, a faint grunting, then the unmistakable presence of a body vacant of its spirit. Death.

Firdos twisted the sole of his shoe on his cigarette butt and lit another. Two men had exited the black car. One went into the trailer, the other was slapping the floor mat on the driver side and dusting it off with his hand, then he went to the passenger side and did the same with that floor mat. Firdos watched him take a tire gage out of his hip pocket and test the pressure in each tire. As he walked around the car, he wiped little splashes of mud from the rocker panel with a rag. Firdos locked eyes with him. The man gave Firdos a half wave with the rag. Firdos looked down at the narrow gravel road between them.

Henry stepped inside the trailer and elbowed Beto out of his way at the kitchen counter.

"What you doin', man?" Beto said, moving away from the counter with the wine bottle in his hand.

Henry reached across the sink and stuck his iPhone under the little curtain against the kitchen window. "I need to get a picture of this guy and show it to you. Hang on a sec." Henry snapped a few digital images of their trailer park neighbor and brought the phone back into the kitchen.

"Wine?" asked Beto.

"Sure, love some." Henry pinched his fingers apart against the glass of his phone to enlarge the picture.

"Look at this guy," said Henry as he traded Beto the phone for a plastic cup of burgundy.

"Huh!" grunted Beto. "What the heck?"

"Don't look out the window," Henry said, "He'll see you. That's why I took the picture."

"What if I went out and said 'hello' to the guy?" said Beto.

"Good idea," said Henry.

Beto left the trailer and approached Firdos. "Hey, guy, how you doin'?"

Beto watched the man raise his gaze from the pavement to Beto's chest. Beto looked down at his tee shirt to see what his neighbor was looking at—just a black tee shirt, fairly clean with no noticeable spills or stains.

"Hey, mind if I bum a smoke?" Beto said.

Firdos handed his pack of Marlboros and his lighter to Beto, eyes still on Beto's shirt.

Beto realized he was addressing a man slightly impaired some way, so he took the pack, tapped out a cigarette, lit it, and gave the pack and lighter back to him.

"Thanks, bud. Hey, you want to stop over for a drink or a sandwich or something *mi casa su casa*, you know? Thanks, bro."

He heard a grunt come from Firdos' throat, but his lips didn't move.

Beto gave him a wave and went back to his trailer and took a drink of the wine. "What are we eatin' tonight, Henry?"

"What did he say?" said Henry.

"Nothing. I think he may have grunted," said Beto. "He must be an actor or something. He's wearing stage makeup on his face."

"Really," said Henry. "Let's take a ride and find a restaurant."

Henry and Beto polished off their wine, washed up, changed out of their fishing clothes, and headed out. Firdos was no longer in the chair.

"You mind driving, Beto? I gotta make a couple calls," said Henry.

"Sure."

As Beto eased the big vehicle out of the trailer park, Henry dialed his assistant at the FBI. "Hey, Tony, it's Henry here. Can you run a quick check on something for me?"

After a couple miles, Beto pointed to an Italian place, Cabrizzi's Family Restaurant. Henry nodded.

"I'll go in and get us a table," said Beto to Henry.

"Yeah, the file is titled 'York, Maine and Vicinity,'" said Henry. "Then go to 'Theater Groups.' Got it?"

Henry waited. "Okay? Any drama productions rehearsing or showing now? No? How about theatrical supplies, makeup, and that sort of thing, vicinity York Maine?"

Henry could follow every step his assistant was taking through the massive database he had built over the past twenty years.

"Anything?" Pause. "Good, you said 'Maine Stage Theater Supply, in Portland?' Okay, Tony, right now give them a call and see if they have a security cam. Give me a call back when you get that. Right, bye."

"I ordered for you, Henry," said Beto. "We're having the *Couple's Special*—a big bowl of spaghetti with pesto sauce and a platter of their mixed grill. They assume we're gay. Just so you know."

"Sounds good, honey," said Henry. "I got a weird feeling about our neighbor over there at View Point. My assistant is doing some research."

The waitress came to their table with two peach martinis. Henry looked at Beto and just shook his head.

"Thanks, miss," Henry said.

CHAPTER TWENTY-TWO

Andrew Johansen wheeled his polycarbonate equipment case into the Bellefontaine Mansion, up the elevator to the second floor and down the hall to Suite 23B. He knocked on the door and Frances immediately opened it and welcomed him in.

"There's sandwiches on the counter there in the kitchen, sodas and beer in the fridge. Help yourself."

Andrew carried his case with him to the kitchen, grabbed two sandwiches, took a Coke out of the refrigerator. Frances joined him in the kitchen. She pulled a chair up to the table and waited for Andrew to speak.

"Good sandwich," said Andrew. He opened the case and pulled out a power strip. "Mind plugging this in for me?"

He removed several digital devices from slots in the hard foam packing and placed them on the table. He plugged each of them into the power strip and connected them together. He pulled out his laptop and connected it to one of the devices with a USB cable.

"With these, I can still keep up with our operations. This one receiver," he pointed to a cube-shaped device with a large round antenna affixed to the top, "monitors signals off one of our satellites from the enemy's locations on the East Coast."

Andrew dreaded having to meet with people. He'd been monitoring his pulse and he took his blood pressure every couple hours. Everything was out of whack.

Here in the kitchen with the one person with whom he had attained some measure of trust, he felt himself calm down. The food helped. If he had such a thing in his life as a "safe place," it was his mouth stuffed with food.

"What else you got to eat, Frances?" he asked.

Frances went to the cupboard and the refrigerator and pulled out four boxes of cookies, two bags of chips, and a half gallon of chocolate ice cream. She put two bowls and spoons on the table.

Andrew thought, *This lady's prepared.* As he ripped open the cookies, Frances filled a bowl with ice cream. After stuffing a couple chocolate chip cookies in his mouth, Andrew spread ice cream on the next one and gulped that down.

"We're suspending all current operations and consolidating our forces on FITO," he said through a mouthful.

"Dumbbell Randal called a meeting with Delta Squad. He met with them via teleconference. Had them all in the same place and he had one of them executed for poor performance. I think he sees himself as the ground commander of the upcoming battle. Bad choice if you want my opinion."

"We have to take a walk," said Frances. "Won't take long."

"I can't leave my receivers."

"We'll be back in a few minutes. Take a bag of cookies with you."

Andrew followed her down the hall to a back stairway and out into the expansive gardens in the rear of the building. He munched on the cookies and watched Frances' back and hips as she strode along the path, past the arborvitaes that formed the back boundary of the garden. *She's put together pretty nice*, he thought.

"Hey, Frances, what's up?"

"This will be fine," she said, and she pulled out a compact pistol.

A shot of fear charged through his gut. He knew that one of the squad leaders had just been murdered a few hours ago at the orders of another director. He also knew that his own performance could be called into question over all the failed operations under his supervision. He decided silence was his best course of action.

"Ever shot a handgun, Andrew?" Frances asked.

A long breath escaped from his lungs. "Nope," he said.

"This is a compact semiautomatic pistol, a Smith and Wesson M&P in nine millimeter. The magazine holds eight, and with one in the chamber that gives you nine rounds before it's out, got it?"

"Eight plus one is nine. Fairly straightforward," he answered.

"You just point and pull the trigger. Now I have a sound suppressor attached while we practice, see this? It makes the gun a lot longer than it will be when you tuck it into your pants. First I'll show you, then you're going to do it yourself."

Andrew watched. Frances pushed the M&P into the waistband of her jeans. She pulled her tee shirt over it to demonstrate how to conceal it. "My target is this tree here. You want to be at least this close to your target when you engage it."

Frances smoothly lifted up her shirt with her left hand, drew the pistol, pointed it at the tree, and with this two-handed grip she pulled off four rounds. The report from the silencer was muted. Andrew noticed that the gun popped upwards after each shot, but not much.

"Look, when you are handling the gun, keep your trigger finger outside the trigger guard, like this. Even when you draw it from your pants, keep your finger outside. You don't want an accidental discharge while it's in your pants, do you?"

She handed him the gun. Andrew tucked it into his pants and let his tee shirt drop over it. "By the way," he said, "why exactly are you giving me small arms training today?"

"Akebe's going to try to kill you."

"Oh," he said, and he pulled the gun out and fired the five remaining rounds at the tree. Two of them hit it.

It took Andrew four magazines to gain enough proficiency to put all his rounds in the target. He unscrewed the silencer from the muzzle, slid a loaded magazine into the stock, and racked back the slide to insert a bullet into the chamber.

Frances said, "We must give Akebe the opportunity to attack you. Not just threaten you, but he has to raise his hand against you with a weapon. We believe he will be using a blade of some sort, sword or knife. I know this sounds risky, but you are younger and quicker and you will not be surprised. But you have to wait until he raises the knife before you shoot him. Can you do that?"

"Well," Andrew said, "it's not like I have much of a track record with armed combat, but if the guy is trying to kill me, I'll shoot him."

They made their way back through the garden.

Andrew said, "Hey, Frances, why do you want me alive and Akebe dead?"

Frances turned to face him. He felt her hand on his arm, her breath on his face.

"Don't worry, Andrew, it's not because I like you," she said and smiled.

"Oh, good," Andrew muttered. "We wouldn't want that."

Sandy wrapped up her operations briefing. "We expect some advanced warning of the enemy's attack. The signal for you all to you to take your battle stations will be a text with the letters in all capitals: ASFTLAFG, for A Sword For The Lord And For Gabriella.

"We should have at least two weeks to prepare for their attack on our position, so Carlos will push you hard to get you ready. Most likely they'll attack our decoy location on Cape Neddick before they move here to attack us.

"My dear family of warriors, I believe in you all, and more importantly, I believe in God. The battle belongs to the Lord. You are dismissed."

The men, women, and youth filed out through the wide barn doors, chatting, patting each other on the back, and a few were laughing. Sandy could not detect a trace of fear in any of them. She was amazed.

"Well, Commander Granddaughter, what do you think?" asked Gabriella.

"Here's what I know," said Sandy, "we will make war with these devils. We will fight hard and how it comes out, well, only the Lord knows. And I know that our family here at Cielavista will become a strong fighting force, prepared to make a stand against our attackers."

"You see, my love," said Gabriella as she reached up with her gnarly hand and touched Sandy's cheek, "you are more than you know. So get some rest and tonight we will go to the rock and see what is impossible to see."

At the kitchen table in the trailer, Henry studied the screen on his laptop.

"Okay, Tony, show me that video," he said into his cellphone.

Tony had uploaded the security video from the Maine Stage Theater Supply Company. Only two customers walked into the store in that week, one male, one female. Tony played a short clip from each one.

"What did you get from face-recognition?" Henry asked.

"Nothing on the male, but you're gonna like this," Tony said. "The female was an agent with the CIA. Left the Agency six years ago, decent record, nothing distinguished, nothing really negative. Name, Wanda Springer. She resides in New Hampshire with no known place of employment. She changed her name to Carlene Wood."

"Interesting," said Henry. "Do you have a license plate number for her?"

"Yeah, it's a Mass plate 440-D85. So what's the story?" said Tony.

"Just call it 'suspicious activity.' How about contacting the police in York, Maine? Give them the plate number and ask them to keep an eye out for her without any face-to-face involvement. Keep it low priority. It will probably lead nowhere, okay?"

"Sure, I'll give you a call tomorrow, Henry. How's the fishing?"

"Divine," said Henry.

"Does he know how absurd he looks?" said Romano Goldstein to Frances as Chairman Akebe Cheron entered the boardroom. "And why does he always have to make an entrance at our board meetings? Can't he just show up and sit down like the rest of us?"

Romano surveyed the faces of the rest of the Directorate's executive board. Andrew sat at a table separate against the wall with his laptop. Donald Snow and Olivia Kingston appeared as exasperated as he was, and Randal Sanford was just grinning as if he thought the whole thing was a circus act. Romano thought *he might be right.*

"Romano, he has no idea," replied Frances. "I'm certain his image of himself is pure fantasy."

Akebe had entered the board meeting strategically late, wearing a black turtleneck jersey, too-tight black jeans, and a black belt with silver studs. On his left hip was an eighteen-inch leather scabbard bearing a short sword with a silver basket around the grip. His jeans were tucked into black snakeskin boots with silver tips on the toes.

Akebe began his speech, pacing back and forth along the far wall. Romano placed a nervous hand on Frances' forearm.

"Men and women of the Directorate," Akebe said in a commanding voice, "our efforts to purify America has taken a new direction. Heretofore we've enjoyed vast success in our pruning operations. We've eliminated thousands of obstructionists who failed to follow our path to orderly living."

Romano observed Akebe through the eyes of a psychoanalyst. He surmised that the source of Akebe's dysfunctions evolved from years of traumatic abuse. Romano concluded that Akebe suffered from extreme delusional disorder. And in his present position as chair of the Directorate, that psychosis threatened the very existence of the nation.

"I am convinced we must execute our plan," Romano whispered to Frances.

"Heretofore," Akebe was saying," we have completed our missions unimpeded. In the last year alone, we successfully carried out three hundred fifty-two attacks on the obstructionists. Most of them have gone unnoticed by the public, but others have received national and international coverage."

Akebe paused and cast an angry gaze at the table of directors. "You have something to add, Doctor Goldstein?"

"Please, continue, Mr. Chairman," Romano said.

"Well, thank you so much for giving me permission. Listen up, children. Things are going to go from ugly to repulsive in a few short weeks. I will lead you through the troubling events that lay before us, but you all must demonstrate absolute loyalty. Do you understand?"

Randal gave a loud sarcastic, "Yes, sir!" The rest simply nodded at Akebe.

Akebe went on, "Three hundred and fifty-two victories. We go back to our humble beginnings in 1984, when we experimented our techniques with our first slave, James Huberty, who successfully killed twenty-one in San Ysidro, California. Then on to our Jacksonville, Florida Operation in June of 1990 where ten obstructionists were removed, and a wonderful series of victories in Killeen, Iowa City, Olivehurst, San Francisco, Garden City, Jonesboro, Columbine, Atlanta, Fort Worth, Honolulu, all before the turn of the millennium.

"Then in the new millennium, we continued our march here in Massachusetts, the town of Wakefield. Remember Michael McDermott, one of your operations, Randal, if I recall?"

"Yes, sir," from Randal.

"I needn't go on," Akebe said, but he did. "Meridian, Red Lake, Nickel Mines, Salt Lake City, Virginia Tech, Omaha, Binghamton, Fort

Hood—again, Manchester, Aurora, Newtown, Boston, Washington, DC, Charleston, Roseburg, and Paris, France.

"The masterful work of our hands, ladies and gentlemen. And these represent only the operations that the media considered noteworthy enough to cover.

"Of course the genius of all our success has been our ability to conceal our organization's involvement in any of these important actions. What other organization would be able to arrange such brilliant operations where even the killers operate under the impression that they were motivated by hatred or religious fervor?

"Do you all realize our privileged position in world history? What an enormous honor we hold, to serve our country and the world community in this way."

Akebe paused. Romano scanned the board members' faces trying to read them for any shock, guilt, or pride. Nothing.

He watched the four caterers wheel in the carts of pastries and beverages. They stood at the end of the hall by the serving counter.

High above the counter near the ceiling Romano noticed a long window, the audiovisual control room. It should have been unoccupied for this meeting, but Romano detected a face briefly in that window.

"With that introduction," said Akebe, "all rise for the Directorate pledge."

"We are the Directorate. We humbly accept our role as the overseers of the free world's institutions, and where necessary we will carry out our duty to prune out those branches that hinder the healthy advancement of the American culture. Duty. Honor. Oversight. Always loyal to the Directorate." And they returned to their seats.

Chapter Twenty-Three

"I thought you were going to take a rest this afternoon," Gabriella said to Sandy.

"Something has come up and we have to go to the rock."

The two women jumped down the rocky steps and sailed over the crevice to the flat shelf of grey-orange granite where the paranormal and spiritual signals coalesced into visions. The women held hands.

"What are we seeing, Nonina?"

"This young lady, Anna Stone, has been equipped as a spiritual transmitter. She is watching a meeting of the Directorate from the AV control booth above the conference room. Apparently the spirit has positioned her strategically so she can act as a human TV camera monitoring the Directorate's activities and sending them to us."

Sandy and Gabriella watched and listened to the action projected on the sky. A man in black with a sword hanging from a studded belt paced around the table. He was giving a review of their diabolical activities, stating them as patriotic victories. The five people sitting at the table were obviously exasperated with him.

"That's the chairman of the Directorate, Akebe Cheron," said Gabriella.

"Why do we need Anna Stone there? I thought we could see these types of events without needing a person nearby to transmit," Sandy said.

"See that young man at the side table, their operations officer? He takes all the commands of the Directorate and puts them into action. He has created a protective dome over the resort that blocks the energy radiating from their meeting. Having Anna there circumvents his countermeasures."

"They're all standing now," said Sandy. "Listen."

"We are the Directorate. We humbly accept our role as the overseers of the free world's institutions, and where necessary we will carry out our duty to prune out those branches that hinder the healthy advancement of the American culture. Duty. Honor. Oversight. Always loyal to the Directorate."

"My God," said Sandy, "They think they're involved in a righteous cause. How perverted."

Gabriella said, "Two of those caterers are angels from our platoon."

"Really, why did you send them?"

"I didn't. Their Boss did."

"Which ones are angels?" said Sandy.

"Oh, come now, Sandy you can tell. It's Thomas and Joe."

Sandy studied the video. "Ah, yes the incredibly handsome ones. You would think they would disguised themselves a little better." She smiled.

Gabriella and Sandy noticed both angels glance upwards at the same time. The women saw what they were looking at. It was a grayish serpent-like form slithering over Akebe's head.

"Do you know what that is?" said Sandy.

"Ogoun, the demon that controls Akebe's mind. It's one of Satan's low-level minions. Stupid, really. It lords over Voodoo ceremonies."

"Akebe is Haitian, right? So that's where he may have adopted the Voodoo religion."

"Well, he's Nigerian," said Gabriella, "but he's been in Haiti for many years. He could have fallen under Ogoun's power either place. Now we know the real mastermind behind the Directorate's horrific plans."

The meeting on Gabriella's sky-screen proceeded. Akebe Cheron addressed the board. "Ladies and gentlemen of the Directorate, I have asked Andrew, our operations officer, to join us at this special board meeting to recognize him for his years of faithful service. You all know that with his ingenious methods he is able to orchestrate our orders without any assistance. Andrew, would you come forward please."

Andrew hesitated. He removed his headphones and slowly stood up.

"Come here, my good lad," said Akebe.

Andrew stepped in front of Akebe. He kept looking over at Frances. She nodded to him.

"Andrew Johansen, it is my honor to present you with the reward that your performance deserves."

Akebe gave Andrew an awkward bear hug and kissed him on both cheeks. Then Akebe stepped back, drew his sword, and raised it over his head. Two of the caterers—large, muscular, warrior-looking men—jumped forward and pinned Andrew's arms behind his back. Gabriella and Sandy saw Frances O'Donnelly grab Romano Goldstein's arm in shock. "Stephen!" she shouted.

"Ah, yes, my dear Frances," said Akebe. "*Peripeteia.*"

Akebe brandished his sword overhead and said, "Death to incompetence!"

As Akebe's arm slashed down toward Andrew's chest, Joe jumped next to Akebe, grabbed his wrist, and bent it back. Bones snapped. A cry of pain barked out of Akebe's throat, his sword clattered to the floor. Simultaneously the two mercenaries holding Andrew fell unconscious at Thomas' feet. In seconds they lay bound hand and foot with zip ties, and Akebe found himself tied to a chair. He was howling in pain and twisting against his bonds.

Andrew drew the pistol out of his pants and fired six rounds in Akebe's direction; all six sprayed the wall. Joe stepped next to Andrew, secured his wrist, and pointed the gun at the floor.

Softly he said, "Drop it now, Andrew."

Thomas and Joe grabbed the fallen mercenaries and hauled them out. No one asked where they were taking them or what they planned to do with them.

Back on the rocky ledge, Gabriella said, "Ow, Sandy, you're squeezing my hand."

"Oh, sorry, Nonina. I'm still getting used to viewing live TV here on your rock." Sandy rubbed the old woman's weathered hand.

"My dear, it's your rock now, too."

The scene in their vision continued. Romano Goldstein stood next to Akebe and said, "It is with the most respect that I speak to you Akebe," he said.

Akebe ranted, "You will all be tortured. You will all be killed. This is an act of mutiny. I am your leader. I am your superior. Release me this minute. Those thugs have betrayed me. Andrew must be eliminated. Untie me this...."

Andrew came behind the screaming ex-chairman and wrapped a two-foot piece of duct tape around his mouth and eyes. Then he stepped around in front of him and began pounding his head with both fists. Randal and Romano ran to Andrew and pulled him away.

"The old buzzard tried to kill me. ME! I'm the one who runs this ship of psychos. I'm the brains behind everything you killers think of."

Frances slammed Akebe's sword down on the conference table. "Enough!" she said loud but calmly. "Drag Mr. Cheron out of the room and leave him there until our security men get back."

Randal and Romano complied with her order.

"Andrew, take your seat at your table and settle down.

"We still have urgent work to do here. Now that we have taken care of the immediate agenda item, we must proceed." She laid the sword on the floor and placed the gun on the table in front of her. Randal and Romano returned to their seats.

"Unless anyone has any objections, I will assume leadership until we have time to consider a transition and elect our new chairman," said Frances.

No one objected.

"Despite Akebe's obvious mental breakdown, his strategy for our immediate future is sound. We will continue on the course we have set out, to suspend our attacks on individual obstructionists and focus all our resources on eliminating this bothersome annoyance that has been effectively thwarting our noble and righteous cause to rebuild America. The very survival of our great nation depends on our complete control of its citizens. We must all be thinking the same way, believing the same beliefs and living our lives on the same pathway to success.

"Do I have your support? Olivia?" a nod in Frances' direction. "Randal?" a thumbs up. "Romano?" another nod. "Donald?"

Donald Snow was reluctant. "Mrs. O'Donnelly, I have the utmost respect for your intelligence and your loyalty to our cause. I just think it's a little hasty to decide on the leadership of this executive board of the most important organization in America and perhaps the world. I cannot give my total agreement to having you lead us. I reserve my opinion."

"Fair enough, Donald," Frances said. "With that, let us proceed with today's business. Andrew is prepared to brief us on a draft war plan to eliminate FITO. We will take a short break and come back in fifteen minutes."

Sandy lay her head against Gabriella's thick black mane of hair. She closed her eyes.

"All this power, these spiritual gifts: Nonina, are we allowed to be normal humans?"

"We must be human, my dear granddaughter. It is through our humble humanity that the Spirit can work. Now watch," she said, "Anna Stone is acting as our camera there at the conference. She has gone into Frances' room."

"You think that will help?" Anna asked Frances.

Frances was pouring an inch of vodka into a glass. "I don't care if it will help or not. I know it will flush out this terror from my bones." She threw the drink down her throat and poured another. Then she sat on the couch and leaned back on the cushions and sipped from the glass.

"My god," Frances said. "Such violence. Look, I'm shaking like a leaf. I have to calm myself down."

"You are responsible for thousands of violent deaths, Frances," Anna said. "Have you never been this close to any of them?"

"No. But when you are convinced that your cause is just, you know you are justified and righteous," Frances said. "In spite of how nervous I am from that mess downstairs, I know we must press on with our surgical operations, eliminating those who obstruct our ultimate goals.

"Anna, I need you to assist us. Call the catering service. Tell them our crew has quit and we will be sending them four more Directorate employees to work for them for the remainder of the conference."

"All right, Frances, I'll handle that," said Anna.

Frances stood up and smoothed out her slacks. "I so appreciate you being here, Anna. You are a comfort to me." Frances reached over and stroked Anna's arm.

"You're welcome," said Anna.

Sandy observed the conversation. "I wonder how Anna has the ability to assist these barbarians," she said. "Knowing what she knows about their wicked business, she still manages to be a friend to Frances."

"Yes," said Gabriella. "Anna Stone is a remarkable person. I have seen the connection she has to the Spirit. It is more powerful than any I have seen. She never wavers."

"They're reconvening in the boardroom. Akebe has been removed," said Sandy. "Our two angels have permanently disposed of him."

"Yes," said Gabriella. "I don't know if you can see them in their angelic state, can you?"

"Where?"

"They're in the sky above the mansion giving Ogoun a severe thrashing. He was Akebe's Loa—his god. It will soon look for another human to demonize," Gabriella said.

"No, I guess my vision doesn't include angelic beings yet. That's fine with me. Whatever I now know about all this paranormal, spiritual, telepathic, telekinesis stuff is all I can handle," Sandy said.

Sandy looked up at the screen in the sky. "Here we go again, Nonina. The executives are gathering."

Frances tapped the table with her fingernail. The board gave Frances their attention. "Everyone take a long deep breath. We must proceed."

"Our operations officer will begin his briefing. Please hold your questions until he takes a break. Andrew?"

"Operation FITO," Andrew began, "will involve all six of our squads. We will mass our forces in a circle around FITO's position, attack them, and crush them."

Gabriella put her arm around her granddaughter. "Ogoun is hovering over the board members. He seeks a body to inhabit."

"Yes," said Sandy, "and it looks like Frances may be slipping away from us."

The two women on the rock looked at each other, their eyes ablaze with strength and courage. The autumn afternoon sun angled over the ocean casting diamonds on the waves.

CHAPTER TWENTY-FOUR

From her command post in the loft of the barn, Sandy looked out at her defense force. They formed up in two companies on the parade filed. Cielavista, once a peaceful seaside estate, now pulsated with the energy of a paramilitary training camp.

Task Force Saber's two companies, Anvil under Captain Roberto Ramos and Striker under Captain Frederick Sanchez, stood at attention before Colonel Carlos Santiago, Ground Force Commander.

Sandy was amazed at Carlos who mounted a wooden platform at the head of the formation, with Company Anvil to his left and Company Striker to his right. Every warrior maintained a rigid position of attention, dressed in olive drab tee shirts, camouflage pants, and combat boots. Their elderly commander barked out his commands for the day's physical training.

Sandy's heart swelled with pride and sadness watching this once happy throng of adults and youths, who should be spending their days home-schooling, gardening, building, farming and fishing, now trained to face a vicious enemy in lethal combat.

At Carlos' command the trainees assumed the push-up position. In perfect unison they counted out each cadence and the repetition. Thirty push-ups—men, women, and youngsters. They held that position and yelled, "A sword for the Lord and for Gabriella!"

Carlos commanded, "Position of attention," long pause, "move!"

The warriors-in-training all popped up into the position of attention as one organism.

"Jumping jacks, in cadence," pause, "exercise!"

Without a break from the push-ups, the unit sprang into the next exercise. Sandy realized the Lord had possessed Carlos with a commander's spirit, enabling him to rapidly form these individuals into one solid fighting force.

The unit broke down into ten-man platoons for their morning run and Sandy joined the second platoon of Striker Company. She fell right in with the soldiers led by their platoon leader, Paul Sanchez, one of Fredrick's older sons. It was a three-mile run through the roads and pathways of Cielavista. The pace of the run was quick, and Sandy had to push hard to keep up. The run ended with the platoons returning to the parade ground and reforming in companies. Sandy stepped to the side of the formation, hiding her exhaustion, and listened to Colonel Santiago lead them in prayer.

"Father in heaven, we give ourselves to you again today. We stand at attention before you and await your orders. We trust You, Father, that as you give us our marching orders, You will also give us all the supplies, equipment, and instruction to carry out Your mission. All glory to You, our Supreme Commander."

And every soldier in the ranks joined Carlos in their battle cry, "A sword for the Lord and for Gabriella!"

"Dismissed," said the colonel.

The trainees broke ranks and jogged to the mansion for their breakfast in what now was a military chow hall.

At the officers' table, Sandy, Carlos, Frederick, and Roberto sat together over coffee, fruit, eggs, toast, and bacon.

"Peter has found a range suitable for our weapons training," said Sandy. "The busses will be here in a few minutes."

Carlos said, "We'll need three days there and we'll be all set weapons-wise. Where is it?"

"It's an abandoned farm about an hour north of here," said Sandy.

"Used to be owned by a retired army general who brought all his old Army buddies there to shoot."

"How'd we get permission to use it?" said Carlos.

"We bought it."

"I trust that our Lord will empower our young warriors with excellent marksmanship abilities.

"For your information, we now have an alliance of angels. I have assigned three of them the task of covering the sky overhead with a protective shield that will prevent any enemy observation of our activities. I believe that shield will help to divert them to our decoy location on Cape Neddick."

Carlos sprang up out of his chair and walked quickly to the stranger who had just walked into the dining hall, a young man who looked too thin for his clothing, whose face was sunken, whose head was shaved bald, and whose eyes looked vaguely familiar.

"Sir," he said to the young man, "you're not allowed in here. Come with me." And he grabbed the man's arm and began escorting him out. The young man was smiling.

"Well, Carlos, this is a fine welcome home," he said.

Carlos looked closely at the intruder's face. Sandy jumped up from the table and ran to him and threw her arms around him.

"What are you doing here?" she asked, still clinging to him.

"Hi, Mom, I'm home," Hank Junior said. "Where's Dad?"

"A vineyard in New Hampshire," said Frances. "Who would have ever thought such a place existed? How long will we have this place, Randal?"

"As long as we want," said Randal. "I've leased it for a year, and if we need it for that long, we'll just buy the place."

From her command post in the main building on the heights of Zolinos, a vineyard-resort, Frances could see nearly the entire property.

Randal had sectioned off the fan-shaped acreage into six encampments, one section for each of their squads. Rows of white modular units had been set up between the rows of grape vines. Frances watched the groups of soldiers slog through the newly graded muddy roads to their training sites. They looked like robots.

Only five days ago the Directorate was finishing up their planning session four hours west at the Canyon Ranch. The buildup for the attack on FITO was rushed and chaotic. Frances took charge of the recruiting network, Randal became the troop commander, and the other three, Romano, Olivia, and Donald divided the logistical and administrative tasks among themselves.

Frances labored under a strange mixture of emotions—resolution of purpose, a sense of patriotism as well as anxiety, mistrust, and fear. She was nowhere as certain of the strategy as Andrew seemed to be. He tried to assure the executive board members that their first priority target would be FITO's location on Cape Neddick in Maine.

Andrew insisted that all his data and all his logic programs pointed to that conclusion. He showed the board that his telekinetic receivers indicated positive human activity and positive energy emissions from Neddick, all identified with FITO's imprint. While the indicators from FITO's previous location near Cape Ann had always been somewhat intermittent, most recently they had faded completely from his recordings.

Frances and Randal accepted Andrew's assessment with some skepticism, so they located their field headquarters equidistant from both of FITO's probable sites. That way if Andrew was wrong, they could shift resources from one target to the other. The vineyard outside the tiny country village of Sandown, New Hampshire, proved to be the perfect isolated location for their training camp.

But Frances' doubts plagued her: too many new personalities, too many loose moving parts to feel the least bit comfortable about the operation. In the past each of Andrew's six squads operated separately. They were experienced in their roles as seers and operators—locating personnel targets, identifying the shooters, brainwashing them, and supporting their attacks on the obstructionists. But they were woefully inexperienced at leading a force of hypnotized warrior-brutes into combat. And they were even less qualified to cooperate with the other squads in a unified attack.

So as Frances looked out over this rapidly assembled herd trudging through the mud, following orders in their mind-numbed states under the command of an obese, erratic commander—Randal Sanford—she groaned in dismay.

Randal burst into the command center, clumps of mud falling from his absurd rubber boots. His face was flushed. He was hyperventilating. "We need twenty more men. Today."

"Randal, we have only four more days before we establish our attack positions outside Cape Neddick. This gang of fighters looks like it's barely capable of any kind of unified operations. How are you going to integrate twenty more new recruits into these units? And how are you going to house them, equip them, and even feed them?"

"See, Frances, I told you. You worry too much. This fighting force is coming along marvelously. You know George Washington fought the British with a militia force that he put together on the fly. Our cause is as important as his at the birth of our nation. We're only talking about three new warriors in each squad, plus two for the headquarters. Our seers are working on finding them as we speak. They should all be on board by tomorrow morning."

"Fine, Randal," said Frances. "By the way, must you keep that silly sword on your belt? It only reminds me of the nasty business we had back at the Ranch."

"This sword symbolizes my command power," said Randal. "And what you call nasty business, I call a significant event in the history of the Directorate. Buck up, girl. We have a battle ahead and a mighty victory for our cause."

With that he tromped out of the command post, leaving his muddy tracks behind. Frances pulled her flask out of her hip pocket and took a long sip of vodka. Before Randal cleared the door, Andrew was pounding on his table and shouting.

Henry and Beto, aboard *Water Walker* on choppy seas, sat quietly with four lines in the water all baited with cut herring.

"Why we keep coming to the same spot?" said Beto. He was on his second pipe that morning.

"I don't know."

"Is it the lighthouse?"

"I don't know."

"How many fish we caught here in this spot—in what?—four days in a row. How many?"

"Zero."

"Just checking. I wondered if my math was off," said Beto. "I wonder where our weird neighbor went. I kinda miss him, you know. Mister Personality."

"Yeah. When did he take off? You remember?" Henry said.

"I think four days ago. The day after we saw him in that stupid disguise. The day you decided this was the best spot in the entire ocean to fish. Off the Nubble Light House on Cape Neddick."

Beto stopped his teasing. He thought he might be getting under Henry's famously thin skin. He loved the rhythm of the boat bobbing on the light chop. He enjoyed the pleasure of good pipe tobacco, especially in the sea air. He wondered about the wisdom of the placement of this well-photographed lighthouse, built on a tiny nub of an island only a couple hundred yards from the rocks on the mainland.

He considered how inconvenient it was to have this lighthouse on an island, especially when there were several higher locations on the mainland where a lighthouse could have been built with even better range for the light beam. Beto imagined how it was, in a storm of long duration, with the furnace out of fuel, the electricity out, waiting for the seas to calm down so someone could come and resupply and repair by boat. *What were they thinking?*

"Hey, Henry, let's go up there," Beto said.

"The sign says no trespassing."

"Let's go up there," Beto said again.

They let down the zodiac launch from the trawler and motored over to the dock in the little cove between the rocks, hidden from the mainland. They walked up the steps to the small storage shed and then up the walkway to the main house at the base of the light tower. Henry and Beto spent over an hour exploring the grounds and the keeper's quarters. No one had lived there since the Coast Guard left in 1987.

———————————————

At the Directorate's command center, Frances grabbed Andrew's arm. "What?" said Frances, "Knock off the noise."

Frances and Randal stood behind Andrew and peered into the screen in front of him.

"Look, see?" Andrew said, excited.

"See what, Andrew?" Randal said.

"Movement at the lighthouse at Cape Neddick. I told you."

"So someone is at the lighthouse—so what?" Randal pushed.

"Those guys are FITO. I have identifiers on all FITO personnel. See? FITO is occupying the same rock where their energy source generates telekinetic radiation," Andrew said. "This proves it. They've moved to Cape Neddick from Cape Ann."

"Not enough evidence for me," said Frances. You will have to...."

Andrew banged on his table again, harder this time. He shouted, "I got it, I got it. I got the evidence you're looking for, Frances."

"What?"

Andrew swiveled around to face her. He took several deep breaths. "Remember, Frances, when you came to my cave? Remember computer seven?"

Frances said, "Yeah, number seven was doing a search for another computer at the FBI that logged on to two sites that you were logged onto. What about it?"

"Seven alerted me that he completed his search. He has untied that web of proxy servers."

"Took him long enough. Where is this FBI computer genius located?"

"Look for yourself," said Andrew. He lifted a laptop computer up to her face with a map of New England on it. A bright red light was blinking on Cape Neddick, Maine, where Henry's laptop sat on the *Water Walker's* galley table.

Andrew and Randal looked into Frances' eyes. They watched her skepticism fade. Randal was certain.

"Okay, Andrew," Randal said. "We'll take that as a confirmation that we've located the right target."

Frances, Randal, and Andrew couldn't stop watching the traces of human FITO movement beaming from the Nubble Light at Cape Neddick.

Chapter Twenty-Five

Sandy's joy at Hank's return pressed hard against her pangs of emptiness at the absence of her husband. She missed her micromanaging, neat-freak of a partner. What was she supposed to tell her son, just now out of psych rehab? The young veteran looked weak and adrift.

Hank had changed so much since he deployed to Afghanistan. He'd been so successful in high school and in every phase of his Army training. Before he left for his deployment, he proudly displayed his Airborne Wings, his Ranger Tab, and the Unit Scroll for the 75th Ranger Regiment on the shoulder of his uniform. Sandy never quite understood the meaning of the insignia, but she certainly understood the pride beaming off her son's young face and Hank's recently acquired strengths: physical, moral, and spiritual.

But when he came home on leave after two years of intense combat against the Taliban, all that strength had drained away. He sat for hours staring out over the rocky ledge where Gabriella stood. Hank put himself in the care of a Veterans Administration doctor who relied heavily on drugs to address Hank's symptoms of posttraumatic stress disorder. Sandy knew Hank was washing down the pills with vodka.

Somehow Hank purchased an old Colt 1911 pistol and ammunition. Sandy and Henry woke up in the middle of the night to the sound of gunshots outside. Henry grabbed the shotgun he kept under the bed and ran out to confront the shooter, and he nearly had a gun battle with his son. Fortunately, Hank had expended all the rounds in his pistol before he aimed it at his father and pulled the trigger. Henry recognized his son before either of them caused any damage.

That incident moved Henry and Sandy to seek better treatment for their son. They found the most highly recommended facility and doctor at the Loving Center in Port Angeles, Washington, supervised by the nation's top psychiatrist, a Doctor Romano Goldstein.

Sandy looked at her son as he nibbled at the sandwich she made for him. "So you are doing better, Hank? It's great to have you home."

Hank looked up at his mother. Sandy wondered if he heard her words. He just stared at her. "Cielavista has changed, Mom. It looks like an Army camp."

Sandy groped for words. "We are having some serious trouble, Hank. There's a secret society that is systematically murdering innocent civilians here in the US and in other countries. Nonina has received some kind of supernatural power to combat their efforts, and she has been very effective. This society, called the Directorate, has located us and is planning an attack on us. We have begun preparations to defend ourselves here. Incidentally, I found your *Ranger Handbook*. It's been very helpful." She tried to smile as she awaited Hank's reaction.

Hank's eyes brightened as if a curtain had been raised. Sandy didn't know whether to be pleased or alarmed. He quickly devoured the ham and cheese sandwich and asked, "You got anything more to eat?"

Sandy warmed up a bowl of chowder and Hank made short work of that and the rye bread and butter she served with it. "Let's see what you got going on," he said.

Sandy took her newly revived son into the barn. The first floor was divided into a briefing room and several work stations for Task Force Saber operations officers. On the second floor was the operations center. Sandy laid the handwritten operations order in front of him. He quickly comprehended everything.

"You think the enemy is moving to an assembly area?" Hank said.

"Right, but we don't know where."

Hank and Sandy leaned over the table with the map of New England on it. "We are here," she said, pointing to a green pin on the coast just south of Cape Ann. "Gabriella has created a dummy location here," she said, indicating the blue pin at the Nubble Lighthouse on Cape Neddick, Maine, "as a decoy to throw the enemy off."

Hank looked at his mother and shrugged his lack of understanding at her.

"Don't ask me how she does these things," Sandy said. "It's beyond me. And even if I got it, I couldn't explain it."

Hank went back to the map. He drew a pencil line between the two locations, running almost due north along the coast about sixty miles long. "If you were the enemy," Hank said, "where would you put your attack headquarters?"

Sandy studied the map. "Somewhere out in here, equidistant from the two pins on the map. That way they could shift forces from one target to the other."

"Right," said Hank, "but that covers a lot of ground."

Carlos came into the ops center and sidled up to Hank and Sandy. He laid a note on the table with numbers on it—*42.93N, 71.19W.*

"What's this?" said Sandy.

"Not sure. My grandson Beto just texted it to me."

"It's latitude, longitude," said Hank. He went to the computer and pulled up a lat-long locator web site. The site dropped a pin on the town of Sandown, New Hampshire, exactly where Sandy had estimated the enemy's location.

"Where in the world did this come from?" Sandy asked Carlos.

He was on the phone with Beto before she asked the question. He clicked off. "Looks like my grandson Beto and Mr. Henry are fishing for more than fish."

"Where did you say Dad was?" asked Hank.

"I didn't, Hank. Truth is I don't know. He took off in a huff a week ago and I got the impression that he may not be interested in coming back. The last words I said to him were, 'I can live without you.'"

Hank looked at Carlos. They let the awkward minute pass. "Okay, so that's out in the open. Good to know," said Hank.

Carlos said, "Well, let me tell you Beto and Henry are visiting a cousin of mine in the little town of Cape Neddick, Maine, near York Beach. It seems...."

"Cape Neddick?" Sandy interrupted.

"Yeah, I know," said Carlos, "some coincidence, right? That they should be staying in the same town that Gabriella has set up as our decoy location. Anyway, there's more. Evidently they got suspicious about a character staying near them in the trailer park. Henry used his FBI buddies to look into him and they identified a woman connected with him. She worked at the CIA years ago. Henry got her plate number and had local police monitor her movements. First in Maine, then New Hampshire. Her car is parked at the Zolinos Vineyard Resort in Sandown, New Hampshire."

"And these are the coordinates," said Hank. "Where are your map pins?"

Sandy handed Hank the little box, and he stuck a red pin on the paper map on the table at a point corresponding to the pin on the website.

"My head is spinning," said Sandy.

"What?" said Carlos, studying the map.

"Henry's gone. Right when we desperately need him here at Cielavista. He has abandoned me. *Us*—he has abandoned *us*. And for some reason he shows up at the decoy site. And he's running down information on our enemy." She seemed dazed.

"We need eyes on the enemy," said Hank.

Sandy heard a new voice from her son's mouth. A commanding power resonated in his words. She was remembering some of the material produced by the Loving Center for families of PTSD patients. Most of these soldiers are compelled to return to the front lines. The explanation is not healthy. She remembered a chapter on the thirty-two chemicals in the brain, and when a soldier encounters combat the adrenal gland secretes powerful druglike hormones into their nervous system. This stimulation becomes addictive. Then when they return home they find themselves still acting in the same mode—hypervigilant, combative, angry, sleepless, startled at loud noises—but since there is no real threat, there is no release of these internally produced chemicals. So they feel compelled to return to where the excitement is, despite the fact that they will suffer discomfort, separation, and exposure to danger.

She watched Hank return to the battlefield, seeing firsthand the warrior in her son resurface right before her eyes. She wondered if he was prepared to reenter combat, but there was nothing she could do about him any more than she could do anything about her AWOL husband.

"Sandy," Carlos said, breaking into her thoughts.

"What?"

"We need you out on the rocks. We can take care of the operations and the troops here," he said.

Sandy took a deep breath and let out a long sigh. She looked at Hank.

"Son," she said, "I am so glad you are home. I am sorry for the chaos we're in. Please take care of yourself. I'll see you tonight. Let's eat together in the cottage. Carlos, tell your wife to come too, okay?"

Hank Baker, former Army Ranger, Andy Santiago, one of Carlos's grand nephews, and Lucille, the wolfhound, low-crawled along the ridge line overlooking the Zolinos Vineyard Resort in the town of Sandown, New Hampshire. Hank's senses came alive in his familiar role—deep recon in enemy territory.

"So the dog talks to angels," said Hank to Andy.

"That's what they say," said Andy, creeping next to the ranger.

"And you communicate with her?"

"Sort of," Andy said. "Not like talking, but I know what she's thinking."

Hank shook his head. "That place has turned into a looney bin since I left."

From their position at the top of a short cliff covered with high grass they could observe the encampment below. Dawn was seeping into the valley with no promise of warmer temperatures. Whistles sounded. Men scampered into six separate clusters on the muddy streets in front of the modular buildings. Doors slammed, the low rumble of voices and a few shouts filled the air in the valley below the recon team. Streams of light mist blew across the vineyard as the morning light ascended.

"We have two angels overhead," said Andy.

"What are they there for?"

"The enemy has the technology to observe human activity at long distances. Kind of like radar, but more dependent on some kind of paranormal power. The angels are providing a shield over us that's deflecting their view. Otherwise they would pick up on our movements and we would be in deep doo-doo."

"This is one strange war," said Hank.

The two men scanned the encampment with high-powered binoculars. Occasionally they would jot down notes in their notebooks. Lucille watched the men.

Andy produced a camera with a telephoto lens and aimed it at the enemy's formations and he shot away. He attached the camera to his cell phone and sent the images to Cousin Ricardo's phone back in Task Force Saber's ops center.

"I've never seen that many huge men in one place at one time," said Hank.

"Not one under six four by my guess. And they all seem to cower to their leaders, the little guys and the women," said Andy.

"Look at the group by the pond," said Hank. Both men focused their binoculars on the thin strip of sand at the edge of the pond. Their binoculars brought the scene in close. A small framed woman with her hands on her hips was yelling at a group of these huge monsters. The men assumed the push-up position at her command. After a while, some of them dropped onto their stomachs and she went over to each one and stomped her boot into their backs. None gave the slightest retort. They just took the humiliation and tried to give her more push-ups.

"Looks like six units, each led by two or three smaller people," said Hank.

Hank and Andy crawled to four different vantage points and collected data until well after nightfall. They made their way through woods, swamp and brush, back to Andy's vehicle parked in a shopping plaza seven miles away. In an hour they pulled into a service plaza for a memory dump. They put their observations into a Ranger format called "Essential Elements of Information"—organization, activities, vehicles, weapons, uniforms, leadership. They looked at each other.

"This is one lethal enemy force," said Hank.

CHAPTER TWENTY-SIX

Firdos sat on a stump and smoked a cigarette. Randal Sanford came up beside him. They watched Firdos's squad practice fire and maneuver under the command of one of Firdos's operators, Sam Farenza. The squad was divided into two fire teams. Team Alpha laid down suppressive fire while Team Bravo scrambled up the hill to a covered position. Then when Sam yelled, "Move!" Team Alpha leap-frogged ahead to a new position while Team Bravo covered them with suppressive fire.

"How they doing, Firdos?" said Randal.

"They do what they're told," said Firdos.

At the top of the hill two telephone poles lay on the ground. Each fire team slung their weapons across their backs and hoisted the telephone poles on their shoulders and jogged down the hill, turned around, and hauled them back up, grunting and shouting all the way. They threw the poles down and each fighter in Team Alpha lifted a Team Bravo fighter over his shoulder and carried him down, shouting, "Death to FITO!" Then the men threw their human burdens down on the ground and put a boot on their necks.

"Recover," said Sam. "Do it again, you pathetic animals. You'll keep doing this drill until you get it right. Forget about eating until you do. Back in attack formation."

"Good training," said Randal.

"You call me a seer," said Firdos.

"That's right. You have a talent for it. That's why we hired you," said Randal.

"I have some blind spots."

Firdos had been thinking about his time in Cape Neddick. He would observe the two men who lived across from him in the trailer park coming and going to and from their rented residence. When they drove off in their SUV he tried to follow them with his telekinetic powers, as he had done thousands of times before. But with these two—he could not "see" them. Their images and their traces escaped his vision.

He thought it was an anomaly. Then yesterday as he panned over the vineyard with his sky-view vision, one blurry spot hung over the ridge to the east like a cloud. As hard as he tried, he could not penetrate it.

When Firdos explained his doubts to Randal, Randal said, "My boy, don't you see? Your trailer park neighbors were FITO soldiers, somehow covering their movements from your eyes. That confirms Andrew's theory, right? What appears as a deficiency to you works as an asset to us at higher headquarters. I'll report this to the board.

"We're preparing for victory here, Firdos; a glorious battle, believe me. Keep up the good work, commander."

Randal walked away to inspect his other squads. Firdos was still conflicted by the warm feelings he was getting from being encouraged.

"Sam," Firdos called out, "Give the guys a ten-minute water break then get them back to work."

Frances O'Donnelly, Romano Goldstein, Donald Snow, Olivia Kingston, and Randal Sanford were enjoying a sumptuous dinner in their war room. They were finishing the soup course, a lobster bisque and sipping apple wine from the vineyard. Andrew stepped up to the platform to begin his briefing.

Frances was reconsidering her assessment of Andrew's competence. Her mind was growing increasingly negative.

"This wine is hideous," said Donald. "What's it made of, iodine?"

"It's their local apple wine, dear; spoils of war, so to speak," said Olivia. "We mustn't complain. We're warriors now."

"Don't they have any grapes up here?" Donald said.

"Here," said Randal, reaching back to the sideboard behind him, grabbing a bottle. "Try this. It's from a vineyard down the road. A white of some kind."

"You guys want me to start or are you too busy fussing over the wine?" said Andrew.

Donald tasted the white. "Hey, this is really good. Go ahead, Andrew. Brief away."

Frances studied the screen behind Andrew, a map with three locations on it—the Directorate's position at the Zolinos Vineyard, the enemy position at Neddick, and their alternate location south of Cape Ann.

"Target number one is the Nubble Lighthouse on Cape Neddick," Andrew said. He aimed the red dot from his laser pointer at the map on the screen marked "FITO Target No. 1." "Target number two is here, somewhere south of Gloucester." He aimed his laser pointer at a large unspecified area labeled on his map "FITO Target No. 2."

"I fully expect that target two is abandoned, but we will maintain a contingency plan in place just in case some of their forces are there.

"The objective is to kill all FITO personnel, no prisoners. I have four intelligence indicators from Cape Neddick: a telekinetic energy force from the rocks beneath their headquarters, traces of human FITO activity on my detection devices, and confirmation by one of our most competent seers, Firdos Gaffardi. He has had eyes on two of FITO's operatives in and around Target One. And fourth, one of my computers conducted a digital search through layers of proxy servers and located a FITO laptop computer at that location. Very sloppy for them to keep that computer online.

"The attack on Target One will be amphibious." Andrew changed the image on the screen from a map to a live satellite view. Cape Neddick stuck out from York Beach, Maine, like a thumb. The "nub" looked like a tiny island separated from the end of the thumb by a narrow channel one hundred yards wide.

"As you can see from the image here, Cape Neddick is thickly populated. A ground attack through these neighborhoods would be foolish.

"I have procured three vessels to transport our attack force onto the back of the island. We will surprise our enemy from the sea, overrun their weak defenses, kill them all and exfiltrate by sea. The unsuspecting residents of Cape Neddick will never know we were there."

"Question." Frances raised her hand. "What about gunfire? Won't that disturb these residents?"

Andrew waved his hand at Randal, "You wanna take that question, Randal?"

Randal was eager to show off his role as ground commander. He wiped marinara sauce from his mouth with his sleeve. "I've trained our crack troops in silent kill techniques," he said. "Run that video, Andrew."

The video showed the target range where the Directorate force had been training. The board members watched as a line of twenty large, muscular brutes loaded their crossbows. In unison, at the command of one squad leader they bent over at the waist, pulled back on their crossbow strings, straining to set them in the cocked position.

Randal explained, "All these men are capable of lifting three hundred pounds. As you can see, these bows are designed to hold two hundred pounds of pull. Each weapon holds three cocked arrows, ready to fire— either all at once or separately. They have an effective range of four hundred yards."

On the screen each soldier reached across his waist to remove arrows from his quiver hanging on his belt, loaded his crossbow, and aimed downrange.

A command rang out from a voice off camera, "Targets, post!" In the distance, a line of twenty men rose up out of a ditch and charged at the bowmen. Frances gripped the arms of her chair. *Human targets.* Rather than being shocked or repulsed at taking innocent lives simply for target practice, Frances felt a twinge of wicked stimulation.

"Kill!" shouted the voice. All twenty live targets fell to the ground writhing in pain. The other board members watched dispassionately, continuing with their main course—veal marsala, steamed vegetables, and mashed potatoes. Frances gulped downed a full glass of wine.

"Pass me that white wine, Donald," said Frances. She refilled her glass.

"Charge and finish!" the voice on the video commanded. The twenty soldiers ran ahead, unsheathed their short swords, and quickly dispatched their victims.

Randal said, "Our soldiers will employ the bow and the blade as their primary weapons in our attack. Squad leaders will be armed with silenced rifles and pistols."

On the screen a box truck drove across the range followed by a crew of men throwing bodies into the cargo box. The warriors had fallen into a file and marched off to the right under the supervision of their squad leader who was beating one of them with a club as they marched.

"We attack the Nubble Lighthouse tonight," Andrew said, packing up his laptop and projector. "By tomorrow there will be no more Fly In The Ointment."

"What about the contingency plan," asked Frances, "on Target Two?"

"I do not expect I will have to brief that plan, Frances," said Andrew. "If, in the very unlikely event we have to attack Target Two, we will have another meeting."

Frances noticed Olivia lean her shoulder into Donald and say, "What do you think of ourselves, Donald? We're a council of war. Out on the frontier. In charge of an army."

"I know," said Donald. "Quite invigorating, wouldn't you say?"

"Yes, as long as I don't have to get my shoes dirty," Olivia said with a chuckle.

Then to the waiter Olivia said, "Young man, where's the dessert cart?"

Frances shook her head in disgust.

"What are you thinking about, amigo?" said Beto to Henry. They were having a cup of coffee in their trailer before setting out for another day in the boat.

"Marriage," said Henry.

Beto just sipped and looked over the sports page of the *Portland Press Herald*. His fishing mate was not as easy to read as the paper. Henry had dug into his FBI data and identified the woman connected with their creepy neighbor. Then he had the police watch her and they found out she was staying at a vineyard in New Hampshire. It was Tobias who told him to text the latitude-longitude to Carlos—for what?

"I can't stand her and she hates me," said Henry.

"Patriots still undefeated," said Beto.

"I bet she hasn't made the bed since I left."

"We gonna go fishing or are you going to keep talking about your wife, like you been doing for the last week?"

"She probably hasn't paid the electric bill or the gas bill."

"We going back to that lighthouse or we going to avoid it like the fish do?"

"I got an idea," said Henry.

"Uh-oh."

Henry laid it out, Beto liked it because it didn't involve fishing at the Nubble Light or grousing about Henry missing his wife, so they got to it. They drove the Tahoe to Beto's cousin's house. They filled the fuel tanks on *Water Walker* and loaded up their supplies and fishing tackle.

"You figure—what?—three days from here to Gloucester Bay?" said Henry.

"About that," said Beto, "let's go."

CHAPTER TWENTY-SEVEN

"Carlos, have you seen Gabriella?" said Sandy. The two command-ers walked together on their daily inspection tour of Task Force Saber's defensive perimeter around Cielavista. They chatted with the fighters, some digging their foxholes into the earth and some building up their fighting position with rocks. Secondary positions formed the next line of defense a quarter mile behind the perimeter in the event the fighters had to fall back. The third fallback position, a ten-foot-high stone rampart protected by a spiked ditch constituted the inner ring. Carlos had designed this fortress to provide the rear guard of Task Force Saber excellent protection for their last stand against the Directorate's attack. The soldiers had dug two escape tunnels from the interior of the stone fortress to the side of the cliff overlooking the ocean.

"No," said Carlos. "She must be out on her rock."

"I just looked out there and she's not there," said Sandy. "I don't recall seeing her all day yesterday. I'm concerned, Carlos."

"We'll cease work on the defenses and conduct a thorough search of the premises," said Carlos. "Which of the horses can communicate with angelic beings?"

"Sadie," said Sandy. "And your niece, Althea, can communicate with Sadie. I want them with you during the search, okay?"

"Right."

"Sandy, we need you out on the rock," said Carlos, and he placed his rough palms on her cheeks. He looked her in the eye, "My courageous sister, 'no weapon formed against us will stand.'"

"I'll go out," Sandy said. "Find my grandmother."

———————

Andrew was a hurricane of frustration watching Commander Randal Sanford try to lead his battalion of robotic warriors—all brainwashed and hypnotized. When the squad leaders ordered their oversized thugs to line up and board the rental trucks that would transport them to the wharf, the big lummoxes stumbled around in confused clusters. Not having detailed instructions about how and where to line up, which direction to go, which truck to board, where to sit in the back of these large enclosed box trucks, and what equipment to carry, they became more and more confused. Their confusion turned into fear and their fear turned into anger and their anger turned into violence against each other.

A simple movement of personnel from barracks to vehicles, which should have taken less than thirty minutes, took over four hours. Andrew noticed that all the Directorate board members with the exception of Randal were sleeping off their feast. He could do nothing but sit in the ops center and observe the chaos from his window overlooking the ruined vineyard.

In a rare moment of neglect, Andrew failed to monitor his security screens where a faint signal representing human movement on the hills above the vineyard was blinking. He paced back and forth in front of the window overlooking the struggling soldiers, where several violent fist-fights had broken out. In one incident, a soldier fatally stabbed his squad mate. There was no punishment, just a reprimand and an order from the leader of that squad to get into line.

Andrew decided he needed to rouse his bosses from their sleep. He went to each of the guesthouses on the far side of the property and banged on their doors with the butt of his pistol grip. It took ten minutes for Frances, Olivia, Donald, and Romano to join him in the gazebo at the edge of the vineyard. A light drizzle seeped into the hazy directors' clothing.

"We are at war," Andrew said, unveiling his rage. "You are the war council. You have failed to witness the incompetence of your leaders, especially Commander Randal Sanford. The soldiers in our so-called army are totally inept. Come with me. You need to observe their failure to assemble for their attack on the Nubble Light."

Andrew and the four drowsy executives walked toward the operations center in the main building. The convoy of trucks was exiting the vineyard. As they watched the line of taillights stream down the driveway, Hank's demolitions exploded into the night. The multiple blasts throughout the camp threw the board members down onto the muddy ground.

The leaders of the Directorate lay in the mud, deaf and paralyzed.

Hank's team of nine saboteurs had reached its attack position under cover of darkness. Silently they separated into three sections and moved to their preplanned observation posts. They watched the troop activity in the Directorate's camp below them. It appeared to them that the entire enemy force was leaving the encampment. Hank was amazed at the chaos.

Eventually the large box trucks loaded with armed brutes lined up on the main road to Sandown. Hank's men moved quickly and stealthily to their targets—the modular barracks buildings and the main hall. Within a few minutes they lay all the demo and set the timers. Hank's commandos jogged back to their rally point on the ridge and gathered to watch the results of their work. The six modular buildings exploded simultaneously. Fireballs flared upward from the massive explosions followed by huge plumes of black smoke. Before the echo of those explosions subsided, ten horrendous charges went off in the main hall, sending the twenty thousand square foot structure splintering into the sky in a blazing ball of flames and thunder. The saboteurs headed back to their vehicles at their rendezvous point two miles back through the woods.

The computer in Andrew's mobile operations center in his van was untouched by the demolitions. It faithfully recorded Hank's route back to Cielavista, pinpointing Task Force Saber's true location.

By late afternoon Henry was finally satisfied that *Water Walker* was ready for the voyage from Cape Neddick to Gloucester Bay. He had Beto follow his exhaustive checklist inspecting every inch of the craft inside and out. Henry triple-checked the navigation instruments. He called the Coast Guard and several harbor masters along their route. He drove to the local marine supply shop and procured two extra marine batteries and had them charged up. He bought bedding and extra clothing, including two sets of wet weather gear.

"Man, we're not crossing the Atlantic," Beto said, "we're skimming the coastline."

"Okay, we're all set, Beto. Let's cast off," Henry said.

"You sure you didn't forget anything? How about a few extra tubes of toothpaste?"

"Actually I have four. They were buy-one-get-one-free at the supermarket," said Henry.

"So what, you bought two and got two free?" said Beto as he untied the bowline.

"Well, yeah, but I had to leave the store after I got the first two and go back in to get the second deal," said Henry. He pushed the starter button on the console.

Beto shook his head.

A steady rain drizzled down from a cold, dreary sky. Heavy, ashen clouds stretched down to the ocean. Henry cautiously guided *Water Walker* out of Neddick Harbor to the open sea. The dim October twilight faded behind the grey curtain.

On his surface radar, Henry picked up several boats a mile out to his starboard front. "Three large boats," Henry said to Beto. Both men smoked pipes now. They concentrated on the instruments and the ocean out the window. The wipers slapped the mist off the windshield. Henry slowed *Water Walker* down to six knots. The radar showed the three vessels creeping toward the Nubble Light, and then halting in a semicircle around the little island.

"Tobias," said Beto, "you see this?

"Your angel does not like the looks of those boats. There's a band of dark angels accompanying them—bad sign."

"I don't know whether to get out of here or stay and see if we're supposed to do something," said Henry.

"Call the Coast Guard," said Beto. "Just tell them what you see and let them decide if they should respond."

"Good idea."

Into the microphone, "Coast Guard Station Portsmouth, this is *Water Walker*. Can you hear me?"

"*Water Walker*, this is Portsmouth"

"I'm reporting some unusual activity off the Nubble Light. Three large motor craft loitering and moving slowly toward the island. Visibility is low, but I have them on radar."

"Okay, we have Coast Guard auxiliary there in Neddick. We'll send out a boat to check them out. Suggest you keep your distance. Thanks, Captain."

"*Water Walker*, okay. Out," said Henry.

In a few minutes a fourth boat showed on the radar screen in front of Henry and Beto.

"That was quick," said Beto, breathing out a cloud of aromatic smoke into the enclosed cockpit.

The shockwave from a blast rocked the *Water Walker*—followed by four-foot waves from the explosion. Henry and Beto could see a faint orange-yellow glow through the thick low-hanging clouds. On the radar, the image of the destroyed Coast Guard boat radiated bright red and disappeared.

"Coast Guard Portsmouth, your auxiliary boat is in trouble. I suggest a rapid response from your location. Notify law enforcement. It looks like one of the unidentified vessels fired on your boat."

"Roger, *Water Walker*. Quick reaction force is on the way. Keep your distance."

"We gotta move, Henry. Look," Beto said, pointing at the radar screen. One of the three vessels was headed toward them at a high speed.

"Tobias," Henry said, "How 'bout making yourself useful and churn up the water around that approaching boat? Sink it if you can."

Henry pushed forward on the throttle and the *Water Walker* retreated to the high sea. They reached top speed but the pursuing yacht was gaining on them. Henry looked back and watched an unnatural mountain of water swell up in the distance between them and the luxury cruiser. The approaching yacht rose up onto the twenty-foot swell and went momentarily airborne. Then it fell back into the ocean stern-first, became half submerged, and bobbed upright full of seawater. The high speed cruiser stalled helplessly behind them.

Henry looked at Beto and said, "I guess our water boy angel is all right after all."

Randal directed the captain of his yacht into Portsmouth Harbor and up the Piscatagua River to the private cove where their disastrous voyage had begun thirty-six hours before. He stomped into the boathouse on the wharf.

The other two luxury boats—one towing the swamped craft—pulled up to their slips and tied in.

"Everyone get in here," he yelled.

The soldiers entered the boathouse. One of the squad leaders ordered them all to sit down on the floor. They looked more like a class of preschoolers after a field trip than an infantry platoon. Mouths open, eyes staring straight ahead they sat, barely aware that they had neither slept nor eaten for two days.

Randal huddled with his six squad leaders in the equipment room of the boathouse.

"You idiots are pathetic," he said. "You couldn't get your soldiers assembled. You did a miserable job getting them on the trucks, and when the time came to mount our attack on the target, you failed to respond to my commands. The only thing keeping you from execution is that I don't have time to train another team of seers and operators, and we have another target to attack in the next three days."

"Sir?" said one of the leaders.

"What, Carlene? What is it?" Randal said.

"The lighthouse and the island were abandoned. Our recon team scoured the place and there was not a soul in sight."

"I don't want to hear any of your weak excuses. You all failed to attack. You let one volunteer Coast Guard Auxiliary crew interrupt our advance. And you, Firdos, you failed to catch that other launch. You let them get away. You're useless." He pulled Firdos to him by the shirt front and punched him in the face. Firdos crumpled to the floor in a heap.

"We will return to the vineyard. We will regroup, retrain, and reequip. And you will be prepared to attack target number two in three days. Now get your worthless animals on the trucks and follow me back to camp."

The men boarded the trucks and the leaders approached their cars when the blue police lights flashed into the marina's parking lot.

"Carlene," Randal said, "Call Andrew, quick. We need these cops hypnotized. Now."

Carlene called Andrew. "Code blue my location, situation urgent."

Randal looked at Carlene and walked over to the police officers. She nodded to him.

CHAPTER TWENTY-EIGHT

Morning broke on York Beach, burning off yesterday's fog bank. Maine State Police Lieutenant Ralph Churchill and York Village Police Chief Rebecca Quigley pulled into the lot of the private marina on the Piscatagua River. As Churchill leaned out of his cruiser, Randal Sanford greeted him with a smile. An unusually pleasant sensation overwhelmed the trooper. Chief Quigley walked up next to Trooper Churchill and smiled at Randal. They listened to the nice man's explanation of why they were there and they waved to him and his friends as they drove away in a convoy of box trucks and cars.

Lieutenant Churchill turned to the York Village Police Chief and said, "What a mix up, huh, Rebecca?"

"Yeah, and to think we might have mistakenly arrested the lot of them. I'm glad we figured it all out before we took any action."

"Just goes to show you some of those rich folks can be really nice," said Churchill. "That they would take the time and spend the money to give those unfortunate veterans a nice cruise in their luxury yachts. And we thought they were responsible for that Coast Guard Auxiliary boat that blew up from a faulty fuel tank."

"Nice people," Chief Quigley kept repeating, "real nice people. Hey, you wanna join me for breakfast, Ralph? We deserve it after this incident."

"Sure, Chief, sounds like a good idea."

The last of the Directorate's vehicles pulled out of the marina's parking lot. Rebecca reflexively pulled out her notebook and checked the license plates against her notes.

"Hey Ralph, there's a BOLO out on this plate, Massachusetts 440-D85, silver Honda. The driver's name is Carlene Wood," said Rebecca.

"Any instructions?" said the state trooper.

"No, just notify FBI."

"Aw forget it. Those feds don't have to know everything our good citizens are doing."

And the law enforcement officers—still in their hypnotized trances—walked arm in arm to the Sea Side Diner for their "Double Barrel Special"—four eggs, four links of sausage, and a double order of home fries. Free coffee refills.

Sandy climbed up the rocks from her ledge. She'd been watching the Directorate's actions at Cape Neddick and Hank's unauthorized attack on their camp. She was forming a revised defensive plan to counter the enemy's new strategies. She knew the Directorate's plans before they wrote them. Sandy quickly trained herself to transform her fear and worry into the mental energy she needed to lead her forces into battle.

Carlos met Sandy when she reached the yard at the top of the cliffs.

"No one has seen Gabriella for twenty-eight hours," said Carlos.

Sandy's appearance slid downhill since Henry left a week ago. She was always casual in the way she threw on her clothing, but now she was just plain rumpled. She dressed in black sweats, and since the fall temperatures on the shore had dipped down toward freezing, she threw a grey hooded sweatshirt on over her unlaundered clothes.

"I don't know what to think," said Sandy. "I refuse to believe the worst. You would think that of all the visions I have seen out there on the rocky neck, I would get some impressions of Nonina's whereabouts, but no. Nothing. Just the actions of that lunatic army and their botched attack on Cape Neddick, Maine."

Sandy's hoody was still damp from yesterday's rain. Overhead, the grey lid of clouds slowly pealed back across the sky from north to south.

Carlos said, "Dear girl, let's go to the cottage and get you a dry jacket, okay?"

He slid his hand under her arm and led her to her house. Carlos's wife was stirring a pot of beef stew on the kitchen stove.

"In the hall closet here," said Sandy, pulling off her hoody. Carlos pulled a cable-knit wool sweater off its hook and held it open for Sandy to slip her arms into the sleeves.

Sandy and Carlos sat at the kitchen table. She unscrewed the pressure valve in her mind and let some of the stress seep out. The homey smell of Yolanda's cooking, the comfort of Carlos's words, and the familiar warmth of the kitchen embraced her.

"My husband has abandoned me and my Nonina has disappeared. God, I hope she's not in danger. My son turns up here, but he's only a fraction of himself. I don't know why they released him. When he's not conducting a combat patrol, he's staring at the sky. And we have turned this wonderful, peaceful place into an armed camp, and your sweet family into a battle-ready infantry brigade."

She crossed her arms on the kitchen table and put her forehead down on them. Her unwashed mop of white hair fell down over her arms. Carlos and Yolanda sat across from her and prayed silently for their dear friend.

When Sandy sat up she said, "How about some of that stew?"

After a few spoonfuls she said, "Carlos, we have a new enemy situation. We will have to restructure our defensive strategy."

The elderly couple watched Sandy as her countenance changed from the defeated, befuddled woman to the empowered commando captain.

"What is happening?" said Carlos. "What are you seeing out there?"

"Two significant enemy actions. One, they have attempted an attack on the lighthouse at Cape Neddick, Maine, the decoy location that Gabriella had created to throw them off. She transmitted an energy source underground from the granite rocks here on our shoreline through a vein of iron ore that runs all the way to the Maine coast. She had your grandson

Beto and Henry to sail to Cape Neddick to fish— establishing a human presence there. Those two elements fooled the enemy into believing that we had moved.

"Well, the Directorate launched an attack on the Nubble Light at Cape Neddick yesterday and it was a total failure. Henry and Beto in their fishing boat foiled their operation. The Directorate discovered that the Nubble Light was uninhabited."

"Okay," said Carlos, "sounds like a victory for our side—gave us more time to prepare defenses."

"It would seem so," said Sandy. "However, my son has put us in danger."

Sandy stood up from the table, her soup bowl empty. She paced over to the dining room and stared out through the bay window at the unclouded sky.

"Hank, in his attempt to eliminate our enemy, took a small team of saboteurs and invaded their camp in Sandown, New Hampshire. He neglected to take Lucille along with him, so he had no contact with our angelic sky guard. The enemy's operations officer recorded Hank's patrol.

"Hank's team crept into their camp, which was almost deserted except for a few of their executive board members, placed explosives on all their buildings, and blew them up."

Carlos and Yolanda could not suppress their involuntary smirks at this audacious move.

Sandy detected their response. "I know," she said, "seems like a good move, but it will prove very troublesome for us. There is among their leadership an ingenious young technician who monitors their telepathic-telekinetic network. He's the one who has been supervising all their murderous attacks over years. He and their executive officers survived the demolition of their encampment.

"This operations officer, I labeled him 'Enemy Ops-1,' lost his primary operations center with its equipment, but he had installed a portable system in the van that he travels in. Within a few minutes of Hank's attack,

Enemy Ops-1 booted up his equipment and he was able to trace Hank and his attack squad."

Carlos' face hardened as he absorbed this new development. "The enemy must have located our precise location. Your prophetic vision is as powerful as Gabriella's."

"Yes," said Sandy. "Let's get over to our operations center and prepare for an attack."

Sandy gave Yolanda a long hug and thanked her for the stew and the love that helped restore her courage.

"Come here, girl," Yolanda said. The stout Hispanic woman took Sandy by the arm and led her into the bathroom.

"Get those filthy clothes off and get in the shower." It was an order. Sandy looked at Yolanda, sighed, and obeyed.

When Sandy stepped out of the shower, she felt another measure of stress drain out of her as she dried off and donned the clean set of clothing that Yolanda set out on the bed.

Yolanda came in and placed Sandy in front of the mirror and said, "Stay."

She took a comb from the shelf and quickly unsnarled Sandy's twisted nest of hair.

After five minutes of work with the comb and brush, Yolanda said, "Well it's not what it should be, but at least you don't look like a bum. My commander must be presentable, you understand, little girl? You gotta take care of yourself or you're no good to any of us."

Sandy looked at herself in the mirror. She was grateful for the attention. Then it dawned on her. This compulsive drive that forced her to work beyond her strength was the same compulsion that drove her son, Hank, as an Army Ranger. He failed to take care of himself because of his misguided drive to expend every ounce of energy on warrior work.

Sandy was experiencing it for herself—to fall into that adrenaline-induced cycle of action-response-reaction without taking any time to stop, mentally process what was going on and pray. Sandy was becoming aware of the blessing that had just befallen her through the kindness and grace of Yolanda and Carlos. Their love for her and attention broke her destructive cycle and woke her up.

"This is how it happens to them," Sandy said to Yolanda as the women walked down the stairs to the living room in the cottage. "Soldiers, cops, firefighters, ER nurses, anyone in a high-stress job that involves traumatic incidents. It's so easy to ignore what's going on inside their minds while they operate under the influence of all these highly charged chemicals in their heads. There's even an addictive kind of enjoyment, I have to admit. I can't explain it, but when you're charging around in a dangerous environment, making decisions, thinking the world is depending on you for survival, facing death in the teeth, you feel superhuman."

On the front porch of the cottage, Carlos was looking out at what had become a military fortress. He spoke into his radio, giving instructions to Roberto, the Anvil Company Commander.

Sandy shook her head violently and felt herself released from under the weight of her dysfunctional obsession.

"Thank you, dear Yolanda," said Sandy, "You're a wonderful friend."

"Only do what God has equipped you to do," said Yolanda. "Do not try to take care of His business. This battle is not yours, Sandy, the battle belongs to the Lord."

Sandy put on the clean jacket over her fresh clothes.

"What have we got, Commander Carlos?" Sandy said.

"I'm directing Roberto to build overhead protection on all the fighting positions. The enemy has indirect fire weapons. The kind that lob high over obstacles and come down from above," said Carlos.

"Where did you get that intelligence?" asked Sandy.

"Same place you do. Evidently, this position of commander in God's Army comes with some of that divine communication that you and Gabriella have. I saw the sky full of arrows, like a cloud, blocking out the sun."

Sandy joined hands with Carlos and Yolanda. They prayed together. A stream of worship rose up from the porch of the cottage and a waterfall of divine courage poured down into their hearts.

"I'll be out on Gabriella's rock," said Sandy.

Carlos said, "It's your rock now too."

Mounted bareback on Sadie, Carlos rode through the network of defensive positions at the Cielavista estate. He and Roberto had laid out the fortress with three objectives: protect their forces, funnel the enemy into one avenue of approach, and provide for an orderly evacuation.

"What are you seeing overhead, girl?" Carlos said to the horse.

Both man and horse gazed out over the ocean where the sky was painted red, amber, rust, and a deep evening azure. Carlos leaned over Sadie's neck and absorbed what she was seeing. The angels were forming a phalanx of defensive lines—clothed in full armor, swords drawn, shields up. Michael sent out scouts to the south where a swarm of demons was marshaling.

"Ask them why they're forming on our southern flank," said Carlos, and he waited as Sadie got the answer and put it in her mind.

"Ah, yes," said Carlos, "All Hallow's Eve in Salem. The witches and warlocks and magicians are making preparations for their Black Mass, scheduled for midnight, October thirty-first. I'm sure the Directorate has included this annual satanic festival in their plans. That means our angels will have to split their forces—some shielding us from the demonic tribes in Salem, some remaining overhead, engaged in the battle against the demons."

The Task Force Saber soldiers were hard at work improving their fighting positions, erecting roofs to protect them from indirect fire. One of Roberto's assistants walked up to the horseman.

"Good evening, Commander Carlos," he said. "We're just getting ready to have our evening meal. Come, join us for supper."

Their field kitchen under the oak trees in the woods on the western perimeter of Cielavista consisted of a simple tarp over a cooking fire next to a table. A black cast-iron kettle hung over the glowing embers from a tripod of steel rods. One soldier was ladling thick chowder from the kettle into bowls and handing them to another soldier who placed them on the table. The men and women ate standing up.

"I want you to pack six inches of earth on your overhead cover," said Carlos. "I am expecting fiery arrows and darts as the enemy's primary artillery.

"I estimate that the enemy will attack in two days, Halloween night. They will be depending on assistance from their demonic allies in Salem. Remember this, my brave brothers and sisters, no weapon formed against us will stand."

Carlos spent the night stopping at all the defensive positions encouraging his troops. His last stop on Sadie was with Striker Company under Frederick's command. There he dismounted and had them review their battle plan with him. Before the morning twilight, a young nephew came up to Sadie and gave her an apple. Carlos put his arm around the youth and asked him how he was doing.

"Uncle, I am proud to be in your service. We will win this battle," he said, "because we trust you and we trust our Lord. A sword for the Lord and for Gabriella."

CHAPTER TWENTY-NINE

Randal and his convoy from Cape Neddick approached the driveway of their former training camp, now a pile of smoking rubble.

Romano flagged Randal down at the entrance to the vineyard. "We have relocated," said Romano.

Randal signaled the convoy to pull over. "Why?" Randal said.

"They blew up all our buildings. No one got hurt. Follow me."

Randal's mouth hung open as Romano walked back to his vehicle and climbed into the passenger seat. They started to pull away, but Randal just sat there in his truck.

"Let's go, Randal, move out," said Romano, sticking his head out the window.

In a few minutes, Randal's wretched attack force pulled into the gate of their new quarters, the Mountain Inn. Romano yelled to them to park the trucks and file into the lobby where they would get their room assignments. The exhausted soldiers quickly complied and the executive board assembled in the ballroom with their key squad leaders.

Randal chose a seat at the table as far from Frances as possible. The chairwoman took her position at the head of the table. The squad leaders found seats on the chairs against the walls of the room.

"We have had two setbacks," Frances said. "One, a failed assault on Target One, which apparently was deserted, and two, we suffered an attack on our previous location. We could hang our heads and feel defeated. But we will not. We could be humiliated, but we will not be. We could fold up our operation, tail between our legs and run away, but we will not. Everyone stand and recite with me our pledge."

In unison, the board members and the squad leaders stood and said, "We are the Directorate. We humbly accept our role as the overseers of the free world's institutions, and where necessary we will carry out our duty to prune out those branches that hinder the healthy advancement of the American culture. Duty. Honor. Oversight. Always loyal to the Directorate."

"Be seated. I want every one of you to sit up tall, heads raised, and take a deep breath." Randal did as she ordered.

"Now listen to me. We have lost nothing. We still have every resource we started with. Our soldiers are all present and accounted for. Our leaders are here in the room. We have an inexhaustible supply of funds and we have this paranormal power to control men in battle and this exclusive technology to see events beyond time and distance and project our will on those very events. Do you hear me?"

Randal fixed his glazed eyes on Frances. He nodded along with the rest of them.

"When I ask a question, your answer from now on will be 'Yes, ma'am.' Do you hear me?"

A scattered, muffled "Yes, ma'am" emitted from the indecisive listeners.

"I can't hear you," shouted Frances. "We will overcome our enemy, this Fly In The Ointment, do you understand?"

"YES, MA'AM," Randal heard the assembled group shout en masse.

"And we have something else, now," Frances said. "We have a very personal reason to be angry. This FITO has thwarted our efforts in Neddick, and they have dared to come into our house and cause devastating destruction."

She peered into the eyes of each executive and each squad leader in the room. She let the silence hang in the air. "Are you angry?"

"YES, MA'AM."

"Are you incensed?"

"YES, MA'AM."

"Are you enraged?"

"YES, MA'AM."

"Will you prepare our warriors for the next attack?"

"YES, MA'AM."

"Will you get them as raging mad as you are?"

"YES, MA'AM."

"Are we going to demolish our enemy?"

"YES, MA'AM."

"You better believe we will. Our purpose is righteous. Our nation needs us to be successful. The future of America is in our hands, and we must be victorious. Executive board and Andrew, remain in place. Squad leaders, you will be given new training schedules at zero five hundred tomorrow. When you wake up in the morning, you will wake up with strength and confidence. Do you understand?"

"YES, MA'AM."

"Dismissed."

The Directorate's squad leaders left the room. Randal and the other executives all gawked at Frances.

Randal Sanford nudged Romano Goldstein. "Where is our chairwoman getting all this Pattonlike command presence?"

"She's plugged in to the powers of darkness," said Romano.

Frances said, "All right, Andrew, let's have the battle plan for Target Two in Magnolia, Massachusetts."

"Let me begin with what I have seen and heard out on the ledges," Sandy said, opening the daily council of war in the loft of the barn. "Whereas previously our enemy has been able to shield their actions with a dome of telekinetic energy, that capability has been penetrated. I am now able to observe their preparations.

"What's the date today?" asked Sandy.

"October thirtieth," said Peter.

Sandy's emotions were conflicted about Peter's transformation from a brainy graduate student to a resourceful operations officer. He'd fine-tuned Task Force Saber's training plan specifically for their mission of ground defense, and he coordinated every activity and every resource for maximum efficiency. On one hand Sandy was amazed at the way he dove into his military assignment, on the other she worried about him losing ground in his progress toward a professorship at MIT.

Sandy assumed her role as the eyes and ears beyond the walls of Fortress Cielavista, and left the overall command of Task Force Saber forces to Carlos.

"Hank and his Special Operations buddies refer to this predawn time as 'zero-dark-thirty,'" Sandy said to the gathered warriors in Task Force Saber's ops center. "Right, Hank?"

Hank slouched in the outer ring of the group. He offered a slight grin, "Yeah. Sometimes it seemed funny. Sometimes it meant something else, you know. Something dark inside you."

Sandy had decided not to rebuke Hank for his rash tactical error—making an unauthorized raid on the enemy's encampment without angelic protection. What was done was done, and she needed to work together with her leaders to analyze their current threat situation and deal with it. She knew that her son, in his fragile emotional state, might buckle under the guilt of an indicting castigation and be rendered ineffective. And she needed every warrior in her fighting force to be at maximum effectiveness.

"Commander Carlos," Sandy said, "would you lead us in prayer?"

"Blessed be the Lord my rock," Carlos quoted Psalm 144, "who trains my hands for war, my fingers for battle; my lovingkindness, and my fortress, my stronghold and my deliverer, my shield and He in whom I take refuge.

"We come to you Lord as your humble servants, simple soldiers in your army and we take confidence that you have already given us the victory over your evil enemies. We ask, Lord, that you guide us and your heavenly angels in the battle to come. And when you destroy this enemy we will give you all the glory, Lord, because we know, this battle belongs to you and you will have your victory. Amen."

"AMEN," responded every voice in the room. The dogs gave a short bark and the two horses snorted their agreement.

"Thank you, Carlos," said Sandy. She launched into her intel briefing.

"In the two days since the Directorate's failed attack at our decoy location on Cape Neddick and the demolition of their training camp in Sandown, New Hampshire, their leaders have reorganized and increased their combat forces to one hundred-twenty fighting men. All huge, very strong, brutal killers.

"They have replaced their previous ground commander with a new man, Romano Goldstein."

Sandy noticed a startled look on Hank's face. What she did not know was that this same Doctor Goldstein was Hank's primary psychologist at the treatment center in Washington. Hank pulled out his cell phone and left the room.

She continued, "Goldstein is much more level-headed in his leadership of this demonic gang of barbarians than their previous commander. Their training has become much more organized and more focused on the specific objectives he has given to each of his subordinate units.

"In addition, they have developed a new weapons system. Still maintaining their principle of silent weaponry, they have come up with a rapid-fire, multiple launcher for their arrows and darts. Basically it's a system of tubes where hundreds of arrows are loaded into launchers powered by elastic bands made of some kind of polymer. They have a range of about a quarter mile, and I estimate that they can fire about a thousand of them at a time and reload in less than a minute. In addition, it looks like they're trying to develop a way to set the arrowheads on fire as they launch."

Hank had returned to the briefing room. He said, "Mom, when you're done, I may have some relevant information."

"Okay, Hank," said Sandy. "Now here is the enemy's attack plan. Peter?"

Peter passed out a one-page sheet to each warrior-leader in the room. He projected a map of Cielavista and the surrounding area on the screen. He said, "You can read the plan and direct your attention to this map as you read. Then we'll take questions when you're done."

As the leaders absorbed the details of the enemy's plan, Hank came to Sandy and told her that the commander of the Directorate's forces was his doctor at the Loving Center, Romano Goldstein.

"I thought that name sounded familiar," Sandy said, "but I couldn't place it. Okay, work up a profile on him and let me have it after this meeting. Thanks."

Peter's order described the enemy's plan. They would be organized into three sections: a fire support company that would soften Task Force Saber's defensive position with a barrage of fiery arrows; an attack force that would launch a ground attack on foot into fortress Cielavista; and the third company will remain in strategic reserve. The map on the screen animated the attack, and the precise tactics of Task Force Saber forces that would repel, delay, and if needed, evacuate Cielavista to the sea.

Sandy gave her subordinate commanders time to process the new information and said, "Commander Carlos will review our defensive operations. Carlos?"

"Force protection is our first priority, ladies and gentlemen warriors. We believe with God's help we can defend our position with no friendly casualties," he said. And he took the best part of an hour detailing every action of every Task Force Saber fighting unit.

After the briefing, Sandy asked Carlos and Hank to join her in her office in the loft of the barn.

"So what do we know about their commander, Romano Goldstein?" said Sandy.

Sandy sat at her cluttered desk, a door sitting on two sawhorses placed against the open-frame wall of the barn. She sat in a straight-back chair, with her right boot resting on her left knee. She was using her Kabar knife to dig the mud out of the sole of her boot.

"Doctor Goldstein conceals a ruthless monster under what appears to be a compassionate, intelligent phycologist," Hank said. "He's brilliant, you have to give him that, but the reason he has risen to the top of his profession and amassed such a huge fortune is that he has systematically removed anyone who would rival him or stand in his way."

"How did you figure out all this?" said Sandy.

"He uses some of his patients as—well, kinda like slaves, I guess. He had me and four of my fellow veterans on all kinds of drugs. I had a way of sneaking some of my pills into my pocket, so I could at least be halfway conscious in that place. So we would do all kinds of chores for him. You know, making copies, transcribing recordings, and other stuff."

Sandy watched Hank's eyes look downward to the floorboards. There was a long pause.

Carlos said, "Hank, what kind of stuff?"

"The five of us that he picked as his 'assistants'—we were all special operators. We all had a certain skill set, you know what I mean?

"We never really knew what was going on with these people that Goldstein had us soften up, but we did what he asked."

"Soften up?" asked his mother.

Hank stared at his mother through tears that began pooling in his eyes. He knew that revealing his moral wounds to her would break her heart, but he felt compelled to continue.

"Yeah," said Hank, "we—the five of us—had been involved in this type of work before. In Afghanistan we worked with a CIA cell that interrogated Taliban prisoners. The prison guards kept these guys isolated in deep holes in the ground two feet wide, two feet long, and eight feet deep. They played all kinds of loud music and crazy noises to keep them awake, starved them, and threw cold water on them. My job, along with these four other operators, was to rough them up before the interrogation sessions and afterward.

"Goldstein knew all about our backgrounds, and he used us on some of the patients at the Loving Center."

"My, God," said Sandy, "he's an animal."

"And then there was the stuff he was writing," said Hank. "This guy, this eminent doctor, was tied in with some of the most violent crime bosses in the world. I saw emails to Whitey Bulger's 'Winter Hill Gang' in Boston, the Russian mobsters in Atlanta and Kiev, and the Mafia in Sicily."

"Nobody knew about this guy's criminal activities?" said Carlos.

"I guess not," said Hank. "I mean my father is a data analyst for the FBI, and the doctor's name obviously never came up on his radar or he wouldn't have sent me to the Loving Center."

"We thought we were getting you the best care," said Sandy. "You would think with all Gabriella's special knowledge and our commitment to avoiding the evils of mainstream medicine we would have realized what we were getting you into.

"I am so sorry, dear Hank," Sandy said and she went to her son and held him in her arms.

After a long spell of tears and talk, the three stood and prayed together. Hank left Sandy's office to tend to the horses.

"You all right there, Mama?" said Carlos.

"No, but I'll get through it. Something else bothers me," Sandy said.

"What's that?"

"How did Goldstein and the staff at the Loving Center conceal their sick procedures from Gabriella and the rest of us? We are better than that. We have identified doctors and medical facilities that harm their patients with drugs and dangerous procedures, and charge obscene prices for them. We looked into the Loving Center, studied everything available about them and Doctor Goldstein, and all the information we got convinced us that the place was a holistic, healthy, healing place.

"Somehow they have succeeded in covering up what goes on there. And the same guy is commanding the forces attacking Cielavista."

"The Center was probably under the Directorate's security shield, wouldn't you say?" said Carlos.

Sandy nodded; the rage in her heart burned in her face.

CHAPTER THIRTY

Halloween traffic in the center of Salem, Massachusetts, was paralyzed. Out-of-state cars jammed the small parking lot behind Firdos' apartment building, so he had to park two miles away from the center of town and walk to his home. He hadn't visited his tiny room in over a month, and he needed to get some cold weather clothing and his mountain boots. He spent a few minutes scanning the *Salem News Online*. The headline read, "Salem's Population Swells from 46,000 to over 100,000." The subtitle boasted, "Witch City's Biggest Business Boon."

The paper listed all the "Festivals of the Dead" that attracted people from all over the country and abroad: "Nightly Seances by authentic Salem mediums, Speaking to the dead, with Salem's own official witch, Lady Crandall, Graveyard Tour with Conjurer, Seth Morris, Portals to the Spirit World with paranormal expert Eleanor Gilford, Witches' Halloween Ball, Death and Rebirth session with High Priestess Salome Wainwright, the Mourning Tea, the Dumb Supper: Dinner with the Dead, and on October 31st, Halloween Night, the Climactic, Salem Witches' Black Mass."

Firdos scoffed at the last line of the article, a quote from www.festivalofthedead.com, "Defying the boundaries of religion, culture, and continent, death captivates our imaginations and ensnares our minds, beckoning us to journey to destinations beyond the tattered shroud of mortality."

Firdos packed a few items in a backpack, slung it on one shoulder, and stepped out into the throngs of costumed people swarming the streets of Salem. His body quivered involuntarily as he walked through the crowds of possessed people, many of whom were warlocks and witches, giving off reflected spiritual energy from the gates of hell.

In the seven months that Firdos had developed as a seer for the Directorate under Carlene's supervision, he had refined his talents. He could mentally flick a switch, turning on or off his seer mode. When he turned it off, he would go about his business like any normal human, but when he turned it on he saw far beyond the physical world through a powerful paranormal lens.

He walked from his first floor apartment in the three-decker wood frame house on Jefferson Avenue, past the metal industrial buildings and parking lots where men were waving flags for motorists to buy parking spaces for ten dollars, to the downtown streets snarled with cars. Charter buses occupied most of the public parking lots in this congested center of Salem.

Firdos took notice of the sky. Even at noonday, a dark grey quilt of clouds obstructed the sunlight. To the naked eye the misty fog in town was natural, but to Firdos' supernatural eye the foglike mist was inhabited by hordes of microscopic unclean spirits.

At the corner of Front Street and Derby Square, where the mob of black-clad pedestrians was thickest, Firdos detected a singular column of clear light. He was just out of earshot of the man with the bullhorn who stood at the base of this refreshing beam. Stationed in a perimeter around the preacher stood a ring of helmeted policemen. Firdos was drawn to the power of the words radiating from the bullhorn. The man read from a thick black-covered book with gold leaf on the edges of the pages.

"Don't participate in the fruitless works of darkness, but instead expose them. For it is shameful even to mention what is done by them in secret," said the bearded man with the bullhorn.

Firdos' head was filled with static, distorting the words of the prophet. "Everything exposed by the light is made clear, for what makes everything clear is light. Therefore it is said: 'Get up, sleeper, and rise up from the dead, and the Messiah will shine on you.'"

Fear possessed Firdos' mind. Carlene's image swirled around in his garbled mental chaos.

"Pay careful attention, then, to how you walk—not as unwise people but as wise—making the most of the time, because the days are evil. So don't be foolish, but understand what the Lord's will is. And don't be drunk with wine, which leads to reckless actions, but be filled by the Spirit—Ephesian 5:11–18."

Firdos got sick and ran down a vacant alley where he vomited and shuddered in violent convulsions. He leaned against the brick wall of a building and looked down each end of the alley to see if anyone noticed him. At one end swirled the grey darkness. At the other end where the prophet was preaching, sharp beams of light pierced down the alley and struck Firdos in the heart. Eyes wide and mouth agape, he sprinted in panic toward the darkness where the screaming voices in his head calmed down and he escaped the discomfiting light.

He made his way through the crowds of revelers and devotees until he reached his car in the lot at the edge of Salem's city limits. He would never return.

Anna Stone pulled into the parking lot of her office in Sherwood, Arkansas, her tires squishing the shards of smashed pumpkins. She said a silent prayer thanking God that no other pre-Halloween vandalism had visited her building. Her cell phone rang as she walked through the waiting room to the kitchenette. Her phone identified the caller as Frances O'Donnelly.

"Hello, Frances," Anna said.

"Yes, Anna," Frances' voice was different—aggressive, angry, "I want to tell you I am on to your schemes, you wicked woman."

Anna was not surprised. She had known that her connection to this powerful woman was tenuous, and that Frances would, at some point, have to make a decision as to which spirit she would follow. Anna's inner voice had become very clear over the past months. It was informing Anna how to respond.

"'The path of the righteous is like the light of dawn, shining brighter and brighter until midday. But the way of the wicked is like the darkest gloom; they don't know what makes them stumble,'" Anna quoted from the Book of Proverbs.

Frances screamed, "Don't try that crap with me, you traitor. You hate your country and you have tried to infiltrate our ranks. You are a liar and a hypocrite. We are America's only hope out of all this chaos. We will lead the sheep into green pastures, not your weak emasculated excuse of a god."

"Good bye, Frances." Anna pressed the "end call" button on her phone, and she found herself involuntarily taking off her shoes and shaking the dirt off the soles into the waste basket.

Frances O'Donnelly continued her rant into her cell phone for several minutes, unaware that Anna had hung up. She was dressed in grey-green digital camouflage fatigues. A tactical holster strapped to her thigh hung from a black nylon belt. Frances wore the Glock 17 nine-millimeter pistol with the same ease that most women wore a scarf.

She paced back and forth in her office at the newly acquired Mountain Inn in the midst of the Pawtuckaway Forest, ten miles north of their former encampment at Zolino's Vineyard. The Vibram soles of her tan combat boots pounded the hardwood flooring.

"Can you hear me, you miserable whore?" Frances shouted. "Answer me, you ignorant tramp!" Spittle flew from her mouth. "Hello? Hello? You coward. You hung up on me. You will be sorry. I will deal with you soon, and it won't be pretty."

Then she realized she was yelling into a dead connection and that Romano Goldstein was observing her from the doorway of her office.

Frances hurled the phone at the nearest wall where it splintered into pieces.

"What do you want?" Frances said.

Romano cocked his head to the side and gave Frances a look that she took to be judgmental.

Frances felt him scolding her with his eyes, then he said, "Nice to see our chairwoman has it all together today. We are ready to move out to our assembly area in Massachusetts. When you come down from your tirade, you might wish to join the convoy."

"You're such a pompous jerk, Romano, you know that? Always the morally superior one, aren't you? Well, let me tell you something: if you had half the...."

Romano stepped close to Frances and grabbed her by the shoulders, "Get ahold of yourself, woman." He shook her violently. "This is no time for emotion. We all need cool heads. We demoted Randal for this very reason. Now Frances, look me in the eye."

Frances restrained herself. Her right hand was on the stock of her Glock, and she knew she could draw it, even with Romano's hand on her arm. Her chest was heaving. Whatever it was that had come over her was sifting away under the weight of Romano's calm authority.

"Okay, Romano, I got it. Get your hands off me."

Romano backed off. "The units have formed up in order of march. The convoy is ready to depart. You must address the fighters."

Frances walked down the long driveway alongside the line of vehicles. She had personally selected the cars and trucks they would use for the drive to their four assembly areas on Cape Ann. No two were alike. Frances had given them fifteen different routes to their assembly area. She had clothed her soldiers in casual civilian clothing, and she arranged each vehicle group to appear like families or students or workers.

As she passed the van driven by Randal Sanford, she caught the vicious sneer on his face. She had found it necessary, upon Randal's demotion to squad leader, to have Andrew reprogram his mind and create a veil of restraining energy around his body as a means of rendering him compliant to Frances' orders and instructions.

With bullhorn in hand, Frances mounted a boulder so all the drivers could see her. She readied herself to address the war party.

Frances was barely aware of the almost imperceptible humming noise that vibrated from Romano Goldstein's voice box. Unconsciously every member of the Directorate's attack force was humming one of the notes in the eerie chord designed by Goldstein to alter the state of the atmosphere around each vehicle and around their brains. Once the discordant notes began vibrating through the air, no one but Romano Goldstein and Andrew Johansen were aware of the noise.

"Soldiers of the Directorate," Frances addressed the convoy. "You are embarking on the most important battle in the history of the United States of America."

Her voice was not her own. It was empowered by a force beyond her control. Over the past few days, Frances allowed herself to become seduced by this strange dark force because it gave her the sense of fulfillment that neither Anna Stone's warmth nor the vodka could give her. Her new spiritual energy gave her the strength to assert herself over everyone. She was well aware of the commanding impact she was having on these men who were driving to their deaths.

"Failure is not an option. Your squad leaders will not hesitate to kill anyone who shows cowardice or reluctance in the attack. You will move forward into the enemy's defenses and drive them into the sea. They are vermin. They are subhuman. They are destroying America and they must be terminated. You are the instrument of the Directorate's wrath to exterminate this fly in the ointment."

Through the windshields of the vehicles near Frances, she could see the eyes of the soldiers bug out, their mouths and nostrils gaped open, entranced by the harsh dissonant harmonic that defied natural acoustics.

"You are no longer humans with natural emotions," Frances said. All of the former beauty of her face was contorted into a mask of raging fury. "You. Will. Obey. My. Commands."

Some of the soldiers were bleeding from their ears and noses.

"Repeat after me," said Frances, "I. Will. Obey."

And she kept up the chant as the company of robotic troglodytes chanted back in that eerie, piercing wail, "I. Will. Obey."

Then to Andrew, "Andrew, reduce the hypnotic chord to operational mode."

The enormous wormlike electromagnetic field around the convoy abated as the drivers started their engines. The soldiers recovered from the intense brain-numbing charge and they entered a relaxed mode, still quietly humming the notes of that horror-movie chord.

Frances' driver held her coat open and she slipped her arms through the sleeves and buttoned it over her military battle dress. She jumped into the command van. Andrew sat in the back, concentrating on his screens, viewing FITO's troop movements at Cielavista. The Directorate's attack force rumbled south through New Hampshire toward Cape Ann.

Henry gave Beto a gentle shove to wake him. "Coffee's on, buddy."

"What time is it?" said Beto, squirming out of his berth in the comfortable cabin of *Water Walker*.

"Zero-five-thirty. I'm going to put on a pot of oatmeal, okay?"

"Yeah, good," said Beto. He shoved his muscle-bound arms into the sleeves of his thick canvas jacket and clomped up the steps to the main deck.

Beto sipped the strong black coffee and looked out over Gloucester Bay. In a few minutes Henry joined him carrying the coffee pot and two bowls of oatmeal with raisins, almonds, and honey. He set them down on the table between the two swivel chairs in the helm and the two fishermen bowed their heads. Beto blessed the breakfast.

"What do you make of that weather pattern?" said Henry, looking out to the south.

"I know; strange, right?" said Beto. He gazed south at the predawn sky.

Henry said, "Those clouds slither around like a swarm of snakes. See how they churn around the full moon, blocking it out and then letting it shine through? Weird."

"Never seen anything like it," said Beto. "What's the Doppler Radar showing?"

Henry scrolled the computer screen to the weather mode and focused in on the shoreline to their south.

"Look. A tight, local weather system hangs steady over the city of Salem. The movement of the pattern is violent, flaring out in all directions like rays of some kind of ionic energy," said Henry.

"What are you planning for today?" asked Beto.

"Well, we need fuel, so we'll run over to Rose's Marine at seven when they open. I'd like to have them look at *Water Walker's* prop too. We may have nicked it when we hit that driftwood yesterday. Probably get underway around—what ?— noon or so."

Beto checked the fishing report, "They say they're getting yellowfin and bluefin out in the deep waters.

"Small craft warnings later today," Beto clicked over to the marine weather website. He read, "In effect 5:00 p.m. EST this evening. Southwest winds 20 to 30 knots, gusts up to 40. Seas 2 to 5 feet."

"So what do you think, Beto?"

"This trawler is made to take those big waves, so I say go for it," he said.

"We got a plan then," said Henry.

Over the rim of his coffee mug Beto looked at Henry's eyes. Henry caught him staring at him.

"What?" said Henry.

"Nothing, amigo, nothing," Beto said. "I'm loving this new Captain Courageous I'm fishing with. The old Henry I once knew and loved would have left the boat at the mooring and headed for the high ground in weather like this. Believe me, I'm not complaining. Those tuna are hungry and we have plenty of bait. Let's get this baby fueled up and serviced and head out."

Henry took their bowls and spoons to the galley, threw them in the sink, and left them there.

Chapter Thirty-One

Sandy began the battle briefing with prayer. "Heavenly Father, we thank you for leading us in all our preparations for this battle against your enemy. We thank you for providing us with these angelic warriors to protect us from evil forces in the heavens. We are Task Force Saber. We belong to you. Amen"

"Amen," echoed the assembled warriors in the briefing room of the barn. Every leader and every warrior was present for the battle briefing except those manning the observation and listening posts on Cielavista's perimeter.

"Each of our commanders will brief his portion of the operation," said Sandy. "But first I want to tell you how impressed I am with you. Our American colonial minutemen would be proud of you. I know that God's grace has empowered you all to band together against our evil enemy. I thank God for your humble obedience to his commands.

"Commander Carlos, begin the tactical review of our mission."

Sandy was so familiar with the war plan she hardly heard Carlos' words. She had combed over every detail, refining, rehearsing, assembling all the resources. She knew precisely what each subordinate unit was going to do every second of the battle. Still she agonized over lethal violence looming on the horizon.

She stood against the wall of the barn, arms crossed over her chest, one boot cocked against the wall. She disengaged her overextended mind from the battle ahead. In these rare retreats from her mental immersion in the battle plan, she felt like an underwater swimmer breaking the surface and filling her lungs with fresh air.

Sandy's mind wavered. She savored her newly found powers of prophesy and telekinesis, but she worried about Gabriella. She admired Carlos' amazing ability to train a family of landscapers into a crack fighting force, but she struggled with Hank's erratic behavior. She relished her role as the senior leader of Task Force Saber, but her heart ached at her separation from Henry. Even as she watched Henry and Beto on Gabriella's sky screen defeat the Directorate's amphibious attack at the Nubble Lighthouse, she craved her husband's presence.

Sandy tuned in to the battle briefing.

Carlos carefully presented the scheme of maneuver. "Anvil-Alpha will take your positions on the perimeter and engage the enemy as he approaches. You will be prepared to fall back to your prepared positions in phases, taking advantage of our natural terrain features." Carlos pointed to the gravel road that followed the valley through the center of Cielavista.

"Striker-Charlie, you will attack the enemy force as it breaches our perimeter, here," Carlos pointed to a section of the perimeter's defensive line. "Conduct an orderly retreat back down the prearranged route, drawing the enemy into our trap.

"Anvil-Bravo, you will occupy these positions at the rear of Cielavista on the ledges overlooking the ocean. You will hold the enemy in place until I give the order to evacuate.

"Striker-Delta, you will take up your ambush positions here," Carlos pointed to the heights on both sides of the valley. After you let Striker-Charlie deploy past you to their ambush position, you will rain down the wrath of God on the enemy with maximum explosives and firepower.

"This is the primary kill zone." Carlos pointed to the section of the valley that had once been his prized flower garden. "The enemy attack force will be trapped on four sides. I estimate that by the time they reach the kill zone, we will have reduced their numbers by fifty percent.

"The battle here will be violent. At my command, we will conduct an orderly exfiltration of the battle zone."

A new image came up on the screen. Carlos pointed out the four escape routes down the ledges to small craft moored at the base of the cliff.

"You all have rehearsed our evacuation procedures, and you all know which set of ropes you have been assigned. As soon as each boat is full, it will take off to the rally point two miles north on the coast.

"God is for us. Who can be against us?" Carlos said and he passed the pointer to Roberto, Commander of Company Anvil.

Sandy's hand fell on Cinnamon's nose as the faithful pony nuzzled her side. She looked over at Hank who sat on the barn floor with the Australian Shepherd across his lap, the Bull Terrier under his arm, and the two Wolfhounds at his feet. He was unconsciously stroking the thick white hair on John's broad chest. His eyes were glazed over. Sandy knew he was far away from the briefing room. Her feelings of helplessness gnawed at her heart.

She shook herself back into the job at hand. The briefing was over. They were all looking at her. Carlos had called on her to pray. She didn't know what to say, so she repeated the warrior's psalm.

"Blessed be the Lord my rock, who trains my hands for war, my fingers for battle; my lovingkindness and my fortress, my stronghold and my deliverer, my shield and He in whom I take refuge, who subdues my people under me."

They all looked into her eyes and she looked back into theirs. "A sword for the Lord and for Gabriella," she said.

"A sword for the Lord and for Gabriella," they repeated.

Behind the wheel of the sixteen-passenger Mercedes van with smoked side windows, Carlene drove to their assembly area. Firdos sat next to her, studying the GPS map on his mobile phone. Twelve large infantrymen sat in the rear, all stoned on Romano Goldstein's pharmaceutical cocktail.

"How you doing there, Firdos?" said Carlene. She glanced at her faithful disciple's unreadable face.

Firdos kept his eyes on his small screen, but his mind chased off in another new direction. He contemplated the implication—that for the first time in his life someone seemed to care about how he was doing. His obsession with this woman swelled up inside him. His imagination took him to scenes with her that sent him into fits of arousal he could not control. Now he perceived something deeper.

"Fine, I guess," he said. "Do you care?"

It was a blunt, simple question, but Carlene had connived every step of her control over her emotionally impaired pawn.

"I am pleased with your performance, Firdos," she said. "You have proven very useful in your role as a seer. Now we expect you to lead troops in combat. I want to know how confident you are in that role."

"I will do anything you ask of me to the utmost of my ability," Firdos said.

"What more could we expect of you?" said Carlene. "Now give me a detailed briefing on what you are going to do in this attack."

Firdos turned to face Carlene. He recited his part of the attack plan in the same digital tone as a recording device. "I exit this van in the field where we park and inspect my men to make sure their weapons are loaded and their arrows are properly secured for easy reloading. Before we leave the field, I make them repeat their instructions to me.

"We take the dirt road from the field to our position at the attack site. My squad will be in the center of the line of attack in the woods on the opposite side of the road from the entrance to FITO's encampment."

Carlene interrupted his recitation, "What are these FITOs?"

"They are insects that must be crushed," Firdos recited. "They have no business taking up the air they breathe, the food they devour, or the space they inhabit. Those filthy worms have infected the noble efforts of the Directorate. We will annihilate these foul cockroaches tomorrow on Halloween."

Firdos looked to Carlene for approval.

"Well done, Firdos," said Carlene, "now continue."

The diagram of the objective appeared in Firdos' mind—a mile wide and a mile deep, mostly thick forest, with the estate at the far end near the cliff overlooking the ocean. Firdos could envision the symbol on the battle map signifying his squad at the head of the attack force. Alpha Company had the sector to his left and Charlie Company had the sector to his right.

"My squad is Bravo Company's lead element of the center sector," Firdos said. "The bell at Saint James Episcopal Church will strike twelve times. At the first toll our artillery begins their barrage. At the third toll my squad advances across the road and charges into the enemy's perimeter. We will engage their defenses and kill them until we reach the cliff where we will consolidate with our adjacent units and secure the objective. No prisoners. We kill them all."

"What else?" Carlene said.

Firdos looked out the windshield. The vanilla fragrance from Carlene's perfume warmed his chest. "The first man in my squad to hesitate in our attack I will kill," Firdos said.

Carlene knew Firdos and his squad had no chance of survival. She looked over at him the same way that a farmer would look at the next pig to slaughter.

Carlene had come a long way under the tutelage of Romano Goldstein. He taught her how to steel her mind against all emotions for the good of the Directorate's cause and the future of America. She learned how to use all the psychological tools the doctor had given her: subterfuge, false encouragement, phony affection, threats, guilt and many more, with one purpose—to mold her seers and operators into killing machines.

"Okay, Firdos, take a nap. We'll be on the road for a while yet."

The young Iranian closed his eyes and slept for the last time.

Sandy selected three young athletes to run messages from her ledge to the command post on the cliff. In Cielavista's mansion, she helped them pack backpacks for the long, boring hours they would spend out there on the rocky neck. In Althea's pack she jammed a down-filled sleeping bag. On the top of Sam's pack she strapped a small nylon tent.

Sandy took Brian aside and showed him the Beretta nine-millimeter pistol. "You know how to use this, right, Brian?"

"Yes, ma'am. I'm one of Commander Roberto's best marksmen."

"Right, that's what I heard. Here's the holster and the magazine pouch." The fourteen-year-old was almost as tall as Sandy. She looked into Brian's eyes. He nodded, pulled off his belt, and attached the weapon and extra magazines.

Then Sandy heard something in the parlor. This sound was important—not sure why, but she just had to investigate.

"What is that?" Sandy asked Althea.

"My silly cousin trying to play the guitar," said Althea.

Sandy walked into the parlor where Frederick was sitting with a guitar across his lap, and one of his granddaughters was struggling as she tried to stretch her little fingers to the right position on the fretboard of her guitar. When she strummed, a strange combination of notes vibrated from the sound hole. Frederick reached over and placed her fingertips where they were supposed to go and she strummed a pleasant, familiar chord.

"Frederick, who is this little musician?" said Sandy.

"This is Ramona," said Frederick. "She and her mother came back to Cielavista to get Ramona's guitar. She forgot it. They tell me she's one of my granddaughters, but I think she's a freeloader that walked in off the street."

The little one gave her grandfather a kick.

Sandy squatted down and smiled at Ramona. "Frederick, the weird-sounding chord Ramona strummed. What was that?"

"It was a mistake, Sandy," said Frederick. "The heavy metal rockers use it a lot. In music theory it's called a discordant. Kind of a spooky, scary sound, huh?"

"So," said Sandy, "would you play it?"

When he strummed the strings, an unpleasant, disharmonious combination of notes came out.

"Then when I drop the E on the fourth string down to a D#, it gets even weirder," and he strummed that combination of E-D#-A#-B.

"Kinda leaves you hanging," said Frederick. Ramona put her little hands over her ears.

"Downright ugly, I'd say," said Sandy. "Okay, thanks. Sorry for the interruption, Ramona. So long."

Sandy turned to Brian, Sam, and Althea and said, "Let's go, my intrepid messengers, we have work to do out on the ledges."

Chapter Thirty-Two

When Sandy and her three young runners reached the ledge, they looked down at the crevice that would separate them from Sandy's prophecy post. Waves crashed through the rocky chasm, shooting up jets of white spray dowsing the youngsters with saltwater.

"Set up your tent back over there, troopers," said Sandy. "You have to be within earshot of me at all times. Your mission here is crucial to our victory in this battle." She was impressed with the young soldiers' demeanor as they stood, heads up and attentive in the early morning wind and spray.

"Set up a watch rotation. I suggest you rotate every hour, two at the most. When I receive a message for the battle commanders, I will jump across and dictate it to whichever one of you is on watch. You will write it down in your notebook and run it up to the command post. Got it?"

All three nodded.

"Okay, now I want all of you to take three practice runs up the rocks to that spot on the heights. Put your packs down." They set their backpacks down, away from the mist spurting up from the crevice, and got ready to climb.

"Now, troopers, listen to me. Safety is more important than speed. Climb quickly and carefully. Ready?"

Brian, Sam, and Althea looked up the cliff and studied the course they would climb from rock to rock. They each looked to Sandy and gave her a sober nod.

"Go ahead," Sandy said softly.

Brian took the lead. They bounded from rock to ledge, scrambled over the slippery, wet stones, and on the final climb up the steep slope to the top of the cliff, they found handholds and footholds. At the lip of the rock they pulled their upper bodies over and rolled up to the top. They turned around and saluted Sandy.

They chose a different way down, making use of the stairlike path that Gabriella and Sandy used. They leaped down like mountain goats. Twice more, the runners practiced their run. Sandy was amazed that none of them was out of breath. *The vitality of youth,* she thought.

As they pitched their tent and planned their watch schedule, Sandy took her leap over the crevice. The three young soldiers watched her jump. They looked at each other.

"Not sure how she did that," said Sam, "but I'm glad we don't have to make that jump."

The first hint of sunlight seeped through the fog and drizzle. The orange-grey granite ledge was slick with a layer of rain and seawater. Sandy sailed over the chasm to her three messengers. They were squatting by the gas stove warming a pot of instant coffee.

"You're up first, right, Althea?" said Sandy.

"Yes, ma'am."

"Where's your notebook?" Sandy said sternly.

As Althea dug her small spiral notebook and pen out of her pack, Sandy said, "You all need to be ready for me," Sandy instructed the runners.

"When I have a word for my commanders, every second counts. I never want to have to wait for any of you again, you understand?"

The three were all standing at attention. "Yes, ma'am."

Althea took down Sandy's message. "This goes to Commander Carlos," said Sandy.

Althea ran up the cliff and gave the note to Carlos in the command post in the barn. The room was a flurry of orderly activity. Carlos took the note, read it, and called to his wife.

"This is urgent, Yolanda," Carlos said. "Please take care of it right now."

Yolanda read the note aloud, "Purchase one hundred harmonicas in the key of C. Distribute them to all battle commanders and have them issue one to each warrior. At my command they will blow them."

Yolanda gave Carlos a quick skeptical look, and he just said, "Now, dear."

In the sky over Cielavista, Michael held a war council with his angelic host.

"Joseph and Thomas, I commend you for your actions at the Directorate's meeting at the Canyon Ranch. It's good to have you back in your spiritual form again. Those human bodies get cumbersome, don't they?"

"Yes," said Thomas, "but sometimes it's fun to put them on. Keeps you in touch with how difficult it is to operate in the flesh."

"Right," said Michael. "Now we have a split mission over the next thirty-six hours.

"This demon-possessed Directorate army will attack our earthly allies at midnight on All Hallows Eve. Satan's forces are aligned as usual, with their rulers at the top of the food chain, authorities having command over battalions, and their subordinate companies divided up between the spiritual forces in the heavens and the dark powers down on the world plane. Nothing new there.

"A demonic battalion will take charge of the Black Mass in Salem, scheduled for Midnight to 3:00 a.m. October thirty-first.

"A second battalion of dark world powers has possessed the barbarian monsters in the Directorate's attack force.

"So our primary target for the first three hours of the battle will be the demons in Salem. They will want to slip over to Cielavista and join forces with the hellions in the battle against Task Force Saber. We have to stop them.

"Thomas and Joe, you take four fighters to assist Task Force Saber. I will command the main body against the demoniacs in the skies over Salem. We will remain in that battle until well after daylight. At some point, my team will break off from the satanic worship in Salem and redeploy in support of your force, Thomas.

"Tobias, you stick with Henry and Beto in the boat. They will be critical in the extraction phase of Task Force Saber's battle plan."

When Michael was done, all the angelic warriors waited in silence. A voice like the sound of tons of water cascading over a towering waterfall boomed from all directions around them. "Bring me another victory."

"That's it for the bluefin," said Beto. "We only get one each."

"How about pollack and haddock? We got a bunch of those," said Henry.

"No limit," said Beto, holding the bluefin tuna on their measuring tape. "Fifty-two inches," he said.

"Nice," said Henry, wiping the mist off his face with his blue bandana.

"Gloomy grey," he said, searching for the horizon.

"I know," said Beto. "We got about a quarter mile visibility. Where are we, anyway?"

Henry went to the helm and checked the radar and the GPS. "We're five and a half miles due east of Marblehead," he said.

"Why don't we just head in to Marblehead? We could have lunch there at the Landing," said Beto.

"What, you don't like my cooking?" said Henry.

"Can you do fried Ipswich clams, lobster bisque, and an Irish espresso?"

"Twisted my arm, Beto. Pull in the lines. I'm getting depressed out here in this dreary soup, anyway."

As they approached Marblehead Neck, Beto pointed at the blurry horizon. The windshield wipers swatted away the film. "What the heck is that?"

"Same weird, dark weather pattern we saw yesterday," said Henry.

Henry strained his eyes through the murky clouds over the Massachusetts coast. His gut churned as he watched the shimmering mass of black air erupt with short bursts of blue lightning. Henry consulted his GPS and expanded the range of the image.

"That thing is hanging over Salem," Henry said.

"That ain't normal," said Beto. "That's demonic activity for sure."

As they pulled into Marblehead Harbor and eased into the slip by the Landing Restaurant, Henry noticed the mask of concern on Beto's face.

After they secured the trawler to the slip, Henry said, "Hey, brother, let's go below and have a few minutes of prayer. How about it?"

———

Squad leader Alexandrea Santiago stopped her golf cart behind Antonio and Jacob's foxhole on Cielavista's perimeter. The infantrymen had constructed their fighting position according to the instructions in the Ranger Handbook, giving them fields of fire to their front in a 180-degree fan. They were concealed and covered overhead with a thick earthen roof. Alexandrea had to low-crawl on her belly to deliver the two lunch boxes to her warriors.

She stuck her head into the back of the foxhole and said, "Hey, heroes, lunchtime."

She watched her squad members open the boxes, take out the sandwiches, and pull out the little plastic box underneath. Jacob opened his up and waved the silver harmonica back at Alexandrea. He didn't say anything, just looked at her. Antonio pulled his harmonica out of his lunch box and blew into it. The same sound was coming from the fighting positions to his left and right. He shrugged and raised his eyebrows at his squad leader.

"Don't ask me, but keep them handy. That's all I know. When I give you the order, blow into them."

Jacob said, "Like the Israelites blowing the trumpets at Jericho?"

"You got me," said Alexandrea. "How many rounds of ammo you got?"

Each man had an M249 SAW light machine gun, an M4 Carbine, and a Beretta nine-millimeter sidearm. "We each have two thousand rounds for the SAWs. Our M4's have a hundred and twenty rounds, four thirty-round mags each."

"Right," said Alexandrea. "Well, eat up and keep those harmonicas handy. You know where I am if you need me." She crawled back to her golf cart and motored to her next pair of fighters on the perimeter.

Frances O'Donnelly sat between Romano Goldstein and Andrew Johansen in the mobile operations center in the extended Mercedes Sprinter Van outfitted with three disk antennas, an external generator, and enough electronic equipment in the cabin to rival a field marshal's command post in modern warfare.

On one HD screen, Frances observed the troop positions of their enemy, FITO, in their location on the coast near Magnolia, Massachusetts. On two other screens she viewed her troops moving into their attack positions in the woods and fields across the narrow road from the estate listed on their map as Cielavista.

She was unaware of the permanent sneer on her lips. Her eyes flicked back and forth from screen to screen and to the rapid keystroking of Andrew's fingers. Her mind was quickly absorbing every detail of her army's movements.

"Andrew, when we get done with this attack would you do me a small favor?" Romano said.

"I doubt it," Andrew said. "What?"

"You really need to take a long shower and change those filthy clothes. The odor coming off your body sickens me."

"Why don't you just get out of my van?" Andrew said.

Romano Goldstein said, "Andrew, behave."

Andrew's head and shoulders shivered and blinked away the tears that welled up in his eyes. "I'm sorry, Doctor Goldstein, for being disrespectful. I will definitely bathe and put on new clothes as soon as we have won this battle."

Frances looked from Romano to Andrew and back. Romano had obviously found a way to hypnotize their operations officer.

"I'm surprised that we haven't encountered enemy skirmishers or scouts. Some of our units are less than a mile from their perimeter. I expected some initial resistance at this point," said Frances.

"They can't see us," said Romano.

"All units in place," said Andrew.

"Can't see us?" said Frances. "These people see activity thousands of miles away. Why can't they see us, so close to their home base?"

"Andrew and I have synthesized two rather remarkable technologies that will revolutionize the way the Directorate does business. We have made ourselves invisible."

"Really." Frances glared at Goldstein's air of superiority.

"For some years now I have been experimenting with the science of dissonant musical theory to resonate forcefields of vibrating ions. Andrew here has discovered that he can magnify this vibrating ionic field in such a way to create a cloud of energy around our forces that renders us invisible."

"So that's why we hum," said Frances through her sneer.

Frances' hand thrust upward and grasped Romano's throat, shutting off his windpipe in a powerful grip. "Never do anything like that without my permission, Goldstein, do you hear me? I am the chairman of this Directorate. Nothing happens in this organization without my knowledge."

Doctor Goldstein's face turned blue. He passed out and fell from Frances' grip.

"That goes for you too, you filthy swine," and she drew her pistol and whacked Andrew across the back of his skull, opening a wide cut beneath his greasy hair. He fell forward onto the console in front of him and grabbed the painful wound on his head. Blood seeped through his fingers.

"Get something to stop that mess," Frances said. "And get this garbage up off my floor. I just relieved Goldstein of command. I'm in command now."

Andrew's mouth hung open, pain in his eyes. "What has happened to you?"

"Do what you're told, maggot."

Frances' body swelled with an infusion of fiendish power. Her arm muscles swelled and her shoulders broadened, straining the seams of her uniform shirt. She took Andrew's seat at the keyboard while Andrew looked for a rag to bandage his head wound.

At 1:00 p.m. her attack force was in place, waiting for the bell at St. James Church to toll midnight of All Hallows Eve.

At the famous Landing Restaurant in Marblehead, Henry and Beto were polishing off a bottle of Sauvignon Blanc.

"We're not far from Cielavista, amigo. What do you think? Wanna give these fish a rest?" Roberto said.

Henry had not shaved in four days. Little flecks of lunch decorated his salt-and-pepper stubble. "This little fishing trip has been good for me, my friend."

"Yeah, I think you've loosened up a bit, Henry. You know, you haven't flown off the handle for several days, now. Maybe you can even put up with those two crazy women who never know what's coming next."

"Right now, Beto, all I want is to lie down on my berth in the *Water Walker* and let her rock me to sleep."

"Then what, Henry?"

"Then we'll surprise my dear wife with a sailor's homecoming."

When Henry woke up it was dark and cold. He rolled out of his berth and prepared to shove off from Marblehead Harbor to Cielavista. He took a shower in the head, put on warm dry clothes, and looked in the mirror. He decided to keep his scraggly stubble.

CHAPTER THIRTY-THREE

Sandy found comfort with Carlos' standing next to her on the granite outcropping below Cielavista. The runners had carried kindling and logs down from the cliff top, and they were sitting around a nice low fire.

"You know," said Carlos, "when the night is flat black like this, you can't see anything. No horizon, no sky, no sea, no nada. These invisible nights deepen the silence."

"Hmm," said Sandy, looking out at the nothingness. A huge, infinite nothing. Not the claustrophobic darkness of a cave, but a sacred void without dimensions.

"Out here this huge blackness is like a gulf that goes on forever with no sign of light or life or substance," she said.

Sandy felt Carlos's shoulder lean gently against hers—sharing the overpowering stillness.

"When are they coming?" Carlos asked.

"I haven't been able to see them. Ever since they departed the Mountain Inn in New Hampshire, they disappeared from my view. Gabriella would be able to see them. She's out there somewhere in that emptiness. Inside my heart, Carlos, that's what it's like without her. A big black nothingness."

Carlos asked again, "When are they coming?"

Sandy leaned away from him.

"If I were to hazard a guess, I would say tonight. They have had time to prepare for an attack. They are bristling from their failure at the Nubble Light and having their base camp blown up. Even the fact that they disappeared from my telepathic view indicates that they have probably moved down here near us."

"The sooner, the better," said Carlos.

"Why's that?"

"In a defensive position, sitting in a foxhole and waiting for an enemy attack is the worst. Waiting is harder than fighting. Our warriors are tough, but if we had to wait in this posture for weeks, we would lose our vigilance."

"Well, I think they're coming tonight and our battle will take place on All Hallows Eve," Sandy said. She gazed out into the black, empty void.

Hank rode Sadie along the perimeter with all four dogs trotting around the horse's hooves. He stopped and dismounted at each Claymore antipersonnel mine to check their deployment.

"Stay behind me," he told the dogs. "These are called Claymore Mines, named after a Scottish sword. I've got them deployed with trip wires, so when the enemy approaches our positions our soldiers will be protected. Each one of these babies has seven hundred steel balls that fire out in a sixty-degree arc for fifty meters. It's like having seven hundred riflemen added to each fighting position."

Hank looked back at the dogs who were all sticking their muzzles into the opening of the fighting position behind Hank. Two gloved hands were reaching out through the gun port to pet the curious animals.

"Thanks, Hank," Antonio said. "That'll slow 'em down."

"Okay," Hank said. "Let's go, pups, we have twenty more of these Scottish swords to check. Remember: stay with me and do not go out beyond the perimeter."

Hank led Sadie back behind Antonio and Jacob's foxhole and the dogs sniffed along behind the horse.

Carlos studied the large wall-mounted satellite image of Cielavista, once the object of his passion as a landscape architect, now an armed encampment. Peter had superimposed military map symbols on the image. The perimeter was divided into three sections, and each section had six fighting positions, designated by a small rectangle with a fan-shape facing outward—their fields of fire. These fans overlapped from one fighting position to the other all along the defensive crescent.

"Excellent detail, Peter," said Carlos. "I see you have posted each soldier's range card under every fighting position on your schematic."

The cards were marked with exact ranges to every significant terrain feature in their range fan. The locations of each Claymore mine was marked there too, with smaller fans spreading outward, showing the killing zones of these antipersonnel mines.

"What's this?" asked Peter, looking down on Carlos' uncluttered table.

"My father gave me this," Carlos said. "General George S. Patton sent these out to all the soldiers in his Third Army as a Christmas card in 1944."

Carlos read the card, "'Almighty and most merciful Father, we humbly beseech Thee, of Thy great goodness, to restrain these immoderate rains with which we have had to contend. Grant us fair weather for Battle. Graciously hearken to us as soldiers who call on Thee that, armed with Thy power, we may advance from victory to victory, and crush the oppression and wickedness of our enemies, and establish Thy justice among men and nations. Amen.'

"Then on the same card," said Carlos, "see here, Peter? 'Headquarters Third United States Army. To each officer and soldier in the Third United States Army, I wish a Merry Christmas. I have full confidence in your courage, devotion to duty, and skill in battle. We march in our might to complete victory. May God's blessings rest upon each of you on this Christmas Day.'

"Then here— Patton's signature."

"Wow," said Peter, "back in those days, generals could actually invoke the name of God and publish it."

"Yeah, Peter. We could use some fair weather for battle. This nasty drizzle and overcast sky favors the enemy, gives him concealment and cover, and makes our troops cold and miserable."

"Well, let's pray, Uncle."

The afternoon sun was powerless against the steel-grey lid clamped over coastal New England. Carlos and Peter went to the back of the barn's loft and looked out over the cliff to the dreary sky and churning black waves. "Lord Jesus, our Savior, we ask you to move this weather out to the sea and give us clear skies for the battle tonight. Amen."

The two men walked outside to the edge of the cliff. They looked down at Sandy, standing hatless with her face to the wind. On the near side of the crevice they noticed the little orange nylon tent with a glowing campfire in front of it. Sandy performed one of her impossible leaps across the wide space and stood next to Brian. He was rapidly writing a message in his notebook. She gave Brian a punch in his shoulder and he took off up the cliff. In three minutes he stood dripping wet in front of Carlos and Peter. They took Brian to the ops center and gave him a cup of soup while he waited for their response.

"When the St. James church bell strikes the sixth toll at midnight, every Task Force Saber warrior will blow their harmonicas," Carlos read the note and looked at Peter.

Peter just shrugged. He called one of the ops center runners and told him to deliver the word verbally to each company commander for immediate distribution to all Task Force Saber personnel.

Brian waited for Carlos to write his message for delivery back to Sandy. Carlos wrote, "Sandy, we need clear weather for battle." Brian left the barn. Ten minutes later Carlos and Peter looked out the loft window and saw a thin line of bright blue open up under the clouds on the horizon.

"Have the kitchen prepare enough rations for the fighters on the perimeter to last them twenty-four hours," Carlos told Peter. "That means tonight's dinner, some nuts and fruit to sustain them through the night, something for breakfast and lunch tomorrow. We won't resupply them with anything but ammo until after midnight tomorrow, maybe later."

"Always thinking of your warriors," said Peter as he wrote out the order for a runner to deliver it to the kitchen.

"Get them into position," said Director Goldstein. Andrew relayed the message to each platoon leader via telepathy. "I thought you had created cloud cover and rain," he said.

"I did," said Andrew. "Seems that the weather is one thing that is more responsive to FITO's cockroaches than my atmospheric instruments. Their local energy force pushed my weather system off to the east."

They looked out the windows of the van. The starlit night was crystal clear. The belly of a half-moon hung over the treetops in the east. "That's not good," said Goldstein.

Frances' voice had morphed into a low, angry growl. "I will not tolerate any negativity in my command center." Goldstein flinched. What unnerved him wasn't so much Frances' words or even her tone: it was the force of manifest evil that inhabited her foul breath. These men, who had been at the source of thousands of killings and innumerable atrocities, had never encountered the level of Satanic presence that possessed their chairwoman.

"Victory is ours," said Romano with as much enthusiasm as he could muster.

In the screen above Andrew's keyboard, they watched their forces spread out along the road at the edge of Cielavista. "We're still invisible," said Romano. "Our umbrella of dissonant energy conceals our soldiers."

"Show me the artillery," said Frances.

Andrew toggled one of his joysticks controlling their satellite camera until the screen showed the artillery emplacements. He thumbed the button on the controller to enlarge their view of the three batteries of dart launchers.

"What's their signal for firing?" asked the chairwoman.

"The first toll of the midnight bell," said Romano.

"And the signal for our units to attack?"

"Third toll, Madam Chairwoman," Romano said. "At that signal, the artillery will shift their fire fifty meters deeper into the target, launch eight volleys, then hold fire until Carlene calls for targets of opportunity."

Unconsciously, the eerie chord breathed out from their mouths. Barely audible—Romano hummed the low E, Andrew the D#, and Frances the A#. On the roof of the Mercedes van sat three grinning demons humming the same notes in an upper register. The three Directorate leaders waited in that dark trance while the clock on the wall above the screen ticked off the minutes.

The half-moon slid upward.

The bell in the tower of St. James Episcopal Church sounded the first toll of midnight, ringing in All Hallow's Evening.

Antonio and Jacob leaned forward against the earthen wall of their fighting position, eyes scanning the woods to their front.

Jacob reached for his vibrating cell phone. He read the text, "A, S, F, T, L, A, F, G. A sword for the Lord and for Gabriella. The enemy is here. Take courage, my brother."

The first toll of the church bell rang out and they heard a loud pattering on the thick roof of their foxhole.

"Enemy fire arrows," said Jacob.

Two more tolls of the bell and they heard the heavy crunch of footsteps tromping toward them.

"Where are they?" said Jacob.

"Harmonicas," said Antonio.

The moment the sixth toll sounded, the notes of the C major scale rang out along the Saber's perimeter. The attackers suddenly became visible—massive, robotic brutes steadily advancing with a discordant humming noise.

"So that's what these are for," said Antonio. "Now we can see the enemy!"

Seconds later the four Claymores covering their front exploded and twelve large bodies flew upwards and backwards, limbs windmilling and dismembering in the flash. Leaves and twigs flew into Antonio and Jacob's goggles from the back-blast. They watched their sector for targets. The battle was on.

CHAPTER THIRTY-FOUR

"So much for your musical umbrella, you idiots," said Frances. Romano and Andrew braced for Frances' next strike. "Our entire first wave is down, wounded or dead. Look at this."

The attacking horde became a chaotic herd. The Directorate soldiers milled around, bumping into each other. Squad leaders screamed and fired their pistols at their men.

Romano grabbed the radio microphone, "Fall back to your attack positions and regroup. Cease firing. Fall back."

"You timid weakling," said Frances, her mouth so close to Romano her spittle sprayed into his ear. "Attack. I say attack!"

Romano held up his hand and said, "Yes, Commander, most respectfully. We need to start over. I will be back."

"Andrew, tell the squad leaders to assemble in the cemetery," said Romano.

Romano left the van and jogged over to the Directorate's original assembly area. When the leaders arrived, he reinforced his discordant humE2` and they hypnotically joined him. They were rattled and horrified.

"My dear children," Romano said calmly, "you have done well. Victory is now ours."

Entranced, the seven unit leaders stared blankly at their commander.

"Your soldiers will follow you on this next attack. Firdos, your squad will combine with Carlene's." Romano reorganized the order of battle and formed six squads from the remnants of the original seven. He dictated a new attack order to his forces when a flash of heat scorched his back.

He turned around, raised his forearm to protect his eyes, and there was Frances. Hovering over her head were six horrific beings, glowing orange and red. From their mouths a fetid odor belched out, and putrid gobs of sludge dribbled down their hairy chests.

"Enough, Romano," Frances said. A deeply hoarse male voice oozed from her snarling mouth. "You will now lead the third squad. I have taken command."

Frances' feet were off the ground. Her body drifted back over the grave markers. The humming grew louder and more heinous.

"Follow me," Frances said and she glided forward to the cemetery wall. The squad leaders lined up behind her.

"Forces of the directorate fall in," she bellowed.

The demons swirled out over the quivering crowd of barbaric fighters and herded them into the graveyard.

"Form this mob into their ranks," ordered Frances.

The squad leaders quickly gathered their charges and lined them up in six separate formations. Each squad had six ranks of eleven men in each rank. The artillerymen—twenty strong—formed another platoon behind the six squads.

Frances hovered in front of a black marble monument. The six demons swooped around the formation.

"Executives," Frances called, "come over here."

Romano and Randal left their units and stood near their demonic chairwoman.

"Where're the other two? Donald, Olivia, get your worthless rears out here where I can see you."

Donald Snow and Olivia Kingston stepped out of their BMW and picked their way through headstones. They stood next to Randal and Romano. Donald's Italian loafers and Olivia's dress heels were covered with mud.

"New lines of authority," said Frances. "I now proclaim myself both president and field marshal over the Directorate. These people in front of you have been inept in their leadership. Sanford and Goldstein have been demoted to unit commanders and you two, Snow and Kingston, are foot soldiers."

Olivia opened her mouth to protest, but Donald grabbed her arm and pulled her away. She stumbled next to him.

"One word and you're a dead woman, Olivia," said Frances.

"The woman is out of control," said Donald to Olivia. "She's a murderer unhinged."

The two former world leaders trudged together into the ranks of Randal Sanford's squad.

"We're going to have to find some kind of outdoor clothing," said Donald to his terrified companion—now a draftee.

"The source of our power has radically changed," said Frances. "The Prince of Darkness has enlisted us into his army. We now have allies in the air above us and nearby in the city of Salem. Our comrades are now performing sixty-six black masses in honor of King Lucifer, our exalted ruler."

Romano watched Frances float off beyond the cemetery. She returned carrying something like a large duffle bag in her right hand. The crowd of entranced soldiers gawked at their leader as she swooshed back and forth holding her burden like a suitcase.

"Pay close attention, you disciples of Satan. I have been anointed by the Devil himself as a priestess in the Church of Darkness." Her arm shot out to her right, and Romano realized she was holding Andrew's inanimate body by the belt. He dangled comatose beneath her powerful grip. "This is what happens to traitors and failures."

She cast Andrew's body off to her right and it smashed against a gravestone carved in the image of a gargoyle typing on a keyboard.

"I will now show all of you how to receive the powers of darkness."

On the divine screen in the sky over her ledge, Sandy watched Frances perform the ritual of the Antichrist—the Black Mass.

Frances' voice surged out like steam from a ruptured sewer pipe. Her body skimmed over the graves, buoyed up by a web spun by the six demons. The "congregation" sat spellbound on gravestones and on the grass.

Holding a cross upside-down, Frances incanted, "Oh Haborym, we worship your unholy name. We exorcise all the forces of Jehovah from among us. We bask in your darkness. Yea, as we walk through the valley of the shadow of death we follow you into its depths. We fear nothing but your authority, oh great Tchort, our black god."

Sandy viewed the ritual without emotion. She prayed, "Greater are you, my Lord, who dwells within me and my warriors, than this evil tribe that inhabits the sky over the earth. I thank you, Lord Jesus, for calling me and dear Carlos's family into this victorious battle. We overcome by your blood and our courageous testimony."

Sandy watched the six demons hover over the satanic priestess as Frances performed the rite of human sacrifice. The cross that Frances held in her hand morphed into a sword.

"Our sacrifice, oh Beelzebub, eradicates the phony sacrifice of God's counterfeit son. Our sacrifice is real. I give you now the body and blood of this human."

Frances raised the sword and plunged it down into Andrew's heart and he bled out.

"Carlene, front and center," Frances said.

Frances gave Carlene a silver chalice and ordered her to hold it at the edge of the altar to collect the blood.

Overhead, under the silver half-moon, a flaming pentagram appeared and cast an orange glow onto the cemetery. Sandy watched the gory ritual continue in the cemetery into the dark early hours of the morning.

Sandy sent a message to Carlos, requesting his presence on the rocky ledge.

"Our angels are engaged in a blocking force, keeping the swarms of demons in Salem from joining the Directorate in their attack. We have only six angels in direct support of our operation here. After daylight, Michael the archangel and his platoon will link up with us here in the battle.

"I just viewed the activities of the Directorate's army. They performed a Black Mass and sacrificed one of their key people, their operations officer.

"A team of demons has been dispatched by Satan to support the Directorate. Remember form the Letter to the Ephesians? Our spiritual enemy is classified into four types. We fight first against the rulers, secondly the authorities, third against the world powers of this darkness, and fourth against the spiritual forces of evil in the heavens.

"The demonic team that controls our enemy is from the world powers. Those are the ones that specialize in manipulating and influencing people, animals, and the weather. Most of the demons dancing around the air over Salem are the spiritual forces of evil in the heavens.

"What you need to do, Carlos, is talk to our angels Joe, Thomas, and the four they brought with them, and coordinate their spiritual fight against the six demons of the Directorate with our battle here on the ground."

Into the air Carlos said, "Thomas, Joe, can you hear me?"

"Right here, Carlos. We're very impressed with your defensive emplacements. Nice job."

"Thanks, guys. Now you've seen what's going on over there across the road in the cemetery, right?"

"Yeah," said Thomas. "Nothing we haven't seen before. Same deal with Hitler, Stalin, Idi Amin, Papa Doc, Yahya Kahn, Saddam Hussein—long list there, so yeah, we have caught their act over there. A high-ranking demon named Botis has taken possession of their chairwoman, Frances O'Donnelly. He got bored with the rituals going on in Salem and decided to see what kind of mayhem he could wreak over here. He's one of their high authorities, an Earl if you will, who oversees a gang of sixty filthy dark angels. The sword in Frances' hand belongs to Botis.

"Sad story with that Frances," said Joe. "We almost had her on our side there for a while with the help of a believer named Anna Stone, but she couldn't resist the kind of power that Botis promised to give her. This type of thing happens a lot with smart, high-achieving people."

"Frances' subordinate leaders have fallen under her control," said Thomas. "Some have become disciples of the dark side. Some, like their troop commander, Romano Goldstein, are simply intimidated by her. The troglodytes that they have enslaved and trained as fighters have no idea what they're doing. Their mental faculties have been destroyed and replaced by the Directorate's control mechanisms. Even their basic functions have been taken over by those psychopaths."

Carlos said, "Hang on a second," and he related the angels' report to Sandy.

"I saw this O'Donnelly woman kill their operations chief," said Sandy to Carlos. "Ask the angels who's running all their telekinesis equipment."

"Nobody," said Joe. "Frances shut it down and she has replaced all those high-tech systems with demonic energy. Satan has taken command of the Directorate through his chain of command—his rulers, authorities, and powers of darkness."

"So what kind of tactics can we expect from her and her attack force now that they are instruments of the devil?" said Carlos.

"These guys will be hard to stop now," said Thomas. "They have no normal survival instincts. That means they have no fear of death. They will charge headlong into lethal fire. When one of their own goes down, they will simply step over them, even use the bodies as shields or sandbags. Think of them as residents of hell in human form.

"Frances has no regard for their lives. She will order them to charge into your defenses in one mass attack and push rapidly until they get to the cliff. Your warriors will take out most of them, but the rest of them will survive and overcome Cielavista."

Carlos listened to Thomas's intel briefing with unimpassioned attention. The courage that the Spirit had imparted in him disallowed worry or panic. This knowledge about their demon-possessed enemy was simply new data for him to consider as he modified his tactical plans.

"Thanks, Thomas," said Carlos.

Then to Sandy, "Our plan for dynamic defense will work well against these demoniacs."

"Yes, I believe you're right, Carlos. What modifications to our battle plan do you see?"

"Nothing major, Sandy," said Carlos. "Company Striker-Charlie will conduct a feint against the charging enemy, fall back as if defeated, and draw them into the valley, forcing them into a confined avenue of advance. Just as we modeled it after Joshua's Battle of Ai.

"Striker-Delta will ambush them from the heights, and Striker-Charlie will counterattack. The only new instructions for our warriors is to warn them that the enemy is on a suicide mission.

"And, Sandy, we must not be reluctant to evacuate Cielavista. Saving the lives of our people is more important than holding ground."

"Yes, Carlos, I realize that. We have the small boats and the Sea Ray launch to shuttle our forces from here to our rally point on the beach north of here. We have vehicles prepositioned there to take us as far away as we need to go," said Sandy.

"This wind," said Carlos. "I'm concerned about how our boats will do in these swells."

"I've been working on that," said Sandy. "This storm's name is Gina. She tells me that she has been sent to assist us in our battle by playing havoc with the enemy's fiery arrows.

"Why are the four angels with Joe and Thomas carrying those trumpets?" Sandy said.

"You got me," said Carlos.

Then to Thomas, "What's with the trumpets?"

Thomas said, "The Directorate army still has the ability to go invisible with their humming. That awful chord they generate conceals their movements from our troops. The notes from your harmonicas in the key of C major won't broadcast far enough to dissolve that umbrella, so these trumpets will get rid of it. One trumpet plays a low C, one plays an E, one the G and the fourth plays a middle C."

"Great," said Carlos. "That way, our attack force, Striker-Charlie, can engage them right at the perimeter and lure them back into the valley where our ambush forces can engage them."

"Yes," said Thomas, "and your warriors will be relieved of their harmonica duty. They will have both hands free to fight.

"Michael and the main body of our angel force will disengage from their fight in Salem before noon today, and they'll join us. We'll have much more impact on the battle here with the whole platoon fighting with you."

Carlos relayed the angels' briefing to Sandy. She said, "Carlos, tell them that we are so grateful that our Lord has sent them to support us in this battle."

"They said they're just doing their jobs. Another day at the office," said Carlos.

"Okay," said Sandy. "You have work to do up top. I'm sending Althea with you. She has a note from me to Hank. Would you have someone check up on him for me? He's a loose cannon, and he has no sense of caution. With Henry gone and Gabriella missing, that boy's all the family I've got."

Carlos looked into his dear friend's eyes. He held her look there for several minutes. Both leaders were exhausted, but their adrenaline was pumping energy into their brains and bodies.

"Sandy, I can tell you know more than you are revealing. Whatever God has shown you is what He desires to happen. His ways are different than ours."

Sandy gave Carlos a gentle shove on both shoulders, "Go back to work, Commander Carlos. Lead our troops to victory."

Carlos and Althea jumped from ledge to rock, up the cliff to the battlefront.

***

CHAPTER THIRTY-FIVE

Henry and Beto decided to sail a wide circle from Marblehead Harbor to Cielavista. *Water Walker* handled the high winds and four-foot swells with poise. Their radar told them the stormy weather system was localized on the coast between Salem and Gloucester and they would have a smoother, safer ride twenty miles out.

"Tanker ahead," said Beto. "Looks like she's anchored."

"We'll swing wide to her port side," said Henry, swinging the ship's wheel to the right.

"*Water Walker* to tanker," said Henry into the radio mic."

"*Water Walker*, this is *Hyundai Spartan*" said the voice in the speaker. "We have you heading wide to our port. Have a good night."

"Good night to you and God Bless," said Henry.

Beto said, "South Korean?"

"No, though with the Hyundai name you'd think so. It's a Greek freighter," said Henry, "made in Korea.

"We'll swing one more mile northwest and then head back into shore at Cielavista. We'll get there around noon."

Beto said, "I'll put on a pot of coffee for you. I'm gonna get some sleep. Wake me up in a couple hours and I'll relieve you so you can sleep for a few hours."

"Sounds good, my friend."

The Greek Tanker, *Hyundai Spartan*, disappeared in the darkness behind them.

Thomas and Joe—swords drawn—circled above the Directorate's forward line of attack. Four demons left their posts at the head of each enemy column and charged upward at the angels. Hovering back-to-back the veteran warriors calmly engaged the raging, drooling fiends, delivering scathing wounds to the first two. The demons were cunning, well trained in spiritual warfare. They charged at the angelic champions from all sides, above and below firing darts from their fetid mouths, flicking arrows from their tails. Thomas and Joe were tireless, almost bored with the same centuries-old tactics they had encountered thousands of time. But they knew the battle had to be waged. And they also knew that as they kept these four busy in the air, they would be of no use to Botis, their boss, down below who was leading the fight against the heroic warriors of Task Force Saber.

The angels nodded at each other, signaling their next move. In an instant they rocketed up beyond the exosphere. The demons were outdistanced, but they followed the angels upward toward the moon.

"They fall for this every time," said Thomas.

"Where shall we lose them this time?" said Joe.

"Dark side of the moon?" suggested Thomas.

"Sounds good."

In a matter of seconds the angels circled the earth's moon and disappeared. The demons were once again confused and searched the cosmos for their spiritual adversaries to no avail.

Thomas and Joe returned to their support role over Cielavista. They grinned as Botis growled at the loss of half his squad. Botis' howl rumbled out of Frances' throat, terrifying her subordinate commanders.

"What was that?" Romano asked. Frances just looked at him with fiery eyes and he skulked away.

Thomas said to Joe, "Look, that's their commander," pointing his sword to Frances. "Remember the change of command at their meeting at the Canyon Ranch? She took charge of the board and Randal Sanford became the ground force commander. Then after the debacle at the Nubble Light they reduced Randal to a squad leader, and Goldstein took charge of the army. But now Frances O'Donnelly has total command, and Botis has her under his demonic control."

"What could possibly go wrong for them?" said Joe.

"Here they go," said Thomas as he watched the four columns of Directorate soldiers take their positions for the second attack on Cielavista.

Randal Sanford ordered his two columns to move down the road to their left and spread out. "Firdos, you take the far left flank. Carlene, form your team to his right. Wait for my order to attack."

Romano Goldstein moved his two columns to Sanford's right and formed them up in attack position.

The dark cobalt sky was slowly yielding to the morning twilight. A violent offshore wind raked across the treetops. Randal's boots were soaked through from the heavy dew on the grass in the cemetery. His flabby body shivered in Halloween's coldest hour. He stood behind his squad, pistol in hand, the stub of an unlit cigar clenched in his teeth. *Let's go, Frances. Let's get this over with. See what you can do with this mob.*

He looked back at Frances. *Where in the devil did that come from?* Randal thought peering through the morning mist. Frances held a goat's horn in her hand. She raised it to her lips and a horrendous noise filled the air over the attack force, amplifying the dissonant humming that buzzed around the assembly. Randal was terrified.

"Charge!" Randal squealed.

Jacob and Antonio aimed their SAW machine guns at the attacking line of giants and raked down their front line. The crack and roar of gunfire filled the woods on their left and right as the Task Force Saber gunners unleashed a lethal wall of bullets. They could hear the crunch of boots on the gravel road in the center of the sector. It was Striker-Charlie charging the enemy line.

The wind caught the enemy's fiery arrows that had rained down on Task Force Saber's positions, and blew them back over the attackers, striking the massive men on their helmets and shoulders.

Jacob reloaded a fresh drum of ammo into his machine gun while Antonio maintained a steady stream of suppressive fire on the advancing enemy. The masses of charging giants were within a few yards of their fighting position and the two fighters looked at each other for an instant. Roberto had not given the word to move back to their second battle position.

"We stay until ordered to move," Antonio said to his battle buddy.

A volley of enemy arrows sailed at them, three of them flying directly into their gunport. Jacob jerked backwards as an arrowhead banged into the shoulder of his Kevlar vest. They returned fire on their attackers.

Antonio and Jacob noticed a pudgy, red-faced soldier stomping through the underbrush behind the charging line of fighters. He was screaming.

"Get them!" yelled Randal. "Move to the right now, fools! They're counterattacking our middle. Move to the right and smash the FITO force that's attacking us."

Through the dim morning light, Antonio and Jacob watched the foot soldiers mechanically obey the screams of their leader and turn to their right and pound through the trees after Striker-Charlie.

"Our strategy is working, Bud," said Jacob. "Let's take out as many of these Philistines as we can and wait for the order to move back to join Anvil-Bravo on the cliffs."

"This might get in your way," said Antonio, and he broke the enemy arrow off Jacob's vest with the arrowhead still imbedded in the Kevlar.

From behind them a familiar voice said, "Time to move." It was Brian, the messenger. He held his hand out to assist them out of the foxhole they occupied for the last twenty-four hours.

"It was a lovely home, wasn't it, Jacob?" Antonio said.

"Yes; we'll miss it, I'm sure."

In a crouch they followed Brian as he rolled up the warriors on the perimeter and led them through their prearranged route to their new fighting positions on the cliffs.

Randal Sanford was sweating and heaving through the thickets and briars of Cielavista.

"Romano," he called, as his depleted squad linked up with the other columns from the right of the attack line.

The two executives, now demoted to squad leaders, met in the cluster of attackers heading down the narrow pass toward the FITO force that was advancing toward them.

"How does it look on your side?" Randal said.

"We seemed to be making progress with limited casualties, but now our dear commander has ordered us to join forces against this counterattack," said an exhausted Romano Goldstein.

Over their heads, what sounded like the roar of a jet engine blasted through the air. The two men looked up to see a fiery ball flying in the direction of the counterattacking FITO force. Clumps of molten fire fell from its wake.

"Oh, god, what's next?" said Randal.

The fireball ascended up and hovered there over the lead elements of the Directorate's column. The distorted face of Frances O'Donnelly, now ten feet in diameter and totally engulfed in flames, scowled down at the confused mass of men charging down the valley at the defenders. From her head a fiery serpent's tail flagged out behind, dripping hot molten liquid onto the attackers.

"Charge on, you fools. They are weak. They are falling back. Push on, you slackers," Botis' voice bawled out from the flaming glob. Two of his henchmen darted in and out of the fireball, moronically laughing and screaming.

Randal was crowded in with the army of the Directorate all massed into the kill zone of Task Force Saber's ambush. He could see that his formation was only eight abreast, with the rest of the force stumbling in a useless herd behind them. In their fury, the mindless brutes began slashing at each other.

Then the forest exploded. Claymore mines detonated on both flanks. A hail of bullets rained down on Randal's unsuspecting foot soldiers. They fell in heaps, wounded, wailing and dying.

Randal fell to the ground beneath two bleeding bodies. He squirmed out from under the weight and crawled after Romano. It was becoming clear to Randal, exhausted as he was, that Romano had figured out the enemy's tactic before they sprung their trap. Randal grabbed Firdos and crawled along with Romano's small patrol back through the woods around the ambushers. They huddled in a grove of pines, some with minor wounds, all of them shell-shocked. Firdos was sitting next to his beloved leader, Carlene. Randal listened to the bedlam in the valley. Romano formed a plan and he briefed his terrified soldiers.

From her post on the ledge, Sandy cried out to God for more protection. So far they had suffered no deaths. The wounded were evacuated down the tunnels to the Sea Ray. The launch shuttled them up the coast to their field hospital.

The battle plan was working. The enemy's force took the bait and chased Striker-Charlie into the confines of the valley and found themselves facing withering fire from Striker-Delta's ambush. Striker-Charlie maneuvered to their ambush position, trapping the enemy in a three-sided casket.

Sandy watched her sky-screen as Botis, Frances, and two lunatic demons glided over the mob. She was amazed at how totally Frances was possessed. And to think at one point she was almost ready to abandon the dark side. But now she was lost to the forces of hell.

A small enemy patrol had deserted the main body and was hiding in the woods. Hank had been right about Romano Goldstein. The doctor had a sixth sense for survival and he was now using it to command a viable commando team. Randal Sanford and his minions, Carlene Wood and Firdos Gaffardi, were part of it.

The enemy attack had become completely unraveled and the enraged demoniac in the form of Frances O'Donnelly took her place at the rear of the decimated column and commanded them to retreat back to the cemetery across the road, hauling their dead and wounded.

CHAPTER THIRTY-SIX

Task Force Saber regrouped at its secondary battle positions on the cliff.

"Alright, warriors, we have accomplished our mission thus far," said Commander Carlos. "We have sustained many casualties. No deaths, but a number of wounded. All have been med-evaced to our field hospital, and some have been taken to local hospitals. We are using seven different hospitals, so no one emergency room will be suspicious of what's going on here. We don't need outside law enforcement involved, as you all know.

"The enemy will be back. Sandy has informed me that their force is under the direct influence of an earl of the underworld named Botis. He reports directly to Satan. So the power that controls them has dramatically changed.

"They will charge without caution. They do not value their lives or the lives of others. Some will keep fighting despite serious wounds. You will wonder why your bullets will not stop them. All these phenomena are the result of the demonic powers that possess these people.

"Do not let the fire over their heads distract you. It will not harm you. It's more like a projected light designed to terrify you. Same thing with that blaring discordant noise that comes from their mouths. That sound no longer makes them invisible. The angels' trumpets are playing the C major chord that cancels out their sickening hum."

"Commander Carlos," Jacob said, raising his hand.

"Yes, son,"

"Why don't we just leave now and let them have the property?"

"Good question, Jacob. I should have covered that," said Carlos. "There are three reasons why we must fight them until ordered to evacuate. One: it is our responsibility to cause as much damage on them as possible; two: the weather is so violent that our flotilla cannot accommodate us all at once. Only our biggest launch is capable of navigating these three-foot waves. The small boats will be swamped. Third, and most important, Sandy is getting our instructions directly from the Angel of the Lord who sits at the right hand of God. We must operate in God's will, even if it puts us at risk. Make sense?"

"Absolutely, Uncle. Thank you. We will fight and we will win," said the young warrior.

"Yes, and because God is in charge, the battle belongs to Him and He will be glorified," said Carlos.

"Now, we have our main body in position at the cliff. Hank will lead his scouts to our front to probe the enemy as they advance and warn us of their movements. Evacuation teams one, two, three, and four will man the four paths down the cliffs and facilitate our withdrawal.

"Before we redeploy, I want to pray a blessing on us."

Carlos removed his helmet from his thick, matted grey hair. The heavy Kevlar helmet left a dark indentation in his forehead. He bowed his head and the others, bareheaded, followed suit.

"My Lord, our great commander, strengthen our bodies, minds and spirits for this final phase of the battle. Pour your Holy Spirit out on us and fill us with your power. Power to fight, power to run, power to stand fast, power to shoot, power to kill, power to protect one another. And most of all, give us your power to stay bounded together with your divine love. Save us all, my Lord and Savior. Yours is the battle, yours is the glory. We follow your every command. Amen."

In unison, Task Force Saber shouted, "A sword for the Lord and for Gabriella."

Sandy watched her sky-screen as Carlos issue the battle order. The battle cry of the army came to her ears and she sighed.

"Oh, Gabriella, with all this power I have to see beyond the horizons and project this miraculous energy to change the course of human events, why can't I see you? Where are you? Where did you go, my dear Nonina?"

Then she felt it, a whisper of uplifting strength in her gut. Like a faint charge of electricity—familiar somehow. She waited, concentrating on the feeling, deep in her soul—willing it to be louder, clearer, but it remained faint and deep. Her mind groped after it, desperate to be sure.

Aloud she said, "This can only be you, dear Nonina. I can almost taste you. Will I ever see you again?"

"So, what do we have?" said Archangel Michael to Thomas.

"Joe and I had a little tussle with four of them—no big problem. Botis is in charge of the Directorate now. He occupies their leader, Frances O'Donnelly, removed her human body, and he now uses her face to terrorize their forces," said Thomas.

"How goes the battle?"

"The enemy has attacked twice and Task Force Saber has done a good job chasing them back to the cemetery. The enemy force is down to half their original strength, so that puts them at about fifty personnel fit to fight. Task Force Saber has lost eleven of their original seventy, all wounded and effectively med-evaced to their field hospital, and some to civilian hospitals in the area."

Michael said, "Well, the fools in Salem have settled down. Most of the humans have retired to their beds. All the chartered busses from out of state have taken off."

Thomas said, "Who was in charge this year?"

"Morax," said Michael. "He's the one who has this power to embolden

Satan worshippers. He makes them feel wise and respectable. Under his leadership, the Satanic rituals this year have definitely revived their enthusiasm for their cause. We expect that those who openly worship Satan will double in number this year."

"America is in for some real bad times," said Joe. "I mean with today's mindset where Christians who worship Jehovah and the Trinity are ridiculed, and cult worshippers are looked upon as sophisticated freethinkers, Satan has an open door for his hellish influence."

"Yes," said Michael. "That's why a decisive victory here at Cielavista is extremely important. Our objective is total annihilation of the Directorate."

Michael drew the Sword of the Lord. He held it out at arm's length and pointed toward the heavens. All the angels stared as the weapon expanded grew longer and thicker.

"Brothers, I will need your help. This weapon will become so heavy that it will take many of us to hold it steady." As the hilt lengthened, Javier came alongside Michael and wrapped his hands around it. Fire from the throne room of the Almighty engulfed the blade.

Michael clung to the radiant, expanding steel. "Here's our plan."

The mid-autumn afternoon sun glared down from the southwest at a blinding angle, reflecting hard and silver off the raging surf. Mounted on Sadie, Hank directed his scout platoon to the front of Task Force Saber's defensive battle line near the clifftop. Since the operations staff in the barn had abandoned their headquarters and joined the ranks of the infantry, Peter became Hank's platoon sergeant.

"You take Lucille and Andy with you," Hank said to Peter. "The wolf-hound is your connection with the angels, and Andy communicates with her." Hank watched Peter's expression to see how he'd react to these bizarre instructions. Evidently even skeptical Peter had come to grips with the realities of the spiritual realm.

"Thanks, Hank. Good to know," said Peter, mounted on Cinnamon. "So, how will you know what the angels are saying?"

"Sadie has the same connection as Lucille. The horse and I have come to an understanding. As long as she gets a couple apples every day, she will keep me posted on all the messages from the angels." Hank gave his horse an affectionate pat on the neck. Sadie snorted her approval.

"This pine grove will be our rally point," said Hank to the twelve-foot soldiers in his scout platoon. "Here we have good cover and concealment from the enemy.

"Our job is to find the attacking enemy and notify Commander Carlos. Do not engage the enemy. Once you get a visual on him, keep your distance and quickly withdraw.

Hank said to Andy and five other infantrymen. "You six go with Peter. Lucille and the bulldog are attached to your squad. The property is divided into two sectors. Sector Green is everything north of the main road into the estate. Sector Red is to the south. I'll take Green. Peter, you take Red.

"Do not use the radio for internal commo. Only come up on the net to inform Carlos of enemy positions or to call me in extreme emergencies. When you see the enemy attack our perimeter, send up a red flare. That's the warning for our forces on the cliff. Everyone got it?"

"Yes, sir."

"All right, warriors," said Hank. "Remember, do not engage. Restrain your instincts. Find him, withdraw, and call Carlos. Peter, you wanna pray for this courageous gang?"

"Dear Father, you have trained our hands for war, our fingers for battle. Thank you for the angelic protection. Yours is the victory, we glorify your name. Amen."

"Good. Let's roll," said Hank, and he nudged Sadie onto the path through the briars. His foot soldiers followed. Mark, the Irish Wolfhound, and John, the Shepherd, sniffed and darted in the brush to their flanks.

"Take the helm for a while, would you, Beto?" Henry wouldn't admit how much pain he was enduring in his back and legs from holding the boat steady through the rolling swells. He took a seat in the mate's chair and watched the instruments and the ocean to their front.

"Look at that big orange ball on the western horizon," said Beto.

"I've never seen a sunset like that before, have you?" said Henry.

"That's not the sun. It looks like some kind of weird band of fire in the sky over the coast. What is that?"

"Ask your buddy up there—what's his name? Tobias?"

"Hey, Tobias, you still there?" said Beto.

"Yeah. You need to hear all this and tell Henry the skeptic everything. This is going to be quite a night for you two," said Tobias.

Romano Goldstein was convinced that Frances could not effectively lead the Directorate's forces in her demonic state. It was clear that she had totally succumbed to the evil influence of Botis, one of Satan's most high-ranking captains. Romano was quite familiar with this evil spirit from his experiences dealing with war veterans. His patients with such severe mental disorientation lacked the ability to relate to other people and the ability to feel any true emotions. They easily fell prey to the wiles of unclean spirits. When he first observed the manifestation of Botis in Frances, he reckoned that it might embolden her and make her a more dangerous leader. But now Romano realized that Frances was totally irrational and ineffective.

As the Directorate's lead elements chased after FITO's counterattack force into the valley, Romano quickly caught on to their tactic. He had read General Joshua's book. He knew it would be useless to try to change Frances-Botis' mind, so he decided to gather a separate force with two objectives: survival and victory over FITO.

Hidden in the thicket where Romano found refuge with his remnant of twenty fighters, he listened to the clamor of the battle in the kill zone of FITO's ambush. The indirect fire from his carefully designed artillery proved utterly inaccurate because of the high, swirling winds. As many arrows fell on his own giants as fell on the enemy. The screaming wails of his huge brutish soldiers was disgusting. The war cry of the FITO fighters was terrifying—"A sword for the Lord and for Gabriella"—reverberated through the hills and treetops. Romano read the horror on the faces of his band of fighters.

"Randal, my fellow executive; Carlene, my valiant leader; Firdos, my brave seer and saboteur; and my tenacious foot soldiers: you are the last hope for victory in this desperate struggle. Do you hear me?" Romano said.

Romano relied on his well-practiced powers of hypnosis and brainwashing. He looked each person in their eyes. The notes of his dissonant chord vibrated in his teeth. Their eyes glazed over. He was reaching their subconsciousnesses.

"Randal, you will command half of this mighty platoon and lead them in a historic battle. Carlene, you will command the other half. Firdos, you will support Carlene and be faithful to her every order."

Romano assigned eight fighters to Carlene and eight to Randal.

"My mighty men of valor," Romano said, ignoring their gender, "you are my children. I love you dearly. When this fantastic fight is over, we will all celebrate for years how we overcame this terrible fly in the ointment. We will tell our children of our heroism and for many generations they will sing our praises."

He watched the panic in their eyes fade, and their obeisance rise.

"The attack force under the command of Frances will push FITO back and force them off this high cliff. Many of our men will die in the effort. Our mission is to wait until the battle is nearly over and only a scant fragment of the enemy's force remains. That's when we will strike. We will kill every FITO soldier and every Directorate soldier. Both sides of this battle will be exhausted, wounded, and decimated. They will have lost their will to fight and we will be rested and strong.

"We will attack from our hiding places in the woods. Randal from the north, Carlene from the south. We will pin them against the cliff and wipe them out. Let me hear you say, 'Victory is ours.'"

Randal's nine and Carlene's ten all peered back at Romano with blank, senseless smiles. "Victory is ours?" they mumbled.

"That's the stuff," Romano said. "Victory is ours."

Chapter Thirty-Seven

Ignoring her exhaustion after thirty-six hours of nonstop enemy surveillance, Sandy stayed focused on her sky-screen. She couldn't shake the pain in her gut as she watched Romano Goldstein. *How could Gabriella have allowed her to place Hank in the care of this monster?* As the question formed itself in her mind, the answer whispered into her inner self. *All part of the plan.*

How many times had Gabriella said, "I only know what I know and I can only do what I can do."

Sandy now realized that a prophet only sees scattered fragments of God's plans. The Lord only lets the knowers know what is essential for them to know. Faith fills in the blanks.

"Sam, you're up," Sandy said loud enough to be heard inside the little tent where her runners were resting.

Sam wrote what Sandy dictated. "Romano Goldstein has formed a detachment separate from the enemy's main body. They will be hanging back until the main battle is over, and they plan to wipe out our force and what remains of the enemy. They will be attacking from the south in two squads of ten fighters each. Distribute to all subordinate commanders."

Sam read the message back to Sandy. "Right," she said. "Up you go, young warrior."

Sandy watched the young athlete leap, run, step and climb up the uneven rocks. At some high ledges Sam jumped up, pulled himself up, and swung his legs over the next level. All smooth, coordinated moves, making the difficult climb look effortless. She had taken that route hundreds of times, but never as quickly and gracefully as her young athletic messengers.

Sandy looked back up into the sky. *I wonder what Michael is going to do with that magnificent flaming sword.*

"Robby," called Hank, "here they come. Pop the red flare."

To the front of Hank's sector, a column of enemy infantry was advancing across the road. Over their heads was a cloud of flame. Hank saw red flares in the sky over Peter's sector, indicating a coordinated enemy advance across their entire front.

Hank deployed his last three Claymores and pulled his recon squad back. He called Carlos on the radio and informed him of the enemy's strength and avenues of approach. He was surprised to find a breathless Althea running up to him with a message from his mother.

Hank, Romano's detachment is just to the rear of your present location. Do not engage. Circle around that thicket to your right front at azimuth 180 degrees. Circle to the north and continue your retrograde. Repeat, do not engage that enemy detachment.

"Jump up on Sadie, Althea," said Hank. "I'll give you a ride to the edge."

The young girl swung up behind Hank and hung on to his waist.

"Hey, Sadie," said Althea. "Good to see ya. Thanks for the lift."

"She says *con mucho gusto*," said Hank. "I guess she's showing off her Spanish."

"I know," said Althea, "I can hear her, too."

Hank gave the hand-and-arm signal to his squad to follow him.

Through the trees to the north of him, Hank heard the enemy crash through the underbrush. The dismal, now-familiar hum snaked through the woods. A wildly flashing ball of flame swooped back and forth over the onrushing horde.

Night fell quick and cold. Sadie picked her way through the dark woods, leading Hank's men behind her. They halted in the tree line near the cliff. Hank could hear the violent surf pounding the ledge where Sandy stood. The night wind roared through the trees and feathered Althea's air across Hank's neck. Any minute now the enemy army would close in on Task Force Saber for the kill.

The column of giants halted in the tree line to Hank's left. He could smell the barbarians' breath wafting through the trees in foul streams of vapor. The voice of the demon master growled out over the restless mob. When he spoke, drops of fire fell from his lips.

"You are a killing machine. Your enemy is a weak coward. You will trample him and throw him over the cliff into the sea," Botis said through the face of Frances O'Donnelly.

Hank grinned and turned to look over at his scouts. He shook his head. "It's all a big show," he said. "These clumsy brutes will be defeated this night."

Althea gave him a hug from behind and slipped down from Sadie's back. "Any message for your mom?" she said.

To Sadie Hank said, "What'd ya see, lady?" Hank leaned over Sadie's warm brown neck and listened.

"Botis will depart the battle." Hank repeated what the horse transmitted to him. "From there on, it will be hand-to-hand combat. Begin to evacuate all our family members who are not essential to the battle."

"Okay, Hank. Take care of yourself," Althea said. "You're the best. God be with you."

The young female commando bolted across the open area between the tree line and rolled off the edge to a foothold below.

"What'd ya think, Sadie, was that cute young lady flirting with me?" said Hank.

He smiled. "Okay, I won't flatter myself."

The dissonant humming grew loud and threatening. The Frances-Botis fiend rose up into the starry sky and cried out at both columns of monstrous brutes, "Victory is ours."

The mob picked up the chant, "Victory is ours. Victory is ours."

The line of enemy infantrymen rocked forward and back with a tension like a bowstring drawn tight. The villainous voice of Botis sounded the command, "Charge!" The horde of giant enemy soldiers lumbered at Task Force Saber on the cliff's edge.

Water Walker pushed hard through the swells and the raging wind. The sun had set but the night sky over Cielavista blazed orange and red.

"Tobias, grab our bowline and pull," said Henry.

The big trawler heaved upwards and sped up to sixty knots. Henry and Beto clung to their chairs as the craft bounded dangerously close to the breaking point. Near the base of Cielavista's cliff, Henry cut the engine and Tobias released the bowline and *Water Walker* drifted to the shore.

"The battle has begun," said Beto. "You can hear them."

Shots and screams, clashing of swords on shields, shouts and the pounding of men's' feet and horses' hooves.

"Get an update from Tobias," said Henry.

Beto stood on the deck for a moment. "Our people are evacuating the estate. They will board the boats and sail up the coast to awaiting vehicles. Our fighters will hold off the enemy and conduct an orderly evacuation."

"Where's Sandy?"

"On Gabriella's ledge," said Beto. "Gabriella has been missing for days.

"Henry," Beto put his hand on Henry's forearm, "your son, Hank, is up there. He's joined the fight."

"Hank," said Henry.

Henry guided the boat to the rocky shoreline. The tide was coming in. Henry approached the natural stone dock where the rock went straight down deep into the water. Secured there were all the boats in Cielavista's fleet—the thirty-two-foot Sea Ray fishing boat, the twenty-three-foot sailboat, and four open Boston Whalers.

Henry called to one of the men manning the granite wharf. "What's going on, Steven?"

"Oh, Henry," said Steven, "Where have you been? We need you. We're at war."

Henry threw the forward line to Stephen, hopped up on the rock, and secured the aft line himself. The boat's bumpers banged against the rock.

"What are all these boats for?" Henry said.

"We need them all for our evacuation plan. Every seat on every boat will be needed to get our people from here to the exfil point up the coast," said Steven.

"The only boat that can take these waves is the Sea Ray," said Henry. "The others would be swamped the minute they left the dock."

"I know," said Stephen. "How many can get on that big trawler?" He pointed at the *Water Walker* and grinned.

"We'll get 'em all on this and the Sea Ray," said Henry.

"Beto, you stay here on the boat. Fill the gas tank from the five-gallon cans. Unload anything that takes up space. We'll be taking on about fifty passengers."

"Right," said Beto.

Henry stepped into one of the Whalers, untied the lines, and started the outboard engine.

"I thought you said this boat can't make it through these waves," said Steven.

"Probably won't," said Henry.

Henry guided the Boston Whaler up each wave and slammed down into each trough, jarring Henry's body with each bound. He motored the open boat around the rocky point to Sandy's ledge. With the forward line in his hand he climbed over the gunwale, thigh-deep in the pounding surf, and secured the boat to a rock. He jumped up onto the granite ledge and stood across the crevice from his wife.

Henry knew Sandy saw him but she didn't turn around.

Commander Carlos directed the fight from his fortified position behind the earthworks and revetments. His warriors were successfully degrading the attackers' ranks with only a few friendly casualties. The savage attackers employed no tactics. They simply charged headlong at Task Force Saber's fortification, firing their powerful crossbows, hurling stones, knives, swords, and spears. They attacked in waves, withdrew, and attacked again.

"Striker-Charlie, pull back. Begin exfiltration down route Apple," Carlos ordered.

As one of Frederick's companies quickly and calmly moved rearward through the protective trench, the three remaining companies tightened their perimeter and moved rearward as planned.

A flight of arrows soared overhead, some burrowing into the earth. Jacob and Antonio fought side-by-side in their shielded gunport and eliminated two charging enemy soldiers. All along the revetments the Task Force Saber soldiers held off the charging animals, but the attackers were getting closer, stepping over the bodies of their fallen fighters.

"Fix bayonets, men!" called Carlos, and he took a stand between Antonio and Jacob with his own bayonet fixed on the end of his M-16 rifle.

"Striker-Delta, exfiltrate now," Carlos ordered. Frederick's other company obeyed and slipped to the rear and down the tunnel. Anvil-Alpha and Anvil-Bravo pulled back to the next series of revetments, a tighter, more defensible position.

Carlos could hear the enemy commander's demonic voice. "Charge the cowards, you maniacs," Botis howled. The demon-prince clothed in Frances O'Donnelly's humanness set the woods on fire behind his line so his men could not retreat. They were trapped between the flames to their rear and the lethal gunfire pouring out from Saber's fortress.

The next desperate wave of giant soldiers stormed the rim of the revetment, and Saber's warriors engaged them hand-to-hand in primitive steel combat. The smaller Task Force Saber men had the advantage of superior firepower, and the enemy could not breach the wall, but the fight was bloody.

Antonio thrust his bayonet into the throat of one monster and he watched the giant's eyes bulge out and heard his last bloody gasps. The huge man fell right on top of Antonio. Jacob slung his weapon and leaned over to pull the dead man off his friend, exposing his back to an attacker. The massive brute held his sword over Jacob and plunged it downward, piercing Jacob's Kevlar vest. Enough of the steel tip found flesh. Jacob whirled upward and caught the man flush in the face with the point of his right elbow. Despite the pain from the wound in his back, he unsheathed his dagger with his left hand and stabbed his attacker in the heart.

"I've been wounded," grunted Jacob.

"Where?" asked Antonio.

"My back. Under my body armor."

"Commander Carlos," said Antonio, "permission to evacuate the wounded down the cliff."

"Take him down," said Carlos, noticing the blood seeping into Jacob's pants. "Good job, boys."

Chapter Thirty-Eight

The brush fire cut Romano's unit off from Randal and his nine. *Forget them.* Romano thought. *Randal is an idiot anyway. I have no use for him.*

Coughing through the intense cloud of smoke that was snaking through the woods, Romano said, "This way. It's time for our attack."

He led his gang of stupefied warriors in a wide circle to the south to skirt the fire and find a position on the flank of the battle. At the top of the cliff, they found themselves a hundred yards from Task Force Saber's fortified perimeter. The Directorate's force repeatedly stormed the perimeter.

Romano watched the Frances-Botis fiend soar in the air behind the attackers, shouting, threatening, and when necessary, strangling any of the fighters who tried to run away.

"Ready your bows," said Romano. "You two stay with me. You four go with Firdos, you four go with Carlene."

The archers loaded their crossbows with three arrows. Their muscles in their massive arms were exhausted from arming their weapons, and they struggled to pull back their bowstrings and cock them.

""Do not shoot until you have a target. You have three arrows, and each arrow must be a kill shot. When you are out of arrows, unsheathe your swords and your daggers.

"We will attack in two units. Carlene, you and your four soldiers will form up on the left and engage the Directorate attackers. You will have the element of surprise. They will think you're there to reinforce them, so wait until you're real close before you shoot. Men, you will obey every order Carlene tells you.

"Firdos, you will form your four fighters to the right of Carlene's. You will storm over FITO's earthwork there. See the weak point?"

"Yes," said Firdos, looking over at Carlene. She gave him a somber nod.

"The enemy will be concentrating on the attackers to their front and you will have an easy shot picking them off from their flank.

"Now get ready for the attack."

When they were in their attack formation, Romano said, "Victory is ours."

The pitiful, battle-weary soldiers repeated a doleful, "Victory is ours."

Peter's scout platoon was screening the northern flank out in front of the embattled fortress. He heard movement in the hedges near the cottage, so he dismounted Cinnamon and crept up on the yard. Ten large enemy soldiers were milling around near the front of the house.

Peter organized his people. "When the enemy soldiers are subdued, approach them, take your zip-ties and secure their hands and feet and duct tape their mouths and eyes. Let's go."

Peter's scouts surprised the enemy giants, surrounded them, and ordered them to kneel. Eight of them insanely charged at the armed warriors and fell to their deaths. The remaining two knelt down and the team secured them for capture.

"How many inside?" said Peter.

"Two," said one of the enemy combatants.

When Peter burst through the door, he encountered Olivia Kingston and Donald Snow at Gabriella's dining room table. Six empty bottles of wine sat on the table and each former director had a bottle by the neck. No glasses.

Peter approached, rifle at the ready.

"Ha-row," Donald slurred. "Wanss-som wine?"

"Ya gonna shoot ussh?" said Olivia.

"Team, come in here and tie up these drunks," said Peter.

"What should we do with them?" said Andy.

"We'll use the cottage cellar for a prison. Bring in the two guards. We'll see what Carlos wants to do with them when this fight is over. We need to get back to our mission. Hurry up."

"Can we take some wine down there with us?" said Donald.

Sandy ignored her husband standing on the other side of the crevice. There was no room in her emotional cauldron for a reunion with Henry. Not now.

Sandy had a full view of the entire battlefield on her sky-screen and her spirit was rapidly forming orders for her commanders.

Her runners no longer sought the shelter of the tent. The three young messengers were fully aware of the importance of their role in the fight, and seconds mattered. Brian was up on the cliff delivering her latest battle order.

"I have another message for Hank. Who's up?" Sandy said.

Sam started to step forward, and Althea gently grabbed his shoulder to restrain him. "I got it," said the young woman.

Sandy leaped across the space and Althea took her place with her pencil and notebook. "Henry, how'd you get here?" Althea said.

Henry just stood silent in the rain.

"No need to write, dear girl," said Sandy. "Here's the message for Hank: Kill Goldstein."

Sandy looked in Althea's eyes. "Go."

Sandy glanced over at Henry. The hood of his rain jacket blew up against his head. The open fishing boat came loose from its mooring, flipped over in the white-capped waves, and swirled out into the open water.

Hank watched Althea stealthily creep toward him through the under-brush. In the open space between the pear orchard and the pine grove where he and his men were hiding, she got down on her belly and low-crawled, like a swimmer in a dry pond. She paused in her progress along the turf to grab an abandoned rifle, slung it on her back, and kept crawling.

Only five yards from Goldstein's attack units, Althea slipped unde-tected to Hank's hiding place.

"Message from Sandy," said Althea to Hank. "Kill Goldstein."

Hank nodded. "Got any ammo for that weapon?"

Althea extracted the magazine from the M-16, weighed it in her hand, and said, "Feels like maybe ten rounds."

Robby pulled three thirty-round magazines from his daypack and handed them to the girl.

"Thanks," she said.

She clicked in the full mag, jacked back the bolt, and put the weapon on safe. She stuck the two extras in her cargo pockets.

"Sandy doesn't need me on the ledge anymore," said Althea.

"Team. Gather round here," said Hank.

Hank's fifteen scouts including Althea lay prone on the ground with their heads together. Mark, the wolfhound, lay between Althea and Hank. Sadie hung her head down between two of the men.

"Goldstein's renegade detachment is planning to kill off everyone."

"You mean he's turning against his own people?" said Robby.

"The man has no loyalties. He's a heartless snake.

"We only have a dozen warriors with Carlos defending the fortress. The rest have successfully evacuated, some wounded, most okay. Our mission is to take out Goldstein's detachment and whatever is left of the enemy force.

"Althea, you will ride Sadie over to Peter. Give him this order: 'You will be the blocking force at the north edge of the battle area. When the enemy attempts to retreat, take them out. At my command you will attack the enemy force on the field in front of the revetment. My signal will be a yellow flare.'

"We will wait until I determine that Goldstein's force is at its weakest. He divided his detachment into two squads. One will attack our fort. The other will attack the Directorate's force."

Hank gave detailed instructions to each scout and Mark.

"Questions?"

"A prayer, Hank, if I may," said Robby.

"Yeah, please," said Hank.

"God brought me to this passage in Nehemiah: 'Don't be afraid of them. Remember the great and awe-inspiring Lord, and fight for your countrymen, your sons and daughters, your wives and homes.'"

The scouts lay quietly for a second and let the power of that Word settle on them.

"Okay, Althea, get going and hurry back," said Hank. "I'll need the horse to communicate with my angels."

"Right," said Althea. Althea gave Hank a warm look, hopped up on Sadie, and disappeared through the trees.

"You think he likes me?" she asked the horse.

Sadie's long neck bobbed up and down in the affirmative.

CHAPTER THIRTY-NINE

Carlos fired his machine gun into the mass of attackers from his protected fighting position in the last ring of revetments. He was satisfied with the progress of the battle so far. Most of his family had safely exfiltrated the battlefield. He still had a dozen fighters with him fending off the waves of attackers. He estimated the enemy was still forty or fifty strong. But the ferocity of their attacks was waning.

The intensity of the hellish fiery cloud over their ranks had diminished. The flaming manifestation of Demon General Botis would leave the battlefield for several minutes at a time. Carlos looked into the night sky and watched as a squadron of Michael's angels engage the demonic force. They swooped down at the Botis-Frances beast and swiped at it with their swords. Botis would rage upward at them and they soared out of his range.

Carlos noticed that when Botis left the battlefield, Frances became powerless, and the Directorate fighters stumbled into each other, so Botis had to reoccupy Frances and take command.

Brian, one of Sandy's intrepid messengers, crawled next to Carlos. "Message from Sandy."

"Hang on a sec, Brian," Carlos said.

Carlos directed his fire at a group of attackers, took them out, and handed his SAW to Brian. "This is my sector of fire, Brian. Got it?"

Brian took the light machine gun and rolled over into Carlos' prone firing position. He sighted down the barrel and engaged the attackers.

Carlos took the note from Brian and kneeled next to him. *A fresh enemy detachment will be attacking you from your left flank in five minutes. It's Goldstein. One five-man team will hit your revetment. Another small squad will attack their own infantry out to your front. Goldstein is making a move to eliminate us and all of his own army including their demon-possessed commander. Our scouts are deployed to counterattack them. Hank has a scout platoon to your left front in the tree line, and Peter has another platoon to your right.*

Also, Henry is here on the ledge with me. Don't know how to act!

Carlos gave Brian a slap on the back of his jacket. "Back down the cliff, boy," he said. "Keep up the good work."

Brian engaged three more attacking giants with the SAW, checked the sector, and rolled to his left. "One of our messengers has joined Hank's scout team—Althea," he said.

"Sounds good. Take care, son."

Firdos and his men crawled from their temporary assembly area to a depression in the ground where he awaited Romano's order to attack the fort. He watched Carlene lead her squad across the battlefield in leaps and bounds. He was surprised to see Frances in her former state, pistol in hand, screaming at her flagging infantrymen.

Firdos glanced back over his shoulder at Romano and his two bodyguards as they crawled to a protected position in the rear.

Firdos caught Carlene's eye when she looked over at him. He knew she was proud of him.

When Frances saw Carlene's squad maneuvering from her right, she signaled them to charge the enemy revetment, but they kept moving in her direction. Carlene ordered her men to open fire. Ten of Frances' huge archers crumbed to the ground. Frances turned and shot Carlene in the neck, killing her immediately.

"Traitors," Frances yelled, "kill them all."

Caught between the blistering wall of machine-gun fire from Task Force Saber's fortress and the wave of charging Directorate swordsmen to her left flank, Carlene's band of robotic soldiers twisted in place, firing in both directions.

The moment Carlene was killed, Firdos screamed in anguish. In that moment of shock, Firdos' mind escaped its hypnotic shell. His survival instincts overcame his mindless loyalty to the Directorate, and it warned him to keep silent. He was momentarily stunned. *What has become of my life? How in the name of Allah have I come to this deathtrap?*

Firdos was not going to rush to his death. He kept his small squad of fighters hunkered down in the depression until Carlene's squad was fully engaged in their attack. It was clear to him that Goldstein's plan was hopeless.

Firdos looked over at the massive hulks of men beside him. The four of them were peering over the edge of the ditch at Frances for direction, but all they saw was her back as she scurried into the tree line. She was pressing her left hand on her hip, trying to stop the bleeding from a bullet wound.

"You men, you are under my command now. Look at me and tell me you understand what I'm telling you," Firdos said.

Their eyes were lifeless mirrors. From their lips came the irritating buzzing hum, and Firdos vaguely understood that somehow this eerie sound controlled these childlike beasts. Firdos felt a twinge of compassion for them and he wondered why. There was nothing he could do to break the spell.

Still undiscovered by the FITO forces defending the fortress, Firdos made a decision. He opened his jacket and ripped apart his white undershirt. He took a sword from one of his soldiers and tied the white flag to it and raised it over the edge of the depression.

Peter's scout platoon began their exfiltration down the cliff when he saw the white rag fluttering up from a ditch near Carlos' earthworks. He radioed to Carlos.

"Commander Carlos, can you hear me?" Peter spoke into the mic clipped to his body armor.

"Loud and clear, Peter. I see you're headed down to the water."

"Roger, Carlos. There's an enemy unit trying to surrender to your left front. I will take them prisoner."

"Ah, good eyes, Peter. They're all yours." Carlos continued firing at the next wave of Directorate attackers. "We should be heading down to the shoreline as soon as we push this gang back into the woods."

"Roger, out," said Peter.

Peter and three warriors quickly surrounded the depression where Firdos and his men huddled.

"Throw all your weapons out here," Peter ordered. His men leveled their rifles at the captives. Firdos complied, but the four brutes just stared beyond them and kept humming their brainless drone.

"Harmonicas," said Peter.

Peter's three fighters fished in their pockets, and with harmonicas to their lips and rifles still fixed on their prisoners, they all blew out the C major notes. The giants in the ditch opened their drooling mouths wide and ceased the throbbing hum.

Peter spoke to the men, "Now listen: lay down your bows, right now."

They obeyed.

"Throw your swords out here, now."

They unsheathed their swords and threw them at Peter's feet.

"Daggers."

They complied again, and they held out their hands for Peter's scouts to bind them with plastic zip-ties. Their clothing was ragged and they reeked of a foul odor.

Peter and his men led them back to the cottage and locked them in the cellar with the sleeping executives. Olivia Kingston woke up and recoiled back into the corner of the concrete room.

"What are you doing? Who are these creatures?" she said.

"They're your new roommates," said Peter. "Play nice."

Botis had about enough of this torment. He was, after all, an earl in the kingdom, not some lowly spirit of the world. His pride had swelled at the role he was filling as the commander of this human army. He even took some pride at being Michael's prime target. It had been a long time since he went one-on-one with the Captain of the Lord's Host. But he couldn't do both.

Botis reported back to his boss and complained about his predicament.

"Hey, Lucifer," he said, "give me a break here. I got this mob of humans fighting these do-gooders. I possess the body of this crazy woman, and now I have to contend with enemy angels sniping at me from the sky."

The voice from the pit throbbed into Botis' presence, "Stop whining and handle it."

"It's Michael," said Botis.

"Oh, why didn't you say that?" hissed the prince. "Forget the idiots on the ground. Kill the archangel."

That's what I wanted to hear. So long, suckers. You're on your own now. And Botis abandoned Frances' body for good and gathered his demons for the battle in the air.

"Look at them, the angelic fools," Botis said to his minions. "They're always smiling when we attack them. Well, we'll wipe those idiotic smirks off their angelic faces.

"Attack!" Botis ordered, and the spiritual clash in the heavens was on.

Sandy faced her husband. "Can you hear me?" she said across the crashing waves. Henry let out a long sigh full of guilt and apology.

Henry nodded. Neither wanted to speak. They just stared at each other.

A ball of thunder and lightning crashed high overhead.

Sandy said, "Michael and Botis are going at it. The angels will win again. I don't know why the demons even keep trying." Her voice was void of any emotion.

"What about our son?" said Henry.

"He's among the last of our fighters up on the cliff. He's going after Goldstein."

Hank and his scouts watched a wounded Frances and her twenty giants occupy the fortress, now abandoned by Carlos and his fighters.

"Ammo check," Hank said.

Robby went down the line of scouts, got their status, and reported to Hank.

"Doesn't look good, brother. No one has more than one extra magazine. The two SAWs have only what's in their drums—about fifty rounds each."

"Okay enough for one attack and possibly a few rounds extra," said Hank.

"Guys, listen up," said Hank. "Be smart with your fire. Expect a sword fight when we run out of bullets. They are low on arrows, too. Do not be impressed by their size. Slash at their legs and guts. Protect yourselves with quickness and maneuver. Pair up, and fight in twos. If your battle buddy is incapacitated, carry him to the exfil point and both of you leave the fight. We will take as many of these beasts as we can and then get out.

"Do not push it. Fight hard and get away. You all got it?" Hank said.

"Roger, Hank," they said.

"Look," said Hank. "Goldstein and his two bodyguards have joined up with Frances. I know what he did. He convinced Frances that Carlene was acting on her own. That's how that snake operates. Always shifting loyalties for his own gain. Remember, troops, Goldstein is mine.

"Everyone ready?" he said.

The warriors nodded. They knew full well that the situation favored the enemy. The Directorate had superior numbers and they were protected by a well-designed earthwork.

"Take courage, my magnificent warriors. The battle belongs to the Lord," Hank said.

Robby and his eight men moved over to their attack position on the right. Hank with seven men and Althea—mounted on Sadie—shifted to the left. The two wolfhounds stayed with Hank, and the shepherd and the bulldog joined Robby's troops.

The wind had ceased. The cold Halloween night was dead still, save for the flashes of blue electricity overhead from Michael's sky war with Botis. The strange dark cloud over Salem had dispersed as the grotesque energy from the revelers and their demonic allies dwindled. Their black Satanic rituals were over.

Hank stood motionless at the front of his scouts, waiting for the precise moment to attack. He ignored his exhaustion and the bleeding graze in his left thigh. He breathed in the clear ocean air, knowing it may be his last taste of life.

He looked over at his faithful comrade, Robby, who was down on one knee at the forefront of his scouts. Hank raised his rifle over his head, muzzle to the sky. Robby stood up and held out his hand to his men, palm up. Hank swung his rifle down and both units crept silently toward the fort.

Without the telekinetic field from Andrew's devices or the support of the demonic forces, Commander Frances O'Donnelly had only her human strength to control the twenty savage brutes under her command. The giant thugs all lay exhausted and heavy against the interior wall of the earthworks.

"What am I going to do with these worthless brutes?" Frances said to Romano. The two executives sat cross-legged next to each other in the dirt, filthy and discouraged.

"Here," said Romano, offering Frances a tablet from a round pillbox he pulled out of his pocket.

"What's this, Doctor? Cyanide?"

Goldstein couldn't restrain the vile grin. "It's our only hope right now, my dear chairwoman." He popped one in his mouth and held the pillbox open for her. "Take one."

Frances swallowed a pill, closed her eyes, and let the powerful chemical concoction course through her bloodstream. When she opened her eyes she was energized, ecstatic, and deeply fond and respectful of Romano Goldstein.

"Wow," she said.

"Yeah, wow," said Romano. "You have relinquished command to me, haven't you, Frances?"

"Of course, of course. You're in charge, Doctor Goldstein. What's the plan, Commander?"

"Arrange the men in two rows, up against the dirt wall there."

Frances ordered the hulks to get into a semicircle of two rows and listen to Commander Goldstein.

Goldstein began the hum again. Frances picked up the next note in the ominous chord.

Romano knelt in front of one of the soldiers and held the man's massive jaw in his hand and peered into his weary eyes. "Look at me," Goldstein sang. "I speak murderous power to your bones and depraved bravery into your heart. Wake up. You will slash your sword into the bellies of our enemy and throw them over the cliff. Now hum, you dumb gorilla."

Frances watched Goldstein go from man to man, expertly manipulating them into his web.

"Frances, get these idiots ready for the enemy attack. Force this fly in the ointment off the cliff and into the ocean."

CHAPTER FORTY

Sandy jumped across the fissure and stood next to her husband. "Henry, I refuse to forgive you for leaving me. Gabriella's gone. I'm alone and our son broke out of rehab and he's in danger up there. Doctor Goldstein is a fraud. He's evil. He's one of the leaders of the Directorate and he's now in charge of what's left of their army on the cliff."

"And I … I don't know if…," Sandy said.

Henry waited, chewing his lower lip, staring at Sandy's face.

"I have the same powers Gabriella has … had—over there across the crevice." Sandy looked up at Henry for a response, but got none.

"I'm directing the battle from here, using these kids as runners." She waved vaguely at the tent. Only Sam stood by with a metal cup of coffee in his hands, keeping out of earshot of the couple.

"I can see the battlefield. I get orders from the Spirit and the angels and I relay them to the troops up there. My last order…," Sandy wasn't sure if she could trust Henry with real truth.

"I don't know if it was from above or just from me. I told Hank to kill Goldstein."

She watched Henry's eyes and she knew he was trying to conceal his anger.

"I have to get over there." She bounded back to her post and looked to the sky. It took her several minutes to process what she was seeing.

"Thomas, are you still with me?"

"Yes, Commander Sandy, what is it?" said Thomas.

"Tell me what I am viewing here in the sky."

"There is an army of enemy reinforcements inbound to this location. Possibly a hundred fresh soldiers. The Directorate has no knowledge of these forces, but they are allies of our enemy. ETA twenty minutes."

"Here we go, girl," said Althea. She pulled her fingernails through Sadie's tangled mane. "Now our job is to hang back from the first attack, and when we see one of our guys in trouble we charge and help him."

Sadie snorted and pawed the ground.

Hank and Robby directed their attack forces against the enemy in the fort using bounding overwatch. Each of their squadrons was divided into two sections. One section ran to a covered position and fired their weapons at the rim of the earthwork. The other section advanced past them and took up a protected firing position. They leapfrogged ahead, attacking the earthworks through barrages of enemy arrows.

Althea watched the enemy fire wildly over their heads. Arrows flew by her into the trees.

"Those big fellas look like they're on some crazy drugs, girl," she said to her mount.

"What's that, Sadie?"

From the horse's mind to Althea's: *The angel Thomas told me Goldstein hypnotized the brutes. They have no idea what they are doing, but they are dangerous.*

"Oh, dear God," said Althea, "these people are beyond evil. Lord help us."

He is.

Hank's squadron and Robby's squadron advanced to within twenty feet of the wall without any casualties. The giants rose up over the wall, swords in hand, and charged down onto the Task Force Saber warriors.

The earsplitting dissonant drone pulsated through the air. Hank's men recoiled at the repulsive blast.

"Tell the angels to blow the trumpets," said Althea to Sadie.

In seconds, the power of the horrific humming dissipated.

The girl and the horse watched as the Task Force Saber fighters regained their calm courage and charged back at the massive swordsmen.

"There," said Althea, pointing her pistol at a giant with his broadsword raised over her cousin David squirming backwards on the ground. Before the enemy could bring his weapon down, Althea put a bullet through his head and he fell on top of David. Robby pulled the dead brute off David, helped him to his feet, and supported him to the exfiltration point.

Pistol in her left hand, sword in her right, Althea controlled Sadie with her legs, but Sadie needed no direction as they charged into the raging melee.

"You're a natural warhorse," said Althea. She leaned forward in the saddle and Sadie kicked back with both hind legs, knocking out two enemy fighters.

The hand-to-hand fight lasted over an hour. Hank was a cyclone of lethal violence. Movements almost too fast for Althea's eye to follow. He fought by executing precise karate movements from a *Shiko Dachi* to a *Fudo Dachi* then he'd fly into the neck of a confused attacker with a *Nidan Geri* and finish him off with a slash of his Kabar knife across the throat.

Hank was covered with blood, wounded on his right side and left arm. Still twisting, crouching, leaping, stabbing in a continuous fluid killing dance through the enemy force. Althea had to force her attention from Hank's devastating onslaught so she could support the others in the fray.

Finally the fight on the field was down to six giants against Hank, the two wolfhounds, Sadie, and Althea.

The dogs had one of the hypnotized swordsmen cornered against a tree. Hank was fending off the other five when a war club struck him in the head and felled him to the ground. Still conscious, he held his sword in front of his bleeding supine body as two giants reared back for the kill.

Sadie charged and rammed one of Hank's attackers. Althea shot another. Suddenly Sadie let out a chilling scream and Althea cried, "No!" as an enemy swordsman thrust his weapon into Sadie's throat. The sword's point pierced through Sadie's neck and stopped within inches of Althea's abdomen. The horse reared back on her hind legs and smashed her front hooves into her attacker, crushing his skull. Then Sadie crashed to the earth next to Hank with the hilt of the massive weapon sticking out of her bloody throat.

Althea rolled free and dragged the severely wounded Hank behind a rock wall. She unzipped her jacket, ripped her tee shirt from her body, and pressed the cloth against the deepest gash in his abdomen. Hank removed his belt and bound the blood-soaked rag to his body.

"Inject this," groaned Hank. He pulled a fat plastic syringe from one of the pockets on his body armor marked with the word "X-Stat." Althea placed the blunt end of the syringe into Hank's open wound and pushed down on the plunger. Hundreds of tiny sponges squirted into Hank's artery and the bleeding stopped in seconds. He gulped down the last of his water and threw his canteen on the ground.

"I'll be okay," Hank said.

Althea read the lie on his face. "Sure. You'll be fine, Hank."

They watched the three remaining crazed monsters howl with maniacal laughter at the wounded warhorse struggling on the ground. Sadie's eyes bulged out. Her tongue hung from her gasping mouth. One of the savages grasped Sadie's back legs in his huge hands and dragged her across the field. The other two crazed soldiers grabbed Sadie's front hooves and they circled around in a demonic dance, whirling the horse above the ground between them.

"Oh my dear God," said Althea. She started to rise up over the stone wall and Hank grabbed her belt and pulled her back down.

The three savages laughed and hummed that satanic buzz—they whirled around faster with the dying animal between them and hurled Sadie over the cliff.

"Go," said Hank. "Get down to the water."

Althea shook her head, tears streaming down her face.

"This is an order, soldier. You get down there now. Run."

Althea clinched her teeth and shook both fists in protest, but she pushed herself up, took a runner's stance, and sprinted to the nearest exfiltration point and jumped down the rocks.

"Henry! Hank's alone up there," called Sandy across the crevice.

"My boy," Henry whispered and he dashed up the cliffside.

Sandy looked up at the three brutes standing at the edge, hands on their hips laughing, humming, screaming into the air as the flailing horse fell to her death on the jagged rocks below. Romano Goldstein and Frances O'Donnelly appeared next to them under the sharp silver half-moon rising behind them.

Then Sandy saw the reinforcements—over a hundred warriors lined up alongside the directors at the cliff's edge.

One of the giants turned from the edge and reappeared holding something aloft. It was a man, kicking and pounding his fists at the thug's arms.

"Hank!" yelled Sandy. "You unholy beast, put my boy down."

The monstrous brute looked up at his captive and laughed. Hank was twisting and kicking, trying to escape the giant's grasp, smashing the enemy's wrists, pulling at his fingers.

"Throw the worthless pig down," said Goldstein.

The giant drew his arms back overhead. Sandy watched in horror.

Then the giant crumbled. Like torpedoes Mark and Lucille flew into his body—Mark hitting him in the left knee, Lucille flying into the right side of his neck. Two sets of powerful canine jaws crunched down—Mark's into the giant's leg, Lucille's into his jugular.

Sandy watched the man fall like a tree, dropping her son at his feet. The dogs reverted to their wolf-killing instincts and tore the man apart while Hank's weak, wounded body rolled over the lip of the cliff. He grasped the base of a sapling in his right hand and clawed at the turf with his left. He desperately scraped his boots against the rock for purchase but found none. He twisted down, clinging with one hand to the bush, but he couldn't hang on. He fell from the clifftop out of Sandy's sight.

Sandy fell hard to her knees on the granite shelf, but she didn't feel the pain. Her face sunk into her hands under her bushy white hair.

"Sandy. Sandy, get in the boat," Carlos said. He had maneuvered *Water Walker* to the deep water on the back side of Sandy's ledge.

"Climb down here and slide on your backside to that little outcropping and you can jump in from there."

The big boat had forty-five Task Force Saber warriors aboard, plus two dogs and Cinnamon.

Sandy took one more look at the cliff where the savages stood proud between the directors, scoffing at her and her retreating army—peaceful Cielavista now occupied by a powerful demonic army. Sandy hesitated there on her rock.

And there was Henry.

Henry was stepping heavily down the uneven rocky stairway with his son embraced in his arms, carrying him like a toddler, chest to chest, one of Henry's arms around Hank's bleeding thighs, the other across his back. Hank's face was nuzzled into Henry's neck, his weakened arms clinging to his father.

"I got him," said Henry.

"Oh, thank God," said Sandy. "Henry!"

A cheer rose up from the crowded trawler.

Henry couldn't make the leap over the wide crevice on Sandy's rock to get to the boat, so he made his way to the shallow water on the near side of the ledge.

"Carlos can't get the boat over there, Henry, it's too shallow," said Sandy. "What are you going to do?"

Henry smiled up to her over Hank's matted hair. "Sandy, I'll be right there. Get in the boat."

"Tobias, you there, buddy?" said Henry. "You know what I need, right?"

Sandy said, "Who're you talking to, Henry?" She was kneeling on the edge of the granite ledge looking down at her husband and her son. "How is Hank, Henry? Is he all right?"

Hank lifted his face up off Henry's neck and gave his mother a weak grin.

"Get in the boat, Sandy. I'll be right there," Henry said. "These women," he said to Hank, "they just don't trust us, do they?"

From the rocks on the tideline Henry stepped out onto the gently rippling water. One step. The second step—lost his balance for a second on the unfamiliar surface—hung on to Hank. Another step, and then Henry walked confidently out on the ocean around Sandy's ledge.

"If Saint Peter could do it, so can I," said Henry.

"Now you know how he did it," said Tobias, swimming under the weight of Henry and Hank. "We angels never got the credit we deserved."

The two wolfhounds were swimming next to Henry.

When Henry got to the boat, Carlos and several of his nephews lifted Hank from Henry's arms. They helped Henry over the transom.

"Now I've seen everything," said Carlos.

Chapter Forty-One

Henry accepted his wife's punishment when he met her on the deck. Sandy grabbed Henry's jacket with both hands and shook him. She banged her forehead against his chest. Then she followed the men bearing her wounded son below into the cabin. Althea jumped down behind her.

Henry was puzzled as the boat slowly backed away from the rock and into the open water, swung around, and accelerated out to the horizon. Carlos, Henry, Roberto, Beto, and Robby looked at each other.

"Say good-bye to our home," said the elder Roberto.

The warrior-family on deck looked up at the cliff receding behind them. On the heights stood Frances O'Donnelly, Romano Goldstein, and over a hundred fresh enemy fighters.

The warriors in the boat whispered prayers. Prayers of thanksgiving and prayers for guidance. *Water Walker* sped out to sea, towing the *Sea Ray*.

"We're all safe. Some with serious injuries, but all alive except for that brave warhorse," said Carlos. "You know, Henry, you went AWOL on us. But old Gabriella told us there was a higher reason for your taking off like that."

Young Beto said, "I think old Henry here had—what'd you call it— an epiphany up there in Neddick."

"Yeah?" said Carlos.

"Look at him, Grampa. He ain't shaved in a week, and he hasn't even changed his clothes in three days. He even quit washing the dishes in the galley. I had to do that."

"Well," said Carlos, "great job, my friend, rescuing Hank. We all thought he'd met his maker. And by the way how'd you do that water walking thing?"

Henry, still silent, looked to each man—Carlos, Roberto, his son Robby and grandson, Beto. "How fast do you think we're going?"

"Feels like thirty to forty knots. Top speed, I'm thinking," said Beto.

"Anyone hear any engine noise?"

They all stood and listened. They were on the deck right over the engine compartment. The trawler was flying through the ocean, leaving a huge wake behind. Each man's brow wrinkled at the same time.

"Who's at the helm?" said Henry.

They all looked at the ship's wheel and saw it unmanned.

"One other thing—where are we going?"

Carlos knelt down by Lucille. She was drinking from a bowl of water and eating a steak. "So, Lucille, how many angels we got pulling this trawler?"

"Seven? Nice. They do a very smooth job. Ask them where we are going."

"What did she say?" said Henry.

"It's a surprise."

Sandy came up from the cabin, stood next to Henry, and crossed her arms across her chest. She bumped him with her shoulder.

"Hank's sleeping. Yolanda applied one of her honey-calendula potions to his wounds and gave him tea from an herb called Star of Bethlehem to make him sleep. Evidently the boy's body is made of Kevlar."

"How about his mind, his soul?" said Henry.

"Hard to tell, but you know, I've never felt more hope for him. Those clouds in his eyes have gone. When he responded to what Yolanda gave him, his breathing became normal immediately. All he could do was smile and joke around."

"What's with the little cutie?" Henry said.

"Yeah, Althea. She's quite the young lady. Sweet as can be, tough as leather."

Henry just looked at Sandy. She knew what he was thinking.

The cliff of Cielavista was dipping into the horizon under the half moon. The hoard of fresh enemy troops remained lined up on the edge of the cliff. The battle in the starry sky was over.

"They'll renew their attacks on innocent victims, won't they?" said Henry.

"Not them," said Sandy.

"What do you mean?" said Henry.

"I only know what I know and I can only do what I can do," Sandy said.

"That used to kill me, you know, but not anymore," said Henry.

"Maybe something clicked *on*," said Sandy. "All I know is this war isn't over. Somehow, don't ask me how, Gabriella will have her victory."

"Henry, did you notice the fuel gage?" said Beto seated at the helm of *Water Walker*. Henry and Sandy sat in the mate's chair next to him.

"No."

"I used the last drop of gas keeping her steady on the shore back there when we were loading the family."

Sandy and Henry smiled at the gage on the dashboard reading empty. "This seat is designed for just one person, you know," said Henry.

Sandy snuggled her behind against Henry's lap and looked at the seven soaring angels easily pulling on *Water Walker's,* mooring lines. "This is the only way to sail," she said.

"Look. It's the supertanker we saw this morning, the *Hyundai Spartan,*" said Beto, pointing through the boat's windshield at the dark shape on the horizon. "No lights."

Henry and Sandy strained their eyes at the line where the sky met the ocean beyond *Water Walker's* bow. The ship they were racing toward grew larger quickly.

"We're not going to ram this tanker, are we?" said Henry.

The angels let their lines go slack. The *Water Walker* slowed as it approached the starboard side of the huge tanker. Henry swiveled around the mate's chair so he and Sandy could face the crowd of Carlos's family standing below them on the main deck, all craning their necks, looking up at the steel side of the giant vessel ten stories high. One collective gasp rose up from the warriors on the trawler as the side of the tanker opened up and the angels pulled *Water Walker* and the *Sea Ray* into the bowels of the ship.

The ship's hull closed behind them and halogen lights banged on overhead. *Water Walker* and the *Sea Ray* bobbed gently on the pool of seawater in the tanker's belly.

Sandy, Henry, and Beto stood in the helm. "Tie her up," said Henry as if docking a fishing boat inside a supertanker's hull was something he did every day.

Antonio and Beto secured the lines to the steel dock inside the fuel tank and the weary warriors disembarked the boats and bunched up like sheep, waiting on the metal dock for Sandy and Henry.

Sandy went below to check to see if Hank could walk. Yolanda had two of her grandsons fashion a stretcher out of blankets and a couple docking poles. Over Hank's objections they made him lie on it, and they carried him to the deck and onto the dock.

Henry led the troops up the metal stairway on the interior wall of the tanker to a landing near the ceiling. A door opened as he got to the landing and a crewman welcomed him aboard.

"Hello, Henry," said the stocky sailor. He shook Henry's hand. "Welcome aboard the *Spartan*. I'm Simon."

"Thanks. Any idea what's going on?"

"Nope. I just work here." Simon gave Henry a big toothy grin. "Follow me."

"Stay close, folks," said Simon to the Santiago family as they fell in line on the expansive deck of the *Spartan*. "There's lots of obstacles on the deck here, so don't wander off."

Simon led the file of haggard soldiers along an elevated pipeline to the four-story-high structure near the stern.

"This is the bridge," said Simon. "Watch your step. There's a lip at the base of this door."

In a minute, they were all seated in comfortable chairs in the recreation hall. Except for the steady hum of engines and electricity coursing through the veins of the ship, they may have been in the ballroom of a five-star hotel.

"Every family or individual gets a room," Simon said. "These guys will show you to your quarters." He waved in the general direction of four clean-cut men in pressed khaki shirts and trousers.

"There's clean clothes for you in these boxes. Before you go to your rooms, just rummage through and get what you need for the night."

"The dining room is next to this room. We'll have breakfast in an hour. Our chef is the best."

Sandy turned to Henry, "Their chef is the best."

"We'll see," said Henry. "If not we'll just take our business to another supertanker."

"Yeah," said Sandy. "One with big doors that open up and swallow fishing boats."

"Plenty of those," said Henry.

"Let's get some clean clothes."

Henry and Sandy clutched their new sweats, socks, underwear and slippers to their chests like refugees. Simon opened the door to their suite. They stepped in over the edge of the doorway. Simon flicked the switch and soft lighting streamed into the plush quarters.

"This is the best you can do, Simon?" said Henry, gazing into the elegant room.

Sandy punched her husband. Simon smiled. "I'll come get you in a few minutes after you bathe and change. The captain would like to have a word before breakfast."

Showered, changed, and lying next to each other on the king-size bed, Sandy said, "Sleep much?"

"Not lately. If this guy doesn't knock in the next two minutes I'm out like a light."

"Gotten any lately?" she asked.

"You're gonna have to wait for that until after breakfast, kid."

Sandy, Henry, and Simon entered the elevator and rode it up to the command bridge. The stainless steel doors zipped open and they stepped out to a hallway lined in teak paneling. Simon opened the door opposite the elevator and they entered the command center. Four rectangular windows offered a 180-degree view of the horizon. On the rear wall behind Henry and Sandy stood a bank of thirteen metal cabinets, each one with its own digital dials, buttons, and radio handsets.

Through the windows all Sandy could see was stars. Between Sandy and the command console were three high-backed leather chairs with headrests and arms. Two looked occupied by large men, the third seemed empty.

"Sir?" said Simon.

The chair on Sandy's right spun around and a grey-haired man in black slacks and a white uniform shirt with black epaulets trimmed with four wide gold stripes slid off his chair and held out his hand. The captain shook hands with Sandy and Henry.

"What a pleasure to meet you two heroes. I'm Skip Blumenthal."

The chair in the middle spun and a younger, blond version of Skip Blumenthal appeared. He stood smiling and greeted the couple with handshakes. "I'm Tom, Skip's son."

Skip seemed enthralled with Sandy and Henry. He looked at them and shook his head. "We've followed every stage of your battle. I'm sure that General Joshua is proud of you."

It took Sandy a few seconds to comprehend. "Oh, yes from heaven. You think he was watching?"

Skip smiled, "Who knows, but your soldiers executed his tactics superbly. And no battle deaths."

"Well, our dear courageous Sadie. She saved my son's life and gave up her own."

"Yes, yes. So sorry about Sadie, the splendid warhorse," said the captain.

Tom interrupted, "And I believe you already know our other captain."

Sandy gave Tom a puzzled look. He reached over and put his hand on the back of the third chair and gave it a gentle turn.

"Nonina!"

CHAPTER FORTY-TWO

Captain Blumenthal got his son's eye and gave him the signal. He rotated his index finger in a couple circles. Tom grabbed the handset from the metal cabinet behind him and gave the order, "Raise anchor, ease her forward 270 degrees. Ten knots steady."

Sandy's heart pounded as she kneeled down and lay her head in Gabriella's lap. Tears streamed down her cheeks. "Oh, God, Nonina."

The old lady looked down at her granddaughter and up at Henry.

Sandy said, "You old lady. Where have you been? Why couldn't you communicate with me? I was going crazy with you gone. I was worried…."

"Shhhhhhh, darling," said Gabriella. "You wanna scold someone, scold the angels. But not now they're busy."

Gabriella stroked Sandy's hair. "We're in the hands of the Lord, my dear granddaughter. He's got plans for us that we don't always understand. I had work to do out here on the ocean, and He knew you were the one to direct the battle at Cielavista."

"But why couldn't I see you. Why did you have to disappear?" said Sandy.

"To build your independence, dear Sandy."

Henry wiped his eyes and his nose with the sleeve of his new sweatshirt. "Who are these people, and where did this ship come from?" he asked.

"One of my nephew's fleet, Henry. From Sicily. They have been our allies in the heavenly war for many, many years. I never knew it until a few weeks ago," said Gabriella.

"Turns out we are one of seven units of spiritual warriors stationed around the globe. That enemy force that came to reinforce the Directorate had been fighting our allies in South America. They were ordered to disengage from the battle down there and join the campaign here in New England. Our mission will be expanded in the future."

Sandy shook her head and took a deep breath. She looked into Gabriella's eyes and said, "Don't ever do this again." And she hugged her grandmother long and hard.

"Now, Sandy, stand up and see what God has planned," said Gabriella.

"Henry, are you able to see into the spirit world?"

"No, Gabriella. I'm that guy that has to believe without seeing. Not as easy, you know."

"Hmmm. Still the wise guy, huh? Okay, Sandy, you want to tell your husband what you see out there?"

The tanker *Hyundai Spartan* pushed steady westward through the flat sea at ten knots. The moon had climbed to her zenith. Cielavista's cliffs rose above the horizon. The entire estate was ablaze.

"I see a doomed enemy army. And I see a new day dawning," said Sandy.

"All I see is our home engulfed in flames—the cottage, the barn, and the mansion," said Henry.

The *Hyundai Spartan* slowed. "Reverse engines," said Tom. And the huge vessel slowly glided to a stop. The details of the clifftop were clear. One hundred and fourteen human figures were silhouetted against the raging fires. They stood glaring out at the tanker.

"I see a strange blue star way, way up there," said Henry.

"Yes," said Sandy. "That blue star is the Sword of the Lord. While we were battling the enemy, Michael has been brandishing it up there. Yahweh has transformed this powerful spiritual weapon into its physical form—no telling what it's made of—but now it has natural properties, weight, and shape. The Sword has been increasing in size over the past six hours.

"As the hilt and blade grew larger, more angels had to join Michael to help bear its weight. That's why we didn't have the whole angelic platoon on the battlefield. After their battle with the demons over Salem, the heavenly warriors were assigned to Michael as sword bearers. And the demons from Salem joined Botis."

"How many of them are hanging on to that thing?" said Henry.

"Let's see," said Sandy. "Hard to tell. They're like a flock of butterflies."

"Forty," said Gabriella. "The hilt is a hundred feet long, the blade is over three hundred."

"Did you notice that the demons left the air over Cielavista when Carlos was making his last stand in the fortress?" Gabriella continued. "Botis got sick of shuttling between the ground war and the sky war so he left Frances' body and led his entire gang of filthy spirits to fight Michael. Michael and his team took one massive stroke with the Sword of the Lord through Botis' charging swarm and that was all they could take. Wounded and sniveling, the cowardly demons flew back to hell where they belong."

"That's one powerful, supernatural weapon," said Henry.

Sandy asked Tom if she could use the ship's public address system. He handed her the handset and punched three buttons on the panel. "Talk."

"Hello, everyone, this is Sandy. God bless you. I hope you have found your clothes and your quarters comfortable. The crew will be serving us breakfast in about a half hour. I want you all to go out on the foredeck so you can witness what God has planned. Stay back against the bridge structure. There will be a big wave coming our way and it will cause this tanker rock. You need to watch the shoreline."

From the command tower, Sandy could see her warriors assemble on the foredeck below them. The sea between the *Spartan* and Cielavista was moonlight silver. Several Task Force Saber warriors pointed up at the shimmering blue star. They all looked up. The massive sword descended steadily down and held it's altitude for a moment over the brilliant smile of the half-moon.

Sandy, Henry, and the crew in the tower watched. Sandy turned to Gabriella, still seated in the captain's chair. Gabriella nodded.

The bright green digits on the 24-hour clock just under the tower's ceiling read 23:59:30.

"Dear family, Gabriella is here in the tower. She is perfectly normal, healthy, and she continues to wage her secret war in the heavens."

23:59:35. A murmur of joy rippled through the family.

23:59:37. "This tanker belongs to one of her Sicilian relatives, all allies in our spiritual battle."

23:59:40. "I will count down from ten. At the first toll of the St. James Church bell, we will sound our war cry."

23:59:45. The woeful humming from the enemy occupying their home slithered across the silver water. Task Force Saber reflexively hummed their C major, canceling out the evil bawl.

23:59:50. "Ten-nine-eight-seven—" they all counted in soft unison, "six-five-four-three—"

23:59:58. The point of the bright blue sword swung downward like the second hand of a watch turning from twelve to six, leaving a crescent of radiant brilliance in its wake against the starry sky. "Two. One."

The St. James church bell rang out.

"A Sword For The Lord And For Gabriella!"

The angelic host hurled the magnificent flaming Sword of the Lord down into Gabriella's crevice in the granite ledge and the entire cliff erupted in a seismic explosion. Tons of rock sheared off the face of the cliff as it crashed into the ocean, creating a tsunami that roared seaward. The *Spartan's* bow surged up on the twelve-foot wave, and the Task Force

Saber fighters leaned back against the bridge. The ship slammed down against the ocean and rocked on the waves that followed. The warriors recovered their stance and watched their flaming home tumble into the foaming surf around the blazing cross. The blade of the Sword of the Lord buried itself deep into the stone seabed, leaving the bejeweled hilt exposed—a memorial of the Lord's victory at Cielavista.

The earth quaked, then calmed. The *Spartan* settled onto a quiet sea. The sword's flame died out and disappeared. The men and the women on the deck breathed.

Gabriella was standing now, her arms linked with Henry's on her left and Sandy's on her right. The last midnight toll from Saint James Church bell rang out into the clear, moonlit sky.

"All Saints Day," Gabriella said.

"Poor man's landscaping," said Henry. He looked out at the two-foot quilt of snow covering the ground on Cielavista.

Sandy threw her hand over his shoulder and fingered is scruffy beard. Through the snow-laden spruce branches, the generator purred quietly.

"I like this little deck you built, Henry," she said.

"Hank did most of it. I just handed him the tools and held the ends of the boards for him."

"Speaking of…," said Sandy.

Cinnamon, with Althea at the reins and Hank riding behind her, trotted into the clearing where their temporary camp was set up. They were pulling three toboggans in trail behind them, loaded with Carlos' and Yolanda's grandchildren.

The young couple waved when they spotted Henry and Sandy.

"She's pregnant," said Hank.

Henry and Sandy looked at each other, then back to Hank. "Really?" said Sandy.

Althea swatted Hank in the back of the head. "Not me. Cinnamon."

Hank just grinned, and the horse-drawn train made a wide circle around the field.

The generator noise stopped. Henry shrugged at Sandy. "Out of fuel, I guess."

Gabriella emerged from the trailer with two mugs of black coffee.

"Thanks, Nonina," said Sandy.

"Quiet, isn't it?" said the old prophetess.

"Ummm," said Sandy, looking out over the soft stillness. "Silent."

They sipped their coffee until the mugs were empty.

"I'll take these in," said Henry, collecting the women's cups.

He watched his wife and her grandmother begin their walk down the path they had trod in the snow, out to the edge of the cliff to their new ledge on the water. Just before stepping over the lip, Sandy turned and pointed at Althea. She jerked her head and the young lady slid off Cinnamon. The three women stepped down the natural rock stairway to the ledge. Sandy and Gabriella leaped across the newly formed crevice.

It was low tide. Althea looked down into the seawater sloshing across the stones at the base of the cleft where the massive, bejeweled cross stood shimmering between the rocks.

Althea caught the eye of a seagull with a sand crab in his beak.

Gabriella looked across to Althea. "Come and join us, dear. You can't see anything from there."

(Data on page 135–136 taken from http://www.gannett-cdn.com/GDContent/mass-killings/index.html#title)

CPSIA information can be obtained
at www.ICGtesting.com
Printed in the USA
LVHW080304251019
635290LV00004B/6/P

9 781595 559128